LUKE IRONTREE & THE LAST VAMPIRE WAR

Book 0 - The Centurion Immortal
Book 1 - Dark Fangs Rising - March 22, 2022
Book 2 - Dark Fangs Raging - April 19, 2022
Book 3 - Dark Fangs Descending - May 17, 2022
Book 4 - Blood Empire Reborn - August 23, 2022
Book 5 - Blood Empire Avenged - September 20, 2022
Book 6 - Blood Empire Infiltrated - October 18, 2022
Book 7 - Blood Empire Burning - November 15, 2022
Book 8 - Ancient Sword Falling - March 21, 2023
Book 9 - Ancient Sword Unyielding - August 22, 2023
Book 10 - Ancient Sword Shattering*

The Luke Irontree Historical Adventures
Rise of the Centurio Immortalis - April 5, 2022
Fall of the Centurio Immortalis - May 31, 2022
The Moonlight Centurion*
The Highway Centurion*

*Forthcoming
    Titles and release dates may be subject to change.

BLOOD EMPIRE AVENGED

LUKE IRONTREE & THE LAST VAMPIRE WAR
BOOK 5

C. THOMAS LAFOLLETTE

EDITED BY
SUZANNE LAHNA

BLOOD EMPIRE AVENGED
C. Thomas Lafollette

A Broken World Publication
13820 NE Airport Way
Suite #K395495
Portland, OR 97251-1158
Blood Empire Avenged
Copyright © 2022 by C. Thomas Lafollette
ISBN 978-1-949410-75-4 (ebook);
ISBN 978-1-949410-76-1 (paperback)

Cover Design: Ravven
Developmental Editing by: Suzanne Lahna
Copy/Line Editing: C.D. Tavenor
Proofreading: Amy Cissell

CONTENTS

Content Warning   vii
Pronunciation Guide & Author's Notes   xi

Chapter 1   1
Chapter 2   11
Chapter 3   21
Chapter 4   29
Chapter 5   37
Chapter 6   45
Chapter 7   55
Chapter 8   65
Chapter 9   75
Chapter 10   83
Chapter 11   93
Chapter 12   103
Chapter 13   111
Chapter 14   125
Chapter 15   133
Chapter 16   147
Chapter 17   167
Chapter 18   171
Chapter 19   183
Chapter 20   195
Chapter 21   205
Chapter 22   215
Chapter 23   225
Chapter 24   239
Chapter 25   257
Chapter 26   275
Chapter 27   299
Epilogue   315
Luke Irontree Will Return In   323

Newsletter 331
Acknowledgments 333
About the Author 335
Also by C. Thomas Lafollette 337

CONTENT WARNING

This book contains some gore and body horror. There is also gun and sword violence. There are also scenes of child endangerment and a description of a kidnapping.

For Tim

PRONUNCIATION GUIDE & AUTHOR'S NOTES

Pronunciation: Latin names and words are mentioned throughout the book and are intended to be read with the classical Latin pronunciation. For instance, "c" is always pronounced hard, like a "k." "U" is always a short "oo" sound. "V" typically sounds like a "w." There are plenty of resources on the internet if you wish to learn more about Classical Latin pronunciation.

- Lucius – Loo-kih-oos
- Silvanius – Sihl-wahn-ih-oos
- Ferrata – Fehr-rah-tah
- Jung-sook — Yoong-sook
- Jan - Yeahn
- Roxiustanta - Roks-see-oo-stahn-nah
- Surena - Ser-rehn-nah
- Selene - Sehl-lee-nee
- Le Mousquetaire - Ley Moos-keh-tare

Latin Words: Latin words are used for effect and to add to the "flavor" of the story, not to reflect Latin grammar/declensions/conjugations.

CHAPTER
ONE

Luke stared out over Luxembourg City, the small city's lights eclipsing the stars above on the clear night. He stood in the eye of a hurricane after their tumultuous exit from Belgium and before their next leap into action to get back home to Portland. At the sound of the balcony door, Luke turned and smiled at the curvy blond woman opening it. She wore a shawl against the cool, fall air.

"Mind if I join you?" Maggie asked, a light Polish accent coloring her voice.

"Of course not." He swept his hand toward the chair next to him. "Can't see the stars, but the city's quite nice at night, especially from here."

Maggie scooted the chair closer to Luke's and sat, taking his hand in hers. "What's got you so troubled?"

Luke took a deep breath and let it out as a sigh. "I'm not sure what to do next, Maggie. My friend was killed by his son. His other son is buried in grief. He's lost his home, and I've been denied the land of my birth and the ability to travel to my sanctuary. The pack I'd been helping is now my enemy, and they have several of my properties under their control and the income that goes with them."

He rubbed a hand over his eyes. "We're in the territory of a pack with dubious loyalties, and we have to travel through another pack's territory to get to an airport when we have no assurances of their loyalty." He looked into Maggie's eyes, his brow furrowed as his anxiety opened a pit in his stomach. "I feel trapped, Maggie. Trapped with no safe escape for the people I'm responsible for."

Maggie leaned her head on his shoulder, bringing his hand up to her lips for a kiss against his knuckles. "I know, Luke. We're in a tough place. We'll figure this out together. We'll get the children to their new homes safely. We'll get back to Portland. Then we can figure out what to do as a pack and as a family."

Luke kissed the top of her head. "Thank you for listening to me complain."

"I wouldn't call it complaining. It's a stark recitation of facts." Lifting her head, she looked into his eyes and caressed his cheek. "Besides, you should be able to complain to someone you care about and who cares about you. You can complain to your..." She hesitated for a moment. "Your girlfriend."

A surge of warmth filled him, bringing a smile to his face. "Are you asking me to be your boyfriend?"

Maggie nodded, her eyes twinkling. "I love you, Luke."

"I love you too, Maggie. I want to have an official status with you." Luke leaned into Maggie and kissed her, running his hand through her silky hair. When he pulled back, mischief sparkled in Luke's eyes. "Although, I'm not sure a nineteen-hundred-year-old man qualifies as a boy."

Maggie laughed, patting Luke on the cheek. "I left my girlhood a long time ago in another century and another country, but I'll still be your girlfriend."

"And I'll be your very old boyfriend," Luke replied. "We feel very modern and contemporary."

They settled back into their chairs and enjoyed the sounds of the city below. When it grew too chilly, they retired to their bed to continue enjoying each other's company and an early night's sleep. Despite his best efforts, sleep didn't come easily, nor was it restful when he found it. Nightmares he couldn't remember plagued his dreams, leaving him fuzzy-headed and bleary-eyed in the morning.

At one point, he rolled over and found an empty spot where Maggie should have been. Jolting up in the bed, he tried to clear his head enough to figure out where she was. Once he heard her voice in the other room and the jingle of plates, he relaxed and slumped into his pillow. Maggie peeked into the bedroom after the hotel suite's door clicked shut, probably behind the person bringing room service.

Maggie moved around the bed to Luke's side and bent over to kiss his forehead. "Breakfast is here, as well as fresh coffee."

Rubbing his eyes, he sat back up and swung his legs out of bed. Maggie handed him a robe and left to set up their breakfast. When he sat next to her, he pulled the filled coffee cup over and raised it to his nose, inhaling deeply of the steamy dark aromas. He was nearly finished with his breakfast and halfway through a second cup when someone knocked at the door.

Laying her hand on his forearm, Maggie smiled and stood up. "I'll see who it is." After peeking through the peephole, she turned back to him. "It's Pablo and Sam."

"Well, if they're both here, I doubt it's entirely a social call," Luke said.

Maggie nodded and opened the door, stepping out of the way for them.

"Morning, Luke! We come bearing gifts," Pablo said.

"Good morning, Maggie. I trust you had a pleasant evening." Sam winked at Maggie. "We have another pot of coffee."

Luke raised his coffee cup to salute his friends. "Morning, you two. I just killed this pot, so your timing is excellent. I'm afraid we don't have much left in the way of food."

"No worries, buddy. We already ate. Heidi's been showing us around a bit." Seeing the puzzled look on Luke's face, Pablo elaborated. "She knows the city since she comes here regularly on pack business."

"Ah. That explains it. What brings you two here this morning?" Luke asked.

Sam grabbed an unused cup, filled it with coffee, and added some cream to it. "Heidi says the local alpha wants to meet with us."

"I guess we should, though I'd rather get everyone moving

toward Portland. Every day's delay is another opportunity for something else to go wrong, and we're quickly running out of resources and allies. Speaking of allies, how is Pieter doing?" Luke blew over his coffee before taking a sip.

"No one has seen him. As far as I can tell, he hasn't left his room since we arrived two days ago," Pablo replied.

"Are you sure he's still in his room?" Luke asked, his eyebrows furrowing.

Pablo frowned. "He's told me to go away a few times, so he was there when I checked, but beyond that, he's said nothing."

"I think he was only holding it together until we got everyone to safety," Sam said. "The need to get our non-combatants and children evacuated superseded his need to grieve. Now that we're all reasonably safe, his pain has taken over."

Luke nodded. "Yeah. He's effectively lost both his father and his brother in the most brutal way possible. I suppose I should go check in on him. When does... I guess I don't know the packleader's name."

"Mathis Heinen," Sam supplied. "As far as time, he's invited us to dinner and cocktails. Heidi says we should dress up. I think she was a little concerned our American informality might inform our choice of dress."

"Hmm, I should make sure my shirt and sport coat are not too wrinkly. I don't have anything besides my best jeans to go with them, though." Luke pursed his lips and as his eyes narrowed.

"Good thing you didn't put your luggage in the truck," Sam said.

Luke snorted. "Yeah. Carrying all that across the forests and hills of the Ardennes would not have been fun."

Pablo laughed. "Don't worry about what you wear, dude. You can get away with whatever. You are who you are. You could probably show up in your birthday suit, and it would be fine. Apparently, you're a bit of a celebrity among the European packs."

"I have nothing appropriate to wear," Maggie said, looking worried.

Sam leaned toward Maggie, patting the back of her hand. "Heidi offered to take us shopping. We'll find you something, then get you all dolled up."

"I just want to look nice if I'm going to represent the pack and be Luke's date." Maggie reached over and squeezed Luke's hand.

He squeezed back, smiling fondly. "You always look lovely, Maggie."

"He's such a nice man," Sam said, smiling at Luke. "He's come a long way since he washed up in Portland at the pack's doorstep."

"Ha ha." Luke shook his head. "I'd better get dressed so I can go see Pieter."

Maggie followed him in to grab some things before heading to take a shower. Before she left the bedroom, she pulled Luke into a hug and gave him a kiss on the cheek. "Good luck with Pieter."

"Good luck with finding something to wear," Luke replied.

Maggie disappeared and left him to finish dressing. When he was done, he gave Sam a quick hug, then waved Pablo after him.

"Let's go see Pieter. He could use some friends," Luke said.

"Later, Sam," Pablo said, before raising his voice to speak toward the bathroom door. "See you, Maggie!"

Pablo and Luke headed to the elevator and waited for it to reach their floor.

"So, you and Maggie are going as an official couple?" Pablo asked.

"Hmm?"

"She said she would be your date," Pablo said.

"We are dating. Why wouldn't I want to go with my girlfriend?" Luke replied, slyly slipping in his status change.

"Wait… I've never heard either of you say boyfriend or girl-friend. Are you two official now?" Pablo waggled his eyebrows at Luke, stepping into the elevator.

"Yeah. We made it official last night."

Pablo grinned. "Congratulations, buddy! You finally asked her."

Luke's cheeks flushed as he looked down at the elevator floor.

Pablo reached out and pushed the button for Pieter's floor. "She asked you, didn't she?"

"Yeah."

Chuckling, he patted Luke's shoulders. "Good for her. You two make a good couple. I'm glad I told her to make her pass at you hard and to just be obvious."

"Me too," Luke said. "I love her, Pablo."

"Wow. The big 'L' word? Have you told her that?"

Luke chuckled. "Yeah. I did."

"After she said it first?" Pablo teased.

"No. I said it first. I couldn't not tell her anymore. It's been so intense. I needed to let her know my feelings in case something happens." Luke shuffled nervously.

Pablo pulled him in for a one-armed hug as the elevator dinged and opened. "I'm proud of you, buddy. Sam was right. You really have come a long way."

"Yeah. It's been one hell of a year, that's for sure." Luke knocked on Pieter's door. "Pieter, it's Luke. Let us in."

"Go away," Pieter called back.

"Come on, dude. We're your friends, and we care about you. Let us in, please?" Pablo added.

Pieter sighed heavily. "Fine."

A few moments later, Pieter let them in. He looked terrible—dark stubble on his face, eyes red, and disheveled hair. He wore a pair of boxers and had pulled a robe over his shoulders, though he hadn't closed it. He flopped onto the edge of the bed, letting his head sink into his hands.

Luke sat next to Pieter and put his arm around Pieter's shoulders. "We all care about you. We'll be here for you. You don't have to go through this alone."

Something in Luke's words broke a dam inside Pieter. He leaned into Luke's shoulder, tears falling from his eyes—first slowly but heavier as he let go of the emotions he'd been trying to hold at bay and failing. As Pieter cried like a broken-hearted child, Pablo sat on his other side and held his hand. They let Pieter cry as he wept for his murdered father and the brother who'd pulled the trigger. When he finally calmed, Pablo fetched him some tissue and water.

Taking a deep breath, Pieter sighed. "I miss my papa."

Luke squeezed Pieter's shoulder. "He was a good man. Have I ever told you about the first time I met him?"

"No," Pieter replied.

"You probably don't remember. You were a squalling little toddler at the time…" Luke regaled Pieter with the story of how Luke commissioned a painting from Pieter's father, Pieter Bruegel the Elder, back when the artists were all in their original life spans.

Pablo, using his ability to meld with people, coaxed stories about Pieter's father from him until they were laughing at some of the stories he told. Luke and Pablo worked to bring Pieter back into the world of the living. They couldn't make his grief disappear—it was too fresh and raw—but they helped him back into the light a little bit. After a while, they ordered room service, then went back to their respective rooms to get ready for tonight's dinner.

LUKE JOINED PIETER, Pablo, and Jamaal in the hotel bar for drinks while they waited for Maggie, Sam, Delilah, and Simone to come down for their ride to dinner with the Luxembourg packleader. Delilah and Simone were the first down the stairs. Delilah wore a simple black suit with a white shirt.

Simone, who'd shown up with virtually nothing when she joined their band of misfits, had gone with Sam and Maggie to get a dress for herself. The young woman with onyx black skin looked stunning in an egg yolk yellow dress accented with a rich blue that dropped to just below mid-thigh. Luke stood and hugged both of them.

A few minutes later, Sam stepped out of the elevator. Luke caught a flash of blond hair behind her. When Sam stepped aside, Luke gasped. She wore a silvery sapphire blue dress with a sweetheart neckline, midnight blue velvet accenting the waist and hem. Five-petaled flowers in the same midnight blue velvet covered the sheer outer layer, with the same material forming three-quarter length sleeves and a wide bateau neckline, teasing her collar bones. Strappy heels and a silver shawl accompanied the dress.

Maggie stopped in front of him, her hands clasped in front of her. "What do you think?"

"You look stunning," Luke said, taking her hands and leaning in to kiss her cheek.

"You're looking very handsome yourself," Maggie replied.

Luke smiled, giving her his flirty eyes. "When we get back to Portland, I think I owe you some fancy date nights."

"You don't owe me expensive dates," Maggie replied, smiling softly.

"I know, but I still want to take you on some. We can afford to treat ourselves. Besides, you'll need an excuse to wear that dress again. You're absolutely lovely."

Maggie blushed, her pale cheeks taking a pink hue

Luke wore dark wash designer jeans with a black shirt and a sport jacket. Jamaal and Pablo were similarly dressed, going for Portland sharp. Pieter wore a suit, as did Heidi. Everyone gathered near Luke and Maggie, talking among themselves and complimenting each other on how nice they looked.

"This is a good-looking crew," Pablo said.

"Yeah. We scrub up pretty good." Sam slipped her arm through Pablo's. Nodding toward the exit and a couple men walking in dressed as drivers, Sam cleared her throat to get everyone's attention. "I think our rides are here."

Luke's chest tightened slightly. Without his weapons and armor, he felt naked. They were putting a lot of faith in a man they'd never met, but they had little choice. It's not like they could arrive packing their usual heavy arsenal.

Heidi strode toward the drivers to check, then waved Luke and his friends after her and the drivers. Together, they headed toward the exit.

"Do you need to take care of the drinks?" Maggie asked.

"No. We put them on the rooms, so we're good." Luke held out his arm for Maggie to take, then led her after their friends.

The drivers held the doors open on the high-end SUVs, taking three to a vehicle. After Maggie slid in, Luke walked around to the other side, while Pieter took the front passenger seat. Once the three

SUVs were loaded, they took off into Luxembourg's capital. He tried to relax but couldn't get his body to untense, not as they drove into the unknown, a small group without their weapons. A few minutes later, the drivers pulled up in front of an elegant-looking bistro, parked in front, and let everyone out.

L uke had been designated as the group's spokesperson by Pablo and Sam since he was their war leader and the celebrity du jour. The Luxembourg packleader was a history enthusiast, according to Heidi, particularly that of Rome. Luxembourg's land had been a part of the empire for four hundred and fifty years after Caesar conquered the local Celtic tribes.

Offering his arm to Maggie, Luke escorted her into the bistro, his eyes flicking around, looking for any signs of danger. A group of werewolves were gathered inside, their leader standing in front of them. Heidi stepped forward and embraced the robust man of medium height with gray mixed into his well-coiffed brown hair. They exchanged kisses on the cheek before Heidi turned and gestured to Luke.

"Mathis, I have the honor of presenting Luke Irontree, the Centurion Immortal. Luke, this is Mathis Heinen, packleader of Luxembourg," Heidi said.

Luke took Mathis's offered hand. "It's a pleasure to meet you. Thank you for your pack's hospitality." He turned to his friends. "These are my friends and packmates."

Mathis raised his eyebrows at Luke's use of the term "packmates."

Luke continued, "Sam Wakamatsu is a council member and the wife of the packleader."

Sam exchanged a friendly kiss on the cheek, leaning into the European style of greeting.

"Pablo Sandoval is the pack's second," Luke said.

Pablo shook Mathis's hand.

"This is Delilah Johnson, the pack's combat instructor, and Simone Ndiaye, a new member of our pack." They'd thought it best to keep her identity simple to keep her out of the center of attention. "This is Jamaal Burton. He's on the pack council. And last but not least, this is Dr. Maggie Rabinowitz; she's on the pack council and is in charge of the pack's medical team. She's also my girlfriend."

"Doctor." Mathis nodded and embraced Maggie, kissing her on the cheeks.

"It's a pleasure, Mr. Heinen," Maggie replied.

"And you know Pieter van den Bergh," Luke said.

"Yes, Pieter. I'm sorry to hear about your father. He was a titan of a man. His influence was felt by us all," Mathis said, taking Pieter's hand and kissing him on the cheeks in greeting.

Pieter clenched his jaw and nodded. "It's certainly a tragedy. The European packs lost a good man and a good leader."

Mathis gestured around the restaurant. "We're safe to speak freely. We own the restaurant, and the employees are pack."

Luke nodded, then listened, trying to file the names away as Mathis introduced the various people from his pack, finishing with his wife, Gabriela. With everything else going on in Luke's head, he did his best to keep his anxiety in check at being surrounded by new people who could be potential friends or enemies.

After the introductions were made, the Luxembourg pack stepped forward and ushered Luke and his friends to various tables, as each of them had been assigned a Portland counterpart. Luke and Maggie joined Mathis and Gabriela at a table in the center of the room. Luke sat to the right of Mathis while Maggie sat to Luke's right, Gabriela sitting across from Luke.

When everyone was seated, servers circulated about the room

with bottles of champagne and filled their glasses. Not waiting until the servers finished, Mathis stood.

"I'd like to welcome our new friends from Portland." He raised his glass and looked at Luke. "If you'll indulge me, I'd like to greet the illustrious Centurion Immortal properly in the language of his birth." Mathis switched from English to Latin. "It is with great honor that we welcome a servant of the great Roman Empire to our territory. New friends bring new bonds and new bonds bring prosperity to all involved. Such honors are rare in life and should be seized upon when they present themselves. Enjoy the food and the drink and be at ease. May the gods be propitious!"

Everyone raised their champagne glasses and clinked the glasses of the folks they shared tables with. Luke, being a dutiful guest, tapped Mathis's glass first then Gabriela's before giving Maggie a flirty smile and touching her glass. Luke took a sip of the champagne, admiring its fine quality.

"Thank you for the welcome and the speech. The champagne is excellent," Luke said. "Your Latin is also quite good."

"Thank you for saying so and being gracious enough to forgive my pronunciation. I was taught by Catholic priests when I was young and it was the church's Latin I learned, not classical."

"Either way, you're quite a skilled linguist. Although there's one small correction—Latin wasn't the tongue of my birth. It was my second language. I spoke a Belgic dialect of the Gaulish tongue spoken throughout Gaul. I was born not far from here, a bit south of where Brussels is. My father actually did business with local Treveri Celts after he mustered out of the legions." Luke gave Mathis a courteous nod.

"That is utterly fascinating. I didn't realize you were a local boy," Gabriela said, turning to Maggie. "And judging by your accent, you're originally from eastern Europe, Czechia?"

"Poland, actually, though I haven't been back since I left in the forties." Maggie paused for a moment, thinking. "I guess I've lived most of my life away from the land of my birth."

"Do you still have family in Poland?" Gabriela asked.

Luke slid his hand under the table, grasping Maggie's hand as it trembled slightly. She set her glass of champagne down and placed the other hand under the table as well.

"No. I don't have any family left in Poland. The Nazis were very thorough about that," Maggie said, her voice small as she looked down at the table.

"Oh. I'm…I'm sorry, I didn't mean…" Gabriela stuttered.

"It's OK, Gabby, dear. We're all living with too much historical baggage here. It's the burden of being who we are." Mathis smiled unctuously.

Luke nodded politely, though the gesture felt forced. Maggie slid her other hand over his, gripping it tightly while he squeezed her other hand.

Leaning over, he whispered into her ear, "Do you need to step outside for a minute?"

Maggie shook her head and smiled softly. Luke returned the smile and leaned into kiss her cheek, then sat back in his chair. But he still kept Maggie's hand in his.

Deciding to find safer ground to tread, Gabriela cleared her throat before taking a sip of her champagne. "How long have you two been together?"

"About six months," Luke replied.

"I always find it odd when people of our age use the terms 'boyfriend' and 'girlfriend,'" Mathis said, then dismissed it with a wave of his hand.

"We live in the world." Luke shrugged. "We have to adapt to the times to blend in."

"The champagne is lovely," Maggie said, taking a sip.

"Thank you. My sommelier will be pleased to hear it was well received. I don't remember the label offhand, but he sources it from one of the grower houses. I hope you find the rest of the selections this evening as pleasing." Mathis leaned back, appearing happy to have his bistro's wares complimented.

"I love your dress, Maggie," Gabriela said. "Did you bring it with you from Portland?"

Maggie smiled and shook her head. "No. Heidi took us shopping today. When I flew from home, I didn't anticipate needing a cocktail dress. Fortunately, Heidi knows some lovely boutiques around town."

"We're not a large city, but we're not without our luxuries." Gabriela reached over and patted Maggie's hand.

"Being a banking hub doesn't hurt," Luke said. "People with money need something to spend it on."

"Indeed. Banking has been good to our pack," Mathis said.

As the servers made a rotation through the room, they refilled glasses while leaving menu cards in front of everyone. A few minutes later, the head chef stepped out of the kitchen to discuss the menu with everyone, describing the various dishes he'd prepared for the pack's guests. Each of the three courses had three tempting options, to followed by desserts and digestifs.

Luke and Mathis filled the space with idle conversation as they got to know each other. Once Mathis grew more comfortable with Luke, he peppered him with questions about the Roman Empire and the people Luke had met and known. Mathis delighted in the interaction as if Luke was there to entertain him with anecdotes of his life. He tried not to show his annoyance, needing the good will of Mathis while they took sanctuary in his territory.

Throughout the evening, Maggie helped keep him grounded with a gentle hand on his thigh under the table. They were two private and serious people, introverts in the modern parlance, and understood each other's needs when it came to space and conversation. Luke didn't want to share his life so openly with people who were strangers with unknown loyalties. He felt like a circus animal performing for the amusement of his host. For Maggie, Luke would tell the woman anything about his life she wanted to know, but for Mathis, it was a struggle.

In between courses, Luke excused himself to get a breath of fresh air, taking his glass of excellent red wine with him as he stepped outside onto the patio the bistro currently wasn't using. Maggie followed him out, taking his hand and leaning her head on his shoulder.

"How you holding up?" Maggie asked.

Luke huffed. "Fine, I guess. I'm not really in the mood to be

Wikipedia for all his questions about Rome, but what choice do we have? If I thought it would get us out of here safely, I'd perform all the answers to his questions in burlesque."

Maggie laughed, the bright pure sound bringing a smile to his face. "I'd love to see that. Should I suggest it?"

Luke pulled Maggie in front of him, bent down, and kissed her. "Don't you dare, Magdalena."

"Don't worry. He seems too stuffy for a good burlesque show. I'm sure you'll be safe continuing as you are."

Luke smiled broadly before leaning down for another kiss. "How are you doing?"

"I'm doing alright. Gabriela is working very hard to keep the conversation between us as surface as possible, which is fine, though I'm not really much for small talk." She reached up and pushed a lazy curl off Luke's forehead. "Your hair's getting a little long. Your curls are starting to show."

"Unfortunately, we didn't think to invite my stylist with us. Perhaps next time." Luke smirked.

Chuckling, Maggie gave Luke one last kiss. "I like it. You look very handsome."

"You look beautiful under the moonlight. It makes your hair look like silver," Luke said.

"Ah, you're just trying to flirt with me," Maggie teased.

Luke raised an eyebrow. "Is it working?"

"Very much so. We should probably go back inside before our hosts think we don't care for their conversation," Maggie suggested.

Luke held his arm out. "Shall we?"

Maggie took it and walked with him into the bistro. While they waited for the dessert course, Mathis broke out some high-end Armagnac and presented it to Luke and Maggie. Luke complimented the quality, although he'd have preferred to take it out on the porch at the pack's farmhouse and curl up with Maggie under a blanket. He was quickly running out of mental energy to deal with the strangers, especially one who was so aggressively keeping Luke engaged, constantly peppering him with questions from his past.

Luke finally perked up when Mathis offered to talk about a topic Luke was most keen to broach.

"After dessert, I'd like to speak with you and the Portland pack council, along with Heidi and Pieter. I think we may have a solution to your problem that'll make your life easier," Mathis said, raising his glass toward Luke.

"That's something I would be very interested in hearing." He tapped his glass against Mathis's, sending up the gentle ring of quality crystal.

When the desserts were served, Luke tried to savor the excellent Tarte au Citron, stopping himself from rushing through it. Mathis was taking his time with his dessert, so Luke rushing probably wouldn't encourage him to speed up for his impatient guest. Luke's patience was rewarded when Mathis cleared everyone from the room except for his second and Luke's people.

"Thank you for joining me for dinner. It's been most excellent to have you in my city and my restaurant." Mathis raised his glass. "Now on to the meat of the matter. I've been in contact with the packleader of Köln, and we've come up with a solution to your problem. We'll be able to move you and the children to Portland along with all your gear without having to leave Luxembourg City."

"That sounds almost too good to be true. What did you have in mind?" Luke asked.

"Together, the Rhein Pack and the Luxembourg Pack have acquired two private jets for you to use. You'll be able to fly from the airport here," Mathis replied.

"Not to be blunt, but how much will that cost us?" Luke asked.

"Nothing to your pack. Consider it a gift in thanks for the opportunity to meet a legend." Mathis smiled and gave Luke a magnanimous nod.

Luke squinted, skeptical. "What's Köln's angle in this? I haven't met their packleader."

"Well, since we're being blunt, this is also out of past friendship for Pieter and his father." He turned his gaze to Pieter. "We're hoping that with such a convenient option, you'll choose to avail yourself of it and join your friends in the United States. It'll put you out of reach of your brother, and frankly"—Mathis turned back to Luke—"both of our packs are eager to avoid the chaos that follows the Centurion Immortal. The easiest solution is to ensure an easy exit from our territories. That seems well worth the cost of two private jets."

"Fair enough." Luke took a sip of his brandy. "When would the planes be ready to depart?"

"We can have them ready to go by the day after tomorrow," Mathis replied, turning to Heidi. "Heinrich said he'll have a courier bring the passports you needed by tomorrow afternoon."

"Might we have a few moments to discuss it in private?" Luke asked.

Mathis nodded and stood. "We'll step outside." He gestured for his second to follow. Heidi, after looking around the room, stood and joined Mathis and his second, following them outside. Once the door closed, Luke turned to his friends.

"What do you think?" Luke asked.

Sam took the seat vacated by Gabriela. "It's convenient and solves all our problems. I'll have to get everyone moved from Cologne, but that's a simple train ride."

Luke looked from person to person, then rubbed his hand over his face. He'd shaved since his beard was in an early awkward stage of its regrowth. "I may be overly paranoid, but doesn't it seem too convenient? Private jets aren't cheap."

"They're pennies compared to war in their territories, even shadow wars. Flying us out of here as quickly as they can is a cheap option and the logical one," Sam replied. "Pieter, you know both of the packs in question. What do you think?"

"I trust Heidi, and my father trusts...trusted Heinrich, the Köln packleader. Mathis?" Pieter shrugged. "His word is usually good, especially when money is on the line. And Sam is right, you are a pretty expensive liability to have in his territory when he has no interest in your cause, especially with what happened to my...with Belgium."

"I think we need to take the chance, buddy. This gets us home and all of our gear with us," Pablo said.

Luke nodded and looked at his friends, getting reassuring looks and nods from everyone. Maggie took his hand and squeezed it, adding her nod to everyone else's.

Luke fixed an earnest gaze on his Belgian friend. "Pieter, will you be going with us? I think I can speak for everyone that you're more than welcome to join us in Portland."

"You can stay in our guest room," Pablo offered. "Tony won't mind."

"It seems I have little choice in the matter if I want to keep the peace here and avoid the wrath of Jan. Looks like Portland it is." Pieter didn't seem excited about it.

Luke knew Pieter liked Portland, but it wasn't his home. He'd been denied his home by his brother. Luke could sympathize with Pieter in part. He didn't want to withdraw from the place of his birth in ignominious defeat.

"Alright. We leave the day after tomorrow," Luke said, trying to reassure himself it was the right move.

Luke woke early and anxious. They were on the home stretch of their evacuation from Belgium. Once they boarded the private jets and took off, they'd be winging their way back to the United States and the relative safety of their home turf, but a lot could happen between waking up and buckling into a plane seat. Luke thought he'd slide out of bed and get some coffee, but Maggie threw an arm over him, stopping him from leaving.

"Nuh uh," Maggie said groggily. "Stay here. Snuggle me."

Luke couldn't deny the request. He rolled over as Maggie adjusted so her back was to him. When he laid his arm across her waist, she scooched back into him so she could be the little spoon.

"Mmm, that's better." Maggie reached over her shoulder and patted Luke's cheek. "Everything is packed and ready. The world can wait for a little longer without you there to worry about it."

Luke snorted. "But what if the world can't manage without me there to be anxious?"

She ran her hand up Luke's thigh. "Well, I guess I'll have to find a way to distract you."

Maggie rolled over and pulled Luke into a serious kiss, causing his heartbeat to pick up as warmth spread through his body.

When they pulled back, Luke smiled at Maggie, moving a strand of hair from her forehead to behind her ear. "I think I might be persuadable..."

"You're incorrigible." She rolled out of bed. "I'll be right back," she said, disappearing to use the restroom.

Luke followed her out to take his turn. When he returned to the bedroom, Maggie was stretched out naked, lying on her side with her head propped up on her hand. With her other hand, she patted the bed next to her.

"I seem to have lost my pajamas, and it's kind of chilly. Can you think of any ways to keep me warm?" Maggie asked, her eyes burning seductively.

"I can think of a few ways..." Luke strode toward the end of bed and pushed down his shorts, crawling into bed with the woman he loved.

LUKE WATCHED as Maggie and her team got the kids situated in the vehicles Mathis had sent to transport them. Luke, Pablo, Sam, Pieter, Delilah, and Simone loaded their gear into the back of a box van. Pablo had volunteered to ride with the driver to assuage Luke's fear their equipment might get lost en route. As was usual, Luke's personal gear was stowed in the back of the vehicle he'd be riding in.

When the children were situated, the adults loaded up, mixing Maggie's caretakers with Luke's team. He wanted to make sure each vehicle had someone that could fight. After the last person buckled in, Luke climbed into the front passenger seat in the lead SUV and pulled his seatbelt into place.

Nodding to the driver, he pointed forward. "Let's go."

The driver started the car and put it in drive, pulling out into traffic with his caravan behind him.

"How long is the drive?" Luke asked.

"Ten, fifteen minutes top. It's not far," the driver replied.

Luke watched the scenery change from Luxembourg City's Haute Ville old town as the driver wound his way through streets that were really just residential roads. In a few minutes, they'd left the houses behind and drove by buildings that looked like they belonged to businesses. As the driver predicted, they approached the airport about fifteen minutes after they left. It was a small city in a small country, and the airport matched.

The driver pulled up in front of a guarded gate, rolled his window down, flashed an ID badge, and was waved through. The rest of their caravan followed without stopping. They were expected. Turning, the driver aimed the SUV toward a series of hangars for smaller planes, passing them by as they drove toward the end of the row. Once they passed the last one, Luke saw the two jets parked and ready to load. Almost there.

When they parked between the last hangar and the jets, Mathis stepped out from one of the buildings and waved at Luke as he stepped out of the SUV. "Good afternoon, Luke!"

Luke closed the distance between them and shook Mathis's hand. "Good afternoon. Everything ready to go?"

"It will be as soon as you load all your people and equipment."

"Excellent." Luke turned to watch as everyone exited their vehicles.

"I do have one favor to ask you before we conclude our business today," Mathis said.

Luke suspected there'd be more than originally agreed upon during their after-dinner conversation. "And what would that be?"

"It's a small favor. I'd like to see your sword and armor. I mean, that's always been part of the rumors surrounding your existence — that you still fight in Roman armor and wield a gladius." Mathis seemed as eager as a child getting a special treat.

"That's doable." Luke walked to the rear of the SUV he'd arrived in and leaned into its back.

Someone's suitcase was still next to his gear case. Quietly, he slid the zipper open on the suitcase, then opened the latches on his custom-made case. Careful to not draw attention, he grabbed the handle of the wooden rudis with its silver cutting edge and intricate silver filigree. Pulling it out, he shoved it through the small hole unzipped in the suitcase, then zipped it shut. He'd show the man his sword and armor, but the rudis was too personal, too important.

He picked up his case and walked away from the SUV, setting it on the ground between himself and Mathis. He opened the top, letting the sun reflect off the polished steel of his lorica segmentata.

"It's beautiful." Mathis practically drooled.

Not wanting the covetous man to reach in and grab it, he pulled it out and held it up.

"It's exquisite. Is it really as old as they say it is?" Mathis asked.

Luke shrugged. "I have no idea how old they say it is, but my father commissioned its construction before I enlisted when I was seventeen."

"May I see the gladius?"

Luke carefully tucked the armor back into its spot, then lifted the panel that covered the gladius and the rudis. He reached in and pulled the gladius out quickly, shutting the panel before anyone could notice the empty slot and wonder what was absent. Luke held it in front of him, hilt in one hand and blade laid across the open palm of his other hand. Mathis reached out to touch the blade.

"Careful. It has silver in the steel alloy," Luke said.

Mathis yanked his hand back. "This is a Mainz classification of gladius, correct?"

"It is. It wasn't long before the legions started using mostly the Pompey class, but these were popular when my father had the finest blacksmith in Belgica forge it."

"I've never seen one in better condition." Mathis looked at the weapon from different angles, moving his head around as if it were on a swivel.

"Usually they're in pretty bad shape by the time they make it to a museum. Then again, this one has been maintained for over nineteen-hundred years."

"Luke?" Maggie called.

Luke turned to see what Maggie needed. "Yes?"

"Everyone's on board. All the rest of the gear and luggage has been stowed in the cargo holds. They've closed them up, though."

Luke nodded, watching Maggie walk toward him. "We can just throw this in the cabin."

"OK."

"I'll be along in a second, Maggie." Luke leaned over and kissed her on the cheek and forced a smile on his face.

"See you in a minute." Maggie hesitated as she turned, casting another look over her shoulder at Luke as she walked away.

Luke watched her walk away, longing in his eyes. As her foot hit the first step, the hangar doors opened, accompanied by the sound of dozens of feet pounding over the tarmac. At the noise, Maggie turned.

"Luke!" Maggie screamed, pointing behind him.

Someone stepped out of the plane, wrapped an arm around Maggie, then shoved a pistol into her temple. Luke sighed and shook his head, turning around.

At the look of venom Luke gave Mathis, the packleader backed away, letting his goons step between their leader and the man with a deadly silver blade. Luke didn't bother counting the number of automatic gun barrels pointed at him. It was more than enough to fill Luke full of bullets before he could close the distance between himself and the man who'd betrayed them.

"I take it this was all a set up? The jets, everything?" Luke asked.

"No. Your friends will soon be departing for the States and their home, as promised. I just never said you'd be going with them." With the line of guns separating Luke from Mathis, he looked much more confident, his hands clasped behind his back as he stood tall, though he still fell a few inches short of Luke's six feet.

As if to answer Luke's accusation, the first jet throttled up and headed toward the runway.

"We're going to need you to put your sword down," Mathis instructed.

"Remove the gun from Maggie's head. As soon as I hear the jet rolling away, I'll set it down."

"Luke… no…" Maggie called.

Luke could hear the tears in her voice. He blinked back the burning in his eyes.

"I'm a gentleman," Mathis said magnanimously, nodding in concession, then barked out some orders in Lëtzebuergesch.

When the door sealed shut on the jet, the air fled from Luke's lungs as his shoulders slumped and his head dipped. Taking a few steadying breaths, he listened for the sound of the jet throttling up. When the jet engines roared their power, he raised his head and squared his shoulders, then bent over and set the sword on the case.

"Now take two steps back." Mathis barked more orders in Lëtzebuergesch.

Luke understood most of what Mathis said since Luxembourg's language was historically a dialect of German, and Luke still remembered all the various forms of German he'd learned over the centuries. The goons with machine guns took a few steps forward, so they flanked Luke's gear case on both sides. Mathis, like he was on an afternoon stroll, sauntered forward and picked up the gladius by the handle. Giving himself some space, he swung the blade around, lunging into a few clumsy thrusts.

Since he could do nothing, Luke turned around and watched the jet with Maggie on it taxi away. He should have said he loved her one last time before she returned to the plane, but thoughts of getting her back onto the plane safely had dominated his mind. The ground crew loading the jets must have had guns hidden on the carts used to move his team's gear and luggage. Focusing entirely on watching the jet taxi to the runway, Luke ignored everything else, vaguely hearing Mathis speaking behind him.

He didn't turn around until the wheels had left the ground. "I'm sorry if you said anything important. I was ignoring you."

Anger swept over Mathis's face as the feigned joviality disappeared.

"Now that you have me, what are you going to do with me?" Luke asked.

"I don't actually have you. I'm merely a middleman. A broker, if you will. I'm fulfilling a client's requisition." Mathis held the sword in his right hand.

"And who might this client be?" Luke asked. Feigning nonchalance, Luke clasped his hands behind his back.

"It's an old friend of yours," Mathis replied.

"I killed the last old friend I had last spring. I have no more old friends, only dead enemies." Luke stared at Mathis, blinking slowly and menacingly.

"Look at you. You're positively dripping with malice." Mathis looked gleeful. "Oh, how you must frighten the vampires and make them scurry about. You are indeed a delight."

"Is Le Mousquetaire the fanger pulling your strings?" Luke asked.

"'Fanger'? I don't know… Oh. I understand." Mathis opened his mouth and rubbed his finger over the point of one of his canine teeth before continuing, "No, you're too important for a low-level general like Le Mousquetaire to arrange and handle." He tapped his chin with his forefinger from his unoccupied hand. "I think we'll leave it as a surprise for you."

Luke rolled his eyes and shrugged. "I hate this rigmarole where you try to be clever. You've already got one over on me and betrayed me and my friends; why rub it in? Don't you watch movies? This is step one in your own death at the hands of a vengeful victim of your machinations. How many villains brag and live to see the end of the story?"

"Oh, Mr. Irontree. Only the ones who get away with it, but then, there's no hero to survive and tell of their tale of dealing the villain's comeuppance. There's just sweet victory." Mathis brought his hand from behind his back and pointed an odd-looking gun at Luke. Smiling smugly, he pulled the trigger.

Luke recoiled as the dart hit him in the upper chest near his shoulder. When he looked down, a tranquilizer dart looked back at him.

Mathis smirked. "Sleep well, Centurion Immortal. It may be the last good rest you get."

Luke reached down to pull the dart, but Mathis shook his head and lifted the gun to point the barrel at Luke.

"Leave it." Mathis turned to one of his goons. "Why isn't he going down?"

The man shrugged. "Maybe he needs more?"

Luke shook his head. "It doesn't work instantly when it goes through the muscles. It takes a few minutes to take effect. Didn't you do your research?" Luke sighed. "Now you've wasted your line, and we have to stand around awkwardly, like a pack of assholes." He sat on the tarmac and laid down, anger coursing through his veins.

"What are you doing?" Mathis asked.

"I don't feel like falling and hitting my head. You'll just have to make your goons pick me up after I pass out." Luke stared up at the clouds drifting across the blue sky. He didn't think any of his friends on the planes had ever been a pilot, so they were in for a long ride with the ability to do nothing, otherwise they'd jeopardize crashing the plane. They had to get the children, split up between the two jets, to safety.

He felt bad for his friends. They'd pushed this plan and now were helpless hostages in jets quickly climbing to cruising altitudes. He hoped they'd be OK and figure out a way to come after him. Yawning, he felt the tranquilizer taking effect.

He owed Mathis and the Cologne packleader. Thoughts of vengeance would be his only companion wherever he was headed. As the world around him grew dim, he thought about the beautiful face of Maggie and her kind eyes. Then, the tranquilizer dragged him into unconsciousness.

Garbled conversation filtered through Luke's hazy brain as he cracked his eyes open. Although the light wasn't intense, it still stabbed into his eyes. Once they adjusted, he tried to see where he was. Without moving his head too much—he didn't want to alert his captors that he was awake—he could see a rounded ceiling, like the inside of a jet. Still disoriented from the tranquilizer, he didn't feel entirely flat. Maybe he was in a deep recline.

He pushed forward, testing to see if he was restrained. Yup. The straps held him firmly in place, chest, legs, and arms. Even his head was strapped down. He couldn't move, even if he wanted to. Out of the corner of his eye, he thought he could see an IV line in his arm, running up to disappear above and behind him.

"Master, I think he's awake," someone said in French. They were somewhere in front of him.

"Give him another dose. We can't have him waking until after he's safely stowed away," replied someone else in a thick, raspy voice. It might have sounded familiar if Luke's brain wasn't still hazy from the drugs they'd been pumping into him. The second speaker wasn't a native French speaker, their words heavily accented, but not in a way Luke could determine.

Someone wearing nondescript black clothes and a mask stepped into Luke's view, holding a syringe. Luke tried to pull away from the seat, but the straps were too tight and too strong.

"Don't worry. The needle won't need to go in your arm. Your IV has a port," the person with the syringe said.

A few moments later, Luke's world faded back to black.

LUKE GROANED, consciousness drifting toward him. Wrinkling his nose, he coughed at the smell of piss and shit. He rolled over, no longer restrained, and felt the cold hard stone of the floor he'd been left on. The move left his head swimming. After it stopped, he returned to his back. He couldn't tell if he'd hit his head at some point or if it was the effect of whatever they'd been pumping into his veins to keep him sedated and unconscious while they transported him to whatever hellhole he currently was in.

He could stretch all the way out, though his foot did bump into something solid—probably a wall. He tried to lay patiently, letting his body work to process the drugs from his system. At some point, he dozed off, the drugs still sedating his body. It was an easy solution that would hopefully solve problems—the drugs and his dizziness.

When he woke again, he was able to raise his head and look around the room. Three of the walls were featureless gray stone while the fourth's monotony was broken up by a solid wooden door with a small wooden flap door near the bottom. On the ground in front of the door, a metal tray and a metal cup sat. At least he wasn't in an oubliette.

Pushing himself into a sitting position, he took a minute to let his head stop spinning. Once the fog cleared some, he wondered where the light was coming from and looked up. A single bulb dangled through a hole just big enough for a wire to fit through. The light was dim, but it was better than nothing. Not trusting his body enough to stand, he crawled the few feet to the tray and cup.

Starting with the cup, he picked it up and sniffed it, then dipped a finger into it and brought it to his mouth—clean water. He took a tentative sip. The water seemed fine, so he took a bigger drink but forced himself to set it aside so he didn't chug it all down. The tray was divided into three sections, like a cafeteria tray. A grain porridge filled the largest section, with maybe a few small chunks of meat or fat scattered about in it. In the other sections, there was some mush that looked like it might have started its life as a vegetable of some kind and a slice of bread. Under the slice of bread, a spoon lay hidden. At least they weren't going to starve him.

He picked up the spoon and scooped a tiny amount of the porridge onto the tip of the spoon and brought it up to his nose. He didn't smell anything untoward or rotten about the food. His only observation was that it seemed kind of bland, but better bland than poisoned or spoiled. He put the food into his mouth and squished around on his tongue to see if he noticed something he might have missed with the smell. Nothing wrong with the food, just boring.

Next, he took the spoon and stirred around in the porridge to see if there was anything hidden within. It was clean, same with the vegetable mash. Whoever his captors were, they wanted him alive and decently fed for now. He'd been in worse situations and escaped, so he slowly consumed the food and water, taking his time to make sure his stomach didn't rebel when mixed with whatever they'd used to keep him unconscious. When he was finished, and since there was no one to see his bad manners, he picked up the tray and licked it clean. Every calorie was critical when he had no control over when his next meal would come, so he ensured he left nothing on the tray. Finished, he returned the tray and spoon to the spot where he'd found them.

Leaning against the wall with the remaining half of his water, he looked around to see if he could spot something he might have missed earlier. In the far corner, there was a bucket and a roll of toilet paper. That would explain the stench. He risked standing up, leaning heavily against the wall while his head spun. The dizziness wasn't as bad as when he first woke, but the weakness was concerning. He hoped it was an aftereffect of the drugs in his system. He doubted whoever put them into his system was a doctor. They'd probably overdosed him fearing he'd wake and take his retribution.

He walked slowly, keeping a hand propped against the stone wall. The bucket was empty, thankfully. The odor must be coming from elsewhere, possibly other cells with other occupants. He completed a circuit of the tiny room; it had to be only seven feet by maybe nine feet. Once he returned to the wall with the door, he inspected it.

It looked heavy and thick. He'd get a better idea just how heavy it was when his jailer came to take his tray. He couldn't see any hinges. They must be buried in the stone. There was a stone lip that ran around the door on both sides and the top, meaning the door opened out.

With the increasing pressure in his bladder, Luke looked across the room at the bucket with distaste. Sighing, he walked across the room, keeping his hand on the wall for balance. He nudged the toilet paper away from the bucket with his foot, pulled down the baggy cotton pants they'd stuffed him in at some point, and relieved himself into the bucket. He hoped they took the buckets regularly.

He'd lived most of his life without plumbing, except when he lived in the Roman Empire and the modern era. By and large, cities had been a very fragrant place for most of history. Maybe that was one of the reasons he wandered so much, seeking open country where the air was fresh and not tainted by the shit of too many unclean humans.

He toddled back to the other side of the room and sat down, leaning up against the wall next to the door. The bucket, in his line of sight, drew his eye. He scooted to sit against the perpendicular wall so he could look across the space and not into the back of his cell at his bathroom bucket.

As he lay against the wall, he receded into his head trying to figure out what he was going to do or if he even could do anything. Sweeping his eyes over the stone wall absentmindedly, a random pattern or shading drew his attention and pulled him out of his head. It looked like a crescent moon. Selene...

Hope surged through him. Sitting up, he closed his and lifted his face toward the ceiling. *"My Mistress, I need you, please."* He waited but felt nothing, no touch of acknowledgement or warmth of her presence. He tried reaching out again, but the result was the same. The flame of hope perished, doused with the reality that he might truly be alone. He returned to staring at the wall, trying to stave off panic and a rising wave of despair.

At some point, sleep and the lingering drugs claimed him again. Besides, he had nothing else to do. Sleep was a safer option instead of focusing on his growing fear and anxiety.

FOR DAYS, Luke lived in silence, only broken when the heavy bar was lifted from the outside of the flap door. The bar lifted, the flap opened, and a gun barrel poked into the open space. The empty tray was quickly taken, a new one shoved in. They fed him twice a day at what he guessed was mid-morning and early evening, based on the light switching off a few hours after he ate the second meal. At midday, in between meals, someone would collect the bucket. He'd learned the hard way when he didn't have his bucket in place and the door opened. The latrine person just shut the door and barred it, forcing Luke to live with the bucket for another twenty-four hours.

So by his reckoning of two meals a day, a bucket pickup, and a cycle of dark and light, he'd been there a week or so with nary a word spoken to him or any change of routine. Three silent visitors every day followed by lights out. All Luke could figure was the visitors were human or werewolf since they didn't set off his vampire proximity senses.

He tried to keep to a regular sleep schedule as best as he could by trying to avoid napping out of boredom during the day. To keep his mind occupied, he talked to himself in his head in the various languages he'd learned over the years, even delving into long dead languages or older versions of the modern ones just to keep variety alive and to avoid walking down the darker hallways of his imagination. When he stumbled on the debris of his past lives and dug into one of the old languages, his mind wandered to those he'd spoken the language with and his movement through their points in time.

He never considered those times as his, even when he lived in them. He was a traveler through time, where everyone else's timeline was finite and fixed. They belonged in their times, were products of it. Luke was a product of hundreds of years, with each person only skimming across his psyche with the barest of touches, altering him by means of many tiny drops that built slowly over time. Whereas time flooded the being of humans with their finite lives until it drowned them, carrying them away and ending their sparks.

He'd been through long stretches of time alone with no company but the horse he rode upon, but at least then he had the wind and birds to keep him company and the scenery to stimulate his thoughts. Here, he had dull gray stone walls with only mild variations in coloring and lighting to feed his mind, which at best was a scanty meal. At least his week's worth of beard growth gave him something to occasionally do, providing an opportunity to scratch at his face.

Periodically, he'd try to reach out to Selene—sometimes he'd try when the light bulb shined and sometimes when it didn't. He had no idea if his keepers kept the light on during the daytime or not. It didn't matter. No matter when he tried to reach out to her, she never replied.

By the end of the second week, he was having trouble keeping his mind straight, often drifting wildly without aim or purpose. When the end of the third week approached, Luke found himself napping to avoid the tedium of nothing, losing track of night and day. Once welcome reminders of a schedule, the noise of the caretakers intruding on his silence caused distress—the noise of the bar being lifted raised his heart rate and caused him to scramble away from the door.

The only bright spot in his life became the weekly pair of buckets, one filled with soapy water and one filled with clean water. With the water, he'd carefully bathe himself, then use the soapy water to clean his room, and finally, rinse his bucket. As soon as he finished his tasks, he returned the buckets with their used water to the door to be picked up.

Each day Luke stared at the wall with the scratch marks he'd been making to represent days, and each day his struggle to add the next tally mark grew more difficult. Sometimes he even told himself it didn't even matter and resolved to stop, but inevitably, he'd scramble to grab the spoon. He used the end of its handle to scrape a mark into the stone next to his other tally marks before dropping it back on the tray.

When he grew tired of staring at the scratches in the stone, he found another patch of stone to gaze at. Cataloging the differences in the various stones forming his cell became his new hobby. If he was lucky, he'd find a pattern or picture to keep his mind occupied for a few more minutes.

After six weeks—or was it five?—Luke could no longer bring himself to count the marks. He began napping most of the day, even missing a meal or bucket stop on occasion. At night, he stared at the ceiling or wall, rolling from back to side to the other side trying to find a hard spot that felt slightly softer, but finding all the stone to be of equal hardness.

It must have been at about eight weeks, or at least Luke thought he remembered eight bathing buckets, when the scratching sounds started. At first, Luke thought he was imagining the noise, his brain finding a way to amuse itself. But after a week of irregular scratching, he came to miss the sound when it wasn't there, longing for the companionship it brought. After eleven or twelve weeks, the scratches just blended with the routine of his tedium, but they never went away. After an additional four weeks, each scratch stabbed into his brain until he spent minutes and hours with his fingers stuffed into his ears.

One night, after the scratching stopped, Luke lay staring at the ceiling when he thought he heard something new, some sound other than the night sounds of his prison. Beyond the occasional foot fall or scuff of a boot, Luke had never heard another noise. Once he thought he heard a sneeze. Then weeks of scratching made their way into Luke's mental routine to be cataloged and added. Now there was something new, or at least that's what Luke hoped.

CHAPTER FIVE

The noise became more frequent and consistent. Luke spent hours trying to find the source, crawling along the floor with his ear to the ground or by the cracks in the door, anywhere he could think to find its origin.

After a couple days of searching, he found the spot that produced the loudest sound by one of the back stones near the floor. It was still little more than a whisper accompanied by the faint scratching noises. At what point he realized the scratches were now happening to a rhythm, he wasn't sure, but once he picked up the steady beat, his brain snapped into clarity as did the whispered sound of a song being sung.

He felt something odd with his face, realizing it was his muscles moving into a soft smile. Music. The whispered noises and now the scratches were music. He lay there letting the faint sounds fill him, though they were only a trickle, and he was a very empty jug. As he closed his eyes, his soul latched onto the barest of threads, clinging desperately to an idea.

He was not alone.

His jailers did not count. How could they? They maintained his physical health only so he would live longer—to draw out the torture of isolation and remind him he had no one in this place. Now there was someone who wasn't one of his tormentors, someone cast into this hellhole like him. For the first time in months, someone who wasn't an enemy.

After the first few weeks, he'd stopped thinking about his friends —Pablo, Delilah, & Sam. He'd pushed Maggie's and Gwen's faces into the deep recesses of his brain. Visions of their eyes had first filled with sympathy and love; now he only saw pity and disgust. He knew the real Maggie and Gwen would never look at him that way —at least he thought so, when his higher logic was available to remind him that they must be worried sick after his kidnapping and disappearance.

But right now, he wasn't alone in this prison, and for the first time in ages, when he thought of his friends, knowing there might be someone here, it brought back the comfort that had abandoned him. When he could no longer hide from the face of Gwen, he reached up and felt his cheeks, his fingers drawing back wet from the tears streaming down his face. He missed her terribly. They'd not even had a year together in their weird little found family, and he'd been ripped away from her. The child had been coming along so well, finally finding joys and happiness in her life. He hoped she was still able to seek out her happiness.

Finally, Maggie's pretty face formed in his imagination. He'd fallen in love with her. The first person he'd truly loved romantically in more than a century, probably longer. Zel had told him not to break her heart, and now he'd failed. He tried to reason with himself that it wasn't his fault; he'd been kidnapped, giving his life in exchange for Maggie's. The image of the gun pressed into her temple drew a sob from his disused throat. He barely recognized the raspy sound as coming from his mouth.

The effort of visiting his friends and loved ones took their toll, draining what little energy he had, pushing him from the peak of his musical discovery back into the deep crevasse of his malaise and into a troubled sleep.

IT HAPPENED SO GRADUALLY, Luke barely noticed the singing grew slightly louder over the week. He only figured it out because he could understand the occasional word. Once he had a word or two, his mind pushed aside some of the fog of his depression and searched through the memories of all the tongues he'd ever learned. After a lot of time spent staring at the ceiling with his ear near the stone where the sound was the loudest, he stumbled upon the right combination of thoughts to link the few words he understood.

Middle Persian.

He'd spent some time trading along the southern borders of the Sarmatian steppes as he roamed with his wife Marpesia and her Wolf Clan. Trading with the Sasanians who'd replaced the Parthians as rulers of much of the old Persian empire could be very lucrative, though he wasn't sure Marpesia cared that much about the actual profit. She more valued the experience of seeing new things and being in new lands. After most of his friends had passed, and then Marpesia… After that, the steppes held nothing but pain for him. He disappeared into the Sasanian Empire where no one knew the Centurio Immortalis.

And though he could trace the few words he'd picked from the soft sounds of song coming through the wall, the others didn't match up quite right with the Persian language that had evolved from the Old Persian of Cyrus's empire. The singer must be from one of the other contemporaneous languages of the Iranian language group. Either they were a scholar of antiquity or they were very old, possibly as old as Luke was.

When the latter option took root in his head, he pressed his body against the stone wall hoping proximity might tell him if the voice belonged to his enemy, to an ancient vampire born in the lands of one of Persia's neighbors. Stone had never been a deterrent to his sense of the enemy, though there were more mysteries in the world than he could encounter even if he had lived for nearly two thousand years. He sensed nothing.

It could be some ploy and new deviltry perpetrated by the vampires, for he knew that was who Mathis Heinen had sold him to, but without anything to back a guess of a fanger next door, he'd have to trust that it wasn't. Besides, why would a vampire spend all day in a cell scratching at stones and singing ancient songs just to torture him?

Now that he was attuned to it, he picked up more words but still couldn't place the dialect or base language. Laying on his back, using his toilet paper roll as a pillow, he listened to the simple melodies accompanied by the rhythmic scratching of something on stone. Gradually, the voice grew louder and the words clearer.

He wasn't sure what he expected or why he hadn't put together the clues as to why the songs became clearer and louder, but when something broke through the mortar joining the stones together, he yelped and scrambled away from the stone, pushing his back against the wall on the opposite side from the tiny new hole in the wall.

"Hello? Is…there?" A feminine voice emerged through the stone, still speaking the language Luke couldn't quite grasp.

"I am here," Luke answered in a barely audible whisper, more meant to reassure himself of his own existence than to answer the question.

"Hello?" the voice said.

Shaking his head, Luke crawled to the tiny hole and spoke into it, answering in the Middle Persian he knew. "I am someone, and I am here."

"What? Can you speak louder?" the voice asked, switching to Middle Persian.

Luke's voice hadn't been used in…months. He wet his mouth and tried again. "I am someone, and I am here."

"How do you know Middle Persian?"

"I lived in Persia for a while," Luke answered.

"That version of Persian hasn't been used in twelve hundred years."

"Who…who are you?" Luke closed his eyes to listen.

"Just another voice in the rock."

Luke chuckled, the harsh sound scraping over his ears. "What language were you singing in?"

"Parthian. I lived there for a while," the feminine voice answered, recycling his answer.

"The Parthian Empire died almost eighteen hundred years ago," Luke replied.

"About that long ago... In fact, in a few more years, it'll be eighteen hundred exactly since the last Arsakid king died,"

"Are you a scholar?" Luke asked.

The voice chuckled. "Not as such."

Luke hadn't talked that much in weeks, months. He grabbed the tin cup with the remains of his water and took a sip. "How...how long have you been here?"

For the first time, her voice sounded less confident. "I don't know. I quit counting."

Luke's eyes flicked over to the lines of tally marks he'd been mechanically scratching into the wall. His eyes would blur after he found a clean spot to make his next scratch. Like his neighbor, he quit counting them a while ago. "Me too."

Silence hung after their confessions, Luke receding back into his mind again. Eventually, the soft sound of sad humming pulled him back to the present.

"Can we find a language other than Middle Persian? It's been a long time since I learned it, and it wasn't a strong language for me even then." The struggle to find the vocabulary and assemble the sentences was proving more challenging than it should have had he been healthy and hale.

"I suppose you speak English?" she asked, switching to English.

"I do," Luke replied in English. "How did you get through the mortar?"

"I found a spoon hidden in a hole. I've been enlarging it. It's something to do to keep from going crazy."

"What can I call you?" Luke asked.

"My name?"

"We don't need to be that personal, but something to call you would be nice," Luke replied, scared she might spook and stop talking to him.

"Call me Roxi," she replied.

"Luke." He had wanted to give her one of his many aliases, but the hunger for human contact created by hearing her voice overrode caution. "You can call me Luke."

"Well, Luke, it's nice to meet you, such as it is, but I think I'm going to go away now," Roxi replied.

He finally placed her accent as Farsi accented British English. "OK, Roxi. Perhaps we can talk later."

"If I'm in the neighborhood." Her laughter faded as she moved somewhere else in her cell.

Yawning, Luke moved to his sleeping corner. Talking with Roxi had drained him. He just hoped she wasn't a new stage in his mental breakdown. Hallucinations wouldn't help, although if Roxi was a hallucination, at least she was a pleasant one.

AFTER LUKE first spoke to Roxi, he found he could stay awake longer. The anticipation of being able to talk to another person made his need to constantly nap slightly less urgent.

After their first contact, Roxi didn't return to scraping at the mortar the next day. On the second day, she remained silent. Luke was beginning to think he really had hallucinated her presence. Except, whenever he looked at the wall, the hole she'd poked through was still there. He began to think he'd scared her off, and he'd never hear from her again—until after the second meal had been served. He heaved a sigh of relief when she returned to singing her Parthian songs, either forgetting Luke was there or not caring. With a smile on his face, he laid down on the floor next to the stone with the hole in its mortar. When the lights went out, she stopped scraping, her song ending along with it.

After a while, she finally acknowledged his presence. "Goodnight, Luke."

"Goodnight, Roxi."

The next day, Luke woke to the sound of scraping and singing. He relieved himself in his bucket, then returned to the hole in the mortar.

"Good morning, Luke."

"Good morning, Roxi," Luke replied.

"Big plans for the day?" Roxi asked.

"Not much. How about you?"

"I thought I might make some dust." She returned to singing.

When their breakfasts arrived, she broke off her song. For weeks and weeks, the food had tasted of nothing to Luke, but now it seemed the best meal he'd eaten in ages. Nothing had changed. It was the same glop they'd been putting on his tray since the day he'd arrived, but not today.

When he'd finished and returned to the hole, he waited for Roxi to finish her breakfast, hoping she'd sing some more. He'd nearly dozed off when she finally returned to her task.

"You know, you could join me if you like," Roxi said, taking a break between songs.

"I don't know any Parthian songs."

"Sing with a spoon, Luke. Let its dulcet tones join mine." She hummed a new tune.

"Won't they get concerned if I don't return it?"

"Just borrow it for a while. Return it at the next tray swap. The mindless drones don't care what shape it's in as long as it looks like a spoon and is on the tray for the exchange," Roxi said.

"How do you know?" Luke asked.

Roxi chuckled. "I kept one once because the one I found was in bad shape. They didn't bring me my second meal. The bastards opened the door and then shut it to let me know it wasn't some sort of oversight. The next day when they came by for the morning meal, I left my old one on the floor and they exchanged it for a new tray. So I borrow their spoons and use them for a while so I don't destroy my spare, then make sure they're back on the tray in time. I'm quick enough and that crossbar isn't quiet when it comes off the door." She made a sound that made Luke think of a shrug.

"Why aren't they more concerned about their spoons being used to tunnel out of here?" Luke mused.

Roxi snorted. "It took me months to get this far. I don't know how long the previous tenant had been at it before me. But there are two of us, so maybe it won't take so long."

Luke sighed. "It seems kind of pointless."

"You got something more pressing to do?" Roxi asked.

Luke didn't, so he rolled over and grabbed the spoon off his tray. Back in front of the wall, he laid the end of the spoon against the mortar. He was about to dig in when he stopped himself.

"Which stone are we working on?" Luke asked.

"My predecessor was working around this smaller one. The stone to the left of the hole I just made—your left. I'll keep working on this seam. Why don't you work on the top seam so we don't bash into each other?" She started humming a melody as she returned to her scratchings.

Luke put his spoon's handle along the top edge of the stone and pushed into the mortar with the edge, creating a trickle of dust. After a few minutes, his hand hurt from the spoon digging into his flesh. Looking down, he picked up the edge of his shapeless tunic but caught something out of the corner of his eye. One of the empty rolls from his toilet paper lay along the other wall. He grabbed it and used it to pad his hand. Soon, his spoon matched the rhythm of Roxi's spoon, and he quietly hummed along to her melody.

L uke and Roxi worked steadily on their stone. As his hands pushed the spoon, pulling it back to reset, and pushed again, the fog slowly cleared from his mind. Everything still felt fuzzy around the edges, but clarity was more evident when he went searching in the vaults of his mind, seeking whatever he happened to be looking for.

While they worked, Roxi hummed or sang, the songs set to the rhythm of their spoons scratching into mortar. After a while, Luke, seeking any stimulation he could get, played with the rhythms he scratched into the mortar, adding syncopations or triplets. As he added complexity to the rhythms, Roxi kept her rhythm steady but added new subtleties to her melodies. Luke, who'd been humming along with her, kept his notes consistent, learning the key changes she made and adjusting his long steady notes to complement hers. It was like he was providing a drone to accompany her melodies like he'd first heard nineteen hundred years ago in the palace at Antiochia, when Trajan introduced him to the two Armenians youths who would become family.

Despite their proximity and coordination in their task, their conversations never lasted more than a few basic sentences to provide status updates. After the first day they'd spoken, neither initiated much in the way of conversation nor did the words they exchange include questions about who they were or what their pasts might be. Their overabundance of caution felt warranted in a prison they'd both been cast into, and when the outside world had forgotten them. It wasn't until several weeks later that Roxi asked Luke something personal.

"You're a pretty natural musician. Do you actually play anything? You know, on the outside?"

It took a while for Luke to process that he'd been asked something personal. "I…uh…used to play piano. I was pretty good too — I mean, for an amateur. Though, I didn't have your average teacher."

"Not some secondary school teacher looking to pick up a couple extra pounds on the weekend?" Roxi injected a note of humor into the question.

"No. He was a virtuoso pianist and composer. We became friends, and he taught me. I kept playing whenever I could, until…" Luke's spoon stuttered for a moment before picking up his previous rhythm. He'd lost the taste for it after World War I.

"You said he was a composer? Anyone I might have heard of?" Roxi asked.

With his mind distracted by bad memories, he didn't apply his usual filter. "Beethoven."

When Roxi's spoon stopped, Luke's attention snapped back to the present.

"As in Ludwig Van Beethoven? Not some guy named Bill Beethoven? Becky Beethoven, the primary school music teacher?"

He picked up his rhythm again. "Ludwig was a dear friend, and my time spent with him in Vienna is one of my fondest memories."

He'd been caught letting information drop; he wasn't going to backpedal it. Of course, she'd been singing Parthian songs. It's not like she was truly pretending to be a standard human, either.

"I doubt it was Beethoven who taught you how to do a proper drone." She returned to scraping at the mortar.

"No, I spent some time in Armenia and befriended a brother and sister who played tsiranapogh. I guess it's known as a duduk outside of Armenia these days," Luke replied.

"I know what a tsiranapogh is. I've spent more than my share of time in Armenia over the years."

They both scraped at the mortar without speaking. The outside of the seam flaked away relatively easily; it just took time and effort. The insides of the seams, though, were proving more difficult without being able to get proper leverage, since so much of the spoon needed to be shoved inside the growing crevice. With both of them working from each side, it would be easier to meet in the middle.

"You should play piano in your cell," Roxi said, breaking the silence.

It took Luke a minute to process what seemed like a non sequitur. "What?"

"Play piano in your cell."

"I'm not sure who to put in the request with. Think they'd bring me a baby grand?"

Roxi chuckled. "No, silly. In your mind. Close your eyes, and let your fingers find the keys. If you need something to stand in for a keyboard, scratch one in the floor."

"Why?"

"It's another place to escape to. I don't know."

He didn't reply, thinking about her suggestion. He'd quit the piano when it no longer provided comfort. He wasn't sure it would do much in here. He went back to scratching at the wall and humming along with Roxi.

Luke wasn't sure he understood their end game. Neither of them could slip through the space the stone's removal would clear. They'd be able to stick an arm through at best, but maybe it was less about the results and more about doing something, even if it ultimately wouldn't lead to their escape. After all, he didn't have a rock hammer and a Rita Hayworth poster, and these weren't old concrete walls.

After a while, Roxi must have grown more curious about her neighbor and fellow spoon deconstruction enthusiast and started asking more probing questions. Simple questions one might ask on an early date, but eventually she started dropping in deeper questions.

"So, Luke, what you in here for?" she asked.

"I'm innocent. Lawyer fucked me," Luke replied. His body gave a little shake of a chuckle, unvocalized. "Don't you know everyone in here is innocent?"

Roxi groaned. "Do all men quote movies to avoid answering questions?"

"I'm sorry. Just had been thinking about 'The Shawshank Redemption' and your question kind of struck the same note."

"I tell you what, if we meet a guy named Red, we need to scrounge up some smokes to trade for a rock hammer," Roxi replied.

Luke snorted and laughed. "That's what I was thinking about. I guess that's only natural, given the circumstances. Although, the more I think about it, I'm feeling much more in line with Edmond Dantès in my goals. You wouldn't happen to have been imprisoned by Napoleon over a matter of gold, would you?"

"Unfortunately, no."

Luke sighed and stopped his spoon. "I was betrayed. Sold out for power and profit, most likely."

"A friend?" Roxi asked.

"No, but he'd offered me and my friends hospitality."

"He violated your guest rights?" Roxi sounded shocked.

"I've been thinking about that. I don't think he ever said the word 'guest' to me or any of my friends. The slippery bastard chose his words carefully, though it shouldn't matter. We broke bread together." A simmering rage Luke tried to keep banked flared up at the talk of Mathis's betrayal.

"And you trusted him?" Roxi sounded skeptical.

"I didn't trust him, but I had few options at the time. I just hope he followed through and my friends made it home safely." That hope had sustained him, knowing they'd be out there looking for a way to free him. Luke restarted his spoon chiseling. "How about you? How'd your lawyer fuck you?"

Roxi chuckled. "No lawyers, though it's possible one of them had a day job as a lawyer—well, a night job might be more accurate—but I was trapped and captured. They caught me in a dead-end alley and filled me with tranquilizer darts. Next thing I know, I'm in this cell."

"Night Jobs?" Luke thought. His "hunter" alarms were going off.

Over the centuries, he'd run into a few hunters like him, anointed by some god or other to carry justice to the undead. If the circumstances were right, he'd team up with them to accomplish whatever common goal they had at the time, then move on. Usually, their varying masters required them elsewhere after they'd cleared their task.

Luke took a chance. "Are we dancing around the same enemies, Roxi?"

"I'm going to move to the top seam for a while. Why don't you see if you can finish up your side of the right seem," Roxi said, avoiding the question.

Since she didn't answer, he respected her wishes and didn't push further.

"I figured you were a hunter, Luke. Why else would you be in here?" She said after a while. "And how else would you be old enough to have learned piano from Beethoven?"

"Well, I haven't seen you around the hunters' guild hall, but nice to meet you," he replied.

"What. There's a hunters' guild hall? I never got my invite…" Even though he didn't know her at all, she sounded genuinely shocked.

"No. I was being facetious. Sorry if my voice didn't convey the right tone. I'm…I'm struggling with"—he gestured around himself even if she couldn't see it—"everything right now."

"That I can understand. It's a…a challenge to be in here, trapped with nothing but silence. It's been nice to have you to talk to." The energy leached out of her voice.

"Your voice and working on this stupid rock have done more to help me clear the fog in my head than anything else." Luke remained silent for a while as they worked, finally adding, "Thank you, Roxi."

"You're welcome, and thank you, too. It's been a two-way exchange." She went silent for a while before taking up one of her hummed melodies.

They didn't speak anymore, taking a break to rest their hands and eat their dinner meal. Neither of them felt like working after, but Luke still chose to lay next to the work area so his ear was next to the small hole they'd punched in the mortar. Roxi must have also been close to their rock because when she began singing, her voice sounded loud and clear. Well, as loud and clear as possible under the circumstances. When she finished her first song, she moved onto another, then another after it before stopping to rest her voice.

"Luke?" Roxi broke the silence.

"Yes?"

"Where did they take you from?"

"Luxembourg," he replied.

"Is that where you're from?"

Luke chuckled. "That's a big question. Where are people as old as we are from?"

"How do you know I'm as old as you are? If you studied under Beethoven, you'd be well over two-hundred-years-old."

Luke laughed. "Oh, I think you're older than two hundred. I don't know many people born in the eighteenth or nineteenth centuries that sing Parthian songs like they were weaned on them."

"Don't you know it's impolite to ask for a lady's age?"

Choosing to ignore the deflection, Luke decided to feel around the edges of their discussion. "I was actually born not far from Luxembourg, close to Brussels."

"Your American accent is flawless," Roxi replied, going with a safer topic.

"I guess the US is my home these days. I've lived there since the fifties. How about you? Where did they snatch you from?"

"Mumbai, but I've been living in London for a while."

"I thought I recognized the accent." Luke tried adjusting his body to find a more comfortable position but didn't achieve much on the hard stone. He didn't press further. It wasn't that important at the moment, and they weren't going anywhere.

After a while, Roxi startled him by speaking. "Luke, would you sing a song for me?"

"What?" he asked. It took him a moment to process her words. "Sing you a song? My voice isn't beautiful and trained like yours."

"That's sweet of you to say. I've been singing for you for weeks now. I'd like to hear you sing something."

"I'm not that good of a singer," Luke warned.

Roxi chuckled. "I've listened to you hum along or hold a drone for my melodies. Your voice will do fine."

"OK. Let me think of something to sing."

An old melody had been bumping about in Luke's head for a while now since he'd been stolen from his friends and those he loved. A song his mother had sung to him when he was little and scared. Later, she'd sung it to remember the times when her son Lucius was small and she could hold him in her arms. As the images of his boyhood emerged into clarity in his head, the words slipped into order. Once he thought he recalled the first couple of verses, he spoke the words quietly, trying to wrap his tongue around the language he almost never spoke anymore. He was the last native speaker of his Belgic dialect of the Gaulish Celtic tongue, at least that he knew of. Hell, he was the last Gaul. For the space of a song, his people could live, his language heard upon the earth once more.

Oh, Cernunnos, you have carried them all away
Now your high horned brow, swaying low
Your back bent under the strain, too many
Carried deep, returned to darkness
All to dust, deep and dark

Where have your children gone
They go to feed the children of the wolf, they go to feed the eagle

Lugus shining, shining and luminous no more
Three faces, all-seeing, six eyes to weep
Who is to learn your truths, when all are gone
Carried deep, denied your bright light
All to dust, deep and dark

Where have your children gone
They go to feed the children of the wolf, they go to feed the eagle

Beloved of blood, Teutates, watcher of the people
Between Dubnos and Albios, astride Bitu

Were our offerings not enough, to you the sap of our lives
Carried deep, watering your withered roots
All to dust, deep and dark

Where have your children gone
They go to feed the children of the wolf, they go to feed the eagle

Lofty Taranis, thunderer and the gentle breeze
And so your wheel spins, be your judgment bolts or blooms
Lofty one on high, so low we are brought
Carried deep, ashes in the stream
All to dust, deep and dark

Where have your children gone
They go to feed the children of the wolf, they go to feed the eagle
Your children they are no more
They go to feed the children of the wolf, they go to feed the eagle

Once he found the melody, the words fell into place. The first verse was shaky, but as his confidence grew and his mother's voice in his ear steadied, so did his voice. By the time he was halfway through it, hot tears rolled down his cheeks, though they didn't interfere with his singing, only adding the shading that brought Luke's love for his long dead mother back to life. When he finished, he moved to the corner farthest from Roxi's stone and buried his face in his hands, letting the tears take him.

Once they stopped, he unspooled a few squares of his toilet paper and blew his nose. For the span of a few minutes, the song his mother had gently crooned to him brought the color back into his life, brought her back, but now the tears had leached away the brief spark of joy. Feeling numb, he stared at the wall, the stones blurring away into a dull gray mass.

"Luke? Are you alright?" Roxi asked.

He sniffed and returned to his previous spot along the wall near their hole in the mortar. "I don't know...I guess. It's been a long, long time since I heard that song."

"It was beautiful and sad." Warmth and kindness infused her words.

"My mother used to sing it to me as a boy when I was scared. I haven't heard it in a very long time," Luke said.

"I don't recognize the language. I don't think I've ever heard it."

"Not unless you traveled very far west, but no one's spoken it regularly in hundreds of years." Luke inhaled, holding the breath and allowing it to expand his chest.

"How long?" she asked.

"Oh, maybe fourteen hundred or fifteen hundred," Luke replied casually, his walls temporarily taken down by the song.

"What is the language?"

Luke smiled at the gentle, probing tone Roxi was using. "It was my local dialect of Gaulish."

"Gaulish? Celtic?"

"Mhm," he replied.

"How old are you?"

"As old as you are, Parthian."

Roxi laughed. "All the little pieces we drag long with us always seem to trip us up, don't they?"

"They do."

"I'm not sure I've ever met anyone as old as I am," she said.

"Me either. Most people like us don't make it this long in the life we lead."

Roxi didn't reply. When the lights went out, Luke lay in the near total darkness, save for a bit of light leaking through the door flap at the bottom. He wasn't sure how he felt about meeting another hunter nearly his own age. His ego wasn't big enough to feel like he was losing his unique place in the world. He wondered if it had to do with her being a Parthian. They'd been his enemies briefly nineteen hundred years ago, but he'd never held grudges against human enemies, certainly not after he'd accepted Mithras's mission.

Roxi broke the silence. "Luke?"

"Yeah?" he replied.

"Thank you for sharing your song with me. You do have a nice singing voice, by the way."

"Thank you for the compliment and also for your songs. They make this place…" He couldn't complete the thought; he couldn't say the songs made this place less of a hell. "They help some."

"I understand. It's very nice to meet you, or at least learn more about my neighbor," she said. "Goodnight, Luke."

"Goodnight, Roxi."

The day after Luke dredged up the memory of his mother's song, he noticed something different about his food—something off. Taking his tray with him, he moved to the wall so he could talk with Roxi.

"Roxi?" When he didn't hear a reply, he lowered himself and moved his mouth closer to the hole in the mortar, speaking louder. "Roxi?"

"Yeah, Luke?" she replied.

"Does something taste different about the food?"

"I don't know. I haven't felt like breakfast yet this morning. I'll go grab my tray."

He waited for her to bring her food over and sample the breakfast.

A few minutes later, she answered. "It does taste different. It doesn't taste like a poison, at least any I know."

"Yeah, it doesn't make sense that they'd bother keeping us alive this long, then poison us. They could have just killed us when they had us tranquilized. Moving high security prisoners like us and keeping us contained and alive is a sizable capital investment."

"Yes. That's what I was thinking. It just tastes kind of... I don't know, vitamin-y? Like they're fortifying the food."

Luke dipped the tip of today's spoon into the porridge and brought it up to his nose, giving it a good sniff before sliding it into his mouth. He squished it around on his tongue, trying to spread it around so he could analyze the tastes. She was right. It tasted like a vitamin.

"I wonder why the change," she said.

"What are they fattening us up for? Metaphorically speaking." Luke's brow furrowed. He looked down at his body and its withered frame. He wasn't in any kind of condition and had lost quite a bit of muscle and fat. The food had been enough to keep him alive, but not enough to maintain his body or thrive.

"They can't feed from me, my blood is toxic to them…" Roxi mused.

"Same," Luke replied.

She chuckled. "And our stories unravel a bit more…"

He shrugged, even though she couldn't see it. It felt more like a regular conversation to him that way. "Well, for whatever reason they brought us here, we might be getting closer to finding out."

"Have you been keeping your physical conditioning up since you've been here?"

It embarrassed him that the answer was no. He'd barely been able to keep his mental health from spiraling out of control, and that was partially only because of Roxi and her songs. "No. I haven't. It's been… I've barely been able to keep my brain from breaking. I don't know if I would have been able to do prison cell calisthenics as well."

Roxi sighed. "Me either. Perhaps we should help each other. If they're trying to feed us vitamins, they might be planning to use us for something physical. And I don't know about you, but I've been fighting the bloody wankers for too damned long to let them beat me down now."

"Of all the ways I could let myself die, vampires are last on that list." He couldn't let himself be taken down now, not after he'd found so many wonderful things to fight for. He had to get back to Maggie and Gwen. He missed his friends—Pablo, Delilah, and Sam and all the casual friends he'd made with the North Portland Pack. "I'm in, Roxi the Parthian."

"Then it's a deal, Luke the Gaul. What do you say, start lightly after our midday bucket pickup?"

"It's as good a time as any." He looked at the tray of cooling food. "I guess we should eat our new and improved prison slop so we can get back to dust making before we kick off our training montage."

"I am not singing eighties and nineties upbeat pop-rock songs while we work out." She sounded firm on the decision.

Luke laughed, and for the first time in ages, it felt genuine. "Fair enough."

After they finished their breakfasts, they returned to scratching out mortar. He was determined to open his side of the hole Roxi had initially poked through. Using the tiny hole as a starting point, he'd been carving around it, widening it. Every once in a while, he'd get a tiny chunk to fall out that was bigger than the steady supply of dust he was creating, and it would bring a little dopamine surge, inspiring him to dig harder.

When the bucket collector made their rounds, they dropped their spoons and started their individual work outs. Luke started simple with some push-ups and squats and other light calisthenics to get his body used to moving. When he was finished after an embarrassingly short time, he stripped off the baggy tunic he wore, laying it out on the ground, and flopped down onto it, facing the ceiling.

"I hope they're not expecting us to dig ditches by tomorrow," Roxi panted. With Luke's vigorous work widening the hole on his side, her voice sounded the clearest it had been since she first broke through. She cursed for a few seconds in what he guessed was Parthian when he picked up a few words similar to Middle Persian curses. "I should not have let myself go like that."

"I'm not sure I can afford to castigate myself right now, Roxi. I was barely keeping it together, and I don't need to find reasons to push my brain back into a downward spiral."

"You're probably right. It's bad enough in here without making it worse for myself." She remained silent for a while. "You're pretty open about your mental health for a man, and an old one at that."

Luke snorted. "I guess so. I've been seeing a therapist for a little while, although I seem to have missed a few appointments lately.

Besides, I don't even have the mental energy to try to front to you. My brain is in full energy conservation and protection mode."

"Good on you, Luke. How did you find a therapist who can help you without being sent to the loony bin for making up stories about how old you are?"

"My therapist is a werewolf."

"Really? You're not pulling my leg, are you?" She sounded incredulous.

He rolled over so his mouth was pointed toward the gap in the mortar. "The honest truth. I fell in with a werewolf pack back home… Oh, about a year before I was captured and thrown in here."

"I've never had more than passing interactions with the children of Tutyr. How did they let you get so involved as to let you use their pack resources?"

"That's a bit of a long story," he replied.

"Unless you're going somewhere, time seems to be the thing we have in spades. It'll stave off the boredom for a while."

He narrowed his eyes, a smirk spreading across his face. "What will you give me in return? Only fair that we exchange a personal story for a personal story."

"My, aren't we feeling bold, but I'm up for a fair trade. Deal."

They still had hours before the evening meal showed up, so he grabbed his spoon and started chiseling at the hole, wanting to widen it. "So let me tell you the tale of how these vamps moved into my neighborhood and got up to no good…"

Luke sketched in the details of how he met Pablo and became involved with the North Portland Pack, though he kept the details to a minimum and didn't mention a city or any geographic information that might pinpoint where he lived. It felt good to talk about his friends and relive some of the things they'd done together, even if the tale was dark. He was most of the way through the story, almost to the part where Gwen showed up at the pack house, when Roxi interrupted him.

"You've got feelings for this werewolf doctor, don't you?" she asked, pausing her spoon work for a moment.

"Why do you say that?" He narrowed his eyes suspiciously.

She laughed. "She's not a terribly important part in this story, but you make sure to always mention her, and your voice changes when you're talking about her. It's the little things, and I'm trained to be observant about those kinds of details."

Luke sighed. "Yeah. I have feelings for her. We'd been dating for about six months before I was taken away from her. Two days before, we'd made the relationship official, not that in the eyes of our friends it wasn't there already."

"That's sweet. The ancient vampire hunter has a girlfriend." Her voice filled with longing.

She didn't sound like she was mocking him, though Luke felt wary about it for some reason. At first, thoughts of Maggie had sustained him. Then, they became too painful when he'd been there for weeks and weeks with no change, but now that he was feeling better, her face was once again a hopeful thought.

"I wasn't teasing you. It really is sweet. She sounds like she makes you happy. I...I hope you can get back to her."

"Me too," he whispered.

"I'd like to hear the rest of the story, if you're still feeling up to telling it."

"It would be churlish of me to leave the story unfinished just as I was getting to the climax," he replied. He picked up the story where he left off, where he, Pablo, and Delilah were growing increasingly frustrated without breaks in their hunt for vampires. She listened raptly as he described their assault on the jail and the rescue of the unhoused people, followed by the battle on the St. Johns Bridge, but skipped the jail exploding and burning down. He was still being cautious about giving too many specific details.

"Wait, wait...wait. So now you have a kid, too?" She sounded angry to Luke. "I'm sorry, Luke. They took you away from your kid and your girlfriend? That makes this all extra fucked up. You had a life coming together."

Luke thought he might have detected a few wistful and jealous notes in the tones of her voice. "It's just as fucked up for you to be here. My life isn't of more value than yours."

"No, but you had so many people relying on you—who care for you. The monsters took you from them too."

"Our enemy has never been known for their kindness. They always bring pain to their victims and the families of their victims." His words sounded bitter in his own ears.

"Who's taking care of your kid?"

"Probably Maggie. She's the doctor, and her partner Zel," he answered off-handedly.

"Your girlfriend has a partner?"

"Yes. They're polyamorous."

"I see."

"Is that a problem?" He tried to keep his tone neutral.

"Not at all. I am the daughter of a concubine. Who am I to judge another relationship?" She chuckled. "Frankly, you're a curiosity. You're a modern man with an adopted child and a girlfriend—and a centuries-old immortal hunter."

"I have a cat, too."

Roxi chuckled, then started laughing, seemingly unable to stop. Soon, Luke joined her, unsure why she found it funny, but enjoying the feeling of the unrestrained laughter, anyway. Once their laughter subsided, he wiped the tears from his eyes and smiled.

"I'm glad my cat amuses you. He's a good catto." Luke sighed. "I miss him. And Gwen. And Maggie. I miss all my friends. Attachments. I've avoided them for so long, now I have more than I can count."

"I'm sorry, Luke. I'm jealous of you. I've lived for a long time with too few attachments in my life," she said wistfully.

"Do you have anyone to miss you?" he asked.

She didn't answer for a while, stopping her work with her spoon.

"You don't have to answer. I didn't mean to pry."

"That's alright. No, I don't have anyone to miss me. There's no one to mourn me if I'm killed." Her voice was low and sad.

"You do. I would mourn your loss, Roxi." He meant it. Over the weeks they'd spent separated by their stone wall, he'd come to rely on her presence in his life. Not only that, he liked her. Her sharp observations and the first hints of a sly sense of humor, impressively kept alive in a place like this, had won him over. "I'd like to consider you my friend."

"Friends are a dangerous thing, Luke. They can betray you for their own interests," she said, sounding wary, but he thought he also detected a note of hope in her voice.

"It's worth it, though. I'd isolated myself for years, pretty much for a century. Deciding to allow people into my life is one of the best decisions I've made in recent history. Well, they kind of decided for me, but I wouldn't trade the last year for anything."

"You wouldn't even trade it to be free of this place?"

He thought about it for a while. Thought about being free, but with no one in his life save for Alfred. The gentle, soulful eyes of Maggie flashed across his mind. Gwen calling everyone "cis devils" as she confidently strode out of the house. Sam gleefully issuing CB handles for everyone for the first mission when she'd joined them. Fighting Delilah in his training room, pushing each other to grow. He thought about Pablo and the first time he showed off his new "quick nude" outfit so he could easily go wolf.

"Rip and roar..." Luke mumbled.

"What?" Roxi asked.

"Rip and roar. My friend Pablo bought this ridiculous warm up outfit he could rip off so he could make the shift to his wolf. They had these snaps up the seams..." He ended up starting the story from the beginning when he and Delilah walked into Pablo's house. He'd never heard Delilah laugh that hard; the sound brought a spark of joy to his heart. By the time he was done telling the story, Roxi was laughing, gasping for air.

After she controlled her laughter, she let the silence hang for a few minutes. "How do you risk the pain of loss?"

"We already have pain. My life has been full of pain—I'm guessing yours has been too—but as I was told, why not seek joy when it's available. Though there's not much joy to be had in here, I could use a friend to make this place less isolating." He wasn't sure why he was so nervous about putting himself out there to her. He liked her and wanted to be her friend.

"Me too," she said, her voice just audible. Speaking louder, she continued, "My name is Roxiustana Surena. As you've rightly guessed, I'm a Parthian, the last to my knowledge."

"Roxiustana, it's a pleasure to meet you. I am Lucius Silvanius Ferrata. I'm a Belgian Gaul, also the last to my knowledge. I was a soldier of Rome for over two hundred years."

"You… You're the Centurio Immortalis," she said, shock evident in her voice

"I've been called such. You've heard of me?"

"All hunters have heard of the Centurio Immortalis. Where you walk, the ground shakes. I thought you'd died sometime before the twentieth century."

Luke was quickly becoming uncomfortable with the amount of awe in Roxi's voice. "Not quite, though the twentieth century nearly did me in. Before my friends forced their way into my life, I was a hollow shell of a man."

"Wait… Were you in Portland?"

"You heard about that?" Luke asked.

"You blew up a jail. Then you captured and sank a freighter. Wow…"

Luke blushed, not sure how to handle that he had a reputation still at this late date in his life.

"Where the Centurio Immortalis walks, the earth shakes…" Roxi said, quietly. "I would be honored to be your friend."

"You're embarrassing me. I'm afraid I'm not that impressive," he replied.

She laughed harshly. "If half of the stuff I've heard about you is true, you've done more damage to the vampires than most of the rest of us combined."

"Yet here we are together, two hunters trapped in a cage." Luke didn't like the potential shift in their relationship dynamic. Closing his eyes, he took a breath and steeled himself. "Roxi, I just want to be Luke, nothing extra. Just your friend."

"I'm sorry, Luke. I just got a little overexcited." She paused for a moment. "Right now, a friend is more meaningful to me."

"Thank you."

He'd never cared for being the hero-type, fawned over by people who only saw the famous man and what proximity might provide. He did what he did because he'd sworn to fight the forces of evil—to protect humanity from the bloodsucking demons known as vampires. He never wanted to be the center of attention, he just wanted to do the duty he'd sworn and live his life. The thought of his fame creating a barrier between himself and his potential new friend tugged him down deeper into the ever-pervasive sadness he lived in, trapped in this hellhole.

CHAPTER
EIGHT

"I see you!" Roxi called.

Luke squirmed down the wall so his eyes were aligned with the seam they'd been working on relentlessly and peered through. When his eye adjusted, he saw a set of dark brown eyes staring back at him. As she blinked, long, dark eyelashes fluttered down to meet with their companions. They had finally punched through enough to open most of the right seam around the stone, allowing them to look through at each other.

"It's very nice to meet your eyes."

He chuckled. "Same!"

Neither of them spoke for a while, just staring through the crack. For weeks, their only human contact had been each other's voices as they shared songs and stories, talking as much for the company as to get to know each other. After a while, he cleared his throat, growing uncomfortable with the intimate gesture.

"So, now that we have this side mostly cleared out, what next?" he asked.

Her eyes sparkled. "I say we work on the top some more. If we remove two seams, we can maybe rock it or move it to force it out."

"It's worth a try, but I think we're getting close to bucket o'clock and work out time. See you after?" he replied.

"Wouldn't miss it!"

He chuckled at the mix of genuine enthusiasm and sarcasm Roxi achieved with those three words. With the added intimacy of eye contact, they spent more time looking at and talking to each other through the seam. He grew to understand the minute shifts in her emotions captured around her eyes, from laughter to sadness, to fear and boredom. He almost hated having to move so he could chip away at the mortar, but the small reveal of her eyes drove him to want more.

After their morning work session on the stone, they took a break to eat their breakfasts, enjoying some silence since Roxi had been particularly chatty that morning. Despite the changes in Luke's life, he was still largely a solitary person, enjoying the quiet around him when he wasn't overwhelmed by loneliness. While he wasn't constantly lonely now that he had friends and a girlfriend, loneliness was still a constant companion. Roxi helped to stave off his spiral back into the worst of his depression, but he still missed his people — the family who found him worth being with and who loved and welcomed him into their lives.

By an unspoken agreement, they didn't talk about escaping and a life after wherever the hell they were trapped, but when he thought about his family, he couldn't help the places his brain led him. He had to hold on. He knew his friends would be looking for him; he just hoped they could find him. In the meantime, he'd try to keep his mind clear and his body ready in case he or Roxi saw an opportunity to escape. While he was mulling over his life, the sound of metal on stone tinkled through the hole in the seam.

"Roxi? You OK over there?" he asked. When he didn't hear anything, he guessed she just wanted some privacy, so he went back to his breakfast.

After he pushed his tray back into place, he grabbed the spoon and laid down to get to work, peering through the space they'd created to see if she was on the other side. "Roxi?"

From what he could see, Roxi was laid out on the ground. He thought he saw her chest moving. Looking toward his door, he stared at the metal tray laying near the flap door. He stared at the narrow strip of her body visible through the seam with his stomach in his throat. What had happened to her? It wouldn't make sense for them to poison her after all this time, but he couldn't discount they'd put something in her food.

Maybe it was something else…

"Roxi?"

He thought he heard a sound from her cell, then light sliced into the dimly lit room. Her body jostled as it slid across the floor, her arms trailing limply behind her. With the slam of wood on stone, the light extinguished.

Roxi was gone.

Luke had no idea how long he stared into her cell. He missed the midday bucket exchange. After the flap closed, he shook his head and forced himself to move away from the crack in the wall. He tried to run through his calisthenics program to distract himself from the growing anxiety Roxi's disappearance had caused. Over the few weeks he and Roxi had been working out, he'd increased his stamina and strength, but he was far from anything considered campaigning condition.

After going through a couple rounds, he gave up, too distracted to keep his mind on his task. He ended up sitting against the far wall, staring at the crack where he'd witnessed Roxi taken away. When the flap opened, Luke waited until it closed again before he stood up. He was stiff and sore from sitting for hours on the stone without moving. Sitting with his legs crossed, he slid the tray between his knees and stared at it.

Their keepers could have dosed his food too, assuming that's what had happened to Roxi. He could dump the food into his bucket and skip a meal; it wouldn't be the first time he'd gone on short rations. He could wait for Roxi to come back and see what she had to report. Staring at the tray, he sighed. Luke wasn't a waiter, he was a doer. Picking up his spoon, he scooped the food into his mouth. He couldn't taste anything out of the ordinary, but a lot of drugs could be disguised easily enough. When his spoon scraped the bottom of the tray and came up empty, he set the spoon on it and slid it toward the door.

As he sat waiting to see if anything would happen, he couldn't tell if his eyes were feeling heavy because he had been drugged or if he was just tired. Like when he'd been tranq darted by Mathis, Luke laid down to prevent his head from hitting the stone. Sleep took him as his world faded to black.

WHEN LUKE CAME TO, his eyes drifted open. If he was still in his cell, he'd expect to see either the walls or the ceiling, depending on which way his head lolled. Now, it was drooping down with his head on his chin—feeling heavy as if something was on it—and the only thing he could see was bright light. He squeezed his eyes shut and tried to regulate the light entering. When they adjusted, he kept his head hanging, sweeping his eyes over the floor to see if he could see anyone or anything.

The tiny room looked empty. The walls, like his cell, were made from the same gray stone, but the floor here was wood—smooth, but unfinished. Since he was alone and he no longer needed to maintain the charade of being asleep, he lifted his head. Metal bands at his biceps and forearms held him to the wall as he sat on a stool. They'd dressed him in the full regalia of a Roman legionnaire. From the ground up, he looked like the Lucius who'd stalked the earth nineteen hundred years ago, down to the plain greaves and caligae. Unfortunately, it wasn't his armor. The quality looked good, though, better than the stuff he'd purchased when he needed replicas for Jorge to create the modifications to his Volvo. They looked like proper, high-quality museum replicas.

After so long in silence with only Roxi's voice, it took him a while to realize the pounding in his ears wasn't his blood, but sound coming from all around him. It sounded like a lot of feet stamping or maybe yelling.

His mind, which normally snapped into focus when he stood on the edge of the precipice, warred with the remnants of whatever they'd used to knock him out. He rested his helmet-covered head against the wall, closing his eyes and running through breathing exercises to bring his mind fully into the moment. The longer he sat, the more his mind cleared as his body flushed the drugs from his system.

As he waited, the dull thudding and roars grew around him, finally crescendoing into an eruption. When the noise trickled down to the lowest levels, Luke opened his eyes. After the noise had settled for a while, Luke wondered how long he'd be strapped to the wall before he learned what his immediate fate was. When a speaker behind him crackled to life, it took him a moment to place that he was being spoken to.

"Human. Human. Wake up."

Not sure if there was a speaker in the room, Luke turned his head toward the sound. With the restriction of the helmet and being strapped to the wall, he couldn't find where the speaker was exactly. He assumed they'd also have a camera. He hoped the movement would be enough to acknowledge that he heard them.

"You will be released from the wall, then elevated into the field of judgment where you shall meet your fate. Step from its confines when you arrive." The static of the speaker crackled one last time, then went silent.

The click of the bands releasing from around his arms and the relief of the pressure let him know the voice was speaking truth, at least about that. He stood up carefully, making sure his legs were ready to bear his weight. After his knees wobbled for a few moments, he grew more comfortable with full verticality as his body continued recovering from the drugging. He twisted his torso and rotated his arms to loosen them after being held immobile for too long. Once he got the blood flowing to his arms and chest, he did a few slow squats.

Did his armor always feel this heavy? Was he just used to it and it'd been too long since he wore it? Was this replacement steel heavier than his? Or was he just that badly out of condition?

He closed his eyes and turned his face up to the distant, blocked sky. "Whatever gods are watching, if you can spare a little grace for me, please do…"

The ground under him rocked and vibrated as his tiny room become an elevator. He spread his legs and loosened his knees to give himself a bit of shock absorption to help his balance. Squinting his eyes in case of bright lights, he prepared mentally, unsure what awaited him. He cast a brief thought to Roxi, hoping she'd made it through whatever trial she'd been subjected to. Hopefully, he would make it through this and hear her voice when he was cast back into his cell.

The higher he rose, the louder the noise grew—a steady thudding like feet stamping. He thought he heard yells accompanying it. Adrenaline flooded his system, wiping clean the last effects of the drug. Looking up, the darkness above him resolved into a ceiling growing uncomfortably close. Nervous about striking it with his head, he lowered himself on to one knee, bowing his head.

With the creak of the doors above him, the full roar of a hurricane pummeled him with nothing left to block its vibrations. In front of him, light brown, sandy dirt covered the ground.

"We give you the vile enemy of the benevolent Vampire, the Scourge of the Night, the Centurion Immortal, the Wood Fanged Demon!" yelled a man on a PA speaker.

The announcement silenced the crowd. Luke thought he heard some gasps and low shrieks that verged on shock and terror until someone started a chorus of boos and jeers, many hissing their disdain at the revelation. Kneeling before them was the infamous enemy of their kind, the man who had ended so many undead lives over his two millennia career.

Luke tipped his head up enough to look around and see how he was oriented in the large circular arena, for that was where he was. Stadium seats rose up, surrounding the twenty-foot walls. Above the wall, some sort of wiring or caging further protected the audience from the monster they booed. He faced toward the center of the arena. On the ground in front of him on low racks, both sticking up straight, lay the tools of his trade, or at least his original trade—a scutum and gladius.

He inwardly groaned. The scutum wasn't the lightest of shields, and he wasn't confident in his conditioning. He could always ditch it later if it was hindering him. He waited for what was coming next, trying, to remain calm. On the opposite side of the arena, a large double door set in the wall opened backwards, revealing a tunnel or hall shrouded in shadows. Luke thought he saw some movement.

Once the booing quieted to a trickle, the announcer's voice started low, rising in intensity. "Now, let's welcome to the arena to defend the honor of Vampyrdom against the vile demon—the deadly wind, the white tiger, the master of the eastern art of divine kung fu, a vampire who needs no introductions, the undefeated warrior, the great wall protecting Vampyrdom from the barbarian horde of hunters, Shifu Chuck Brannigan!"

Luke snorted, trying to hold in his laughter. "What the fuck?" he mumbled.

The movement in the darkness resolved into a figure wearing a silky black kung fu outfit that looked like he bought it at a Quentin Tarantino garage sale. When he cleared the shadow of his entryway, he yanked a jian from its scabbard, tossing the scabbard aside. Luke rose and strode toward the gladius and scutum. He was skeptical, but the weapons were there to use. Standing between the two, he wrapped his fingers around the hilt of the gladius and pulled. Nothing.

"You didn't think we'd make this easy for you, did we?" Shifu Chuck Brannigan taunted.

Sighing, Luke stepped back, placing the sword and shield rigidly between himself and his opponent. It figured that the vampires would put weapons just within reach but make them unattainable. Anger and annoyance trickled into his gut.

Chuck stopped before getting too close to Luke. "We should at least observe the proprieties," he said, and bowed respectfully.

Luke bowed his head in the barest of acknowledgment. "Bring it, *Chuck*."

Dressed in full armor, he at least had protection of a sort, but the weight would put him at a supreme disadvantage against a fast vampire with a sword. Chuck raised his jian, moving into an elegant en garde position. He couldn't tell if this whole setup was to humiliate him in the weird mismatch, or what. There were plenty of weaknesses in the armor and more than enough flesh with no protection for Chuck to choose from. He was thankful for his time sparring with Delilah. Her unarmed kung fu was excellent and had really pushed Luke's skills forward with the discipline.

Taking another step back but not getting quite into a ready position, Luke waved Shifu Chuck Brannigan forward. "Come on, *Chazz*. I don't have all day."

Anger flashed across the fanger's face just before he launched his first attack, a lunge aimed at the center of Luke's stomach. Moving into action, Luke pivoted backward on his left foot, catching the flat of the blade with his hand as he knocked the sword aside. Chuck's momentum carried him too far, bringing him into reach of Luke's fists. As Chuck tried to correct for his mistake, Luke continued his spin until he planted on his right foot, the hobnails of the caligae biting into the dirt, and pushed up, turning on his hips, to deliver a hay maker of an uppercut to the edge of Chuck's jaw. The crowd went quiet with a gasp.

If the angle had been slightly better, Luke would have practicality torn his head off with the punch. As it was, Chuck staggered away, trying to regain control of his body, the tip of the sword dragging in the dirt. Not wanting to let Chuck recover, Luke followed through, rotating into a back spin. Bending over, Luke nearly lost his balance with the weight of the armor on his torso. He planted his palm on the ground and completed the spin kick, catching the kung fu master in the ribs. The loss of balance and recovery had cost Luke some power, but the hobnails made up for it. Luke thought he heard the crack of ribs.

Chuck dropped his jian and staggered back, falling onto his side. Luke dropped to his knees and spin around instead of trying to force his body back to his feet. As he rose to one knee, he scooped up the hilt of the jian and stood. Chuck cradled his ribs as he tried to scramble away from the now armed vampire hunter. Sacrificing some pain, Chuck rolled away on his side until he landed on his hands and knees and pushed himself to standing.

Twirling the sword in his hand, Luke kept his inexorable advance, a stone visage of irritation plastered on his face. Shifu Chuck was Luke's first chance to strike back at the vampires who'd orchestrated his kidnapping, stealing him from his life. He thought about playing with the vampire, making everyone watch as he slowly disassembled him, but he didn't have the conditioning. A quick and brutal kill to remind them who he was would be better than growing tired and weak in front of his enemies.

Luke feinted toward Chuck's injured ribs, causing the vampire to pull away and cringe around his ribs. Chuck staggered and whimpered in pain. Pulling the sword back, Luke stepped into another backspin and brought the sword around in a deadly arc with the tip of the jian dipping down, then rolling back up to its apex before it screamed into its final downward trajectory through Chuck's neck.

The headless torso of the vampire collapsed to the ground as its head rolled away. The crowd had gone silent with the ignominious defeat of the first champion they'd thrown at the Centurion Immortal. Luke stepped over the torso and prodded the head over so its face stared toward the nearest section of the crowd. Making sure he had its placement correct, Luke looked down at it before staring into the front row of the crowd. He raised his caligae covered foot and stomped down on the head with a small hop to bring as much force as possible into contact with the skull. The cracking of bone reverberated off the walls of the arena as it collapsed under Luke's weight, cracking and popping until it transformed into a shattered mass of shards and pulped brains.

Not looking at what he'd done, he turned and walked back toward where the elevator had disappeared. The ground split apart, the elevator rising from the arena floor. Luke hopped down into it before it finished rising and sat on the stool he'd woken on. With his back straight and his head held high, the jian's point rested between his feet as he laid both hands on top of the pommel.

As soon as the elevator reached its apex, it started the return journey into the bowels of the arena. The crowd, reviving from its stunned silence, sent up the first jeers and boos. Luke didn't move, holding his pose, looking like a victorious king as he disappeared into the ground from whence he'd come. As soon as the roof folded closed, he slumped, drawing in deep breaths. He barely had the conditioning to manage even that short of a fight. Even if he played with the jackass they'd sent to fight him, he wouldn't have had the energy for much more. A faint tremor ran through his limbs.

When the elevator's descent arrested, the crackly speaker came to life. "If you wish to make this easy on yourself, drop the weapon and place your arms in the restraints. Either way, you will be rendered unconscious and returned to your cell. The choice is yours as victor whether you want to return unharmed and unconscious or kicked to shit and unconscious."

He gave a moment's serious thought to seeing what would happen but decided to go with the smarter choice for the moment. Laying the sword respectfully on the ground, he sat back and felt for the restraints. He held his arms in place as they pushed out of the wall and around his biceps and forearms, restraining him. As soon as they locked in place, he felt a sharp jab in his ass, then nothing. A few minutes later, as the tranquilizer took effect, Luke slumped as his vision faded away.

CHAPTER
NINE

"Luke? Luke?"

A voice filtered through the foggy dream scape he inhabited. He'd been lying next to Maggie on the grass next to his house on the Meuse River, staring at the stars, joy and contentment in his heart. He could almost feel the warmth of her hand in his.

"Maggie?" Luke mumbled.

"Luke, are you alright?" the voice asked.

The ground felt too cold and hard to be the grass of his property. Groaning, he rubbed his eyes and opened them to find dimly lit stone. The events of the last day returned—the drugged meal, the arena, his brutal defeat of Shifu Chuck Brannigan. It was Roxi's voice calling to him, not Maggie's. Relief and sadness washed over him—relief that Roxi was alive, sadness that he wasn't free with Maggie. A pit opened in his stomach as his situation reasserted its dominance.

Luke yawned. "I was having the most wonderful dream. And then I woke up here."

"Sexy dreams? I heard you call out to Maggie," Roxi said.

"No." He chuckled. "We were lying in the grass by the Meuse River south of Dinant at my house just staring at the stars."

He'd been returned to his simple cotton prison garb of a baggy, tunic-like garment and baggy pants. As he sat up, he could feel soreness and chafing where the armor had rubbed him. They hadn't exactly fitted the armor to him nor put it on him in the best manner. He stretched, raising his hands above his head and spreading his fingers. He felt something pull in the palm of his right hand. He found three stitches. The blade must have caught him a bit when he deflected it aside. Three stitches weren't bad. He'd had far worse, though he didn't have his rudis, and he doubted his hosts would toss him a fanger to use if he did.

He availed himself of the bucket and walked around a bit to loosen up his body, stiff from lying on the floor for who knew how long while drugged. When his stomach rumbled, he checked for the tray on the ground, hoping a meal had been delivered while he'd been asleep. Nothing. Deciding he'd had enough of walking around his tiny cell, he returned to the patch of floor near the hole in the wall.

"Roxi? Are you OK? Are you hurt?" Luke asked.

"I'm fine, a bit sore. I'm sure I've got a few bruises, but I'm whole. What about you?"

"I'm glad you're OK. I got worried when you fell to the ground and didn't respond," Luke said, staring at his stitches. "I'm fine. I've got three stitches on my palm, but other than that, I didn't take any wounds. What happened? Did they take you to the arena?"

"Arena? No. It was more like a Mixed Martial Arts cage—an octagon. They threw me in there with some burly female vampire and forced us to fight. Well, forced me to fight. She seemed very eager to have a go at me. I snapped her neck then they tranqed me, and I woke up here. Tell me about the arena."

"It was pretty sizable. Not sure the floor was as big as the Colosseum, but it was a fair approximation of a Roman arena. It's got elevators. They raised me through the floor into it. They had a gladius and scutum, but they were locked down, so I had to fight unarmed. Did they give you armor?"

Roxi snorted. "No. A sports bra and Lycra shorts."

"They had me dressed up as a full Roman legionnaire in decent quality replicas." He sighed, sad at the loss of his equipment. "I imagine my gear is decorating some Vampire lord's trophy room. Hell, it could have been the price for my capture. Heinen claimed to be a Roman history enthusiast. I feel naked without my armor. I've worn it for too long to be without it when I have to fight against fucking fangers."

"Yeah. I don't wear mine as much as I used to, but if I can fit it under whatever outfit I'm using to blend in, I wear it. What happened after you entered the arena?" Roxi's voice relayed her sympathy.

Luke laughed. "Shifu Chuck Brannigan."

"What? What is a Shifu Chuck Brannigan?" Laughter filled her voice.

"He was the vampire opponent they sent out to fight me. He thought he was a kung fu master, complete with the full outfit. Came out with a jian. Either he thought he was good enough to take me despite my armor, or he was some asshole the vamps wanted to dispose of."

"Why didn't you have access to weapons? Did they want to torment you by showing them to you but not giving you access?" Roxi asked.

"I don't know. Maybe I just didn't make it deep enough into the fight for them to release them to me." He shrugged.

"How long did it last?"

Luke snorted. "I don't know. Minute. Maybe two? Jackass lunged at me and tried to stab me in the stomach. Maybe he thought he could hit the central seam in my armor and gut me up the middle. I deflected the sword with my palm—that's how I got the stitches—punched him, kicked him in the side and broke his ribs, then took his sword and beheaded him. And because I was pissed at the whole thing, I stomped on his skull and crushed it, then walked back to the elevator." He chuckled mirthlessly. "Left the crowd silent."

"Damn. I wish I could have seen that. I admire the brutal efficiency of it all."

"I don't think the crowd got what they wanted out of the fight. Their boogie man walked away virtually unscathed and crushed their champion in only a few moves. Can't say I feel bad for disappointing them." He smiled, savoring the vicious pettiness of striking back at his captors.

Roxi laughed. "Yeah, I got the same feeling. After I put their champion down. Did you notice any previous activity? Any signs you weren't the first person in the arena?"

"No, but I really wasn't looking for them. What about you?"

"Yeah, I think there were some blood stains that looked fresh and poorly cleaned. How many hunters do you think are down here?" she asked.

"I didn't even think of that. I guess I've just been too focused on myself. This seems too elaborate of a setup for just us two to be the entertainment. Who knows what other amusements this place was built to provide?"

"Why do you think we sat in here for so long before they threw us out into their arenas?" She sounded worried.

"It must take a while to get enough hunters of various stripes to put on something like this. I wish we had a way to get to the others." He hoped none of his friends had been captured and dragged here. Before he could fixate on that too much, he pushed it to the back of his mind before it could take over, though he couldn't bury it entirely. It would niggle at his awareness.

"Yeah, that would be great, but they keep us pretty separated. Who knows how many others could be trapped down here waiting to be the playthings and amusements of those monsters?" Roxi exhaled angrily and remained silent for a few moments. "How did they return you to your cell?"

"Same way I left. Back into the elevator, then they tranqed me when it hit the bottom. Woke up back here. What about you?" Luke asked.

"There was a chair I woke up in, strapped to the side of the cage. They made me go back to it, then jabbed me with a needle. Next thing I know, I'm waking up here."

"How did they 'make' you?"

"They pointed several machine guns at me. I chose to sit down rather than test their resolve. I'm not exactly equipped to overcome that kind of damage right now."

Luke chuckled. "Me either. I stashed my rudis in someone else's bag when I was being abducted. As far as I know, it's back in Portland. I'm sure whoever's bag it was gave it to my friends."

"Your rudis?" Roxi's voice was intent, probing.

"Yeah. It's a wooden practice sword, except this one has a silver alloy cutting edge with silver filigree on the flats of both sides of the blade, and a silver core that runs from the tip to the pommel button."

"About fifty centimeters long? Shaped like one of your Roman gladii?" The questions were pointed, guiding him toward an answer.

"Yeah. Made from Persian Ironwood. Why?" He rolled his head so he could look through the hole. Roxi stared back intently.

"I have one too, though mine is more reminiscent of a Parthian sword in shape. Where did you get it, Luke?" Her eyes bored into his.

"In Armenia, in the Caucasus Mountains. Why?" He guessed she was driving the conversation to a specific destination, a destination he was beginning to suspect they might have in common. "Roxiustana, who gave you your wooden sword? Who is your master?"

"I am my own master or mistress, if you prefer, but I serve the divine will of Mithra."

Luke closed his eyes. She was not only a divinely powered vampire hunter like himself, she literally served the same god as he. Luke could never quite escape the fate he'd tied himself to nineteen hundred years ago in the mountains of Armenia. Even in this deep pit, hidden from the silvery light of Selene, where he'd been thrown into by Mithras's enemies, there was a firm reminder of who he was and who he served. There was no escape or hiding from his past or destiny.

"Whom do you serve, Lucius?" she asked, using his original name as he had hers.

"I serve the mission of Sol Invictus and his divine sister Selene as guided by Mithras." Between them, silence dominated. Even when their food was delivered, neither moved nor spoke. It wasn't until Luke's stomach growled that he shook himself free of the revelation. "It would appear we have more in common than just being prisoners in this vampire amusement park."

"It would seem so."

Luke stood up and worked out the stiffness in his muscles, then grabbed his tray and scooped the food into his mouth, cleaning the tray as if it were the most delectable of delicacies. After he set it down, he paced back and forth in his little room, ostensibly to get the blood flowing and work out the soreness from the fight, but after learning who Roxi was, he felt fidgety.

"Luke?" Roxi's voice drifted up from the hole in the mortar. "Are you alright?"

He wasn't sure how to answer. If he were being truthful with himself, he didn't know how he felt about meeting another hunter of Mithras. He'd never assumed he was the only one Mithras had ever made, but after nearly two-thousand years, he'd assumed he was probably the last.

He'd always felt like a loner, moving about the world, often where Mithras wasn't worshiped or known, or in the case of Europe after its Christianization had been secured, erased from history. After his time spent in the Sasanid Empire, he'd moved on, returning to western Europe and the lands of his youth. The next time he'd moved through the lands where Mithras had been strong, the strength of Islam had displaced most of the former worshipers of Mithras, Mehr, Mithra, and Mitra. It was reasonable that as the world grew, and more people filled its lands, it would be harder to find the old ones, those who'd lived long enough to keep serving their divine masters. Blending in became the commodity of the day, especially in lands ruled by religions where pagans were viewed as particularly loathsome.

Taking a steadying breath, he sank to the ground and lay on his back. "I don't know, Roxi. I haven't met another devotee of Mithras, the one we know and follow, in centuries. It felt like there were fewer and fewer hunters in the world, most of whom I'd never meet or interacted with." He shook his head at himself. If Delilah had been there, she would have told him it was his own fault for isolating and not letting anyone in, and she would certainly have a point. "It's...unsettling. I don't know why. I know it's stupid, but I feel like I'm being manipulated."

"That would be absurd in the extreme," Roxi replied. "We are Mithra's divine will on Earth, empowered to protect humanity from the evil of the vampires. I'd be lying if I didn't say that at times, I've felt the weight of it more than others, but we were chosen for this task—"

"I wasn't chosen," Luke interrupted. "I survived. I was the only one left to walk into his temple and receive his 'blessing.' It's been nearly two-thousand years, and I'm still here. I've bled gallons of blood. Buried legions of friends. Watched loved ones gray and die, if they were lucky enough to meet a peaceful end. I am not the naïve young man who walked into that cave in Armenia. I'm tired, Roxi. Tired of being someone else's pawn. I feel so hollowed out."

He turned his head away from the hole, afraid to see the judgment in her eyes—see his failings in the disappointment in her eyes staring back. She lay silent for a long while, breathing steadily.

"I know. Believe me, I do. I've lived for a long time on the edge. I can't let myself fall over. I can't afford to get trapped in that downward spiral. It's paralyzing and lonely. I live alone. I travel alone. I hunt alone. Neighbors will wave at me when I'm back at my flat, but they're casual acquaintances. My faith in Mithra and in my mission is all I have, Luke. I had to believe, or... I have to believe..." Her voice faded into silence.

He felt terrible for assuming she'd somehow made it through the centuries without sustaining the same emotional wounds. Mostly, he didn't like looking inside himself and seeing the empty place where his faith used to reside, and he'd projected that onto her, assuming she felt similarly betrayed. He'd wanted the peaceful gray of no gods but knew that was impossible in his unique circumstances. However, the serene visage of Selene formed in his mind, her benevolent and loving smile filling the empty place in his soul where he might have held the love for a deity. She'd always looked on him kindly, providing comfort. Mithras's will was iron, but Selene's gaze was gentle.

He'd held himself separate from her embrace because he too closely linked her with Mithras, but she'd understood his soul and the pain of the life Mithras's mission had placed on him. Whenever she appeared before him, her light soothed the soreness of his soul. She'd looked after him for nineteen centuries, and he'd not given her her proper due, yet she'd never held it against him.

"I'm sorry, Roxi."

"I understand. Do…do you not have faith anymore? Faith in our mission?" She sounded timid and weary.

"I don't know. No, that's not true. I haven't had faith in the mission in a long time, and with it, I lost my faith in Mithras, but he doesn't care. He only cares that I do my duty, and so I have. He doesn't require my love, only my obedience. But I feel shame for pushing Selene's embrace away. She has been nothing but kind to me, seeking to fill me with the gentle touch of her light." Luke sighed, tears tickling the corners of his eyes.

"The Greek goddess of the moon? The one who saved the were-wolves from the dark ones?"

"Aye. In my heart, I have bound her too close to Mithras, where I should have let her love fill me and sustain me." He snorted. "What a weird life it is we lead, Roxiustana Surena. We walk by the sides of gods, yet we are cast down into a pit by their enemies." He sighed again. "I'm sorry for dragging you down. I'm still struggling despite making some progress, and these walls feel like they're starting to close in on me. The worst thing that happened to me in that arena was that I got a taste of open space."

"Can we work on our stone for a while, Luke? We've got to be close to a point where we can break it out. I need to do something, even if it's as small and petty as breaking their stone wall just a little."

"OK, Roxi. Let me grab my spoon." He could join with her on that shared goal.

Together, they worked fiercely on the mortar over the week after their first forays out of the cells, tearing out chunks where they could and thinning it so they could perhaps break it without having to chip away every bit of mortar. Luke couldn't tell if the stone was actually feeling a touch wobbly or if it was wishful thinking.

"Luke, I want to give it a try," Roxi said, tossing her spoon aside with a clatter of metal on stone.

"Sure. It'll be awhile before any of our keepers drop off our food, so we'll have privacy. How do you think we should go after it?"

"I've been thinking about it. I'm going to roll up my pants and lay them along the stone to pad my heel, then try to shove it toward you with my foot. See if I can break it out of the seam on the other side." Roxi shuffled and scrapped on the other side.

Luke caught some movement and shifts in the light until the view was blocked by her rolled up pants. "Good idea. I'm going to try it from my side. We should tell the other when it's safe to go, so we don't kick it at the same time." Luke stood and dropped his pants to the ground, before rolling them up and laying across the stone to pad his own foot.

Roxi grunted a couple times. "Go."

Luke positioned his heel at the edge of the rock and shoved. He hissed as the stone reverberated up his leg from his heel, but at least he'd felt the stone give a tiny bit. He gave it another shove. "Go."

Roxi grunted a couple more times before giving Luke the go ahead. They went back and forth for a while until she called a halt.

"My heel is starting to smart," she said. "Let's see if we accomplished anything."

Luke pulled his pants away from the stone. Once he spun around so he faced the rock, it looked a bit crooked. Pushing on it, it gave some.

"Shall we try pushing it back and forth? I think we're close," Luke suggested.

"You start, then me. Back and forth."

Luke shoved the edge, then took the tension off so Roxi could shove back, the stone grinding as it moved. Back and forth they went until a loud crack caused them both to pull back. Excitement and nervousness warred inside him.

"I think we've about got it!" Roxi clapped. "Let's see if we can finish it up."

A few more hard shoves back and forth and the last of the mortar crumbled, releasing the stone. She carefully worked it out of its slot. The removal of the stone left a hole in the wall about eight inches high and about two feet wide. One side was slightly higher than the other.

Luke stretched out so he could look through. The space was empty, but he could see into her cell. The room looked like a mirror clone of his own. The sound of someone moving across the floor caught his attention. A moment later, Roxi's face blocked his view of her cell.

She had messy, black hair that looked like it might have some waves and curls in it. Her eyebrows were thick and dark, and the eyes under them sparkled with curiosity. She had a full nose with a bit of a curve at the bridge and full lips under them. Her skin was light tan with an olive undertone only marred by a few bruises from her fight. She'd probably be darker if she hadn't been trapped in this sunless prison.

He thought about what he must look like after being in the cell for months. His hair was beyond shaggy and hung wildly over his neck, the waves and curls disorderly. He wished he'd thought to drag his fingers through it to at least attempt to get in some semblance of order. His beard was thick and bushy.

"Hi," Roxi said. She smiled nervously.

"Hello."

"It's weird. We've been talking to each other for weeks, yet it feels like we're meeting each other for the first time."

Luke chuckled. "I know, right? It's nice to put a face to the voice and the eyes."

"I like your beard. It's very luxuriant." She winked.

Laughing, he shook his head. "I usually keep it much better trimmed, though before I was captured, I'd shaved it off as part of a disguise."

"Yeah, I don't know that either of us are at our best here. I think we can let each other slide this time. You know, the circumstances and all." Her lips split into a broad grin. She had a small gap between her upper front two teeth.

Luke thought she looked charming, even in the plain prison tunic and dull gray stone surroundings. They stared at each other for a while. Eventually, she blushed and rolled over, shifting her gaze to the ceiling.

"It feels weird. You're the first friendly face I've seen in too long —I already said that, didn't I?" she sighed.

"Yeah. Sorry if I was staring. I've gone most of the twentieth and twenty-first centuries with minimal human contact, but now that I've made friends in the last year, I miss it and crave it."

Roxi slid her hand and arm through the hole. "Can I hold your hand? I just need to feel the warmth of another human. Only for a minute…"

Luke rolled over and adjusted his body so he could take her hand in his. The warmth of her skin against his felt amazing. He felt Maggie's last ghostly touch against his cheek and choked up. With his other hand, he wiped his eyes. The wall he'd been trying to construct to protect himself from his own loneliness crumbled under the warm touch of Roxi's hand. He'd tried to hide from his need to be with other people for too many years, afraid of the pain of losing them and the guilt of potentially being the cause. Instead, he'd only hurt himself.

Roxi squeezed his hand. "Hey, Luke. I think I hear the bucket people coming."

He squeezed back and let go of her hand. When he heard scraping, he looked down as she slid the stone back into the wall. With his bucket in place, he stepped away from the door and found a spot to do some stretches to loosen his muscles. Once the bucket was exchanged, she pulled the rock back out.

"Hey. Exercise time?"

"Yeah, we better step it up some. I don't know how long before they make us dance for them again."

THROUGHOUT THE WEEK, Luke and Roxi split their time between working out and holding hands while taking a break from anymore deconstruction. But with each meal that showed up, they both approached warily, unsure whether it could be the one to send them back to the arenas for their next fight. It was the only reason they'd received nourishment for so long. The food could have been far worse and far less balanced, even if it wasn't enough to truly sustain them. The hunters were prized pets to be trotted out for the amusement of their vampire overlords.

Still not looking at his wall of marks save for only to make them, Luke added a slash to the mark of the day he'd first gone up to the arena. It wasn't until just over a week later that their next date in the arena arrived. They'd sat down next to their hole in the rock to chat and eat together when Roxi hastily shoved her tray aside and fumbled to get the rock back into the hole.

"Luke…I'm starting to fade," she warned.

Starting to drift himself, he set down his tray and slipped his fingers into the space between stones. He worked the stone the rest of the way back into the hole before laying out to let the drugs carry him away into unconsciousness.

AS LUKE STRUGGLED to come to, he had trouble identifying the noise pummeling him. When he'd woken up in the arena elevator strapped to the wall, it had been fairly quiet. Wherever he was now was not.

The indistinguishable buzz of dozens conversation filled the room, punctuated by the occasional shout or raucous peel of laughter. The clink of glassware and silverware and ceramics sauced the main course of the voices. Tipping his eyes open, he saw the floor of a fighting ring. Apparently, today was his turn in the octagon. He didn't feel the weight of the armor they'd put him in before. He was strapped into a chair in nothing but shorts. By now, they'd probably guessed he was awake, so he lifted his head to look around.

He was in the octagon, probably the same one Roxi had been in. The floor was a bright red canvas, though Luke could easily see the marks blood stains had left, both human and the darker ones of a vampire. Unlike a typical MMA ring where the walls were made with vinyl-covered chain-link fencing, this cage looked to have coated steel cables, interwoven and reinforced. The walls were also probably twice the height of a normal human fighting ring, maybe more, and instead of an open top, the ceiling featured steel bars welded together. Luke guessed the underfloor was probably also reinforced beyond standard practices. This was a cage meant to host epic battles with humans and creatures who possessed strength and abilities far beyond those of a stock human.

Luke hoped his opponent would be as similarly lackluster as Shifu Chuck Brannigan. He didn't want to duke it out with some musclebound fanger looking to make a name for himself on Luke's body. The thought of having to punch it out with some goon nearly sapped his will; he still didn't have the conditioning for this kind of excursion.

Shaking his head, he tried to adjust his body so he could get comfortable and focus his mind. If he didn't get his head right, he'd end his career here, pounded into paste for the amusement of soulless, bloodsucking assholes. He closed his eyes and took in a deep breath, holding it before exhaling slowly. He repeated the cycle. It had two effects—helping him rid his body of the last effects of the drugs and allowing him to center himself for the coming struggle.

Not wishing to become distracted, he left his eyes closed as the steady din of the room washed over him. The longer he sat, the more anxious the noise around him grew as the number of voices increased along with the number of vampires he sensed. He couldn't get an idea of exact numbers, but he could feel the density increasing. When the audience started clapping and stomping in rhythm, Luke knew it was nearly time. After the bands holding his arm against the post opened, Luke stood and hopped around, rotating his arms to get the blood flowing. He couldn't go into this totally cold.

"Welcome to the Octagon!" the announcer yelled. After letting the roar of the crowd dissipate, he continued, "Tonight, we have a special one for you! In the red and gold trunks, we have the Cockroach of Portland, the Butcher, the Cruel Destroyer, the Scourge of the Night, the Centurion Immortal, the Wood Fanged Demon!"

"The cockroach? Cassius must have come up with that one," Luke thought.

The announcer left a pause so the audience could hiss and boo. Luke took a moment to look around. The audience looked like any Vegas fight crowd with the rich VIPs in the front in cordoned off boxes. Though unlike Vegas, the attire was far more varied. There were the usual bespoke suits, but there was a variety of flashy period garb depending on the vampire's heritage or mood.

He saw a variety of garments that would have been at home in many a European court worn by the wealthy and aristocratic elite. Who knew, some of these vamps might have even been those elites at one point. He also saw plenty of attractive blood donors on their arms. The majority of those who looked in charge of their little spheres of influence appeared to be men, but a few vampire women held court with their minions as well. Women in skimpy dresses—thralls, probably—moved through the crowds delivering bottles of blood, some in beer-style bottles, while others might have been mistaken for champagne bottles save for the viscous blood visible through the clear glass. The ice buckets and champagne flutes were a nice touch though.

"And now, Ladies and Lords of Vampiredom, please welcome your champion tonight—the Enforcer of the Fang, the Rock *and* the Hard Place! The Beefcake who's not afraid of the stake, once a knight of the Holy Roman Empire and now your favorite brawler— Gunther the Mauler!"

Luke had to admit; the announcer had flair. He clearly had watched "A Knight's Tale" and taken Chaucer's lessons to heart. The crowd had returned to their steady clapping and stomping, but this time it was punctuated by rhythmic chants of "Gun-ther-Maul-er, Gun-ther-Maul-er."

Luke found the shadow of his opponent working his way down an aisle starting on the opposite side from where his seat had been situated. When he turned around, his chair was gone. Someone must have pulled it through the cables. Walking around to warm up, he returned his attention back to his opponent. As Gunther strode down the aisle, letting his adoring fans touch him as he slowly bounced toward the cage, Luke moved and stretched, using every moment to prepare. When Gunther entered the light illuminating the ring, the knight of the Holy Roman Empire indeed looked like the stereotypical German.

Tall, muscular, and blond, he was the poster child for the Aryan race, complete with his Third Reich haircut, sides shaved with the top long and swept back. There was just enough slightly longer hair above the shaved portion around the crown of his head to allow for a mechanically straight part on one side. He wore a gold robe, and when he turned around, it bore the black Reichsadler Imperial Eagle of the Holy Roman Empire.

Looking down at his own trunks, Luke found them much plainer, though someone had gone to the trouble of getting them made in the gold and red often depicted as the colors of Rome. He pressed into the fighting gloves to check the padding against his knuckles. They protected the first knuckles but left the fingers and thumbs uncovered for grappling. Normally, Luke carried a bit of weight around his middle, but the months of just enough rations in the cell had eaten away at that. He'd also lost muscle mass from the forced sedentary life. When Gunther reached the cage, one of his handlers helped him off with his robe. Gunther looked sculpted from stone.

After he was let into the cage, he stared daggers at Luke, a faint unnatural gleam in his eyes. A moment later, a vampire wearing a referee's shirt stepped into the ring before the door they'd entered from was closed and locked.

"Come to the center of the ring," the referee said.

The mountain of vampire flesh swaggered forward. Shaking his head, Luke faced across from him with the referee on his left. Next to the tower of Teutonic tonnage, Luke felt like Rocky Balboa lining up against Dolph Lundgren's Ivan Drago. Gunther had a good three or four inches on Luke's six feet. The vampire had Luke out-muscled and had a better reach to boot. He also couldn't rely on the bigger man being slower. Any speed sacrificed by that much muscle mass would be more than made up for in supernatural vampiric speed. Gunther had probably drained a few juice box thralls, so he was at the peak of his powers.

"Gentlemen, I want a nice fight. If I tell you to move apart, do it. The bell sounds to end the round, return to your corners." The referee looked toward Gunther. "Don't end it too quickly. The finest vampires of the world have assembled here for a show. Give them a good one." He looked back to Luke. "You may go pray to whatever pathetic god has forsaken you before you die. Touch fists, return to your corners, and come out fighting when the bell rings."

The referee grabbed Gunther's fists and pulled them toward the middle. Luke reached out and bumped his fighting glove covered knuckles against the vampire's and turned away, walking to his corner. Gunther turned toward a tall, platform shrouded in darkness deep in the crowd and bowed respectfully before returning to his corner. The referee had told Luke to pray to whatever gods…

He sank to his knees and bowed his head. *"Selene, My Mistress. Please watch over me and give me the strength to survive this."*

The sound of the arena faded to nothing, and he heard a sweet voice in his ear. *"Where are you, my brave soldier? You are shrouded from me. I have not seen you in too long. I feared the worst."*

"I am alive but trapped in some prison of the vampires with other hunters. I know of another of The Wanderer's acolytes here—Roxiustana Surena. The vampires make us fight vampires for their amusement," Luke prayed into his mind.

"I know of her, though she doesn't pay honors to me. She is a fierce servant of The Wanderer's."

Luke couldn't see Selene, but he felt her light upon his soul, bringing peace and centering him.

"Lucius, I give you my blessing and what strength I can muster through the veil you are hidden behind."

Luke felt a kiss on his forehead and a hand run along his jaw. *"Thank you, my mistress, and forgive me for not paying more honors to you. I have been lacking in my devotion to your kindness."*

"It was a hard burden we placed upon you. You have acquitted yourself well in my eyes. Now go fight for our honor, yours and mine. Survive so my light may shine upon you once again."

Luke bowed his head to his goddess. *"As you wish, My Mistress."*

The bell rang.

Luke rose and turned to face Gunther. He could feel Selene's blessing upon him and coursing through his body. Flexing, one corner of his lips tipped up, and he wished everything would be black with green streams of characters everywhere, bending to his flex. Gunther looked less cocksure than he had a minute ago, moving cautiously forward.

Luke extended his hand and curled the tips of his fingers in a few times. "Bring it if you dare. The Centurio Immortalis awaits his next victim."

He'd always preferred that nickname—he'd earned both parts of it—although he did like "The Wood Fanged Demon." Few nicknames given by enemies were so evocative.

Luke decided caution was the best tactic. He didn't want to rush in and try to overwhelm the behemoth, not until he had a plan to go with it. Surviving long enough to find Gunther's weaknesses and exploit them seemed the wiser course. Luke moved clockwise around the octagon, keeping a respectable distance between himself and the German vamp.

"You talk big, but dance away," Gunther taunted through a thick German accent.

"We can do this in German, if you'd like," Luke said in modern German, before switching languages. "Or in Middle High German, if you can remember it, you blood-addled, fang-mouthed meathead."

He didn't think the pathetic taunt would land, but Gunther growled and changed his approach to cross the octagon instead of dancing around it with Luke. The hulking fanger looked like he wanted to grapple, where he could use his superior strength to crush him.

Luke let him, standing taller and taking a half step further away from the cage wall so he had room to work. The German lunged forward but aimed too high. Luke dropped under Gunther's arms and shot to the side, delivering a punishing left-handed punch to the vampire's right obliques. Gunther grunted and cringed. The punch also caught the vamp with his weight on his right foot, so he wasn't able to follow Luke when he continued around behind Gunther.

Luke guessed the vampire hadn't expected to already be on the defensive. He was slow to recover, so Luke took advantage of it, putting a vicious right followed by a left punch into Gunther's right kidney. He didn't know if it would cause the vamp to piss blood, but he knew it would still hurt like a hot poker shoved into him.

Grunting in pain, Gunther stepped forward and spun the other way, aiming a sloppy swipe at Luke. It didn't strike, but it encouraged Luke to move back, allowing Gunther a brief moment to recover. Luke's efficient and brutal punches had taken a bit of the starch out of the crowd, turning down the decibels a few notches.

With a little room to work, Gunther tried to straighten out but cringed as he twisted his torso. The three punches had clearly affected him. Luke backed up, pulling Gunther away from the cage's wall. Once he'd drawn the vampire closer to the center, Luke sidestepped, forcing Gunther to adjust and move until they were both circling the center of the ring clockwise. Luke threw a couple exploratory jabs with his left hand, threatening Gunther's already wounded right side. Gunther dodged the first, cringing at the compression on his torso, and parried the second jab, turning it with his gloved fist.

Luke dropped and spun a low kick toward Gunther's right calf and ankle. Raising the leg, Gunther dodged the slow kick and lashed out at Luke with the leg. Anticipating the counter strike, Luke rolled to his right and delivered a sharp uppercut to Gunther's hamstring. Between Luke's punch and the earlier momentum of the counter kick, Gunter twisted away from Luke clumsily.

Tapping into the strength and speed Selene's blessing had given him, he leapt up and pushed Gunther between the shoulder blades to keep him moving forward and off balance. Placing two more quick punches into the vampire's kidney, Luke drew a pained grunt from the huge vampire.

Instead of trying to turn and swipe at Luke, Gunther stumbled forward and fell into the cage's wall, then rolled along it until he once again faced Luke, using the cage's wall to protect his softened kidneys.

While Gunther's glare had been vampiric rancor at the beginning of the fight, his eyes positively burned with hatred now. Not only had Luke caused him pain, he'd been humiliated in front of the vampiric horde who'd arrived to watch him deal pain and justice. The referee had instructed them to make it a nice fight, but this wasn't what the vampire probably had in mind.

The Mauler shifted to a lower stance with his fists in front of him, head ducked between his shoulders. Stalking toward Luke, he threw a couple tentative jabs. Luke, trying to get him to start rotating again, ducked under the jabs and stepped to his left, but instead of pivoting, Gunther stepped right to block Luke and punctuated it with a right jab.

The vampire was trying to stop Luke taking advantage of his maneuverability and lure him into a slug fest. If it came to that, it would be a losing proposition for Luke. When he failed to move the stack of vamp meat or find a new opening, he dropped back and kept moving, randomly stepping in to throw a punch to try to keep Gunther honest, but the big vamp solidly held the middle of the ring.

The crowd was growing restless, the occasional jeer or boo floating from the audience to the ring along with encouragement to do something—or complaints of boredom. Gunther the Mauler was here to entertain the bloodsucking bastards; Luke was there to survive. He didn't give a shit about the entertainment value of the fight.

As Luke tried to formulate his next move, he wasn't particularly a brawler or a fighter in this sense, his heel caught and he fell backwards into the cage's wall. Gunther leapt upon the opportunity, delivering several hard body blows to Luke's stomach and knocking the wind from his lungs. Hunching over, Luke gasped as he tried to deflect the vampire's fists. Gunther tried to close in so he could grapple with Luke and get him tied firmly in his clutches, but Luke couldn't allow that if he wanted to get out of this alive.

Casting dignity to the wind, he dropped to his knees, dove between Gunther's legs, and rolled onto his back to deliver a two-footed mule kick to Gunther's ass. The vampire slammed into the cage's wall, falling. Luke scrambled to his knees, then his feet, and delivered a series of hard punches into the already tender kidney of the vampire. As Gunther arched his back, trying to pull his middle away, Luke snaked his arm around Gunther's neck and caught his throat in his elbow, flexing his arm to pinch off the blood flow to his head, if there even was much in a vampire. He caught his fist in his other elbow so he could lock his arm around the vampire's neck, then wrapped his legs around Gunther's torso, clasping his foot under a knee to lock himself in place.

Luke drew in a full breath and clenched his body, anticipating what was next. Fortunately, Gunther didn't stand up before flopping onto his back, only doing it from his knees. Still, the force with which he slammed backwards, combined with his weight, pushed the air from Luke's lungs with a grunt. Gunther rolled around, trying to smush Luke against the floor like a berry. Luke used the clench he had with his legs to kick with his heel, unsure what part of the mount of vampiric meat he was digging his heel into.

Despite the tight crunch Luke was putting on Gunther's neck, the vampire's growl of fury rose as he tried to reach behind him to grab for anything of Luke's. Wiggling while keeping his legs and arms locked around Gunther, Luke tried to evade the grasping hands of his opponent. Vaguely in the background, he heard a metal bell chime. Despite the sound telling him it was time to break off, he couldn't do it. Nearly two thousand years of fighting vampires said he couldn't let a vampire go when he had them under his power—he finished them so they couldn't kill him.

The bell sounded again, but this time accompanied by the referee screaming into his ear. "Let him go or I'll break your arm off and you'll have to fight the next round like that. Do it!"

Luke loosened his grip around Gunther but didn't let go all the way. Feeling Luke's grip slackening, Gunther sat up abruptly, breaking Luke's grip, and rolled away from him. Not trusting the vampire to follow the rules, Luke rolled the opposite way and sprang up, ready to go if he had to. That was probably a good idea—the referee had stepped in between Luke and the vampire and was currently holding Gunther back.

"Back to your corners. Now!" the ref called.

Giving Gunther a wide berth, Luke returned to his corner. The seat had been returned to the inside. Luke gladly sank onto it, heaving heavy breaths, still not recovered from the body blows Gunther had delivered.

"Human. Here," someone said behind him.

Luke was shocked at the lack of venom in the speaker's voice. Turning, he saw someone shove a sports bottle between the cables forming the cage's walls. Luke took the bottle and squirted the liquid onto his hand to check it out. It looked and felt like water. Cautiously, he squirted a drop into his mouth. It tasted fine, so he filled his mouth and swished it around before swallowing it. He wanted to down the whole bottle, but that would be a poor choice. He squirted more into his mouth, then over his head. He handed the bottle back to the human—Luke was close enough to tell that much —and took a towel from the man to wipe himself down.

"Stand up, please. I need to move the seat."

Luke nodded and stood with a groan and a sigh.

"Thank you."

"Thank you," Luke replied.

A moment later, the bell rang. While Gunther had looked mean at the stare off before the first bell, now he looked positively wrathful. Luke had embarrassed him. If this had been a sanctioned bout in the human world, Luke would have won that round, landing the most blows and keeping control of the fight.

Luke slid into the versatile ready position he often used with Delilah when they were sparring. It would present a different look to the Mauler, who'd returned to his hulking stalk, head hunched and fists ready to strike. Luke took the offensive and kicked out, catching Gunther by surprise and landed a blow to the vampire's waist. Absorbing the kick, Gunther jabbed out with his right fist. Luke saw it coming and deflected it back across Gunther's body. Using his own momentum from the block, he caught the vamp along the right cheek with a solid punch, then shoved himself away and around the vamp's back to deliver a brutal uppercut into the kidney he'd been working all night.

Gunther fell forward and dove to the ground, rolling away from Luke and springing up near the far side of the cage. So far, the vampire had shown him little beyond an attempt to pulverize him with his fists or grab him to be crushed. Luke had centuries of fighting experience and had learned martial arts from cultures throughout Europe and Asia. He couldn't try to out hit the vampire, but he could keep Gunther from getting a grip on him long enough to find a solution that would result in returning to his cell in one relatively whole piece.

As Gunther approached, Luke moved into a different pose where he could attack with either fists or feet. This time, however, Gunther anticipated Luke's attack and swatted it aside, pulling him in close. Off balance, but desperate, Luke tried to punish the vampire with fast punches to the stomach. Unfortunately, he hadn't studied the three-inch punch with Pei Mei. Either that, or Gunther's abs were far harder than a wooden board.

Luke's only resort was to keep slippery and wiggly. It prevented Gunther from getting solid hits, but a partial blow from the muscular vampire was enough. Luke cringed away, trying to keep the vampire's fists away from his ribs. He'd lived through enough broken ribs over the last couple years, and they were slow to heal without his rudis to aid him. Unable to break Gunther's grip, he wrapped his arm around Gunther's free arm, drew back his head, and flung it forward into the vampire's nose. Light exploded through Luke's skull, sparks flashing across his eyes. Blood gushing from Gunther's shattered nose followed the sound of crunching cartilage, and the vampire loosened his grip. It freed enough space that Luke could draw back his knee and bring it up into Gunther's stomach. The vampire's grip released entirely.

Without Luke to hold him up, Gunther hunched over and tried to flail. Pushing the vampire's hands away, Luke grabbed Gunther's head and brought it down into his knee. The vampire staggered backwards, trying to get out of Luke's reach. With some space, Luke moved back, cradling his stomach where Gunther had hit him, and struggled to get air into his lungs. The roar of the crowd washed over him as his ears flowed in and out of function, still ringing after plowing his forehead into the vampire's rock-hard head.

He gave his head a shake, trying to snap his mind back to attention as he worked to orient himself. Gunther charged at him like a bull. Air whooshed out of Luke's lungs as a shoulder slammed into Luke's midsection. The vampire kept moving until they both slammed into the steel cable walls. Luke's body opened up, flattening against the cables until they snapped both fighters back. Together, they tumbled in a heap.

Gunther tried to get his body in a dominate position while still grappling. Partially powered hits rained onto Luke's back. Between the hits and the vampire squeezing him to keep him from escaping, Luke struggled to pull in oxygen. Feeling his leg freed as they rolled around, he brought his knee up into Gunther's stomach as many times as he could until the vampire's grip slackened. Luke slammed his elbow into the side of Gunther's head, opening more space.

As Gunther scrabbled to reestablish his hold, Luke twisted around until he could get his arm around Gunther's neck. Instead of trying to choke him out by cutting the blood to his brain, he cradled the vampire's chin, gripped the other side of his head with his other hand, and channeled all his strength, his own and that bestowed by Selene's brief blessing. He wrenched the vampire's neck until he heard the sickening sound of Gunther's vertebrae snap. The vampire went limp. He kept twisting until he nearly had the head wrenched all the way around so it was looking backward.

Gasping for air, Luke shoved the motionless vampire off of him and rolled away, lying flat on his stomach. Every part of his chest, stomach, and back throbbed from the pummeling Gunther had given him in their last desperate struggle. When the thunder of his blood pumping through his ears calmed, he could hear the crowd. Or, rather, their lack of reaction. They appeared stunned into silence by Luke's defeat of their mammoth champion.

He struggled to his hands and knees and forced himself into a standing position. Just the effort of standing had his blood pumping again. He'd need some time to rest and recover, but all he had to look forward to was a cold stone floor. Not exactly what one would call prime sleeping.

Staring out at the crowd, they largely sat motionless, staring back. The few eyes he could make out in the light, closer to the ring, burned with hatred and no small amount of fear. They had every right to fear him. If he weren't tightly contained within the cage, he'd try to slay every last one of them. He'd destroyed the vampire they'd judged able to kill the Wood Fanged Demon. Despite a few hitches, Luke had pretty much dominated him.

"And...your winner is the...Wood Fanged Demon." The announcer sounded just as shaken as the audience at what they'd probably viewed as a not only improbable outcome, but a nearly impossible one. As soon as the announcer finished the short sentence, the crowd came to life, hissing and booing until it grew into a raucous din. A few people even threw bottles that shattered or bounced off the vinyl-wrapped steel cables to explode on the concrete surrounding the ring.

The referee stomped over and roughly grabbed Luke's wrist, thrusting it into the air before dropping it like it was a viper. "Go sit in your corner and don't move," he hissed between clenched teeth.

Luke sauntered back to the corner where the thrall had returned the seat to the inside of the cage. He leaned against the post, his back straight, posing like a king on a throne.

Someone behind him cleared their throat, then spoke just loud enough to be heard over the crowd. "If you sit still and let me inject you, I won't have to cuff you."

Luke gave a small nod. A hand grabbed his upper arm, and a moment later, he felt a needle jabbed into it.

"Thank you," the thrall said.

"Will he live? Gunther?" Luke asked.

"Why do you care?"

"Morbid curiosity."

"They'll straighten his neck and get some blood into him. He'll be fine in a few months," the thrall whispered loud enough for Luke to hear.

"That's too bad." Luke shook his head.

The thrall made a disgusted noise.

Whatever the thrall had pumped into his arm was taking effect. Not wanting to fall forward and hit his head and fuck up his neck, he moved to the canvas floor and leaned up against the post, resting his head against it as he let the drugs take him.

TWELVE

He woke sometime the next day in his cell, but unlike all the previous days he'd woken there, this time he lay on top of a thin foam camping sleeping mat. He groaned as he moved, every muscle in his body aching. Worst of all, his entire rib cage was one dull throb from Gunther slamming into his chest, then into the cage and all the pummeling as they tussled on the canvas mat. His eyes shot wide when he ran his eyes over the wall where the loose stone was.

He slid the mat over to that section of the floor and rolled onto his hands and knees, working the stone from its hole. "Roxi?"

He saw her body stretched out on the floor. His heart in his throat, he watched her chest, relief flooding through him when he saw it steadily rising and falling. He adjusted his angle. She wasn't wearing the baggy prison trousers, but she did have a white bandage wrapped around her right thigh. He stared at it, his eyebrows furrowed and mouth drawn tight in worry. He hoped it wasn't too bad or too deep. He didn't trust their jailers to allow her the time to heal properly, and he definitely knew they wouldn't allow her to use her rudis to feed off a vampire, no matter who that vampire might have offended.

Once he'd reassured himself that she at least lived, he looked her over to see if she might have any other noticeable injuries. He couldn't see anything, but he could only see her back and a bit of her side since she lay with the injured leg on top. He'd have to wait until either she rolled over or woke up to assess her true condition. While he looked her over, the door flap opened, and the attendant slid in his tray, distracting him from his worrying.

He sat up, groaning in pain, and grabbed his tray to eat. When he licked the tray clean, not worrying about manners where no one could see him and every calorie counted, he returned the tray to its spot in front of the door. Instead of laying down on the hard floor, even though the mat helped, he decided to stand and do some gentle movements to see how badly he was truly injured.

He tried a few easy stretches to determine what was normal muscle soreness versus muscles bruised from fighting. His legs felt fine, save for a touch of soreness, but his back and ribcage were tender and beat to shit. He pulled up the baggy tunic to examine his chest and stomach. He snorted, impressed by the pastiche of bruises resembling the work of a blotchy, abstract expressionist canvas. He imagined his back looked just as bad.

"Luke," came the groggy sound of Roxi's voice.

Carefully, Luke lowered himself to the ground, creaking and groaning like an old man with way too many miles on his body—which, in a very real sense, he was. He was the oldest man he knew, and he probably had more miles on his body than any other human alive today.

"Roxi? You alive over there?"

"I don't know. I feel funny," she replied.

"It's probably whatever they pumped into your system. They might also have you on a pain med as well. You have an injury on your thigh."

"Yeah, that's true." Her voice sounded lazy and a bit slurred.

"What happened? Your wound, I mean." He didn't want to force her to retell the whole tale until she was ready and more alert.

"Slash across the thigh. I don't think it's too deep, at least I hope. It bled plenty, though. Probably just stitches."

Luke's body unclenched slightly, some of his worry and tension dissipating at hearing her voice and her initial assessment of her injury. "Good. If you're up for it, your food should be there. Might help get you settled some."

She tried to sit up but groaned and returned to her previous position lying on her side. Instead, she moved around, facing the door so she could eat. When she finished, she pushed herself backwards to face Luke.

"I think the food is helping." She smiled weakly, her eyes still partially hooded.

"Good. I'm glad you're alive." He meant it. He didn't want to think about what would happen if she died, leaving him alone.

"Me too. I wasn't sure I was going to come out of that one alive. Frankly, I'm lucky this slash was the worst of it, save for some bruises."

"I'd love to hear about it, if you feel like telling it," Luke replied.

Roxi yawned. "I'm not sure I'm up for it at the moment, but if you want to tell me about your fight, I'm assuming you had one as well…"

He smiled gently. "I can do that." He wove the tale of his smiting of Gunther the Mauler, trying to make it humorous. When he got a couple big laughs from her, it warmed his heart, except when she laughed hard enough to then groan in pain.

Luke stopped the story. "I'll try not to be as funny for the rest of the story, if you want me to continue."

"No, please make me laugh. My ribs are a bit sore, that's all. The laughter feels better than the ache hurts," she replied.

"OK." Luke picked up the tale with the referee's threat. When he arrived at the point where he grappled with Gunther, she gasped, caught up in the story. After he finished the story, she sighed in relief.

"You have a way with a story."

"Thank you."

Roxi yawned. "I think I want to take a nap."

"Sure." He rolled onto his back, squishing into his mat. "Roxi, someone gave me a padded mat. I think I can roll it up small enough we can slide it through to your side. It might be a little easier on your leg and hips."

"How did you get a mat?"

"No idea. I woke up on it," he replied.

"I can't take your mat." She shook her head, her messy hair falling across her face, only to be swept out of the way by her hand.

"Please. I'm just beat up some. You need proper rest to heal that slash. I insist." He didn't wait for her answer, rolling off the mat.

He rolled it up tightly and shoved it into the hole. Squishing it down to fit the wider profile of the hole, and with Roxi's help pulling it, he transferred it to her cell. It was a delicate operation getting it rolled out, since Roxi's mobility was limited as she tried to avoid moving her injured thigh. Luke helped by shoving his arm through and holding it in place by the wall as she shimmied her way onto it. Once she got centered, she arranged herself as best as she could under the circumstance. She gave a big sigh and let her eyelids drift closed.

She pushed her hand toward the hole. "Will you hold my hand while I fall asleep?"

"Sure, Roxi," Luke replied, snaking his hand through the hole to take hers.

"Thank you…" she mumbled, drifting off to sleep.

He lay there, the warmth of her hand in his, soothing the turmoil churning inside him. He wasn't sure how long it was before he fell asleep, but he woke up and Roxi was still asleep. He rolled over and got up, working the kinks out of his body and took the time while she was asleep to use the bucket. Shaking his head, he walked to the other side of the cell. He could barely do more than touch her or hold hands, but the proximity of the bathroom bucket felt far too intimate in the confined space.

When she finally woke from her long nap, she told Luke about her duel in the arena against another burley vampire, this one heavily armored. "I only survived because I've been doing this for so long. Her movements weren't natural. I don't think she was terribly practiced."

"Yeah, Gunther the Mauler relied on his strength and size. If he actually knew how to use martial arts beyond some boxing and maybe some grappling or wrestling, I might have been a dead man. I don't think vampires spend a lot of time on their martial skills, certainly not in this day and age when they can just sneak around and glamour their meals or let modern vices lure in their victims. They've gotten sloppy."

Roxi laughed. "All things considered, I'm glad they're not up to snuff. As long as we have to keep fighting them, I want them to keep falling far short of the Centurio Immortalis's exacting standards."

Luke blushed, then started laughing. "Yeah, that's a good point. If I had a beer, I'd offer to toast to their continued poor training. Though, they do have elite warriors."

"Oh?"

"I ran into a pack of them, oh…" Luke paused to think about the time. "I don't know what time is anymore. The spring before I was captured. They had a dozen of them in Portland to try to take me out. We left most of them dead by the time we broke up the vamp's operation. I think only one or maybe two made it out alive. Don't know for sure. I wasn't conscious for the wrap up of that one."

"Why were you not conscious?" Roxi asked, concern tinging her voice despite the fact that Luke had obviously survived that incident.

"An old friend had unloaded a full magazine at me. Broke most of my ribs—though several were already on their way—my collar bone, and put two into my left arm. Already had a slug in my leg. Then he nearly choked me out. Crushed my windpipe." The recitation all sounded very clinical, even to his own ears.

"You should be dead after all that…"

"I would have been if not for the quick thinking of my friend Delilah. She's the one who killed my old pal." Luke loaded the word "pal" full of all the venom he felt for Cassius. "She had one of our friends drag my body into position and held my hands on my rudis. At least I got to drain the bastard. It healed me well enough to survive until the pack's medical team could stabilize me."

"Whoever that is doesn't sound like a good friend…"

"He was my best friend. We joined the legions at the same time. Made it all the way through Trajan's second Dacian war, but he was murdered in a cave, or so I thought. Ran into him in Portland for the first time a couple years ago and wrecked all his operations." Despite the bitterness of their fight against each other, Luke's feelings about Cassius were still mixed. Cassius had been his friend until jealousy of Luke's achievements put the first wedge in their relationship.

"It's always hard when you run into people you knew in life who were turned into vampires, though it really drives home the insidious evil of vampirism to see the person you knew versus who they've become," Roxi said.

Luke nodded. "Yeah. It does." The joy in her companionship and relief that they'd both survived another day turned hollow in his stomach as all the faces of those who'd been friends before being turned drifted through his vision. He'd killed many of them. He thought about Hersch and his lost leg and the death of his friend Archie. "Seems like being friends with me is dangerous. It makes them targets for the vampires who hunt me."

"Yeah. It's hard to let people into your life when you know they could die just by proximity to you, but it gets lonely." She reached through and squeezed his arm.

Luke bent his arm so he could grab her hand. "It does. If I hadn't been taken in by a wolf pack, I don't know where I'd be. Well, that's not true. I'd be dead by now. Maybe on the streets of Portland or dragged off to this place a couple years earlier."

"Yeah. That was lucky. Usually werewolf packs are standoffish, at least the ones I've encountered.

He chuckled. "I kind of didn't have a choice. One night, I was having dinner and beers down at my local brewpub when some vampires wandered in. I followed them out to the alley when they tried to abscond with some local college coeds. The owner stepped out to help me. He didn't want predators in his bar, though he just thought they were some creeps who'd roofied some girls. Well, when they went vamp, he went full on bipedal wolf, and there I was, stuck in the middle."

"Wow. I'm surprised you didn't get mauled."

"I think werewolves' lack of control is highly exaggerated. He knew exactly what he was doing and was a fine ally for the fight.

When it was done, we cleaned up and got the girls out of there, then he took me back into the bar and bought me a couple beers so we could talk. He set up a meeting with the packleader to introduce us to each other."

"Just like that?" Roxi's voice contained volumes of skepticism.

"I couldn't get rid of him. He'd decided he wanted to hunt vampires and be my friend. When I told him no, he teamed up with a human hunter I'd run across, who I'd likewise told no, and they started following me. They ended up saving my life when I was trapped by a fuck ton of fangy bastards. We've been friends and a team ever since. Everyone in my life, except Delilah, is a werewolf. My ward, my girlfriend, my best friends. I'm actually a member of the pack's council now."

"That's unheard of," she said, astonished.

Luke adjusted so he could be on his side and look through their hole. Once he was situated, he returned his hand to Roxi's. "I would have thought so a few years ago. I've hardly had any interactions with werewolves over my life, and now I'm neck deep in them. At this point, we're recruiting soldiers from other local packs to sweep the vampires out of Portland. At least we were..."

She squeezed his hand. "I'm sorry, Luke. They sound like a wonderful group of people." She paused, not speaking for a while. "I'd like to meet them someday."

"I'd like that very much." He pulled her hand the few inches to his face, moving his lips the last few inches to kiss the back of her hand.

"What was that for?" she asked, not sounding offended but curious.

"I don't know. I guess... You're the only reason I haven't lost my mind in here, Roxi. Although I'd been hiding from others for decades, they were always there. But in here, there was no one else. Not even word from our jailers. Just silence and nothingness. Even though the result is the same, no people in my life, they're entirely different kinds of loneliness. I'd felt my mind slipping away to hide, then when I heard your scratching, I thought I had gone around the bend. But when I figured out the other noise was a voice, it was like an oasis in the desert." Luke squeezed her hand and rested his forehead against the back of it.

"I know. The only thing that kept me going was scratching the mortar from that rock. Then when I heard your voice, I broke down and quietly sobbed. I wasn't alone anymore." Roxi sniffed, fighting a quaver in her voice. "I hope we get out of here someday so I can hug you properly."

"I would like that more than anything," Luke replied.

CHAPTER
THIRTEEN

Luke's head felt heavy inside and out. He'd been drugged again. As he rolled his chin over his chest, the brass-rimmed cheek guards scraped against the steel of the lorica segmentata he'd worn for his first bout in the arena. Leaving his eyes closed, he tipped his head back, doing his best to rest it against the wall in spite of the neck guard. It would have been a lot harder had it been his helmet with its wider, deeper neck guard.

When he heard someone groan, he froze, peeling his eyes open. He wasn't alone. On the wall next to him, someone else was propped against the wall. They wore scale mail that rested over their thighs just at their knees. The conical helmet had cheek guards similar to Luke's, though smaller, and a spike on top that ended in a streamer of white horsehair. It fell down the sides and over the face of the wearer since their head was slumped down on their chest. They were both strapped to the walls like Luke had been the first time.

He didn't know if they were to be his ally or his enemy, though it didn't make sense that they'd put his opponent in the same elevator with him. He didn't sense vampire from them. They roused. When they lifted their head, he could see little besides their eyes. The face was covered in a chain mail veil with a nose guard jutting down from the rim of the helmet, though when they sat up all the way, he thought it might be a woman in the armor.

"Luke?"

Luke's stomach dropped through the floor. "Roxi?"

"What's…what's going on?" she asked, groggily.

"I think we're both fighting in the arena," he replied.

"Oh." She looked around their little elevator. "Well, this wasn't exactly how I wanted to meet you in person."

Luke let out a harsh bark of a laugh. "No. It is decidedly not how I pictured this meeting going. Though we should probably not say much. They could be listening."

"Right."

They sat staring at each other for a couple of minutes until the armbands strapping their upper arms and forearms to the walls clicked open. Luke stood and offered a hand to Roxi, helping her up. He didn't let go of it immediately. With her other hand, Roxi reached up and ran two fingers down Luke's nose and over the little piece of cheek not covered in beard or cheek guard—the touch sending thrills through him.

At first, she took a half step backwards, then lunged forward, shooting her arms under Luke's and wrapping her scale mail covered arms around his waist. He froze, wide eyed, before he wrapped his arms around her shoulders. Every time they moved, Roxi's scale scraped over the steel bands of Luke's armor. They held each other in their awkward armored embrace. Vaguely, he felt the elevator vibrate to life as it ascended toward the floor of the arena.

In the back of his mind, he knew they should part, not letting their captors know there was any connection between the two of them, but he couldn't bring himself to do it. Even with layers of steel between them, it was the closest he'd been to Roxi, the most he'd felt of another human in too long. When the roar of a full arena washed over them as the elevator breached the floor of the arena, he knew it was too late. The dice had been cast.

"Roxi, whatever happens. We stick together." He wished he could kiss her, but it would have to remain a wish for now.

"Right. Together, we survive."

He sighed. "Let's face our fate."

They parted, though they still held each other's hand.

A new awareness filtered into Luke's mind. The air felt fresh and crisp. His spine straightened as he found his full height, Selene's gentle embrace alerting him to her presence. He lifted his face toward where there had been a ceiling during their previous fight. The arena must have a retractable roof. The full moon beamed down on them, filling his heart.

"We are not alone," Luke said. "Selene is here with us."

Like his first fight, they had a scutum, and a gladius stationed not too far from their elevator, sticking up out of stands that probably retracted into the ground, if they ever released the weapons held within. Next to the Roman gear waited a simple straight sword and a round shield.

Luke led Roxi to their weapons, then dropped to his knees, his hand wrapped around the hilt of the gladius. Like last time, it was still locked in place, as was her sword.

"Roxi, do you trust me?" Luke looked up at her, finding her eyes just above the top of her mail veil.

She nodded. "I do."

"Join me. Open your heart to Selene. Let her light fill you and bless you."

Nodding, Roxi fell to her knees. She gripped the handle of her sword, matching Luke's position. He took her hand in his and bowed his head.

"Welcome!" the announcer said, greeting the audience. "In tonight's special bout, we bring you a unique opportunity as two ancient enemies join forces in an exciting match that you'll be talking about for ages!"

Luke cast his prayer to the goddess of the moon, his gentle protector. *"Selene, My Mistress, I open myself to you wholly. Protect and guide me in this trial. Please embrace Roxiustana and share your blessing with her. Together, we will honor you with our survival."*

The announcer continued. "For the second time in the arena, the

Murderer of Mumbai, the Terror of Tehran, the scion of a dead empire, the Deadly Demon, the Shrieking Wind, the Parthian!"

The crowd booed, hissed, and jeered, though Luke only perceived it in the background.

Selene's voice reverberated through his mind. *"You always have my blessing, brave soldier. I welcome Roxiustana. She, too, has my blessings. Fight well and keep my light in your heart, even in the darkness."*

"Save some of your boos for the Cockroach of Portland, the Butcher, the Cruel Destroyer, the Scourge of the Night, the Centurion Immortal, the Wood Fanged Demon!" The announcer's voice rose into a fever pitch.

While Roxi's greeting had been loud and harsh, the roaring boos and screams of hate forced all sound from Luke's ears and awareness. When the gladius in his hand unlocked with a click, Luke didn't hear it so much as feel its vibrations up his arm. He carefully let go of the sword, pulling Roxi's hand gently so he could get her attention. She saw what he was doing and nodded, letting go of her sword. He doubted the swords were supposed to be unlocked yet—another gift from Selene.

Luke reached over and took hold of the scutum's rim and pulled himself up, helping Roxi as well. He stepped around their weapon stations so they stood between them and their opponents' gateway into the arena.

Once the thunderous noise lessened, Luke leaned over and whispered into Roxi's ear, "Let's hold off on pulling the weapons until they're committed. I don't think we're supposed to get them until a later round."

"Right."

"How's the leg? Are you handling the extra weight of the armor OK?" he asked.

Roxi wobbled her head a little from side to side. "It was a little weak, but I think I'll be alright as long as I'm not pressed too hard on it."

"Was?"

"I don't know if it's the adrenaline or what, but it's feeling pretty solid right now. I'll be careful, though."

"And now for your champions!" the announcer called to the arena. "Their bite is worse than their bark! Give a warm howl for the best pets a vampire could have! Bring on the werewolves!"

The crowd erupted into laughter and wolf howls as the door blocking the entryway flew open. Luke stepped behind his shield while Roxi moved behind hers.

She leaned toward him. "I've never fought a werewolf before."

He reached out and squeezed her hand. "You can't out-damage them, and we don't have silver. Watch the claws, they're as dangerous as their teeth and have better reach. Try to dodge or deflect their hits, don't try to take them—they hit hard. Best bet is to aim for their legs. Take out tendons and muscles. Remove their mobility as fast as you can. Then take their head. And don't get separated; we'll need to watch each other's backs."

Roxi's mail veil rustled as she nodded.

The entire arena had taken up the wolf howl. Luke stared down the dark tunnel leading deep into the arena, waiting for the wolves to make their appearance. It didn't take long for the hulking shadows to resolve into four bipedal werewolves tearing out of the causeway. They weren't fanning out, instead charging straight at Luke and Roxi.

"Shit!" he yanked the gladius and scutum free, backing up.

A quick glance out of the corner of his eye told him Roxi had followed suit. She stood about five feet from him on his left, giving herself plenty of room to work with her sword. Seeing two swords and two shields facing them, the wolves skidded to a halt, save for one, and took a moment to assess the situation. The one who hadn't slowed headed for Luke.

He called out in middle Persian, "Open a little space and drop back. Let him take me, then when he's committed, attack!" If the werewolves could communicate with their pack link, he and Roxi could use a language he was pretty sure none of the wolves would know. He doubted many—if any—wolves were that old.

"Right!" Roxi replied.

The wolf loped toward Luke on all fours, accelerating as it neared. Raising his shield, Luke lowered his sword, holding his arm wide. He needed to time his move just right. He watched the creature's muscles bunch and lengthen, waiting for the telltale movements he wanted to see, learned from observing his friends in their bipedal werewolf forms. When the wolf crouched and uncoiled, leaping at him, he stepped right and crouched, raising his shield.

The werewolf hadn't anticipated Luke's sudden movement, possibly guessing the big, bad centurion would try to out muscle the wolf and take him head on. Luke left his joints bent and loose so that when the wolf hit his raised shield, the wolf wouldn't get a solid bounce, instead falling to the side as he landed off kilter on the shield.

His timing was perfect. The wolf hit his shield and dropped to the side in an ungainly heap as Luke tumbled away from him. Dropping the heavy scutum, he stopped his momentum and threw himself toward the wolf, plunging his gladius into the left side of the wolf's ribcage just under its arm. With a savage twist, Luke yanked the gladius out and rolled away in case the wolf lashed out or spasmed violently.

Roxi, waiting until Luke was out of the way, darted in and brought her sword down on the back of the wolf's neck twice, mostly severing the wolf's head from its body. By the time she was done, Luke had scooped up his scutum and was once again facing the rest of the werewolves, sword and shield raised.

"Let's get to clear ground," Luke called in middle Persian, backing up and sidestepping away from the werewolf's body as it made the final shift back into its human form.

Roxi backed up until she cleared the splayed arms of the body and jogged over to Luke, taking station just off his left side. "I don't think the wolf was expecting that!" Roxi laughed, a bit of frantic nervousness in it.

Two of the werewolves, standing on their hind legs, stalked toward Roxi and Luke, opening some distance between them.

"Where's the third one?" he asked.

"Shit," she replied. "Found it. Sneaking around the side."

"Can you keep an eye on it without looking like you're watching it?" He kept his gaze focused on the pair moving toward them from the front.

"Yeah. I think I understand."

"Good." Luke stopped moving backwards. "I'll keep the other two off you."

Giving his sword a twirl, he stepped forward, feigning a relaxed approach as if he wasn't really worried about the wolves. He hoped the quick and efficient dispatch of the first wolf would remind them just who they were dealing with. The legend wasn't just rumor, but brutal hard fact. They slowed their advance, looking toward one another. He wanted to check on Roxi but couldn't risk turning his head for a second as he closed the distance between the two wolves. She knew what she was doing after this long of a life fighting vampires. He'd have to trust her to hold his back.

Luke picked up speed, moving into a trot and aiming for the one toward his left so it couldn't flank him or pin him toward the arena's wall. The wolf's eyes grew wide as it stopped. Luke charged forward, bellowing loudly. The wolf scrambled backward. It must have put a paw down wrong, catching some dirt as it fell onto its ass with a surprised yelp.

Pouring on more speed, he aimed for the fallen wolf, hoping to get to it before the other wolf could adjust. The wolf on the ground tried scuttling backwards on its hands, but it wasn't having much luck getting away from Luke. Just before he came within striking distance, he rolled his head to the side just enough to see the other wolf loping toward him.

Luke slid like he was going into second base feet first and raked the edge of his gladius along the knee of the werewolf. It yelped loudly as blood bloomed just under its kneecap, dribbling down its leg. Luke slashed at the wolf's ribs, drawing another yelp as a shadow flew above him.

He pulled in the scutum so it was laying flat on top of him and brought his sword arm in so it was tight against his body. He rolled toward the wounded wolf and under the flying shadow. The maneuver worked, in that he didn't get pounced by the wolf as it overshot him, but the only thing separating him from the wounded and enraged wolf was the thin wood of his shield. His feet and legs were dangerously close to the business end of the wolf's mouth as spittle splattered against the bare skin of his calves. He pulled them back, relying on the metal greaves covering his shins to provide some protection. Pushing off on the shield, he tried to roll away so he could get up, but the wolf had snagged the shield in its powerful claws. Two options were available: either out-power an enraged werewolf and yank it away or abandon it and rely on his speed and sword.

The former option was neither wise nor even possible, so he leaned back into the scutum, then shoved himself away with all his might. He rolled away, timing the tumble and extending his hands and knees so he skidded to stop on all fours. He pushed himself up and sprinted back towards Roxi.

She'd wounded the third wolf, but not enough to render it immobile or slow it much. Luke could see a long bloody gash in the wolf's back, but all its limbs looked intact. He risked a look over his shoulder at the uninjured wolf. It had skidded to a halt a ways from its companion, its momentum carrying it further than it wanted without a human body to land on and slow its movement. It wouldn't be long before the wolf would pelt after Luke. There was no way he could outrun the wolf in a straight sprint.

Hoping his lead would hold, he poured on everything he had, trusting the hobnailed caligae would keep him from slipping in the dirt of the arena as he ran toward Roxi and the wolf she was fighting. She saw him coming and backed away from the wolf, periodically jabbing or slashing at the wolf's muzzle or claws to keep its attention.

"Luke! Duck!" Roxi screamed.

It took a moment for her command to filter through his head with his blood pumping hard in his ears. When it hit him, he stumbled and dove to the ground but not quite in time. Claws scraped over the back of his armor and helmet, driving him into the ground and knocking the wind from his lungs.

As his face plowed into the ground, he inhaled dust, then coughed and hacked violently. As the momentum of the wolf carried it past Luke, he scrambled to push back, his eyes watering as he coughed and sneezed, trying to clear the dust from his mouth and nose. He dragged his hand over his face to help clear it but drew back blood from his nose. He didn't know if it was broken or not; there was too much going on to check it.

The wolf that had nearly crushed him swiveled around, standing on its hind legs, and towered over him, bellowing its rage. Luke slid into an en garde position. The wolf wasn't going to wait for him clear his face, even if he asked nicely.

He couldn't see Roxi with the hulking wolf blocking his view. He heard a periodic feminine scream that sounded more like effort than pain, interspersed with an occasional yelp of pain or a growl. He backed off, trying to keep some space between him and the wolf as it stalked toward him. His lungs were finally coming back under his command, only giving a weak cough here and there. Trying to blink his eyes clear, he halted and stalked toward the wolf, menacing it with his naked blade.

He wanted to turn the wolf so he could link up with Roxi, but every time he tried to shift the engagement, the wolf would swat out with one of its massive paws, forcing him to duck and back step. Attempting to turn it the other away, he failed, drawing a swat from the other paw. The wolf wanted him moving backwards, probably toward its downed pal.

Luke didn't know how fast a wound like that would heal. The slash to the ribs might already be drawing to a trickle and sealing up, but he didn't know if a severed tendon would take longer. It didn't really matter, though. If the wolf trapped Luke between itself and its pal, he'd be royally fucked. He needed to take a risk if he was going to escape his impending doom.

When he attempted to move to the right to slip around the wolf, he anticipated the swat and lunged forward and dropped to his knees, bringing his sword across the wolf's knee. He nearly severed the tendon, but the wolf had dipped its leg, trying to bat Luke away. The sword cut a deep gash in the wolf's thigh, pulling an angry yelp from between its fanged jaws. Luke tried rolling to the right but was too slow. The wolf caught him with a partial backhand to the helmet, ringing his bell.

Luke, stunned, tried to control his roll, but he dropped. The wolf's lowest claw, coming back around, scraped along the back of his helmet, screeching. If he hadn't fallen, the wolf would have taken his head off.

He slid the sword over to his left hand and lashed out with it, weakly catching the side of the wolf's foot. The wolf jumped back, yelping, and hopped on the other foot until it slipped and tumbled away from Luke. Scrambling up, he collapsed again, but managed to push himself onto his knees, then his feet. With a shambling walk, he picked up speed, half stumbling and half falling toward the wolf Roxi still held at bay.

He had to reach the wolf. Flipping his sword into a reverse grip, he focused on his target. Closer. Almost there. With a final push, he tripped and dove onto the back of the werewolf with a great scream. His sword raised high, he plunged it deep into the werewolf's back, sinking it to the hilt guard.

The werewolf rose, convulsing and shaking. Luke clung to the hilt of his sword with his left hand and scrabbled to snake his right arm around the wolf's neck so he could hold on. Gurgling, the wolf sprayed blood from its mouth as it coughed, coating Luke's arm in hot, sticky blood. Roxi, taking advantage of an exposed belly, lunged in and slashed deeply across the wolf's stomach, spilling its guts onto the dirt of the arena.

Losing its power, the wolf staggered and fell to the side, sending Luke tumbling away, his sword still stuck in the wolf's back. Roxi leapt over the wolf as it quivered on the ground, expelling its last breath with a splutter of blood from its mouth. She slid to a stop and put her back to Luke, placing herself between him and the other two werewolves, both of which were hobbling toward them.

Luke, winded from crashing to the ground, crawled toward the downed werewolf, now a man, and placed his foot on the body's ribcage. He used his whole weight to pull the gladius. At first, it felt stuck, possibly in some bone. When it gave, Luke's force landed him on his back, but at least his sword was free. He rolled over, his lungs aching for air, and staggered back to his feet. He moved up to Roxi's right side, letting her sword cover his left.

"You alright?" Roxi asked, slowly advancing.

"I will be for now." Luke's lungs still burned from lack of air, but his breathing had slowed.

Seeing the hunters advancing on them, the two werewolves stopped and backpedaled.

"Now!" Roxi shouted.

She sprinted toward the werewolf on their right, the one with the slash in its paw. Catching it off guard, she slammed into it with her shield. The paw buckled under the force, and the wolf tumbled to the ground. Luke, a split second behind her, swiped his sword, cutting deep into the same werewolf's forearm. As it drew it away with a yelp, Luke plunged his sword into its chest and through its powerful heart. Luke felt the organ shiver against his blade as it pumped out the wolf's life force. Sparing a quick glance for the other werewolf, he was glad to see it backing away from them, falling onto its front paws to add more mobility to its retreat.

Roxi stepped up and brought her sword across the wolf's exposed neck, severing it to the spine. With a second hack, the head tumbled away, gushing blood from the neck as the body shifted into a human.

Luke yanked his sword free from its chest and stood up, stepping around the dead werewolf. The last werewolf hobbled away as fast as it could, resorting to running along on three legs as it dragged the leg with the severed tendon behind it. When the wolf made it to the door to the tunnel it had come out from, it sank against the door and shifted back into a human. Luke walked slowly along the arena wall, Roxi still on his left side.

He wasn't in a hurry to catch up to the werewolf, not after it had given up and surrendered. The crowd noise which had blasted them like jet engines taking off had quieted to a murmur, revealing the sound of the door creaking open. Luke couldn't hear what the werewolf said as it lay on the ground groveling to a shadow that moved out of the door. Luke couldn't tell who the man was when he stepped out of the shadows of the tunnel and into the lights of the arena.

The man reached down and took the wolf by the head and wrenched the poor creature's head around, ripping it from its body. Luke turned his head, trying to find somewhere where the naked bodies of dead werewolves covered in blood wouldn't haunt his gaze. He had no luck. Roxi stepped into him, lowering her head onto his shoulder so he blocked her vision.

The man, either a vampire or a werewolf with the strength to easily remove a head that way, tossed it into the arena, then turned around and walked back down the tunnel, the doors closing behind him. Luke looked toward where their elevator should be coming up. Sure enough, it rose from the arena floor, lifting the body of the first werewolf they'd killed, tumbling it aside.

"Are you OK, Roxi?"

"I think so. Maybe a few shallow cuts. I took a swipe to the ribs, but I think the armor turned most of it. Doesn't feel like anything's broken. You?" Roxi replied.

"I don't know. My head's fuzzy and everything hurts." Sighing, he walked gingerly toward the elevator.

Roxi took his arm, slung it under her shoulders, and slid her arm around his back so they could support each other on the way back to the elevator. When they reached it, Luke nudged the wolf's leg out of the way so it wouldn't get caught in the elevator door as it descended into the ground.

Once they were inside, Luke tossed his sword to the floor and yanked his helmet off, dropping it to the ground. Roxi threw her weapon in the corner and pulled her own helmet off as the elevator shook to life. Pulling the sleeve of her tunic out from under the sleeve of her armor, she carefully cleaned the last few spots of blood from under his nose. Then, she stepped into Luke and rested her head on his shoulders, her nose poking into his neck. He wrapped his arms around her and stroked her sweaty hair.

Lifting her head, Roxi placed her hands on Luke's cheeks. "Kiss me before they tear us apart and throw us back in our cells."

Luke nodded, leaning forward, and his eyelids dipped closed. Roxi brushed her lips across his before pulling him in and pressing them firmly against his lips. For the space of the elevator ride, Roxi's lips took him far away from the hell of their cells and the arena. He didn't want to stop kissing her, the touch and kiss sending acceptance and desire burning through him. They only parted when the elevator stopped and the speaker buzzed on, telling them to return to their chairs. They gave each other one least squeeze before they reluctantly stepped away from each other, sitting in the two chairs where they'd be bound and knocked unconscious.

L uke groaned, trying to shift into a more comfortable position but failing.

"Luke? Are you awake yet?" Roxi asked.

"I don't know. Maybe?"

The dim light of his cell's single light bulb burned through his eyelids as he became aware of the dull throbbing in his head. He heard a scraping sound. Turning his head toward it, he cracked his eyelids to see Roxi shoving the camping mat through the hole in the wall.

"Your ribs," he said, remembering her comments from the night before, after the arena battle.

"They're just a little tender on one side. You need it more this time. Please take it."

Luke took the end of it and pulled it through, rolling it out next to the wall. Seeing a full tray by the door, he pulled it alongside the mat and laid back down, groaning again. But this time, there was a bit of contentment with the padding mixed in with his general dull body ache.

Looking at the food, his stomach rumbled loudly. "How late is it, Roxi?"

"The bucket exchange has come and gone. Maybe a couple hours after?"

That would explain his hunger. He'd been out for a long time. He noticed a couple pills in the corner of the tray. That was new. He picked one up and inspected it. It looked like a real, commercially manufactured pill complete with markings on it, though he had no idea what they meant.

"Roxi, were there some pills on your tray?" Luke asked.

"Yeah. Pain pills."

"Heavy duty?" He didn't want to be knocked out or rendered too dull, but if he got much sorer, he'd have to risk it.

"Not narcotic level, but pretty good."

"Well, they seem to want their pets well taken care of." He popped the pills into his mouth and swallowed them with a swig of water from the tin cup.

"At least us anyway…"

The last moments of the poor werewolf who'd surrendered flashed through his mind. "Yeah."

Neither of them talked while Luke scarfed down his meal, licking the tray clean. By the time he was done and laying on the mat, the pills had taken the edge off his pain, letting him think a little clearer. He didn't believe anything was broken, but he'd sure taken a beating. All things considered, they'd come off light against four bipedal werewolves.

"Luke, you were brilliant last night. You must be a truly amazing fighter when you're at full strength," Roxi said.

"Thank you. You were fantastic yourself, keeping that wolf occupied. You were always in the right place at the right time and did what needed doing. It was a privilege fighting beside you."

He meant it. She was one of the finest fighters he'd ever seen. No wonder she'd survived for nearly two thousand years. At full strength and health, she'd be a true terror in battle. She was fast, nimble, and decisive—and she had kissed him.

His mind kept drifting back to the feel of her hands on his cheeks and the first soft touch of her lips. When he thought about the second part of the kiss, when she'd fully committed, his heart rate picked up, and heat flushed his cheeks. He was glad the light was low and his head wasn't in easy view of their hole. As pale as his northern Gallic skin was, he'd probably be as red as a tomato right now.

Then Maggie's face appeared to him. He loved Maggie, but he'd kissed another woman. It didn't feel wrong that he'd done it. It'd felt natural in the moment, yet now confusion filled him. He was getting used to what he and Maggie had and understood the dynamics they'd developed. He even had the approval of Maggie's partner, Zel. The longer he lay there in silence, the kiss running through his head, the weirder he felt about it, until he realized he was feeling loopy.

With a deep yawn, realization dawned on him.

"Roxi. I think the pills they gave me are a bit stronger. I might pass out," he mumbled.

"Oh no. Luke, don't forget your tray."

"Thanks," he slurred.

He looked down at the tray; it seemed to magically shift shape, the dim light twinkling and dancing over it. He giggled, then sent the tray sliding across the floor to stop against the door with a thud, the metal spoon clanking around the tray.

"Bullseye!" He threw his arms into the air, letting them hang there above him. "Oh, that hurts."

Roxi chuckled. "Well, lower your arms, silly."

"That's a good idea." He giggled and lowered his arms.

"Oh, those pills must be strong if you're past pain management into silly."

"I'm the silliest," he said around a yawn.

"Really?" she asked.

"No. Not really. I'm usually lonely and sad."

"Even with all your new friends and your girlfriend?"

"I've been lonely and sad for far longer than they've been in my life, but I do like being with them. None of them try to make me be someone I'm not. Well, that's not true. They encourage me to be the best version of myself—the best leader I can be for them—but they never tell me I shouldn't be sad. I do feel happiness with them, but…"

"I think I understand," she replied knowingly. "It's possible to be both happy and sad at the same time, to feel alone with people."

Luke liked the sound of Roxi's voice, its relaxed quality mixing with the richness of her combination of English and Farsi accents. The combination added a world of depth. Her voice had been the only friendly sound he'd heard in months. The phantom sensation of her lips distracted him, sending heat through his body.

"Roxi…"

"Yes?"

"Why did you kiss me?"

"I wanted to." She paused for a moment, taking a deep breath. "Did you not like it?"

The uncertainty in her question tugged at his heart. "I liked it. It was a very good kiss. I…I just wasn't expecting it."

"I don't know. I just needed a little tenderness after the brutality of the arena." She sighed. "Fuck it, what do I have to lose?" she mumbled. "We could die any day. They could decide they're tired of us and poison our food. They can walk in and shoot us. They can keep stacking more and more obstacles in front of us in their arenas until we're crushed. We could get an infection they don't treat well enough. Our lives hang on a fraying thread, and we're only alive through the sufferance of our enemies." She slid her hand through and grabbed his arm.

He adjusted so he could hold her hand.

"You're all I have in life, Luke. This tiny cell, a bucket, and the kindness we've shared. I wanted to kiss you because I needed to feel your lips against mine. I needed to share your breath. I'm so scared and lonely all the time, and your presence is the only thing keeping me from screaming out my sanity."

Luke lowered his lips and kissed the back of her hand. "Thank you, for the kiss and telling me. I think I needed it just as much, even if I didn't recognize it until you asked. I hate this place so fucking much. I was just getting my life together. Being taken from my friends and family and stuffed in here feels like a cruel trick. The only good thing in here is you."

They lay in silence, holding each other's hand until Luke succumbed to the power of the pills.

THAT FIRST DAY after they fought together and shared their kiss was the only day they spoke about it while diving deep into their emotions. Together, they continued stretching and working out while being mindful of their various injuries. Although they didn't talk about the kiss, Luke thought about it almost constantly, and every time he did, he could feel her breath against his lips the moment before she made contact. He found himself smiling about it more than once, but after he realized why his cheeks had tugged up his lips, he inevitably scowled upon the vision clearing and revealing the infernal gray stone walls.

As the days ticked by, Luke continued marking scratches on the wall even if he didn't look at them or even know why he continued. They both grew increasingly nervous, holding hands often as they waited for their next drugged meal so they could wake up in whatever arena for their host's amusement. As each day came and went and their meals were clean, the tension of not knowing their fate grew thick. Luke's sleep grew troubled—not that it was ever great lying on the cold stone floor—even if they shared the mat, exchanging it back and forth.

"Damn it." He dropped his spoon onto his tray with a clank. "I just wish they'd get it over with."

"I know," she said. "The waiting for our next doom is nearly as bad as before we knew our fate when we just had nothing but time."

Luke was about ready to slide the half-filled tray back toward the door, but couldn't bring himself to waste the resources, and forced himself to scoop the slop into his mouth. Done with the tray, he slid it away roughly, sending it clanging into the door. Scowling at it, he got up and paced back and forth across the small room. He was halfway through his eighth or ninth pass when he stumbled. He thought his foot had caught the mat, but when he looked down, he remembered it was Roxi's turn with it.

His knees trembling, he struck one when it collapsed under him, his vision fading around the edges. He fell onto his hand, his other knee joining its companion on the ground.

"Roxi…" he slurred.

"Oh no. The rock!"

He rolled onto his side and grabbed the rock, shoving it toward the hole. The first time, he rapped it against the edge, smashing his own finger between it and the wall. After a couple more near misses, his vision fading further, he shoved it into place. The last thing he heard before he succumbed to the drugs in his food was Roxi calling his name.

"HE WAKES."

Luke was pretty sure the voice was not in his dream, and he was the one who was waking. Something was different about this drugging and waking. No one had spoken about him before. Also, it was quiet, quieter than either of the arena awakenings or the cage fight. As he inhaled, he picked up a faint whiff of tobacco. Not cheap cigarette tobacco, but high-end, loose-leaf pipe tobacco.

"He plays false," a man said in a raspy voice.

"Let him wake up fully. It's annoying to try to talk to someone still in a drug-induced brain fog," said a second voice. It sounded aristocratic, with a British accent.

Whoever they were, they were correct. Luke wouldn't be able to hold a conversation of any intelligence until he had more time to rouse. Cracking his eyes, he noted a rich rug covering the floor. Without lifting his head, he could see the bottom of a large wooden desk stained dark. They knew he was awake; there was no reason to really feign sleep.

He lifted his head and opened his eyes a little wider, letting them adjust to the light. The desk looked like a giant executive model. It was even bigger and fancier than the one he'd seen in Fred Bealer's office…whenever that had been. Behind the desk stood a bookshelf with many leather-bound books strewn about.

The other walls held a few pieces of art. Luke didn't take the time to figure out what they might be. At a round table in a wingback armchair, a man with wild gray hair wearing a black cassock sat, his elbows resting on the chair's arms as he steepled his fingers in front of him.

Luke's eyes caught on the old man. He looked vaguely familiar. Trying to reach into his mind to see if he could place the old man, he gave up when all he drew was a blank surrounded by fog. Movement in the corner of his eye pulled his attention behind the desk. The other man must be sitting in the high-backed leather office chair turned away from Luke. The chair had moved earlier, though not enough to see who might be occupying it. The only thing Luke knew for sure was that they were both vampires. Well, and he was strapped arms and legs to a chair, much like he'd been strapped into the elevator and the MMA cage. At least this chair was cushy and comfortable.

With an audible click, the clasp holding his right wrist unlocked and opened.

"There's water on the table next to you," the man behind the desk said.

Rotating his wrist to loosen it up and get some more circulation going to it, he reached to the small side table by his chair and picked up the crystal glass with a hint of condensation fogging its brilliant clarity. He put it to his lips and took a small sip to test it. The water was cool and clean—the best water he'd tasted since he'd been there. He assumed "there" was still wherever he and Roxi were trapped. The walls of the room looked constructed of the same gray stone as their cells. Satisfied the water wasn't noticeably poisoned or tainted, he drank deep, sighing happily as the cool water washed the dust and dryness from his throat. Once he drained the rest of the water, he set the glass back on the table.

The sound of a striking match followed by a rising stream of smoke and the scent—sulphur, chemicals, and a faint trace of wood —to accompany it filled the silence in the room. A few puffing noises and the aroma of burning pipe tobacco drifted toward Luke.

"So what do you think, my old friend, is it him?" the man in the office chair asked.

"I don't know. It's hard to tell with all the hair, and you spent more time with him than I did. There's something of him around the eyes, but that was so long ago, and time can do a lot in the intervening years." The man in the cassock spoke without taking his eyes off Luke.

"Should we send for my valet and give him a shave and a cut? The night is long."

The man in the cassock sat back in his chair, resting his arms on the chair's arms. "If it amuses you. He's yours to play with as you please, Dominus."

Luke, who'd been looking around the room while they talked, snapped to attention, his gaze locking on the man in the cassock. That was a title long out of use in the world. He squinted at the man in the black cassock. He was pale, as most vampires were, but he still had a bit of cast to his skin tone that said he might be from the Mediterranean. His eyes—that's what had thrown Luke off initially. When last he'd seen him, his eyes had burned with the zealotry of an early Christian fanatic. Now, they held the dead, soulless void of all vampires. It had been nearly seventeen hundred years since he'd last seen the man sitting across the room from him, one thousand six hundred and eighty-eight or nine—Luke wasn't sure how long he'd been hidden away in his cell—since he'd last traded words with Eusebius of Nicomedia.

"Ah, I think I see recognition in his eyes. It may indeed be him. The universe, it seems, has a sense of humor," Eusebius said.

The man in the office chair chuckled. "You've never struck me as a great appreciator of humor, my old friend. I guess I'll have to see if I understand your cosmic joke."

The chair spun slowly. Luke half expected to see a pale bald man with a Persian cat—Blofeld or Evil, either would do. He was disappointed to only find a younger man in an impeccably tailored bespoke suit. His eyes flashed to Eusebius and back to the young man. His disappointment intensified when he realized the man in the chair, smoking a pipe, was none other than Flavius Claudius Constantius, known in the history books as Emperor Constantine II, the man who'd betrayed his father's word to Luke, tortured him, and planned to kill him.

CHAPTER
FIFTEEN

The blood drained from Luke's face as he stared at a man he thought had died in the year 340 CE, killed by his brothers in a fight for the empire. Luke had smiled smugly when the news had made its way to him, deep in the heart of the Sarmatian lands he traveled over with his wife Marpesia and her clan.

"Lucius Silvanius Ferrata. It looks like I have you in my clutches again," Flavius said with a smirk on his face. "You don't look so smug now without that barbarian whore to fight your battles for you."

After seventeen-hundred years, the boy was still holding a grudge from when Marpesia punched him after she helped free Luke from Flavius and his legions. But to be fair, the loathing for the boy who'd betrayed him, killed some of his friends, had Marpesia beaten, and tortured him still burned hot, rekindled instantly after all these years. The boy had been involved in several early humiliations, but Luke thought he'd gotten the last laugh after his brothers killed him at the age of twenty-three.

"I liked you better when I thought your brothers killed you for overreaching your grasp," Luke replied, molding his face into a stone mask.

"Oh, he's still quite saucy, Eusebius." Flavius's smirk sharpened.

"Just think how history would be different if our assassins had killed him in Constantinopolis, Dominus."

"Or if I'd just executed him when I captured him instead of trying to find out his secret to immortality…" Flavius sat back in his chair and released a bark of a laugh. "Ah, the indiscretions of our youth, but he has led us a merry chase all these years without us even knowing it was him. I'd just assumed he'd died somewhere off in the northern steppes raiding sheep with his barbarian whore."

Every time he referred to Marpesia as a "barbarian whore," he stared at Luke, hoping to elicit a reaction. Luke, not wanting to give him the satisfaction, kept his face as calm as a pool of water on a windless day. It still angered him to have his wife called such things, but he was far sadder that she wasn't here to defend herself and punch him again. The memory of her laying out the boy Caesar with a swift and brutal punch brought a warm smile to his face.

"He smiles," Eusebius said.

Constantius huffed.

Luke'd give anything to see her face again, to hold her in his arms, to hear her call him a silly Roman. She'd burned so bright in his life that after her light was extinguished, his life had felt dimmer ever since, with only a few points of brightness along the way. Maggie was one of those lights, as were his friends, their faces drifting through his mind. To his surprise, Roxi's face was among the lights.

"So I hear you've found a new barbarian whore." He turned to Eusebius. "Is that correct?"

"He seemed quite cozy with her, Dominus." Eusebius never took his eyes off Luke.

"I suppose everyone has their vices. The centurion's prime vice appears to barbarian whores."

Luke rolled his eyes.

"I'm sorry, Lucius… Can I call you Lucius? I'm going to call you Lucius. I feel like we're old pals having a chat after not seeing each other in a while. Is something I'm saying bothering you? Do you object to me calling your barbarian whores barbarian whores?" Flavius smiled smugly, tilting his head while he waited for an answer.

Luke stared at Flavius. "Well, after the first few times, it ceases to be original. After all this time, I'd have thought you'd put some time into coming up with something better…or at least more interesting. Now, you're just being dull and repetitive."

"We could always cut his tongue out. He doesn't need a tongue to fight for our amusement," Eusebius suggested.

"It's an idea." Flavius looked like he was considering it. "But it would be a shame to deprive him of such a well-honed weapon. He duels with it nearly as well as he duels with a gladius, or so I hear. Besides, it'll take all that time to heal, and I won't get a chance to watch him fight. I only have so much time to spare for this merry diversion before I must get back to overseeing the consolidation of our new territories."

"As you wish, Dominus," Eusebius said.

"So, I'm here to dance for your amusement? Are you going to dangle the carrot of freedom in front of me only to betray me at the last moment?" Luke asked.

"Oh, no. This isn't one of those kinds of arenas and you're not that kind of gladiator. The only freedom you will know is your death when it comes. You will fight to entertain us until you are killed. If you manage to live awhile, I'll enjoy the delicious taste of your captivity as we continue taking territory and rounding up hunters without you to foul our plans." Flavius laughed.

"With the exception of a couple of the dogs, you've done no permanent damage to any of your opponents, and with the bounty on your head, someone big enough and mean enough will step forward eventually to claim it. In the meantime, we get to watch you struggle for our enjoyment while we laugh and point at you as we pull your strings." He turned to Eusebius. "Is it about time for my next appointment?"

Eusebius pulled a pocket watch out and checked the time. "Almost, Dominus. Are you finished with him for the moment?"

"I think so. I have other matters to attend to, and I think we've exhausted the limited wit of the centurion here." He reached down and pushed a button on his chair.

The cuff snapped shut over Luke's right wrist, trapping it against the chair's arm. He sighed—probably not the best place to have rested it. Flavius reached forward, pulled a drawer open, and reached inside, pulling out a tranquilizer gun.

"They gave me this fun toy to play with, Eusebius. I think I shall..." He took aim and fired a dart that thunked painfully into Luke's stomach.

Gritting his teeth, he stared lazily at the young man, trying not to give him any satisfaction at the pain the dart caused. Finished with the gun, Flavius tossed it onto his desk where it slid, stopping just before the edge. "Well, I'll leave you to clean up here, Eusebius. Send him back to his cell when he passes out." He stood and walked by, then left out a door Luke couldn't see.

Luke sat while Eusebius stared back at him, unmoved by what had just happened between his master and their enemy. It seemed that seventeen hundred years later, the once fiery zealot had settled into a cold malevolence. Luke's eyes felt heavier, his breathing slower. It would only be a matter of time before the tranquilizer sent him all the way under.

His head was bobbing when Eusebius finally stood, walking toward Luke. The old zealot bent over, placing his face in front of Luke's, then reached out and patted him on the cheek a couple times before walking to the door.

LUKE PACED BACK and forth in his tiny cell, his mind still muddled a bit from the tranquilizer. It felt like the gun was dosed with something different from what they were spiking their food with when they wanted to move them about the arena. He hoped the movement would work the drug through his system. Suffering from terrible cottonmouth, he'd drained the water left for him in his cell.

"Luke?" Roxi's voice drifted up from the hole in their stone wall. "What's the matter?"

Looking down at the hole in the wall, he took a deep breath and lowered himself to the ground, rolling onto this back. "I don't know what's the matter. Or rather, there's a new problem, but I don't know what it's going to cause and how it's going to affect us."

"You're going to have to give me more details. You're not making any sense." She reached through the hole and rubbed his arm.

The feel of her hand rubbing over his arm lowered his heart rate and brought a small smile to face. "That feels nice, Roxi."

"I'm just happy you're back. When I wasn't drugged as well, I started worrying. I was scared, I didn't know what they were subjecting you to."

"I'm not entirely sure what I was subjected to. I woke up in a plushly appointed study. It looked too nice to be an office. When I woke, there were two men. Once my mind cleared up, I figured out who the one was. I met him about seventeen hundred years ago, then when his associate turned around, I recognized him too, also from seventeen hundred years ago." He rubbed the heel of his free hand over his eyes. "I'm not making any sense, am I? The drugs are still making me fuzzy and after being trapped down here with no idea what's going on beyond our occasional forays to the arena, which aren't terribly informative..."

"No, they are not."

"I'm just struggling to put together what's going on."

"I can understand that, but who were they?" Roxi asked.

"Flavius Claudius Constantius and Eusebius of Nicomedia."

"Who are they? I'm not terribly familiar with Roman history, other than Parthia's clashes with Rome," she replied.

"Eusebius was an important figure in the early Christian church; he baptized Constantine the Great right before the emperor's death and was a key adviser to his son Flavius, Constantine's oldest surviving son. It was an intense time in my life. I'd been summoned to Constantinople by Constantine. He was preparing for war against the Goths, and I'd been requested specifically by Rome's Roxolani allies. That's when I met my wife..."

Luke told Roxi about the Gothic War and meeting his wife Marpesia, and he told her about Eusebius and Flavius and the kind of men they were as humans. It seemed like he'd been talking about these events a lot lately, first telling Maggie and now Roxi. She was silent for a while after Luke reached the conclusion of his story.

"That's a hell of a year of activity. I guess you know who sent those vampire assassins into the palace," she said finally.

"Yeah. Most of my time during Constantine's reign had been spent along the borders hunting vampires, and they were pretty quiet since they were marshaling their strength in the land of the Goths. Then, all the sudden, I'm marching to war which turned into multiple wars for me against the Goths, the vampires, and finally my own empire. I'm still amazed I came out alive. In all honesty, I wouldn't have were it not for Pisakar and Marpesia." Luke stroked the back of Roxi's hand.

"They sound like wonderful people."

"They were. I loved them both very much. I've been blessed to have some truly wonderful friends." Now that he'd told the story, he wasn't ready to talk about what Flavius and Eusebius might have in store for him. With the temptation to disappear into his past, he let the feelings of his life with Marpesia suffuse his being, letting her memory warm his soul and place a bandage over the damage his life had done to it. He wondered what Roxi was doing in the early fourth century.

He thought about it for a second. He didn't actually know if she was a part of the Parthian Empire or just ethnically Parthian. The Parthians continue to exist within the Sasanid Empire after the last Arsacid king died. Hell, as far as he knew, she could be older than he was, born under the Seleucids.

"Roxi, tell me about yourself. I want to listen to your story. My mind is too turbulent right now to effectively think about last night's revelations. Please?"

"I can do that. What would you like to know?" she asked.

"Anything. Tell me about your childhood."

She inhaled and exhaled noisily. "Let me see…"

Luke guessed she was gathering her thoughts during the pause.

"I was born during the reign of Pakur. My father was named Rustaham Suren. He was one of Pakur's generals—a spahbed." She snickered. "My father was named after a famous ancestor of our clan, the general who defeated Crassus at Carrhae."

He chuckled. "Crassus was good at making money but shit at commanding legions. What a waste of Roman soldiers."

"It was good for the fortunes of my family, though."

Luke rolled over and adjusted his body so he could look through the hole in the wall. Roxi smiled back; she was already facing toward him.

"I bet. I'm not familiar with the Parthian kings. When was Pakur?" He asked.

"It's rude to ask a lady's age, but seeing as we're two of the oldest humans—probably the oldest—I'll let it slide. I think he overlaps with your Domitian and Trajan. His death and the fight for who was going to rule after him was what brought Trajan knocking on our door."

"Oh, wow! We're about the same age then. I was born during the reign of Domitian." He laughed. "I was one of the Romans Trajan brought knocking." He shoved his left arm through the hole. "That wound was caused by a Parthian arrow. Took it while crossing the Tigris."

Roxi took his arm and prompted Luke to rotate it for her. "Bloody hell, all the way through, too."

"It punched through my scutum and into the arm. I broke it off and shoved it all the way through."

She let him have his arm back and gave him a smile. "Now you're just showing off."

"It was either that or go into the Tigris. I can swim in full armor, but I didn't fancy giving it a go with only one arm. Anyway, what about your mother?"

"She was one of my father's concubines—one of the ones from a less prominent family. I grew up with a lot of half siblings. I was kind of what they'd call a tomboy these days. I always wanted to play with my brothers' swords and bows. I turned out to be a natural with a bow, so they trained me. I became an assassin and commander in my own right."

"Impressive." Luke already admired Roxi as a fighter and a

hunter. Though he'd never had the opportunity to see her hunt in the wild, her skills and ability to survive were undeniable. He tried to a hide a smirk when a realization hit him. He always seemed to find women with bows and horses.

"I spent a lot of time in the saddle riding around the empire carrying out my father's will, and by extension, Walagash's will. He succeeded Pakur. I was quite busy dealing with his rivals in Parthia and undermining the Roman rule in Armenia. That's actually when Mithra made me one of his hunters. When the priests of Mithra came to Walagash with their request to send warriors to answer Mithra's summons, Walagash ordered my father to handle it. He sent me."

Luke's mind ground to a halt. They'd been in Armenia about the same time, maybe even at the same time, fighting on opposite sides and trying to counter each other as agents of their Empires.

Roxi's brows furrowed as she pursed her lips. "Luke, what's wrong? You're as pale as a ghost, which is a trick after being trapped in here for so long."

"Roxi, think carefully, do you remember what year you were in Armenia on Mithras's summons?" he asked, his voice low and serious.

"Let me see. I've done the math a few times. I was in Armenia off and on frequently while you Romans were roasting in the deserts, but I found Mithra's temple in 117 of the common era."

Luke's jaw dropped open, his stomach churning into a hollow pit. His mouth went dry. "Were you chasing a cohort of legionnaires with black banners and wearing black cloaks?"

The blood drained from her face as her eyes widened. She nodded. "Yes."

Luke rolled onto his back and started laughing. To his own ear, it had a touch of an unhinged quality to it. When the laughter finally subsided, he shook his head and rolled back over to face Roxi. Emotions rioted over her face so quickly Luke had trouble telling what was going on, though confusion and disbelief seemed to war for dominance.

"I think you tried to kill me in Armenia." If it was possible, he thought she had grown even paler. "Do you remember deep in the northern mountains of Armenia, a centurion, another legionnaire, and an Armenian boy?"

Roxi nodded shakily.

"That centurion was me."

Blood flushed through Roxi's face and a light perspiration burst out on her forehead. Her breathing sounded shallow and quick. Opening and closing her mouth several times to speak, she failed to find the words she wanted. Luke couldn't see what he looked like, but he was pretty sure based on the heat of his face, a lot of the same emotions were running through him as well.

He didn't know why there were so many emotions fighting inside of him. The incident had happened when he was thirty-one, over nineteen-hundred years ago. They'd been enemies fighting their way through Armenia. At the time, Luke had just assumed they were only there to undermine Rome's influence in Armenia and to prepare the way for replacing Rome's puppet with a puppet of their own. He hadn't realized that the fierce woman he'd bandied words with across a chasm was also there in search of Mithras.

Roxi found her voice before Luke. "You were rescued by that Armenian girl who brought a small army. We never did find her after you slipped away, and I was ordered to look."

Her words enabled him to find his own voice. "You weren't looking in the right place. Once the mountains thawed out enough for us to leave, I took her and her brother north with me through Iberia and Colchis and then to Belgica."

"Did you marry her?"

Luke laughed. He wasn't sure why she'd asked that question first of all the possible questions to ask. "No. She was a child, almost half my age. I knew they'd never be safe in Armenia, no matter who controlled the country. I owed them my life for guiding me to Mithras's temple and for saving me afterward, and they'd become my friends."

"Who were they?" Roxi asked.

"They claimed to be the last direct heirs of Tigranes the Great. I don't know if they actually were, but enough people believed they were to make their continued existence in Armenia foolhardy. Ariazate saw the writing on the wall. Their days were numbered if they stayed. I convinced them a peaceful life as merchants in Gaul was better than being beggar royals with a price on their head."

"Did you set them up as merchants? That was generous of you."

"No. I took them home to my parents, and they adopted them. I realized after committing to Mithras, I would never be able to take over my father's business. There'd be no retiring from the legions or from Mithras's service for me. Their descendants have been serving me all this time."

"You didn't have any brothers or sisters to take over the business?"

"No. I was an only a child," he replied.

Roxi broke eye contact. "Luke, I'm sorry for trying to kill you."

"There's no need to apologize. I was trying to kill you too. We were at war. I'm just flabbergasted that after all this time, you and I are here together, trapped by our enemies." He laughed. "If Mithras's temple was a school, we'd be classmates."

Roxi snorted. "Should we get t-shirts made to commemorate our class reunion?"

"It's the thing to do, I hear." He shook his head, frowning. "All this time, there was another person in the world like me, and it took me almost two millennia to find you." He barked a humorless laugh. "And even then, we're here because of our enemies throwing us in adjacent cells."

"The irony is not lost on me. I should have tried to find you. I knew you existed, or at least I'd heard the rumors and myths."

"Why didn't you?" Luke asked, feeling a little hurt she never tried.

"I don't know. Maybe I was afraid of not finding you. Maybe I was afraid of finding you."

"Why would you be afraid of finding me? I'm a nice enough person, I guess."

"You're a legend. When hunters meet up, they swap tales about you over drinks. I've never run into a hunter that's met you first-hand. Always a hunter who met a hunter who met a hunter. Half of us used to joke you were a bogeyman story conjured up by vampires to scare each other, except the things you did were too big and too well documented. I guess the other half thought you were still a myth and that it was easier for the vampires to blame one imaginary super villain than to admit they let various hunters defeat them." She sighed. "I didn't even know if you were real, or if you were real, you'd want to associate with me. Romans weren't renowned for their respect for women outside of a few gendered roles."

"I'm afraid I'm a bit of a disappointment. I've been old and worn out for centuries. I've been fighting anxiety and depression for most of it. This little stay isn't going to help either. I'm going to need to book daily therapy sessions if…"

Neither of them talked about life after or mentioned the words "if" or "when we get out." Not talking about it was their defense mechanism. He hoped… He had to hold hope in his heart, or risk it shriveling and dying. He had an image he never talked about and rarely brought out except when he felt his hope withering, and he needed to water it and nurture it a little to nudge it along and keep it alive for a bit longer. Like a plant, he was careful not to over water it, for that would kill it just as much. Day in and day out, his heart walked the tightrope of hope, trying not to plummet to his death on either side of the wire.

Right now seemed like a good time to bring it out—Maggie under one arm, Gwen under the other with Alfred spread across their laps and Delilah, Pablo, and Sam sitting across from him. The simple scene of domesticity both hurt and felt good. But lately, Roxi appeared in the image along with everyone else. He hadn't put her there intentionally, nor was she there all the time, but on the occasions she was missing from the scene, it felt incomplete, causing Luke more distress than comfort. Her face and voice, along with her gentle touches, were becoming fixtures in his life he didn't wish to have removed. Right now, he needed her; they needed each other. Though, he'd be lying if he said he'd be OK with them going their separate ways if…

"Luke?" she asked, pulling him from his little fantasy realm.

"Yes, Roxiustana?"

She chuckled. "I like it when you use my full name. It sounds good coming from your lips. Um, why didn't you try to find us? Us other hunters?"

"What did the rumors say?" Luke asked. The few hunters he'd met over the years had never mentioned anything like Roxi said. He was genuinely curious. It's not often one gets to delve into those sorts of mysteries.

She gave a nervous laugh. "Are you sure you want to know? Some of them aren't too flattering."

"Lay it on me."

"Well, I kind of classify them into a couple categories—rumors from those who didn't know you and rumors from those who might have met you. In the first category, you were a glory hound and didn't want to share your fame—"

Luke interrupted, "I didn't even know I was famous, at least not once I left the empire. Sorry for interrupting. Go ahead."

"Alright. Some said you weren't actually doing the deeds attributed to you but were merely good at starting rumors. Some even said you paid vampires to spread the rumors. I chalk those up to the jealous hunters who had little in the way of good reputations. The ones that seemed more realistic then or the ones I've moved to the latter category after getting to know you..."

She paused to take a sip from the tin cup. "Those rumors—you weren't very friendly. You're cold. Afraid of attachment. Some were afraid of you. Said you were suicidal. Scary to fight beside. After seeing you in action some, I can see the latter, and maybe the suicidal thing goes with it. You throw your body into a fight with an intensity and ferocity that can be intimidating, to say the least, and you're not even up to full power after being in here for so long without your rudis."

"What do *you* think?" Luke asked tentatively.

"Of you? Based on what I've witnessed and our conversations? You're a sweet man who's faced too much death and lost too many loved ones, and all the pain is hard for you to bear, so you've isolated yourself while dedicating your life to the mission. You've lived a life filled with trauma, and some of the wounds aren't really fully healed."

Her kind honesty punched him in the gut hard. Nothing she said was wrong, but he could hear the tenderness and understanding in her voice. He struggled to keep his emotions in check as his chest rose and fell unsteadily.

"I'm sorry, Luke. I didn't mean to hurt you," she said, sympathy filling her voice.

"No, that's OK. You're not wrong about me." He squeezed his eyes shut tightly, intentionally working to keep his breathing deep and steady. "I'm a mess. I've spent a lot of my life alone and hiding from the world. If you'd found me, I would've probably tried to drive you away. At the time, loneliness felt less painful than loss, or so I thought. It was easier to be cold and unwelcoming, and frankly, to be a dick, so people didn't want to be near me. I felt I was an express ticket to their death. I was a liability to anyone else."

"Depression is a liar, Luke." She reached through and wound her fingers through his, squeezing his hand affectionately. "If I had found you, I wouldn't have gone away. I would have stayed by your side."

Luke clenched his teeth as tears burned his eyes. The sincerity of her words cut through his inner defenses, crumbling his walls until the deep pool of his emotions overflowed, his body shaking as tears fell. He covered his eyes with his other hand and clung to Roxi's hand with the other. As he sobbed, her gentle voice drifted into his awareness as she crooned a soft song in Parthian. As his breathing calmed and the flow of tears slowed, she started a new song after the first one finished.

Wiping his cheeks with his hand, he dried it on his pants, rested it on her arm, and let his eyes drift closed, the gentle sounds of Roxi's beautiful voice soothing him into a deep slumber.

CHAPTER
SIXTEEN

T he sound of Roxi's groan nearby pulled him further toward the surface of awareness. Tipping his eyes open, he saw the floor of the arena elevator.

"'Once more unto breach, dear Roxi…'" Luke mumbled.

"Luke?" Her voice sounded off, the drug's grip on her still firm, even as it weakened.

"I'm here." He longed to reach out to her, but he was still attached to the wall of the elevator.

"Are we fighting again?" she asked.

As Luke's eyes finally adjusted to the low lighting, he saw they were both armored as they'd been when they fought the werewolves. "I think so, based on the sartorial choices made for us."

"I'm tired."

"Try to breathe deeply. Maybe that'll help your body metabolize the drugs out of your body and get some oxygen to your brain."

Roxi giggled. Furrowing his brow, he worried about her lack of clarity. If she were impaired in the arena, it could mean her death.

"Do you know you look cute in your armor?" Roxi fixed a serious gaze on him.

Although he couldn't see her face through the chain mail veil, other than her eyes, he heard the light note of a smile in her voice. "Thank you. I think you look nice in your armor, too."

Roxi tipped her head back against the wall, her chain mail veil rattling as she tried to get comfortable while strapped to the wall. After complimenting Luke, she focused on her breathing. Luke did the same, letting the air fill his lungs only to be expelled. With no clock on the wall or anyway to tell time, he had no idea how long he sat there breathing into a meditative state. When the metal bands holding his arms to the wall clicked open, Luke opened his eyes, his brain focused and sharp.

He stood and rubbed his wrists, taking a step toward Roxi. "How are you doing?"

"Help me up." She extended her hand.

When she made it to her feet, she kept Luke's hands in her grip, bringing them down to her hips. She released her grip and reached up around Luke's neck and pulled herself into him, resting her helmet-covered head against the steel covering his chest and shoulders.

She sighed. "This is the only contact we get, and we're forced to embrace through iron."

Luke wanted to stroke her hair, but it was tucked into her helm. "How are you? Are the drugs clearing?"

"I think so. I still feel weird."

"If their roof is open again, let Selene into your heart. Her light should help clear the last of it."

"What if the roof's closed?"

"It's easier if Selene can see into the arena, but she should be able to hear your voice if you call to her," Luke replied.

Leaning back, she used one hand to lift the chain veil. "Kiss me for luck."

The corners of Luke's lips tipped up as he leaned in, trying to avoid her nose and cheek guards while also navigating his cheek guards. He gave her a brief kiss once he found the angle. He would have kissed her more, except the elevator shook to life, climbing toward the arena floor.

"It's not easy to kiss in these helmets."

Roxi laughed. "I guess that's why maidens fair were always giving only chaste kisses to their handsome knights."

He grinned, laughing with her. With a last squeeze through their armor, they stepped apart, facing toward the exit of the elevator, still holding each other's hands. When the elevator halted with a jolt, they stepped out into the arena to greet their fate.

To their right and left, more elevators lifted out of the arena's floor—two on each side. Each elevator disgorged two warriors in various styles of armor. Luke and Roxi looked around warily, unsure who they were. They'd entered the arena through the floor like Luke and Roxi, not through the tunnel entrance on the other side of the arena like their opponents in previous fights. The others stared around, stopping at Luke when they saw his distinctly Roman getup.

Roxi leaned closer. "It appears you're drawing some stares."

Luke smiled and waggled his eyebrows. "You did say I looked cute in my armor. I guess they're just checking me out."

She snickered. Once the ten different people had stepped from their upward conveyances, the elevators returned from whence they came. Unlike last time, the arena floor wasn't clear. Running in a ring around the arena stood a dozen obelisks, each one made from a different material—either stone, metal, or wood.

"They've got something interesting planned for us this time," Luke said.

"Yeah, they're nothing if not creative," Roxi replied, the short statement loaded with sarcasm and scorn.

In the center of the arena, weapons were arrayed in a circle, including a mix of shields, swords, a few bows and quivers of arrows, and some guns—both handguns and automatics.

Seeing the weapons, Roxi shook her head. "If the announcer says anything about odds being in our favor, I'm going to find him and gut him."

Luke snorted. "The Hunger Games" had been one of Gwen's early book requests. "Do you recognize any of the others here? Are they hunters?"

"I don't know. It's hard to tell with everyone geared up. I haven't run into any real hunters in a long, long time. I stumble on an amateur now and then."

"I guess we're about to see which these guys might be—amateurs or pros." Unless he was mistaken, she was the only woman on the arena floor.

"Welcome to tonight's special event!" The announcer's voice cut across the arena. "Not only do we have a special fight for you, but we also have a special guest to witness it. Please, click your fangs for Ancient Rome's first citizen, Dominus Flavius Claudius Constantius Alamannicus!"

The eerie sound of teeth clacking together made Luke shiver. He snorted a derisive laugh and rolled his eyes. "The little shit wants every title used. It probably galls him that he has so few to choose from. Didn't live long enough to have the Senate vote him more. He was the lesser son of great men, killed the way he lived—conniving and grasping for that which he had no right."

"Hmm. I'm not sure how you really feel about him. You shouldn't keep your feelings so bottled up." Her veil rattled as she looked around.

"Ha!" He squeezed her hand. "No open roof tonight. No moon."

He sank to his knee; Roxi joined him. He called to Selene, thanking her for her blessings. Her warmth filled him as she kissed his forehead. When he felt her presence wane, he stood with a soft smile on his lips.

Roxi exhaled explosively. "Even without the moon, she can make her presence known."

They stood up as the announcer launched into a jeer-accompanied rundown of the identities of the ten combatants visible on the arena floor, finishing with Roxi, then Luke. Most of the others had epitaphs similar in nature to theirs, denoting what cities they might be based out of and their various nicknames bestowed upon them by their vampire enemies. The vampires didn't appear too creative; there were a lot of "butchers" and "murderers" and "thieves of vampiric innocence" collected in the arena for their amusement.

"Luke, why aren't the other hunters coming to join us? We've obviously been set up as the central point," Roxi asked.

"I don't know. I hope it's not a free-for-all."

"Or a small team free-for-all." Roxi stared into Luke's eyes. "I won't draw a weapon against you, no matter what."

Luke gave her a soft smile and nodded. "Me either. We'll watch each other's backs—you and I together." He refocused his attention back on the weapons cache in the center of the arena. "I hope you're feeling fast. We need to get in, grab whatever, and get out. These obelisks should work well for fighting around."

"I could always outrun my brothers," she bragged.

"And now!" The announcer cut across the noise of the crowd's boos after he finished the mildly insulting names applied to Luke. "Your champion! Le Mousquetaire and his Mousquetaires Noirs!"

"You're shitting me…" Luke mumbled.

"What?" Roxi asked.

Luke shook his head, scowling. "This is the asshole that routed me and my friends out of Belgium. I think I killed a couple of his protégés."

"What kind of challenge is he going to be?"

"Tough. I have no idea if he's an original Musketeer, or if he's just adopted the facade, but he's strategic and tactical. I haven't seen him fight, but his students were more than proficient with their rapiers."

The doors to the tunnel opened, and fifteen vampires marched in a column three wide and five deep, muskets on their shoulders and rapiers on their hips. Behind them, six bipedal werewolves followed, carrying huge spears with crossbars just below the spearhead and werewolf-sized rapiers as sidearms. Both groups wore classic muske-teer tabard, except instead of the traditional royal French blue, it was black. Bringing up the rear, a man rode out on a black Friesian horse. As soon as he emerged from the shadows of the tunnel, the crowd launched to their feet, clapping, cheering, and stamping. The horse shifted and sidled out sideways with a dancing prance. Before the column breached the inner circle marked by the obelisks, the soldiers stopped.

"That's a well-trained animal," Roxi commented.

"Yeah. It can handle werewolves and this crowd noise. It's been a long time since I've been on the back of a warhorse."

Roxi sighed. "Me too. Not a lot of roving gangs of horse vampires these days. I miss riding regularly."

The vampire on the horse, presumably Le Mousquetaire, dismounted and handed the reins of his mount to an attendant who'd followed him out. Le Mousquetaire was the only one wearing a blue tabard. Beyond the tabard, he wore thigh-high boots, folded down so the fold landed just below his knees. He even wore the fancy, wide-brimmed hat with its voluminous feather associated with the look of a classic French musketeer. Unfortunately, a large ornate masquerade mask covered most of his face.

"Muskets. This is going to be fun." Luke looked down at his replica lorica segmentata. "I have no idea if this will turn a musket ball. Damn, I miss my proper gear."

"Me too. This stuff feels pretty solid for quality, but it's nowhere near as good as our enchanted armor," Roxi said.

"You can say that. Mine turned a high-caliber sniper round a couple years ago. The round broke the shit out of my ribs, but the armor was fine."

She tilted her head and stared at him. "Damn! I've never taken more than small arms fire with mine. You ready?"

"As I'll ever be," he replied, his nerves still building in intensity. He knew as soon as things started, his body would calm for the fight, but for now, he vibrated with anxiety.

Together, they crept forward trying to look inconspicuous. Luke looked over the weapons one last time and decided to make straight for the scutum and gladius combo standing roughly in his line.

"Combatants to the ready!" the announcer called out. A blaring air horn marked the start of the festivities.

Luke and Roxi took off at a dead sprint. He groaned at putting the stress on his weakened and not properly warmed up legs as she slipped ahead of him. Digging deeper, he poured on more speed, sliding to a halt and ducking down behind the scutum and gladius.

"Take your own weapons!" someone shouted nearby.

"Ready!" Le Mousquetaire shouted in French.

"Come free," Luke mumbled. The weapons clicked loose from their stands.

"Aim!"

Checking to his left, Roxi was already pelting back toward the pair of obelisks they'd just ran through. He tore after her, the scutum in his hand but held over his shoulder to give partial coverage of his back and all of his head.

"Duck!" Roxi screamed.

"Fire!"

Luke dove to the ground, sliding forward on his armor-covered stomach. He felt an impact on his back as metal pinging off metal filled his ears. It must have hit the boss of his shield. A few screams sounded from behind him.

"Advance the line!" Le Mousquetaire ordered.

Roxi dashed out from cover and grabbed Luke's arm, tugging him up as he struggled to his feet. As soon as he was upright, she took off, running for cover. He followed in her wake.

"Ready!"

Roxi disappeared behind an obelisk; Luke was only a handful of steps behind her.

"Aim! Fire!"

Luke dove behind the obelisk as Roxi reached out to slow his slide, so he didn't pop out on the other side. He pushed in against her body, the scutum still over his shoulder.

"Are you alright?" she asked as her breath puffed in and out.

"I think so. You?"

She nodded, her veil flopping against the armor over her chest and shoulders. "Yeah, I told you I was fast."

He chuckled and tipped his nose down to kiss the bump in the chain mail formed by the tip of her nose. "I sure hope they don't have a pocket full of musket balls or this could get annoying."

"What's the damage so far?"

"Advance the line!"

Luke poked his head around the stone obelisk they were hiding behind as Le Mousquetaire's musketeers shifted their line, the front line with their smoking muskets backing up behind the middle line, who was busy reloading their muskets. The middle line, now the front line, dropped to their knees and raised their muskets.

"Ready!"

"I see two bodies down. One is not moving. The other's trying to crawl away, looks like they got him in the leg." He laughed harshly. "All the firearms are still there."

"Aim!"

Roxi tugged him back into the protection of the obelisk. "They were never going to unlock guns for us. Those two idiots probably stayed out there trying to pull them out until they got their dumb asses shot."

"Fire!"

The last five muskets belched out their iron balls.

"Fire at will!"

"Great. I'd almost prefer an organized firing line. At least we'd have warning."

"Spears, advance!" called out Le Mousquetaire.

She groaned. "Now we get to deal with the werewolves too."

"Let's stick together and watch each other's backs," he said.

"And keep an eye on those muskets." She stood on her tiptoes and tapped the rims of their helmets. "I need some space to string my bow."

Luke backed up, trying to keep in the shadow of the obelisk. The werewolves had split into two squads of three, each advancing around the outer ring. One of the hunters, hiding behind an obelisk nearest to the vampires' position, broke cover and sprinted away. A couple shots barked out, followed by a scream.

"Oh no..." His eyes grew wide as the hunter fell.

The werewolves nearest him growled and loped forward. The hunter screamed again as three spears skewered him.

"Three down," Roxi said. She had her bow strung and the quiver attached to her hip, an arrow in her hand as she inspected it. "Luke, where's *Le Mousquetaire?*" She sneered his name.

"Opposite us, between the two obelisks and behind his musketeers, maybe ten feet back from the obelisk line."

Roxie nodded, nocked her arrow, and took a deep breath. She pivoted into the open, drew back her arrow, took a split second to aim, and let loose. As soon as the arrow was in flight, she reversed her pivot and tucked behind the obelisk. Luke leaned his head out, risking it to watch her shot.

He smirked as Le Mousquetaire jolted and stared in shock. A moment later, Luke groaned as the arrow struck the vampire's chest over his heart and bounced off.

"Breast plate?" Roxi asked.

Luke nodded.

"Bloody hell."

"It was worth a shot," he said, consoling her.

"I guess. But I don't have that many arrows to waste."

Occasional musket shots cracked the silence, though none were accompanied by a hunter's scream.

"The other hunters are working their way back. Looks like one has a bow of their own."

The one with the bow slid behind the obelisk nearest to Luke and Roxi. "Nice shot! Too bad he's armored."

"Yeah. We should assume if we can't see their chest, they've got a breast plate on," Roxi called to the other archer. She nocked another arrow and sent it flying toward the musket line. Luke peeked around the obelisk. A musketeer tumbled over, an arrow sticking out of its eye. The others edged away from their fallen comrade and toward the obelisk.

"Hold your lines!" Le Mousquetaire barked out.

The arrow probably wasn't silver. After the fight was done, they'd pull it out and let the vampire's magic heal itself. The breast-plates prevented them from getting the shafts through their hearts, but if he was right, the arrows were probably all composite materials and non-deadly to the vampires. Luke hefted his scutum and eyed the hunters falling toward him on his right. There were two remaining hunters on the left, not counting the archer, and only two on the right.

Roxi took out another musketeer. The other archer joined her and took one out himself. If they had time, the archers could pick the musketeers apart, but with the werewolves advancing on each side, they were quickly running out of time and space. With a deep breath and the twirl of his gladius, he broke from behind the obelisk and sprinted toward the werewolves advancing on his right, his scutum held up to block any musket balls. He didn't know if it would stop them, but it'd slow them down and hopefully let his steel armor do its job.

They had no room for caution if they wanted to even the numbers. Luke bowled forward. Once the werewolves saw him coming toward them, they stopped, lowering their spears in front of them. Luke kept his aim straight down the middle until the last moment when he leapt to his right and shoved out with the scutum, catching the edge of the spear belonging to the werewolf nearest to the wall.

Luke shoved in toward his left, pushing back toward the center of their formation now that he was inside their guard. As he closed, he dragged the edge of the gladius low and across the knee of the right most wolf. With the tendons in its knee severed, it screamed and shoved back with his good leg to escape. Tucking in low, Luke slammed into the middle werewolf with his shield and exploded up. As he caught the chin of the werewolf with the iron rimmed shield, he plunged the gladius into its neck at the junction with his torso. Letting gravity take him back down, he shoved his shield into the chest of the werewolf, pushing himself back.

The last wolf backpedaled, trying to get his spear back into play after Luke had eaten up all their stabbing space and his two companions. Luke pulled in the shield to his side and carefully tucked the gladius into the cingulum belt they'd outfitted him with. It wasn't meant to hold a sword, but it would have to do in a pinch. With his hand empty, Luke scooped up the dropped spear of the werewolf he'd stabbed in the neck. He tucked the spear under his arm and advanced on the last werewolf.

"Luke! Pull back. Incoming," Roxi yelled.

Her warning halted his advance as he darted behind the nearest obelisk. The three werewolves from the other side were working their way across the center of the arena to join their compatriot. Luke only had one more thing to do before backing up. He jumped out and rammed the spear into the skull of the first werewolf he'd downed with a slash to the knees. He didn't know exactly how fast werewolves healed, but he didn't want the wolf coming back around if his knee healed enough. Once the spear crunched into its skull, Luke yanked it out and backed up, taking advantage of the werewolves fouling the musketeers' shooting lines to cover his retreat.

The yelp of a werewolf followed by another drew Luke's attention as he backed up. A couple of the werewolves had sprouted some arrows—one in the knee and another in the thigh.

"Centurion, what should we do?" called one of the hunters, his English thick with an accent Luke couldn't discern in the chaos.

"Form up on me!" Luke turned and ran back, ducking behind the obelisk to the right of Roxi's position.

Taking a moment, he smiled and winked at her. The remaining hunters darted from hiding place to hiding place, risking it with the werewolves in the middle. Once they were close enough, Luke ran out from his hiding place toward the center of the arena, advancing with his spear leveled and ready. He heard feet behind him as the two hunters joined him on either side. One of them had snagged the other werewolf's dropped spear and tucked in behind one of the hunters with a shield.

The wolves, with yips and growls, turned to face the new threat.

"Now!" Luke yelled and charged forward.

He took the first spear shoved at him on his shield and turned it aside, metal scraping wood. The wolf's eyes bulged as Luke plunged the spear into its neck. It opened its mouth to yelp, but only blood came out. With a twist, Luke yanked it free and rolled his shoulder, the head of the next wolf's spear grinding against the strips of steel protecting his shoulders. Tipping his head toward the spear, he used the neck guard to block the spear in case the wolf drew it back, hoping to catch his neck. When the wolf pulled back, the sharpened lugs on the side of the spear caught Luke's ear guard and twisted his head, releasing the spear.

Luke stepped back to collect himself and reset. He whipped his head around as one of the hunters next to him let out a scream. A wolf had gotten through his defenses, spearing him in the guts. The wolf, exacting its revenge for its fallen comrades, lifted the spear and the hunter into the air, his body catching on the cross bars. With each violent shake of the spear, the hunter screamed, though each one got weaker and more ragged. Luke surged forward and rammed his spear into the wolf, pulling it back and sticking the wolf again. One of the other hunters leapt forward and slashed at the wolf's legs with a saber.

The spear and the skewered hunter tipped to the side and fell, the hunter weakly thrashing on the ground as blood poured out of his ripped-up abdomen. As the hunter brought his sword down on the wolf's neck, a musket barked to life.

"Fuck!" The hunter stumbled back, struggling to keep his shield up on his left side.

Luke ignored him, letting the man tuck in behind as he and the other hunter with the spear harried the last two wolves. One of the wolves tried to stab the hunter without a spear, but he got his shield up in time, the spear tip sticking into the wood of the shield. The other hunter lunged forward, taking advantage of the open wolf, and rammed the spear into its neck. The wolf crumpled. Seeing his last comrade go down, the last wolf chucked his spear at Luke and dashed away. Raising his scutum, Luke staggered backwards under the impact of the spear on his shield.

"Withdraw!" Luke yelled.

Now that the wolf was out of the way, the musketeers took aim and fired. Luke ducked as a ball sparked off the metal rim of his shield. With the resumption of firing, Roxi and the other archer sent arrows flying across the arena. Two musketeers fell, followed by a couple more. The archers could put more firepower into the air more quickly than the musketeers. The muskets took too much time to reload, even for experienced shooters working at vampiric speed.

"To cover!" Le Mousquetaire yelled as the archers decimated his musketeers.

If they'd been smart, they'd have given both quivers to Roxi. She was the far superior archer of the two. She knew her business, but how could a Parthian assassin and commander not know the bow? Their bows kept Rome at bay for three hundred years.

Once Luke backed up past the obelisks, he darted behind one and drew close to Roxi. "That was some good shooting."

"Child's play. Nice work on the werewolves."

"Thanks. Mind peeking around the corner to see what they're doing while I catch my breath?" he asked between huge gasps for air.

She winked at him. "Sure thing, handsome."

Luke chuckled between gasps for breath. "Are you flirting with me in the middle of a life and death struggle in a vampire arena?"

"I'm glad you picked up on it. I have a bow in my hands, I'm fighting beside the Centurio Immortalis, and I'm alive for the moment. It's a good day." She patted his cheek guard and turned to see what was up. "I'm not sure what they're up to. They seem to be milling about. Wait... A few of them are tossing their muskets back toward the doors in the wall and are drawing their rapiers."

"What about the mouseketeer?" Luke asked, his breathing calming.

"His rapier is out, but he's still behind his men," Roxi replied.

"How're your arrows looking?"

She looked down at the hip quiver. "I'm down to a handful." She turned to the other archer. "Oi, you there. Arrows?"

The other archer rifled through their quiver and held up a hand with four fingers raised.

"You any good with that sword you picked up?" Luke asked the archer.

"Yeah."

"Toss the quiver here and draw steel. She'll handle the arrows until she's out. We're going to be outnumbered here in a minute."

The archer lashed down the flap on the quiver and tossed it to Roxi. It landed on the dirt and skidded toward her. After she integrated the arrows into her quiver, she tossed the extra quiver toward the wall so it would be out of her way.

Luke set the scutum down and pulled the spear out of it, then placed the scutum against the obelisk. "Anyone want a spear?"

"Sure," replied the archer.

Luke slid it across the ground to him. He peered at the scutum but decided its weight would only slow him down. He was far from full strength—the fight needed to end soon. His body wasn't recovering very quickly and his energy flagged hard. If the vampires could buy more time, they might wear him down. He'd need speed and two hands to fight the rapier-wielding vampires.

"Alright, let's stick together and keep from getting surrounded." He leaned forward so his lips were near Roxi's ear. "Shoot straight, beautiful. Follow behind. I don't want us getting separated. There's not enough of us to split up."

Roxi nodded. "Stab true, handsome."

Luke smiled, took a deep breath, and ran toward the left side this time. The vampires had sent the majority of the musketeers down the right side since most of the remaining hunters gathered there, pushing strength against strength. Roxi broke cover and followed Luke, stopping at each obelisk to use it as a shield if she found a chance to fire. The rest of the hunters ran after Luke, passing Roxi.

The vampires slid to a stop when they saw Luke barreling at them. They fanned out, taking up a post near one of the obelisks so it could hold one of their sides. As the vampires set themselves, Luke judged they might be competent with their weapons, but he'd find out shortly. He leveled his spear and swung wide, carving an arc in front of him. The rapiers lashed out, deflecting his spear to the side. Other than carving a few tiny slivers, the thin blades did virtually no damage to the wood of the thick spear. He'd have to thank the vamps for making the spears werewolf sized. It was one sturdy weapon. His only concern with the bulky weapon was the encroaching fatigue — he was already feeling its edges.

He focused his efforts on the one on the outside near the obelisk, trying to turn him and bunch the fangers against the wall. Luke pushed the vamp back, swinging the spear wide to keep the others back as the hunters engaged. Two spears plunged into the first vampire, one in the head and the other in the chest. The distraction allowed Luke to swing the spear up, slicing through the neck of the vampire he'd been fighting. The other two hunters took down the last vampire of the three.

"Luke!" Roxi cried out.

Luke spun around and charged back to the other side as Roxi fired off another arrow. It missed as a vampire darted out of the way using all its supernatural speed. The few other arrows she'd fired off hadn't missed, leaving several vampires motionless or crawling away from the action.

Passing Roxi, Luke thrust out with the spear, but several vampires darted out from behind the obelisk and grabbed the shaft. Yanking it from Luke's hands, they pulled him off balance. He stumbled forward as he let go of the spear, losing it to the vampires. Dropping to his knees, he pulled back to slide to a halt, stopping too close to his awaiting enemies. He yanked the gladius free and blocked the incoming rapier. Two spears thrust over his head, pushing back the first wave of vampires.

With some space, Luke got onto his feet. The vampires had thrown the spear they'd taken from him away from the action.

"Cover me," Luke said to Roxi.

Luke waded in, thrusting and parrying. His gladius wasn't made for this kind of fight, but it was light and he knew the weapon intimately, even if it wasn't his personal sword. Off to his side, a vampire went down with an arrow in the face, distracting one of its comrades and allowing one of the other hunters to take it down. Although Luke hadn't struck any blows so far, he was doing all he could to get inside the guards of the engaged vampires. He hoped the battle didn't last much longer; the burning in his arm grew more intense by the minute.

He couldn't figure out Le Mousquetaire's plan, other than standing behind his greatly diminished squad of vampire musketeers. Luke's concern grew when their leader backed away, mumbling something only the other vampires could understand. Once he'd opened up a decent amount of space, and a few of his boys joined him, he put fingers to his lips and blew a shrill whistle. As one, the vampires broke and ran away to join their master, the lone werewolf loping up to stand between Luke and Le Mousquetaire with his rapier drawn.

Luke advanced cautiously a couple steps.

"Luke! Behind you! Betrayal!" Roxi screamed.

Betrayal? Luke dove to the right, but not nearly quick enough to entirely dodge the spears thrust at his back—one ripping a gash along his hamstring just above his knee while the other scraped along the back of his armor, slashing the back of his left arm. He scrambled to rise and defend as the hunters made another run at skewering him. Behind the two spearmen, Roxi dueled with the last of the hunters, though it looked like she'd been wounded already. She limped, trying to keep her attacker at bay.

Luke swatted the first spear aside with his gladius and knocked the second one off target, slapping the haft of the spear with his hand. A low growl behind him warned him of the approaching werewolf. He lunged forward, aiming between the two spears, shouldering one aside while trying to grab the other with his left hand. Despite grabbing it, he couldn't keep a grip on it with his weakened left arm. Ultimately, it didn't matter. He needed to break through them and away from the hulking werewolf and its massive rapier.

Warm blood seeped from his wounds, dribbling down the back of his leg and arm. As he pushed himself forward, he hoped the leg didn't give out, each step shooting burning agony up and down his leg. Anger rose inside him, spreading up from his stomach and out his throat in a ragged growl that quickly turned into a bellow of rage. The wide eyes of the two betraying hunters gratified him as he lifted his gladius and shoved it under the raised arm of the one on his right. The sword grated against bones as Luke planted on his right foot and shoved himself into the body of the hunter on his left, twisting and pulling out the gladius as he went by.

Luke's fierce and foolhardy charge provided Roxi the momentary distraction she needed as she flicked a quick slash across the neck of the hunter trying to slay her. The hunter stumbled backwards, dropping his sword and grasping at his throat as blood welled from around his fingers. Pulling back, she rammed her sword into his eye socket, giving it a twist and pulling it back out again. The hunter dropped to ground.

Luke kept up his mad, stumbling shamble until he drew level with Roxi and slid to a halt, putting his weight on his good leg. Together, they turned to face the other two hunters. Except now it was only one as the other hunter—the one Luke had stabbed under the arm—was lying in a growing pool of blood. Luke must have severed the traitor's brachial artery.

The last hunter wasn't sure what to do with Luke and Roxi united again and the massive werewolf closing the distance. He retreated from the wolf, sidestepping away from both parties toward the nearest obelisk.

Luke and Roxi backed away. He didn't want to fight around the body on the ground and risk tripping.

"You got any more shots left?" Luke asked.

"Yeah, but no bow. I used it to block that traitor bastard."

"Better the bow than you. Are you OK?"

She lifted her hand from her side and showed Luke the palm coated in her blood. "I think the armor took most of the force, but I don't know how bad it is. It hurts like hell. How are you?"

"Nothing my rudis wouldn't fix right up..." he grated out.

"So not great."

Luke grunted in pain. "No. The werewolf and the remaining hunter are spreading out. We need to get that wolf down before we're surrounded."

"Right," Roxi said, taking a few deep breaths. "Let's do it. Let's go fence with a werewolf. I'm psyched for this plan."

Nodding, Luke advanced toward the wolf, exaggerating the limp, but not by much. His heel slipped and stuck in his caligae as the blood trickled into it. Roxi struck first, grunting through the pain and lunging with her saber. The wolf parried and counterthrust, but she deflected it. Luke circled away and attacked with his gladius. The lightning reflexes of the wolf deflected the blow but opened the wolf's side to Roxi. She lashed out with her saber, piercing its side just above the hipbone.

The wolf yelped and staggered back, trying to position its wounded side away from Roxi, and knocked her blade away with its weapon, exactly what Luke was waiting for. He darted to the side, using his good left leg, and swung into the wolf's hamstring, severing it. Screaming, the wolf went down. For good measure, Roxi slashed at the tendons along its ankles. With no good legs, the wolf abandoned its rapier and tried to shove itself backwards on his paws. As it neared the vampire musketeers, it lashed out with its teeth, snapping to clear its retreat.

Luke sucked in air, keeping his weight on his unwounded leg. Roxi tucked around, her hand on her side, glistening red blood trickling over her hand and down the silver leaves of her scale mail. The vampires fanned out, Le Mousquetaire standing behind them in the center of the arena. Luke couldn't tell if the noise running through his ears was pumping blood or the thunder of the crowd growing increasingly unruly, excited as the fight neared its climax and their champions neared victory.

Roxi cleared her throat, spitting into the dirt of the arena. "Luke, it's been… I only wish —"

He interrupted her. "Don't say it. We're not done yet."

With that, Luke charged toward the nearest vampire on the edge of their formation. The vampire's eyes went wide, but before Luke finished the attack, he pivoted and spun, taking the head of the vampire next to him. Collapsing to the ground, the vampire's head rolled away as he dropped the rapier. Luke scooped it with his foot and lifted it into the air, almost tumbling over as his bad leg nearly gave out on him. He snatched the rapier's hilt out of the air and extended both swords out to his sides, backing up toward Roxi.

Roxi was doing her best to deflect blows aimed at her while using the obelisk to shield herself. As the vampire's backed off from Luke, he swapped hands, shifting the rapier into his uninjured hand. When a vampire tried to sneak up on Roxi, Luke lunged toward it, coming up short on his bad leg, but driving the vampire back just as Roxi smashed the head of her vampire into the obelisk, stepped back, and severed his spine.

They were down to three musketeers and Le Mousquetaire. As their leader backed away, he barked orders to his men. They must have been in code, because even though he spoke in French, Luke didn't understand the words. At Le Mousquetaire's last command, all three lunged forward. One of the vampires dove into Luke's left side, but he managed to raise his gladius in time to parry it, only taking a shallow slash to his thigh.

Roxi screamed and collapsed into the obelisk, blood running down her leg.

"No!" Luke bellowed.

Heedless of injury, he bowled into the vampire in front of him, thrusting with the rapier, he caught the vamp out of position and took his leg off at the knee with the gladius. Spinning to reach Roxi, his leg gave out on him. He dropped to his knee but forced himself up, staggering toward the vampires circling her. They weren't paying attention to him. The one nearest turned at the last minute, lashing out at Luke. He contemptuously knocked the attack aside and crowded the vampires together. As he swung a brutal slash at the vamp's neck, Roxi stabbed up from the ground, taking the other vampire in the groin. Luke bodied the nearly beheaded vampire aside, turning it into a pez dispenser with its head flapping loosely from some tissue, and shoved the rapier into the groin-slashed fanger's ear, piercing him through to the other side.

Falling, the vampire pulled the rapier from Luke's hand as it tumbled limply to the ground. Stumbling back, Luke turned to face where he'd last seen Le Mousquetaire. The vampire in the blue tabard was gone. A brief flicker of silver caught Luke's eye as the vampire disappeared down the tunnel, leaving his fifteen musketeers and six werewolves bleeding on the arena floor along with the eight other hunters that had initially been on their team. Luke's leg gave out, and he slumped to the ground next to Roxi.

Luke wheezed, trying to get air, until it resolved into a hoarse laugh bordering on unhinged. A hand weakly grasped at his arm.

"Roxi…"

"Luke…are…you alright?" Her voice sounded weak.

He pulled himself along the ground, pushing with his good leg to get to Roxi. "Shit. They're going to make us move to the elevator ourselves."

She chuckled softly. "Assholes."

"Do you think you can hobble over with me?" He squeezed his eyes shut, trying to push the pain to the back of his awareness.

"If you help me, I think I can," She said, gritting her teeth in pain.

As Luke sat, trying to catch his breath, he noticed the rising noise in the crowd. They'd gone quiet after their certain victory had turned to ashes in their mouths, their hero retreating ignominiously into the tunnel and out of the arena, leaving the two hunters alive and victorious. The noise rose to boos as the vampires in the audience stamped their feet.

"I don't think they find the results to their liking," Luke said, his breath starting to come under control.

"No. They don't."

"We better get to the elevator before something else happens." Luke forced himself up and reached down.

Roxi grasped his forearm, groaning in pain as she pulled herself up with his help. He slid his good right arm under her arms, and together they hobbled their way to the elevator, leaking blood. Fortunately, they'd sent up an elevator close to their location. Once they arrived, Luke helped Roxi into a seat before collapsing into his own. He reached over to keep Roxi from tumbling forward.

"I don't feel good, Luke." Her voice sounded thin as she tried to contain her weariness and pain.

"They'll fix you up." He barked a humorless laugh. "They like to keep their pets alive so we can continue entertaining them."

He pulled off his helmet, then helped with hers. Her skin looked paler than usual after all the blood loss. He hoped they'd take care of her. They'd provided medical care before. He needed her. He couldn't live in that cell without her companionship. He leaned forward and kissed her forehead as she leaned into him, letting him bear her weight.

"Luke, I'm so tired. I'm scared." Her body shook lightly in his arms.

"Me too. All the time. I'll do anything I can for you." He stroked her sweaty hair. "I'd go to the ends of the world for you."

When they reached the bottom, the elevator shuddered to a stop, and the voice commanded them to sit back. Luke pushed Roxi into place until the straps clicked over her arms and held her in place. Once they locked, he sat in his spot and forced his tired limbs into position, waiting to embrace the drugs to carry him into darkness.

Luke woke in his cell, every inch of his body a dull ache punctuated by areas of burning fire. With a foggy head, he wiped at his eyes, the crust locking his eyelids shut abrasive and prickly. Once he got them opened, he let them adjust to the dull light of his cell.

Roxi!

He forced himself over to the wall with their stone-blocked hole. Slipping his fingers into the space where the mortar used to be, he worked it out and peered into Roxi's cell. He couldn't see her. He adjusted, trying to find a new field of vision, but every angle he tried revealed nothing and no one.

"Roxi?" He paused to listen. "Roxi? Are you there?" When he didn't hear anything after waiting for a response, he raised his voice. "Roxi!"

Nothing.

As his breathing grew shallow, he pulled his knees up and curled his back. His chest grew tighter, and his vision blurred. His heart thundered in his chest as he struggled to catch his breath. If he closed his eyes, maybe the walls would stop closing in on him. But with nothing to focus on, his head spun. He opened his eyes wide, focusing on a point on the wall, then rolled onto his back, straightening out to see if it would help him draw air into his lungs. Above him, the bare bulb dangled, a lone point of light. He stared at it, trying to breathe through what was becoming an intense panic attack.

In the months since he and Roxi had discovered each other's presence, he'd never been alone except when rendered unconscious against his will. Now, he felt totally bereft without her in the neighboring cell. What if she'd succumbed to her wounds? What if they'd determined her wounds weren't worth treating at this point? She could be dead…

Luke scrambled to his hands and knees and made it to the bucket just in time to puke some liquid, which turned into a dry heave with nothing else in his stomach to give. When he got his stomach under control, he looked at the door to see if they'd delivered his water. He crawled to the tin cup and swished some water around his mouth. Then, he collapsed onto his side, sobbing.

IT HAD BEEN THREE DAYS—AT least Luke thought it had been three days—since he'd woken after the last arena bout, and Roxi still hadn't returned to her cell. His food showed up regularly with pain medication and material to clean and treat his wounds with anti-microbial gel, but her cell still remained unoccupied.

He tried to burn off his nervous energy by pacing, but his bad leg only allowed it for so long before he had to sit or lay down again.

When he couldn't lay still any longer, he turned to his imaginary keyboard and tried to disappear into music, but that fizzled into nothing but smoke and anxiety.

By the fourth day, he'd shoved the stone back into the hole in the wall and refused to look at it, laying curled up on the floor staring blankly at the opposite wall. By the time a week passed, at least as far as he could reckon, he'd been losing track of day and night, sleeping when the dangling bulb above him shone and waking in the darkness.

Maybe they'd discovered the hole and moved her to a different cell? What if they'd not treated her and tossed her into a cell to die slowly of blood loss and infection? Luke, no longer able to control his mind's dark paths, imagined scenario after cruel scenario in which Roxi was tortured or dead or allowed to suffer the pain of her wounds.

She could be a figment of his imagination, a conjuration of his brain to keep itself occupied and clinging to the surface of sanity as he bobbed powerless in the hell his life had become. But her lips. He could still feel her warm lips when he closed his eyes—the phantom sensation flooding his body with dopamine, oxytocin, and serotonin. All those light touches and hours holding hands couldn't be a hallucination.

After being alone in the world for nearly two thousand years with only brief respites of love and friendship, he'd met someone who uniquely understood the world he moved through. He needed for her to still be alive, still somehow existing in the world so he could find her again. He needed Roxi.

Together, they'd avoided talking about a life after escape—after this hellhole. It had been a self-preservation decision. Luke had harbored a small flame of hope, but he hadn't let it burn him. It was only after someone was gone that he realized how much they'd meant to him. Roxi couldn't be gone. He'd dreamed of a time when they could walk under the sun together. He could practically feel the warmth of the sun on his back when he woke from such dreams, a smile on his face. She'd become as much a part of his life as the others in his inner circle. He knew without a doubt they'd be here with him, bonded in the struggle.

Luke missed each of them in their own way, and with Roxi gone, every one of his loved ones felt that much further away. She'd become a proxy, standing in for Pablo, Delilah, Sam, Maggie, and Gwen, but she'd also become more than just a friend of proximity— she'd become dear to him, a friend and…

He dare not say it, or he'd only widen and deepen the wound of her absence. He missed her painfully. For the first time in days, he removed the stone and reached his arm through, just to have the feel of the stone hole's edges against his skin. He lay there, disappearing into his memories and fantasies, until the scrape of the crossbar against the wooden flap announced the evening meal, followed by the scrape of the tray against the stone.

CHAPTER
EIGHTEEN

As Luke surfaced from his latest meal drugging, he tried to remember if he pushed the stone back into the hole before succumbing to the drugs. He thought so. He didn't want it discovered, so when he returned to his cell after the latest fight, he could still find Roxi on the other side.

Without opening his eyes, he knew he was in the elevator, waiting to be lifted into the arena. The air was too still and quiet to be heading into the MMA cage, plus he'd come to know the feel of being strapped to the elevator. The only difference today—he wasn't wearing his armor or helmet. He was dressed in heavy cloth, he could feel that much.

He almost felt eager to meet whatever they'd throw at him in the arena, so he'd be able to take out his frustration and growing fury at Roxi being taken away. He drew in a deep breath and held it, letting his expanded lungs stretch the tightness in his ribcage. As he exhaled, he opened his eyes and looked down.

He was dressed like the mid-seventeenth century musketeers he'd fought a few days ago, except his tabard was red with gold highlighting, and instead of the traditional cross in the center, his bore a laurel wreath.

Chuckling, he shook his head. They did like to put on a show.

Whoever his costumer was, they'd done a good job making him look like a Roman musketeer as they might have appeared in an alternative history. Now, he had a good idea who his opponent would be when he reached the arena floor.

When the straps released, he checked his left arm and right leg. The stitches remained in both. Using the time, he stretched and tried to get some blood moving through his muscles, paying special attention to the injured limbs so they'd be more resilient than if he went in cold.

The elevator finally ground to life, taking Luke to his next date in the arena. He hoped the roof was open today; he'd need the warm embrace of Selene's silvery light if he actually hoped to make it through this fight. He was sure Le Mousquetaire would be fully juiced up and ready to go, and Luke wasn't even all the way healed let alone at full power, not after who knew how long he'd been trapped here in his cage without his rudis or the ability to do any real conditioning.

When the elevator reached the top, he stepped into the arena. Unlike last time, the arena floor was free of obelisks. In front of him, sticking out of the ground like in all the previous fights, waited a gladius and a rapier.

"Of course…"

He looked up, breathing in the stagnant air of the closed arena. Grunting at the pull and twinge of the muscle in his injured leg, he sank to a knee behind the gladius, wrapping his hands around the hilt. He closed his eyes and bowed his head.

"My mistress, please watch over me in this struggle and please protect Roxi wherever she is. May your light envelop and bless her."

"Fight well, my brave soldier. I shall watch over you both."

Luke felt a warm brush across his forehead. He pulled himself up. Selene's brief benediction would have to do. Standing between the rapier and the gladius, he rested his hands on them, waiting. He ignored the announcer and the mildly creative verbal abuse leveled at Luke as he warmed up the crowd. Luke kept his focus squarely on the door where his opponent would emerge.

"And now for your hero, the dashing and engaging, the right

hand of Richelieu, the terror of France, the only thing sharper than his rapier is his wit. He's enough musketeer for all three, plus a couple bonus musketeers. He's killed more hunters than the plague. He's the vampire of your heart and the vengeance of all the victims of the cockroach — Le Mousquetaire!"

The crowd erupted in cheers, hands clapping and feet stamping. Le Mousquetaire strutted out from the tunnel waving aristocratically, rolling his hand slowly as if he were the queen riding by her peasants. When he drew near Luke, he looked over Luke's head.

Tipping his head toward Luke, Le Mousquetaire spoke toward him. "Turn and bow to your emperor, cockroach. He has a special guest tonight."

Luke turned, following Le Mousquetaire's gaze to a box at the edge of the arena. Flavius, wearing the purple toga of a Roman emperor and a gold laurel wreath on his head, sat in the center of the box in a chair elevating him above the rest of the people in his box. Below him and to the left sat Roxi, strapped to a chair. She looked paler than usual, but she was alive. His heart soared at finding her there. Luke stared into her eyes. She looked weak and terrified, but also relieved to see him. Or, maybe, he was projecting his own feelings on her, but he'd stared into those eyes for months — it'd been their only contact. He thought he knew her eyes well enough by now.

Luke tipped his head toward Le Mousquetaire. "I hope you're better with that rapier than your pupils were, or this won't provide much entertainment to the blood suckers cheering for you."

"The Mistress was one of my finest pupils and Guillaume was not too far behind her." He kept his voice lofty and disinterested, as if he were above it all.

Luke snorted. "The Mistress was killed by a nine-year-old child, and Guillaume died fast and hard."

"One cannot be blamed for the fickle changes of fortune and over-confident pupils," Le Mousquetaire replied.

"Do your friends call you Le Mousquetaire? At cocktail Parties? 'Do you need a beer, Le Mousquetaire?' Seems kind of pretentious." Luke chuckled at his own joke.

"Vampires don't have friends, only inferiors and superiors." He spoke the words with disdain for Luke's attempt at humor.

"Then I guess I won't feel bad since no one will mourn you."

"Ha! At least you'll die confidently and with bravado." Le Mousquetaire fixed his gaze on Roxi. "She looks like a tasty little morsel. I can't say I've ever tasted from a hunter as old as she's reputed to be. I look forward to draining her blood slowly and making her beg for my blood in return. Too bad you won't be around to see how powerful of a vampire she'll become."

"I wish you the best of luck. If you survive me, I don't fancy your luck with her." Luke laughed.

It was meant to be the worst way a vampire could threaten a hunter. And though he had no evidence to back it up, he was almost certain no hunter touched by Mithras would be able to rise again. Mithras had planned his hunters too well to allow someone invested with such powers to rise as his enemy.

Le Mousquetaire pulled his rapier from its scabbard and brought it up so it was in front of his face in a salute to Flavius.

"I should have killed that little shit when I had the opportunity. It won't be a mistake I make again," Luke said.

Le Mousquetaire turned and walked toward his starting position. "It's good to have goals and dreams. It'll make it that much sweeter when you spill out your life on my sword."

"I doubt you're vamp enough to accomplish what no other vampire has managed to do in nearly two thousand years."

Now, it was Luke's turn to be saluted by Le Mousquetaire. Luke pulled on both the gladius and the rapier. The gladius came free of the stand while the rapier was locked into place. *My mistress, the rapier?* He felt its locking mechanism snick, and the rapier come free. Lifting it to his head, he saluted Le Mousquetaire. A brief flash of consternation came and went across the vampire's face as his eyes flicked to the rapier. Apparently, like in the first fight, it was only there to tease him.

The gladius would make a good parrying dagger and second attack option to accompany the simple rapier they'd supplied. Le Mousquetaire's rapier, like The Mistress's, was a work of art with spirals of elegantly engraved and bejeweled metal swirling around the handle and up the forte of the blade. He'd love to add it to his collection and pair it with The Mistress's sword. At least, he hoped it was still in his collection. It might not have made it back with his friends. The thought of his friends sent a crushing wave of sadness to his guts, forcing him to fight the desire to just curl up on the ground.

The sound of the air horn snapped him out of his head, dumping adrenaline into his system as he slid into an en garde position. His world focused on just him and Le Mousquetaire—the crowd noise disappeared as did any details other than the vampire in front of him.

Le Mousquetaire started with a quick but basic set of attacks. Luke easily parried them, giving the appropriate responses, guessing the old vampire was testing Luke's actual abilities with the long, thin sword. Finding an opening, Luke launched a different series of attacks from one of the various French rapier schools he'd studied. Le Mousquetaire met them easily.

If the contest weren't in earnest, Luke would've been having fun. Le Mousquetaire appeared to be a well-schooled student of the rapier, at least in French rapier techniques. When the next opportunity came to press his own attack, Luke shifted to the German methods he'd studied in depth at the time. Luke caught him off guard, pushing him back and drawing the first less than perfect responses. If Le Mousquetaire had only devoted himself to the French schools as a French partisan, Luke might have a chance to end this with the right mix of German and Italian techniques.

While Luke thought he could beat Le Mousquetaire's technique, he could already feel his body flagging. The slashed leg tugged at him if he moved too quickly. While the gladius made for an effective defensive weapon, its weight—heavier than an appropriately paired dagger—tired his injured left arm. If Luke was going to end this before Le Mousquetaire, he was going to have to take some chances.

Luke slipped in a combo of a couple different techniques that had always drawn touches when he'd been training with the best swordsmen of Italy and Germany. When the sound of slicing cloth silenced the crowd, sucking the air from the arena, Luke followed with a killing thrust that Le Mousquetaire barely parried, resulting in the first blood drawn of the night. A blossom of deep red drenched the edges of the cloth along the fanger's shoulder.

Le Mousquetaire used his vampiric speed to disengage and re-approach Luke, a look of stern concentration on his face. Luke was glad he'd forced the vampire to stop underestimating him, but he'd rather fight an overconfident opponent. He drew in a deep breath and exhaled it violently, darting in with a new series of techniques. This time, the fanger was ready, countering with an interesting combination. Somehow, either Luke's arm failed him or Le Mousquetaire had slipped through his guard, opening a line of blood in Luke's left forearm.

Luke hissed in pain, countering instantly to drive the vampire back while trying to keep a grip on the gladius. The cut was shallow, but it burned like hell. It was time to end the rapier games. Luke went looking for what speed and power he could muster from the reserve Mithras had given him and shifted to a unique hybrid style he'd spent his lifetime developing.

Le Mousquetaire's eyes opened wide as he gave ground, trying to keep up with Luke's sword, barely parrying or deflect the heavy blows and sneaky thrusts and slashes Luke intermixed to keep the vampire off beat. When he opened a bloody gash, seeping the thick reddish-black blood of a vampire across Le Mousquetaire's thigh, Luke sidestepped the vampire's counter and opened another shallow line across the fanger's ribs.

His lungs heaving, Luke tried to press further to keep Le Mousquetaire from disengaging and resetting, but his initial burst of power was reaching a premature conclusion. It'd been months since he'd topped up on a vampire, and his time trapped in this vampire prison combined with his injuries had robbed him of his vitality.

Le Mousquetaire, sensing the shift, disengaged but didn't reengage, instead setting up an organized retreat that kept Luke from getting any serious attacks but forced him to follow the vampire. Time was on the fanger's side as his wounds trickled to a stop. The shallow ones looked like they might be sealing themselves and starting their healing process. The vampire'd topped up on blood before the fight and was in full form; soon, he'd be back to nearly one hundred percent while Luke only went downhill.

Letting the vampire open a gap, Luke wiped his sleeve across his forehead to clear the sweat threatening to drip into his eyes. Instead of following along, Luke stopped, breathing hard. If Le Mousquetaire wanted him, he'd have to come to Luke. The grin on Le Mousquetaire's face turned feral as he circled Luke, occasionally darting in to lay down a new series of attacks. Sometimes Luke countered them, sending the vampire skittering back out of range, but with each successive attack, Le Mousquetaire drew blood more often than not.

Luke was being played with—a mouse the cat was torturing for the cruel amusement of his master. The roar of the crowd with its jeers steadily broke through into Luke's awareness, adding another distraction.

He had little time left if he didn't do something about it. Looking deep in his soul for any reserves, he cast a quick prayer to Selene and attacked. The fierce brutality of the gladius-led attacks drove the vampire back, hushing the crowd slightly. Luke could see the fight in front of him, see the counters, and knew he'd land the blow he needed in just a few more moves. Adjusting to the counter he expected, he planted on his wounded leg and thrust forward, only to have the leg collapse under him, dumping him into the dirt of the arena. It was over. Le Mousquetaire had run Luke out of energy until his body had failed him. The fanger could finish him at any time.

Le Mousquetaire initial shock at Luke's collapse quickly turned to feral glee as he circled his downed prey.

"Hold on, my brave soldier, just for a little longer…"

Selene's voice sounded through his head and soul, numbing his body but only just around the edges. Swatting aside a tentative trust from Le Mousquetaire, Luke struggled to his feet, trying to keep as little weight on his wounded leg as possible. His body shook from the exhaustion and exertion.

Each parried thrust, each deflected blow, Luke struggled to meet. When the Mousquetaire pierced Luke's left shoulder, he dropped the gladius, no longer able to grip it. As the vampire made his next attack, he went high. Luke deflected it, but the tip grazed across his forehead, warm blood dribbling out of it. He wiped it away with a sleeve already bloodied from the wounds in his arms. He had nothing left. The next pass by the fanger would be Luke's last.

Le Mousquetaire prepared to make his next attack when a series of explosions ripped through the stadium. Screams rose from the crowd, the shaking of the arena sending Luke back to the ground. He wiped a sleeve across his bleeding forehead and looked up. Someone had blasted holes around the edge of the arena's ceiling, and whoever they were repelled into the stadium like commandos — werewolf commandos.

Luke laughed weakly. When the wolves reached a comfortable level, they let go of the ropes, landing nimbly in the stadium. Once their feet hit the ground, they grabbed the nearest vampires and tore them to shreds. Shotgun blasts rang out from various points around him. It was the sweetest music at that moment.

He checked on Le Mousquetaire, but only saw his back as he ran toward Flavius's box.

"Save the emperor! Get him to safety and get that fucking hunter out of here!" Le Mousquetaire yelled.

Roxi! Luke tried to rise but only collapsed in a heap. His body was torn, leaking blood from too many shallow cuts. He didn't know which was the best arm/leg combo to stand and move. When he finally found it, he staggered after Le Mousquetaire.

"LUKE!" Roxi screamed.

He wiped blood from his forehead again. "Roxi! ROXI!"

Someone was trying to move her as she struggled against her restraints. Luke saw the glint of metal as something was injected into her.

"No!" Luke yelled, losing his muscles again as he tumbled to the ground.

Chaos reigned around the stadium. As a cluster of werewolves tore through the crowd, aiming for Flavius, Le Mousquetaire looked at Luke, then at his emperor. Deciding, he sprinted across the arena floor and out the tunnel, which swiftly closed again. A minute later, he saw the vampire struggling through the arena seats to protect the emperor and organize the vampires he'd rallied. Some had weapons, but most didn't.

"Roxi…"

"Hold on, Lucius." Selene's voice was strong as beams of moonlight tainted by dust fell through the holes the werewolves had blasted through the ceiling. As he tried to watch what was going on, he noted a cluster of wolves protecting someone with a heavy pack on their back. A moment later, when the pack was set down, Luke realized what it was when a tall, thin Latino fired up a cutting torch and started burning through the steel cage separating the arena from the audience's seats.

"Jorge?" Luke muttered. He started to laugh. His friends were here.

A couple minutes later, several werewolves ran across the arena floor toward him. He didn't recognize them, but one of them slid in next to him and pulled a bag off their back. Rustling through it, they pulled out bandages and wrapped up the most obviously egregious of Luke's wounds.

"We have to find Roxi," Luke said, having trouble forming the words and making them clear, the exhaustion and blood loss robbing him of even the most basic abilities. "Roxi…"

The wolves looked at each other, shrugging and shaking their heads. A moment later, a tall black woman in a leather three-quarter trench coat joined them.

"We need to get him out of here. I've got his rudis, but we need to find some vampires for him." She pumped her shotgun and turned toward the arena's door when it groaned open, but relaxed. "Good. They've found an easier way out. Pick him up. We'll carry him out."

"Delilah?" Luke mumbled.

"What're you saying, Luke?"

"Delilah. Roxi." He couldn't tell if his tongue was working or not. His tongue felt like dead weight in his mouth.

"What? I can't understand you."

He swallowed, trying to concentrate. "Roxi."

"I don't know what that means, Luke. We have to go."

"No…" Luke struggled as one of the wolves tried to pick him up.

"Damn it, Luke. Quit fighting or we'll have to sedate you," Delilah ordered, irritation staining her voice.

"Roxi…" Luke stopped struggling. If he were sedated, he couldn't save Roxi.

He felt like a prisoner in his brain. Control over his body was lost to him, but Selene's touch kept his brain semi-alert. Luke tried to hold his head steady as the werewolf ran after Delilah into the tunnel Luke's opponents had emerged from for his fights. It was dark as it sloped downward to turn into a dimly lighted hall.

"There's a vamp body up ahead. Set him down by it." Delilah pulled the backpack off and retrieved his rudis from it. With a calm efficiency, she plunged it into the heart of the vampire. "Prop him up."

Luke weakly lifted his shaking hands to the rudis. Delilah took them, covered them with hers, and held them in place around the hilt. He lowered his head on its wobbly neck until his forehead hit the pommel button. Taking a deep breath through burning lungs, he exhaled and concentrated. The incantation he'd spoken more times than probably any other words in his life ran through his head, too ingrained to slip from even his blood-loss addled brain. When he finished, a pure, white light danced its way down the sliver filigree and silver alloy cutting edges to disappear into the vampire's body. It reemerged a moment later and retraced its journey to disappear into Luke's forehead.

The aching in his body lessened slightly, but his head remained foggy and disconnected. After the damage his body had taken and the time since his last vampire top up, it would take way more than one measly fanger to render him whole again.

"Pick him up. He's still going to be too weak." Delilah stood and yanked the rudis from the vampire, sending it dissolving into the red-black goop of a decomposing young vamp after being staked for a true death. "We'll find more vamps along the way if we have time."

"No, Delilah. Roxi. GottasaveRoxi…" Except for the incantation, which was almost always clear even in times of bodily distress, Luke still couldn't get his mouth to work right.

"Luke, I don't know what you mean. We have to get you out of here. We're outnumbered, and if they get weapons, we're going to be in deep shit." Delilah tried to keep her voice calm, but her bunched eyebrows spoke of her irritation. "Now let's go. Time isn't on our side."

Tears streamed down his face, tracing tracks through the blood drying on his face. They couldn't leave Roxi, not after he'd found her. He needed her to be alive and free. He needed her.

"No..." He tried struggling, but the werewolf's hold was too firm, despite the apparent gentleness of the wolf's grasp.

"Damn it, Luke. Stop it," Delilah waved her group forward, only stopping to pull a piece of paper from her pocket. Once she checked on it, she took the next right then left.

When they found another vampire, they stopped so Luke could siphon it off. Even with a second, he couldn't make himself understood, even if he had more strength to struggle with.

"I warned you, Luke," Delilah said. She nodded to someone behind the wolf holding Luke.

Someone held his arm immobile as his sleeve was ripped open. A moment later, he felt a prick in his arm. "No..."

They'd put it into his vein. He had no more fight to give—nor could he, with yet more drugs in his blood, this time put there by his friends. Tears streaked out of his eyes as his eyelids drifted shut, ignoring Luke's struggle to keep them open.

CHAPTER NINETEEN

A cool breeze played across Luke's face. He'd been dreaming about bluebells and the forest outside the village he grew up in, but the air didn't smell right. It smelled dusty and dry and felt thin in his lungs. As his eyes cracked open slightly, the velvety night sky felt close as stars glittered brightly, bouncing in the dark.

Only it wasn't the stars bouncing, but Luke's head. The heat of a large, hairy body held him aloft at the back of his knees and along his back under his shoulders, his feet swaying with the motion of whoever was doing the carrying. He was being carried, but why?

He'd been fighting, which would explain why his body ached and burned. Delilah had been there, rescuing him from the arena after nearly being killed by Le Mousquetaire. Someone was taking him away from the arena. He tried to speak, but only a weak moan escaped his lips. He couldn't muster any strength or coordination to his body, he may as well have been made of rags for all the control he could exert over his own body.

The moon. He didn't see the moon.

"Selene," he called out in his fuzzy mind. *"My Mistress…"*

"I see you, but barely, my soldier."

"Where are you?" Luke asked.

"I have waned for this cycle and am at my weakest on this the night of the new moon," Selene replied. *"Why do you sound so distressed?"*

"In pain, drugged."

"I feel you under the free sky…"

"My friends have come for me," Luke replied.

"I rejoice at your freedom!"

"Roxi… Roxiustana…"

"I do not feel the child under my sky… Oh, no. She calls your name and mine, she weeps. Lucius, she must be freed."

"Help me, please…" Luke pleaded in his mind, trying to break through the fog of the drugs. His was heart breaking, but in his own mind, he sounded devoid of affect.

"I have little help I can give; I am weak until I can wax strong again."

"Please my mistress, I need her…" The words sounded true throughout his being, but he couldn't let them be said. *"To be free."*

He thought he heard the goddess sigh, but he wasn't sure what the noise was. The one who carried him breathed heavy, grunting occasionally under the burden of Luke's weight.

"I will do the best I can for you…"

Some life returned to his body, his mind clearing a fraction. He thrashed weakly, trying to get up, but only caused the arms holding him to squeeze him tighter.

"Rossiii…" Luke slurred.

The wolf holding him yipped and gave a low growl. The wind blowing over his cheek chilled the line where a tear ran down his cheek as he bounced along, robbed of his agency by his friend and a syringe. Giving one last effort to regain control, he tried to lift his arm, but only succeeded in lifting his hand before gravity reclaimed it and his limb went limp again.

Voices drifted on the cool night breeze, growing louder as the wolf steered toward them.

"Set him on the gurney, Pablo," a woman said.

The wolf laid him on a narrow, soft surface. "He struggled a bit a minute ago and tried to speak."

"He should be knocked out cold after what I gave Delilah to use." The woman clicked on something.

Light poured over his face and into his slitted eyelids. He tried to turn his head, only managing to shift a few degrees away.

"Luke? Oh my, he's covered in blood. Is it all his?" the woman asked.

"Yeah. I think so. He was in bad shape when we found him. The vamp they'd forced him to fight cut him to ribbons."

"Oh, Luke…" The woman said.

Finally, the sound of her voice clicked in his foggy brain —Maggie.

"Maaaa…" Luke said, failing to complete the sounds of her name.

A gentle hand stroked his hair off his forehead. "My poor Luke. What have they done to you?"

"Maggie, I've got to get back and help with the rest of the evac. Anything else you need from me?" Pablo said. He must have transformed back to his human form after setting Luke on the gurney.

"No, Pablo. I can get a couple of people to help me load him into the van," Maggie replied.

Off in the distance, Luke heard an engine rev accompanied by a high-powered machine gun. "Rosssiii," he mumbled.

"I need some more light here. He's still bleeding from some of these deeper cuts."

When Maggie turned away from him, he heard splashing. A few moments later, she turned around and started cleaning his wounds. He twitched in pain, unable to pull away.

"I'm sorry, Luke," Maggie said while she worked. "I have to clean these and get them closed up. You've lost a lot of blood already. Patrice, can you get an IV into his arm? We need to get some plasma into him. I have some O-positive for him."

Someone, he assumed Patrice, grabbed his arm and lifted it gently. "This arm's pretty bad, Maggie. How's that one look?"

"Yeah, it looks better. Let's swap sides," Maggie replied. "Hold on Luke. We have some frozen vampires stashed for you. Just stay with me."

He moaned. Maybe the vampires would heal him to neutral, or close enough he could get everyone's attention. He just hoped it wouldn't be too late for Roxi. He'd promised her he'd stand by her, and now he'd been forced to abandon her. He ignored the needle piercing his arm, the drugs aiding him.

"When you're done there, start cutting him out of these clothes so we can make sure we get all the cuts. Ugh. There's just so many of them."

"Hey, Maggie. He's a tough bastard. He'll pull through this," Patrice replied.

Luke tried to speak again. "Maaag…"

"Should he be conscious?" Patrice asked.

"No, he shouldn't, but I don't understand how his body works. It's not like a wolf's or a human's when it comes to healing," Maggie replied.

"You want some more sedatives?" Patrice gently tugged off his boots.

"Nooo…" Luke mumbled.

"This is going to hurt, Luke."

"Nooo…"

Maggie sighed. "It's probably for the best. Two doses might be too much after this much blood loss."

The night air grew colder as Patrice exposed his skin to it, cutting the rags of the costume.

"What did they do to you?" Anguish filled Maggie's voice.

"He's so skinny. He was such a robust man," Patrice said.

"Fucking vampires. They starved him and then made him fight for their entertainment." Anger banished the anguish from Maggie's voice. Luke had never heard her curse.

"Maggie, you almost done there?" a woman yelled.

"Almost, Sam. I want to get some butterfly bandages on these cuts. We can wrap him up on the road. I just want to stop as much of the bleeding as I can before we move."

"Good. We're getting the last few people out now." Sam sounded winded.

"Any casualties?" Maggie asked.

"Nothing serious. I think we caught them completely off guard," Sam replied.

"Good." Maggie moved to a different cut. "Patrice, I want to tip him onto his side so we can check his back."

Luke groaned as they rolled him.

Patrice gasped. "He's got so many scars…"

"Hold him steady, please." Maggie inspected the cut on the back of his leg. "This one looks like it split open from a previous fight. Yeah, but a lot of these scars were already there. He lived a hard life before his whole deal. These will all disappear once he can drain some more vampires, then he'll just be left with his oldest scars. Alright, that's the last one. Help me get him into the van."

They laid him carefully on his back, then fixed a strap around his waist and his chest where he didn't have any cuts, and collapsed the gurney, lifting him into the back of the unmarked Sprinter van. They pressed him up against the side of the van and tied down the gurney to tie points installed on the van's wall.

"Need any help back here, Maggie?" Patrice asked.

"No, I've got it from here. Go make sure no one else needs medical attention. Fetch me if it's more than you think you can handle," Maggie replied.

Patrice patted Maggie's forearm. "Sure thing, Doc. I'm glad we got your boy back. He's a good man."

"Thanks, Patrice. I'm happy he's alive."

Patrice shut the back of the van on her way out. Maggie turned on a light in the back of the van as the engine fired up. The van bumped and swayed as it moved slowly forward. Maggie covered Luke's wounds with a mixture of gauze and tape. When she finished, she pulled out a damp cloth of some sort and wiped down his skin, cleaning the dried blood from his body, starting with his head. Once she cleaned his face, she leaned over and placed a gentle kiss on his cheek.

She sniffed and wiped her nose with her sleeve. "I've missed you so much, Luke."

"Maggie, missed…" The words almost sounded intelligible.

She traced her fingers along his hairline. "Don't try to talk yet. Let me get some fluids into you, and once we get out of these mountains, we've got some frozen vampires for you. Hopefully, enough to get you on the mend. Gwen will be so happy to see you."

Maggie kept up her steady stream of innocuous talk, speaking more to soothe Luke than to relay important information, which would have been useless in his current state. When she finished cleaning him up as best as she could under the circumstances, she pulled a blanket over him and sat next to him, carefully holding his hand as he fell asleep despite the constant shaking of the van moving over rough terrain.

"LUKE?"

Someone gently shook him.

Maggie's face appeared above him, her long blond hair pulled back in a ponytail. "Luke, we're here. We're going to take you to the freezer trailer so you can heal up. Then we'll go into town and you can get some rest."

"K," Luke said.

Maggie unsnapped the straps holding him down and helped him sit up on the gurney. When the blanket tumbled off of him, he realized he was only wearing the filthy underwear from before going into the arena.

"Do you have any clothes for me?" Luke asked, his voice still a bit sloppy and slurred, but much clearer than last night.

"Yeah, I'll help you put them on." Maggie grabbed a duffel bag.

The act of getting dressed exhausted him, so he laid back down on the gurney and caught his breath. The back of the van opened, letting the bright light of day filter in. It stabbed his eyes.

"How's our boy doing?" Pablo said. He looked the same as ever with the same haircut and his signature tear away warm up suit.

"Stable," Maggie replied.

"That's good. You ready to move him?" Pablo sounded relieved.

"Let's just move him to the ground. We can bring the vampires to him," Maggie replied.

Pablo and Maggie shifted Luke's gurney to the ground, then

helped him sit up, Maggie holding him steady. Sam, wearing black stretch pants and a jacket, stepped into view and waved Pablo over. After they disappeared, they brought over the first headless corpse. They'd already shoved his rudis into the chest of the corpse. Maggie helped him lift his hands to the hilt as they tipped the pommel toward his forehead. The words of the incantation formed in his mind, sending the light down the sliver of the blade into the frozen vamp.

He inhaled, his body feeling better.

"How you feeling, buddy?" Pablo asked.

"Like shit." Luke's voice sounded weak, the words less slurred.

"Well, we have more fanger pops for you." Pablo smiled.

He and Sam moved the body to a pit in the ground. Sam grabbed the handle of the rudis as Pablo shoved the corpse into the hole. It hit the bottom with a squelching noise as it dissolved into reddish-black goo. They ran Luke through the remaining four bodies.

"Sorry we couldn't get more. It was short notice when we moved out, and it was the best we could do," Sam said, sitting on the bumper of the van.

"How are you feeling?" Maggie asked.

"Can I... Can I sit in the van, please?" He squinted tightly, his eyes twitching up to the open blue sky, then back to the ground. The vast open space terrified him, his mind still foggy and locked in his cell. And the intensity of the light burned in his eyes.

"Of course," Maggie replied.

Sam moved off the bumper, making room for him. Maggie and Pablo helped him stand, then guided him to the back of the van. He sat on the edge and pushed back until the van's roof was over his head. Looking around the interior of the van, he shook his head and chuckled mirthlessly.

"The cell they kept me in wasn't much bigger than this." He looked his friends in the eyes, holding their gaze. "We have to go back."

"What?" Pablo asked. His eyes flew open wide as his body went rigid. "We got lucky getting you out of there without more than a few injuries."

Sam leaned closer, her lips drawn into a thin line as concern filled her eyes. "Luke, what's going on?"

Maggie slid in next to Luke, taking his hand in hers.

"There are other hunters trapped there. There's one like me…" He pleaded with his eyes. "She's a, uh, she's a servant of Mithras, or Mithra, as the Persians called him. We have to get her out."

"Is she a Persian?" Sam blinked hard several times. Seeming unsure of where to take the conversation, she'd chosen the simple question.

"Parthian," Luke said. "She's nearly as old as I am."

"How do you know her? From before?" Maggie asked.

Luke shook his head. "Well, I mean, I guess. It's a long story…"

"Well, give us the highlights." Pablo reached in and patted Luke's knee.

"Do you have anything to drink? I'm so thirsty. They didn't give us much in the way of water."

"Oh, sure. I'm sorry for not thinking of that earlier." Maggie turned around, pulled forward a cooler, and handed Luke a bottle of water from it. She pulled out three more for the rest of them.

Luke drank half the bottle, sighing happily. "Cold, clean water. They didn't give us much. Just enough to keep us alive. The same slop, day in, day out. Just that tiny cell. Scratching hash marks on the wall until I stopped counting but still kept scratching them. I nearly went insane."

He snorted. "I probably traveled a ways down that road. Then I heard scratching. Well, I thought that was a hallucination, too, thought I was losing it when I heard singing. At least it wasn't being alone, even if it was all in my head. Then I wasn't alone. She'd been scratching through the mortar and had punched through finally."

He looked up at all his friends. "We only had each other. I joined her digging out the mortar until we removed the stone. It wasn't long after that, they started us in the arenas…"

"Who was she?" Sam asked.

"Is," Luke emphasized. "Her name is Roxiustana Surena. She was the daughter of a Parthian general." Luke chuckled. "She actually tried to kill me in Armenia. Well, we tried to kill each other.

Rome was at war with Parthia at the time. We'd both been given the same mission from Mithras."

"Did you recognize her?" Sam asked. "When you finally saw her in the cell, I mean."

"No. We didn't discover it until a week or so ago. A month? Two?" He shook his head, his brow furrowing in confusion. "I don't know. It's time..."

Maggie wrapped an arm around Luke's shoulder.

He looked down at the ground. He didn't want to ask, but he had to know. "How...how long was I in there?"

Maggie, Pablo, and Sam exchanged looks.

Maggie kissed his cheek. "Luke, you were in there over a year and a half."

"A year...and a half?" He hung his head. What was a year and a half in a two-thousand-year-old life? But it was a year lost with the new girlfriend he loved. A year he missed from Gwen's life growing up. A year with his friends. A year of living.

Maggie pulled him in, cradling his head. Avoiding his friends' eyes, he stared out of the van, focusing on nothing, trying to keep his breathing steady. He didn't want to look up and see the pity. The only thing that brought him out of his frozen stupor was the sound of a truck crunching over gravel, then sliding as it braked.

Pablo stepped away from the back of the van. "Hey, Delilah."

"He alive?" Delilah asked, her jaw clenched while squinting at the sun. Her leather coat still had some dark smudges and dirt on it. She now wore her hair in a series of elaborate braids. There was something else about her that Luke couldn't quite put his finger on.

"Mostly," Pablo replied. "He's explaining why we have to go back to the arena."

Sam groaned. "Pablo..."

Delilah stepped forward, joining everyone. "The fuck you say? What now? I know you didn't just say he wants to go back."

Luke still didn't look up. Partially, he couldn't deal with Delilah's irritation, but he was also having trouble with the day sky.

"It sounds like there are some hunters still left in there, including a special one like Luke," Maggie said, stroking Luke's hair soothingly.

"Like Luke? What does that mean?" Delilah crossed her arms, standing with her legs spread and one foot forward.

"As in an 'ancient Mithras vampire hunter' hunter," Sam said.

Luke finally raised his head, catching Delilah's gaze and pouring his heart into his eyes. "I could talk about the practicalities of having another powerful hunter to add to our cause, but I just…I just can't. Delilah, she's my friend and I can't leave her there."

Delilah, pursing her lips, inhaled through her nose, then exhaled noisily. "This isn't going to be easy, Luke. We really kicked a big hornet's nest over to get you out."

"I know. I'm grateful, but we need to get her out…and the rest of the hunters," Luke said, tacking the last part on.

"We really can't leave them to that fate," Sam said, giving Luke a comforting smile.

"Shit." Delilah turned and looked to the northwest into the brown, sagebrush-covered hills. She nodded to herself and turned around. "What are the chances of them even still being there?"

"Probably pretty good. It was late in the night when we struck and that place is a long way from safe harbor from the sunlight." Sam shrugged. "If they've already evacuated, then it won't be that dangerous with everyone gone."

Delilah nodded, pursing her lips. "We better put everyone on alert. We still have Owen and his crew up there, keeping an eye on the road out. I'll call him on the satphone to get an update on the situation there and let him know to stay put."

"Are you going to be strong enough to go in with us?" Pablo asked. "You look as frail as an old man."

Maggie's body went rigid next to Luke. "He can't go in, not in this condition."

"I have to, Maggie." He mixed pleading and force into his voice.

Maggie pulled back and stared at Luke. "Why, Luke? You said you never saw anything but your cell and the arena? You can't afford to get hurt more."

"Conversely, it's also the only place I can regain my strength faster. I can't abandon her. She was the only one I had for months. She's the only reason I managed to keep my mind together enough to survive in the arena. I told her I'd do anything for her, and I can't break my word."

"Do you love her?" Maggie asked, quietly.

He hated the vulnerability as well as the hurt around the edges of her eyes — hated that he was causing it. He loved Maggie, his feelings burning just as strongly today as the morning they made love before he was captured. "I don't know what my feelings are for her. Everything is too chaotic in my head to do much, other than keep putting one foot in front of the other. Maggie, I love you. You and Gwen, and Pablo, Sam, and Delilah, the thought of seeing you all again was the hope I'd drag out when I was suffering the most. Even though I'm weak and unwell, I'm still the best suited to find her and get us out of there alive."

Maggie looked like she was about to argue more, then thought better of it and closed her mouth. "OK, Luke. Just promise you'll not charge in recklessly without getting stronger first."

"I promise. I don't know how many vampires it'll take, but I'll stay back and not try to do everything." Luke tried to fill his eyes with appreciation and love, but he felt only slightly less bone-crushingly sad and wrung out. He pulled her into his arms and held her for a moment. "Gods above and below, I missed you, Maggie."

"I missed you too, Luke. So much." Maggie squeezed him gently.

He carefully levered himself to his feet and took in his friends. "I missed you all. You're some of the best people and friends I've ever had, and that's saying something, because I've known some pretty spectacular people over two millennia."

Pablo pulled him into a gentle yet crushing hug. "I missed you too, buddy."

Sam and Delilah came in for a hug, surrounding him with the gentle affection of his friends. When they finally let him go, he stepped back, wiping a tear from his cheek, then crossed his arms. "I love you all."

Pablo clamped his teeth together as his chest heaved. Delilah looked down at Luke's lower half and started snickering.

Luke squinched his eyes closed and stared up toward the sky. "The reason it's suddenly breezy is because my pants just slid off, isn't it?"

Pablo burst out laughing. Delilah turned around to let out a laugh before trying to stifle it.

Sam, hiding her mouth with her hand, tried to control her giggles. "Yeah, Luke. It doesn't look like your clothes fit you very well anymore."

Luke sighed and shook his head, then laughed weakly. "Is there a belt in that bag?"

Maggie fetched him a belt and helped him get pulled back together, allowing his friends a good laugh. It had felt good to laugh with them, even if it was at his own expense.

His stomach growled. "I am starving."

"I brought you some gentle food so it wouldn't upset your stomach. I wanted to be safe since we had no idea what condition you'd be in." Maggie pulled out another cooler and removed a storage container with rice, chicken, and sweet potatoes in it. Popping the top off, she handed it to Luke and pulled a fork out for him.

It was the best tasting thing he'd eaten in ages. He made it halfway through before he had to stop, his stomach filling too easily. "I'll have to save that for later."

"Sorry we didn't have anything more exciting for you, buddy. Doc wanted to keep it safe," Pablo said.

"That's OK. It tasted amazing after what I've been eating for months." He looked around at the arid scenery. "Now that my stomach is taken care of, where the hell are we?"

"We're a little ways outside of Thermopolis, Wyoming," Sam said.

CHAPTER
TWENTY

Patrice had volunteered to drive the ambulance van so Maggie could ride with Luke in the backseat of Pablo's pickup. Pablo's black Toyota Tundra crew cab looked brown from the dust and road grime accumulated during the process of Luke's rescue.

It felt amazing to be with his friends and girlfriend again, but also surreal. Luke had been so disconnected from the world he rebuilt, he half thought he was asleep and dreaming, plugging Maggie into a scene that had replayed through his brain countless times since his abduction—Luke driving around hunting for vampires with his best friends, Pablo, Delilah, and Sam.

"So they kidnapped me and flew me all the way to Thermopolis, Wyoming?" Luke stared out the window, watching the arid landscape through the dust their caravan raised as it moved northwest toward the Shoshone National Forest.

"Best as we can figure," Pablo said.

"Why here?" Luke asked.

Sam, sitting next to Maggie on the other side of the seat, turned to angle toward him. "You can get away with a lot in Wyoming if you have money. There are plenty of places to hide, few people to see you, and even fewer regulations if you grease the right palms."

"Plus there's a couple smaller airports nearby in Thermopolis and Worland," Pablo added. "They can fly their private jets in and look like just some more rich assholes flying in to go hunting or fishing."

Pablo turned slightly to speak into the backseat. "There are other airports, but Owen says they're not using the ones near Riverton or Lander."

Luke tore his gaze away from the scenery and looked at Pablo. "Why not?"

"They're on the Wind River Reservation or you have to drive through it. Owen says the Shoshone and Arapaho keep the vampires out of their land. The vamps don't push it since they're eager to stay under the radar, and they have the other two airports, or the ones up near Cody if they want to drive a ways. Owen knows a few were-wolves from the two tribes here, so they've been helping out. They know the land around here and would rather not have their new neighbors."

"And we can trust them?" Luke asked.

"Owen assures us we can, and they've been nothing but friendly and helpful. They're good people, Luke," Sam replied.

Luke, replaying what he'd just heard, perked up. "New? How long have they had that arena?"

"Three or four years is the best we can figure," Delilah replied.

"How did you even find me? I thought I was going to die in there."

"You can thank Heidi for that," Sam said. "Partially. But mostly, it was Gwen's doing."

"What?" Luke was shocked to hear that. He'd chalked Heidi up as part of his betrayal since her packleader had been part of the setup with Mathis Heinen. "I thought she'd betrayed us."

"So did we," Maggie said. "Pieter was devastated. Then she showed up in Portland out of the blue and put herself at the pack's mercy and offered to help free you. She's been playing the double agent since, working her way into the good graces of the vampire masters until she was invited here. As soon as she confirmed you were here, she relayed the information to us. We didn't have the location—they'd kept her from seeing the ultimate destination—but she was able to give us an estimate and some rough maps of the inside of the facility."

"I guess I owe her an apology." Luke chuckled. "She's been high on the list of people who need some comeuppance."

Sam reached across Maggie and patted Luke's knee. "You'll have to save it for now. She's still undercover."

"Wait? How did Gwen help?" Luke asked, remembering that bit Sam had tacked on.

"We'll have to hold off on that and let her explain," Maggie said.

Luke nodded and furrowed his brows. "If you insist..." He sat silently, letting the random thoughts flit about his poor attention span. "I hope they don't take the hunters with them." His eyebrows closed together pensively.

"I doubt it. We sabotaged every vehicle we could. It's going to be a slow trickle to get anyone out of there." Pablo laughed merrily at the thought of destruction. "They'll be spitting mad, that's for sure."

Luke, some of the fog lifting from his brain after eating good food and getting as much liquid as he needed, thought to bring up a second objective. "We're going to need to find my armor and sword. Roxi's too."

"How do you propose we do that?" Delilah turned in the passenger seat to stare at Luke.

Before Luke could answer, Sam's satphone started ringing.

"Yellooo?" Sam said into the phone. "Hey, Owen. Mind if I put you on speakerphone?" Sam pushed a button on the touch screen and the speaker crackled to life. "Hey Owen, you're on speaker."

"Hey, Luke! Finally got you off your butt after your little vacation?" Owen said.

"Yeah. It was a real Club Med. How do things look up there?" Luke asked.

Owen laughed. "They're flying choppers rigged out with dark chambers up here to evacuate some of the high muckety-mucks. Want me to do anything about it?"

"Owen." Sam sounded concerned. "What can you do about it?"

"Well, I have this .50 caliber machine gun and a fuck ton of ammo…" Owen made machine gun noises, followed by the sound of a helicopter going down and exploding.

"Owen. Put Lauren on the phone," Sam replied.

Owen laughed, as did Pablo in the front seat.

"Yeah, honey?" Lauren spoke into the phone.

"He's not serious, is he?" Sam asked.

"It would make for pretty fireworks."

"Um, Lauren, it's Luke. We should probably avoid shooting down anything for the moment. It might attract local authority figures and pesky FAA types. They don't have much of a sense of humor for things like that."

"And we kind of need to keep as low of a profile as possible, especially after we set off explosives to break Luke out last night," Sam said.

"Not likely anyone heard them that far into the mountains, Sam. You city wolves are always trying to harsh our fun."

"I don't think Lauren is the voice of reason you thought she was going to be, Sam." Maggie grinned.

"No shit," Sam said, shaking her head.

"Don't worry, Sam." Lauren said. "We won't shoot down anything. What about cars? If they get anything running, should we stop them?"

"We don't particularly want to meet them out here. Blast away, I guess." Sam was a little off her game, trying to handle the combination of Lauren and her brother Owen.

"Good. The truck gets better mileage without all the weight, and .50 cal ammo is heavy."

"Here's to your improved fuel economy," Luke added. "Lauren, keep an eye out for any thralls trying to slip out. I'm guessing there will be some rats fleeing the sinking ship, especially the easily replaceable ones without a precious seat in a helicopter." He looked at Delilah. "They might be a handy source of information for our next operation."

"Copy that, handsome. What about any runaway strays?" Lauren added a bit of contempt to the last two words.

"Pick them up. If they're disloyal to their current masters once they see their low value to them, they might willingly provide valuable insights." Luke muted his end and gazed toward Sam.

Sam took the phone back. "Anything else, Lauren?"

"No, we'll let you know if the situation changes. What's your ETA?"

"About an hour, hour-and-a-half?" Pablo replied. "These roads are crap and some of these vehicles weren't made to move fast on rough roads."

"No hurry, we have a bit before sunset. No sense busting an axle being stupid. Hey, Luke. Look forward to seeing your handsome mug again."

"It's a bit shaggy these days," Maggie commented.

"The resort's barber was booked out, so I couldn't get in." Luke knew that was the joke everyone expected, whether he felt like joking or not. For now, it was easier to keep appearances. He could fake it and sooth everyone's concerns for one more day. When Roxi was free and they were headed away from here, he could break down then. Keep it together, finish the mission, heal later.

Sam leaned over the phone. "We'll see you soon, Lauren."

"Drive safely!"

Sam hung up the phone and stashed it.

"Hey, Pablo. Since we have a little time, mind if we pull over for a few minutes? I need to stretch my legs for a minute." Luke fixed his stare forward, trying to dispel the motion sickness threatening his stomach's ability to keep the meager meal he'd eaten earlier.

"Totes. I'm sure some folks would like to find a bush to water. Just be sure to check it for nope ropes first," Pablo replied.

"Nope ropes?" Luke asked.

"You know, danger noodles? Sneks?"

"Ah." Luke chuckled.

"The kind around here play maracas at you if you get too close," Pablo added.

"I'll be sure to be careful to avoid any nope ropes," Luke replied.

LUKE DOZED in and out as they wound their way up the rough roads leading deeper into the forest and Absaroka Mountains. When they stopped, Luke piled out of Pablo's truck, his long, messy hair flopping into his face. Sweeping it away, he stretched quickly, then went looking for a long-haired teammate.

"Hey, Sam, Maggie, do either of you have a spare hair tie I could borrow?" Luke asked. He figured one of the women with the ponytails might have a spare.

Maggie was the first to retrieve one from her bag. Luke pulled the top and sides of his hair back and cinched it down with the stretchy hair tie. Everyone except him and Maggie had already stepped out of the truck to carry out their tasks, leaving them alone, standing by Pablo's truck.

"Are you going to be OK, Luke?" Maggie leaned in and kissed his cheek just above his shaggy beard.

"I must smell pretty bad, especially with a wolf's sense of smell." Luke looked down in front of him.

Maggie chuckled softly before getting serious. "You don't smell great, but I don't care. I'm so happy to have you back. I just don't want to lose you again."

"I can hold it together for one operation." He looked up, caressing her cheek. "I'll try not to do anything stupid or foolhardy. Seeing your face…it's like a dream. I don't want this to be the last time I see it. I'll do what I must to come back."

Maggie nodded and leaned forward, kissing him softly. "I'll have the medical van ready in case your friend or the other hunters need it."

"Thank you." He leaned in for another kiss, then stepped away from the pickup, Maggie following.

"Hey, buddy. I found a spare bullet-proof vest for you. Owen says they've been getting a little of small arms fire." Pablo handed Luke a Kevlar vest.

"Yeah. Looks like mostly pot shots at anyone trying to run away. I don't think they have any idea if we're out here." Owen patted Luke on the shoulders. The man's long black hair ran loose down his back over a brown flannel shirt with the top couple of buttons unbuttoned and the sleeves rolled up. "You look like shit, man."

"Good. That's how I feel too." Luke smiled at the handsome Chinook man. "Do you think any of the choppers saw you as they went over?"

"Not likely." He hitched his thumb over his shoulder.

His truck was covered in brown camouflage netting with sagebrush stuffed artfully into it so it blended with the background. There were a few other vehicles similarly hidden. A tall young man with similar hair and a few similar facial features stood centennial behind the .50 caliber machine gun mounted on the bed of the pickup.

"Is that Toby?" Luke asked. "He's gotten taller."

Owen laughed. "Yeah. The boy is about to eat Lauren out of house and home. If he has any more growth spurts, he'll be taller than me. He's still not as handsome as his old uncle, though."

Not even bothering to look toward the cluster of men, Toby raised a bird at them while he kept watch.

Owen shook his head, a smirk on his face. "No respect for his elders."

"Holy shit, Maggie. You weren't kidding about that shaggy face. Give him some leather clothes and a fur hat and he'd look just like a damned fur trapper." Lauren grabbed his shoulders, holding him at arm's length. "I'm glad you're free, handsome." She pulled him in for a hug. "So what's our plan?"

Sam, Delilah, Pablo, and Pieter gathered around Luke.

"Pieter?" Luke said.

"Hey, Luke. It's good to see you." Pieter smiled warmly. He looked far more casual than Luke was used to seeing him in Europe. If it wasn't for the accent, he'd blend in perfectly as an American in his hoodie and jeans.

"I'm glad to see you too." Luke hadn't thought about it. It had been decided right before he was abducted that Pieter was coming to live in Portland, but he'd not been part of the move and hadn't seen it. It had moved to the back of his mind during his captivity.

"So, about that plan?" Delilah asked.

Simone wandered over and slid in front of Delilah, pulling Delilah's arms around her.

"Are you two…" Luke pointed between Simone and Delilah.

"Yes, we've been together since not long after I moved to Portland," Simone answered.

She looked more relaxed and confident than when she was still learning her place in the world, without her pack and its rigid dominance. He'd watched their tentative touches and secretive hand holding when they thought they were being sneaky. The fact they'd continued and were still together genuinely warmed his heart. He moved his gaze up to his friend Delilah. With her arms wrapped lovingly around Simon, there was a contentment in her eyes he'd never seen before.

Smiling, Luke nodded. "I'm glad it worked out. I was hoping it would."

"What do you mean?" Delilah asked.

"I saw all the signs while we were in Belgium and France. The looks, the touches. You two weren't quite as secretive as you thought you were. Why do you think I engineered reasons to give you two time alone? Once you two showed up in Cambrai after being at my house, I knew something had shifted when I caught you holding hands that first morning at the apartment. Why do you think I left to be elsewhere? Or arranged things so I could send you two out to dinner."

Delilah's eyes widened and her jaw dropped. "You devious old man." She smiled broadly. "Thank you."

He turned to Sam and Pablo who seemed shocked by the revelations. "See, I'm not totally oblivious when it comes to people flirting."

Pablo patted his shoulder. "You're just oblivious to it when you're personally involved."

"That I can't deny," Luke replied. "So…plan. Owen, did you pick up any thralls?"

"Yeah, and a few wolves. We've got them separated."

"Take me to the thralls," Luke ordered.

Owen waved everyone after him. They walked along the edge of the hill back the way they'd driven in earlier until they found a wash winding between hills. With guards posted along the ridge, the thralls sat or sprawled out along the bottom of the wash. Most of them looked fearful and anxious, worried what their captors would do to them, wondering if they'd be as cruel to the thralls as their vampire masters had been to those in their mercy.

"Just grab any thrall?" Delilah asked, waving her arm to indicate all the humans sitting on the ground.

Luke looked over the crowd, watching heads dip to avoid eye contact when he stopped on one whose eyes widened with recognition. "The cage…" Luke pointed at the thrall. "That one."

Delilah pointed. "You, thrall. Come here."

He leapt up, walked through the seated crowd, and stopped in front of Delilah, his head bowed and his shoulders slumped. "Yes, ma'am?"

"Come with us," Delilah ordered, turning to walk away.

Everyone fell in behind her. The thrall threw furtive looks at Luke. When he caught a glance of the man's face, Luke thought his eyes were filled with terror. Maybe he thought Luke was taking him aside to exact vengeance on him. Delilah led them into the center of their little caravan where they'd have a secure spot to talk.

"Do you have a name, thrall?" Luke asked.

"Jimmy, sir," the thrall replied. He kept his hands in front of himself, wringing them nervously, and refused to make eye contact.

"I'm not going to harm you. You were the one creature in this hell that wasn't cruel to me, but I'm not just going to turn you loose either. I need you to lead me to the cells where the hunters are kept and to the cell where I was kept. Do that, and we'll take you away from this hell if you want—or set you free, if that's your preference."

Jimmy risked raising his eyes to Luke's. "Really?"

"I swear it." Luke held the man's gaze.

The young man licked his lips nervously, thinking about it. "I don't know where exactly your cell was. You weren't kept with the other hunters. I can take you to them easily, but I only have a vague idea where your cell was."

"Why not?" Luke asked.

"Only the oldest and most trusted thralls were allowed down with the special prisoners."

"Were there any with you and the other thralls?" Delilah asked.

Jimmy looked down. "No, ma'am. They'd be involved with evacuating their masters and their households. All the thralls you captured were not that important. We were supposed to sell our lives to slow you down."

"Well, if you see one, point them out so we can snag one of them," Luke said.

Jimmy nodded.

"Can you draw some maps of the arena complex? I need to know about three locations—the hunters' cells, my cell, and the armory." He thought for a moment. "Would they keep the special armor with regular stuff?"

"What?" Sam asked.

"Did I say that out loud?" Luke asked, his cheeks flushing red. "I'm not used to people around," he mumbled, hanging his head and clasping his hands.

Maggie rubbed his shoulder and leaned up toward his ear. "It's OK, Luke. Everyone here understands."

He nodded, pursing his lips, and looked up. "Do you know where they kept their special prizes, Jimmy? The stuff they took off hunters. My possessions and the other special prisoner's stuff."

"Yeah. I know where that's at. One of the higher thralls showed me one time. It's a little museum dedicated to the masters' victories," Jimmy replied.

Someone held out a pad and a pen for Jimmy.

"Put them on the map," Luke instructed, before turning to Delilah. "Let me know when you have the team assembled. I'm going to go sit down and see about the rest of that food Maggie packed for me."

CHAPTER
TWENTY-ONE

Luke dozed in the back of Pablo's pickup, his container of chicken, rice, and sweet potatoes balanced precariously on his leg.

"Luke?"

Maggie's voice drifted through the haze of his sleep.

"Luke? Delilah's ready to go soon." Maggie tried to coax him awake.

He startled, knocking the container to the floor of Pablo's pickup truck. Breathing quickly, he raised his hand to his chest as his heart thudded against the inside of his ribs.

"Sorry for startling you," she said, rubbing his leg soothingly.

"That's OK. I shouldn't have fallen asleep." He looked down awkwardly. "And now I've made a mess in Pablo's truck."

He stepped out of the truck, careful not to smash the food. Picking up the container, he cleaned up the fallen pieces and did his best to scoop up the stray rice. Once he got it cleaned up, he tossed it under the truck.

"Where's Delilah?" Luke asked.

Maggie picked up the Kevlar vest. "Let's get you into this before you go."

Luke nodded, unzipping his hoodie. He let Maggie help him with the armor, the ritual of being dressed for battle by his loved one bringing a sense of continuity to the moment. When finished, she inspected her work, running her hand along the edges over his chest.

"It's not as sharp-looking as your armor, but it'll at least keep you somewhat safe," Maggie said, smiling softly.

"I hope I won't need it." Luke brushed a strand of hair off her forehead and tucked it behind her ear. He tried to muster a smile for her, but barely got the corners of his lips tipped up at all.

"You look so tired." Maggie rested her head against his chest.

"I am." Luke wrapped his arms around her, squeezing her. "It's getting chilly."

"Luke?" Delilah called.

"You should get going." Maggie picked up his hoodie and handed it to him.

Reaching out, Luke tipped Maggie's chin up and leaned down for a kiss. "I'll see you in a bit."

He stared into her eyes for a moment, wanting to make sure she was indeed real and not a dream. The poorly contained worry in her eyes served as a poignant reminder that he needed to restrain himself from heroics if he wanted to get back to her alive. He'd dreamed of being with her too many times to waste himself on stupidity. A soft, tired smile spread across his face. "I'll do my best to come back to you in one piece."

Maggie nodded and squeezed his arm before letting him go.

He turned and walked toward Delilah, giving Maggie a last wave. When he rejoined the attack team, Pablo handed him his rudis in a scabbard. Luke buttoned it onto his belt, then tied the strap around his thigh. They helped Luke on with a couple ammo bandoliers and handed him a shotgun.

"That was smart work stashing your rudis in my suitcase," Pieter said, a smirk spreading across his face. "Though you sliced one of my good shirts."

"Sorry about that. I'll replace it when we get home. Hiding my rudis was about the only action I could take, considering the circumstances," Luke replied.

Delilah waved everyone to silence. "Everyone up on the plan?"

When she saw everyone nod, she pointed off into the distance. "Then let's go."

Luke assumed the arena was off that way. The sun's last rays shone over their destination as it tucked into the western horizon. He scanned the sky, looking for his mistress and her moon chariot.

"Selene, my mistress, are you there?"

"Yes, Lucius, I can see you now. Where is your companion? Roxiustana?"

"I couldn't get them to listen last night. I was too drugged. Is she still... there?" Luke felt sick at the thought of the word dead and couldn't even voice it in his head while speaking to Selene.

"I think she is. There is a veil blocking her, but it vacillates. When last I had contact, she still called out your name. She wept."

Luke's heart, already weak, broke. *"Can you tell her I'm coming? We're coming to free her?"*

"Her heart is not open to me, or the veil obscures it. I can almost see her because of our first touches, but she is closed off. Alone."

"Luke, buddy, pay attention," Pablo said as he caught Luke and kept him from tripping.

"Sorry, I was checking in." He cast his eyes toward the sliver of crescent moon on its first waxing after the new moon.

"Ah. Anything worth reporting?" Delilah asked.

"Only that Roxi is still alive," Luke replied.

Delilah nodded and reached out, squeezing his hand. "That's good news. How are you doing? Keeping up?"

Luke nodded, unsure at first but then more firmly as he thought about it and looked inward. "I think I'm getting a little help from..." He gestured toward Selene again.

Delilah turned to the rest of the team. "Alright, we're getting close. I want to angle around and come at the entrance we blew in the wall from the side so we're not in view of it for too long. All silent from here on out."

Pablo took a moment to strip down and shift to full wolf. Simone followed suit, and together they loped off into the darkness to meet up with the advance scouts and sniff out the rest of the way to the arena. As they worked through the brush and winding hills and boulders, Luke concentrated on putting one foot in front of the other.

Even with the addition of Selene's strength to bolster him, he still felt weak and slow and wanted to preserve whatever strength was available for the coming search for Roxi.

Delilah held up a fist, bringing the group to a halt. A few minutes later, the wolf Luke recognized as Pablo jogged around the corner and blurred into his man shape, whispering into Delilah's ear. She nodded, and Pablo blurred into his bipedal form. Waving them forward, Delilah tucked in after Pablo as they made the last jog to the arena.

Luke hadn't seen the arena last night when he'd been drugged. This was his first chance to see where he'd been held prisoner for so long. Most of the arena was subterranean, save for a little that rose above the ground, carefully camouflaged with dirt berms and local plants that ran along the eight feet or so of wall and over the roof, making it look like part of the surrounding landscape. If Luke hadn't been a prisoner there for over a year and a half, he'd have admired the ingenuity and sheer effort it would have taken to build way up here in the middle of nowhere. No wonder the wolves had blown their way through the ceiling to rescue Luke. It was the fastest way in.

In pairs, they crouched low and worked their way to the outer wall of the arena, meeting up with the advanced scouts. As soon as they all backed up against the wall, the wolves, still in their full wolf form, shifted to their bipedal form. When they were ready, they sprinted into the gap in the wall blown apart last night.

Once they disappeared into the darkness, everyone else followed them in. Growls and screams poured out of the darkness as Luke and the rest of the team joined the wolves. He held back until his eyes adjust to the darkness, not wanting to hit one of his teammates. Besides, he'd been ordered to hang back, and he didn't want to blow all his energy early and come up wanting later when he truly needed it. The wolves acting as shock troops and his trained friends could secure the entrance well enough without him.

"Go!" Delilah shouted.

Drawing in a deep breath, Luke jogged after his friends as they advanced down the outer rim of the arena complex—a handful of people stayed back to guard their exit. Up ahead, he heard the occasional blast of one of their shotguns accompanied by a flash of muzzle fire or the growls of his wolf friends. They were moving pretty fast, and Luke struggled to keep up. Keeping his head down as he huffed and puffed his way forward, he ran into the back of someone who'd stopped in front of him.

"Sorry about that…" Luke mumbled.

"Hey, Luke. There are a couple vamp bodies up here. Want a refresher?" Delilah called.

"Yeah. That would be amazing." He pulled his rudis and walked through the crowd to find the bodies Delilah mentioned. He set about draining them. After the second one, he felt mildly refreshed, at least enough to keep up.

"How you doing, Luke?" Delilah asked.

"A long way from human, but better." Luke pulled the rudis out of the vampire, letting it puff into dust.

The ancient vampire had done a lot to fix the last of his wounds, leaving pink scars where visible. He still felt weak as a kitten, but maybe a healthy kitten. They'd take a little time for Luke to drain a few vampires they'd found along the way, though Luke had requested they leave some headless bodies unstaked for the return trip.

He chuckled. "Still half sure I'm going to wake up back in my cell, and you'll all just be figures in a dream."

"I've put too much work into getting your ass out of here for this to be a dream in your head." She reached out and lightly flicked the back of his hand.

"You're a very mean dream." Luke chuckled. "I missed you, Dee."

"I missed you, too, Luke." She squeezed his shoulder.

"Alright, we're heading down these stairs. Two floors down should be the museum." Delilah turned her gaze to Jimmy.

"Yes, ma'am." The thrall was doing his best to be polite and stay out of the way. As someone who had been expendable food and labor, he seemed genuinely interested in helping them so he could help himself out of this life. He worked his way up so that he was next to Delilah.

"OK, lead the way, but if you lead us into a trap, you're the first one shot. Understand?" Delilah towered over him.

"Understood, ma'am." Jimmy, looking a bit green, nodded nervously, and turned into the stairwell and disappeared down the first flight of stairs.

When he stopped to the door leading out to the level they wanted for the museum, Jimmy ducked his head out and pulled it back in. A gun fired, chipping stone from the wall where the bullet missed his head, hitting the wall instead. Delilah yanked him behind her, leaning out of the door and firing off her shotgun. She waved forward someone Luke didn't recognize, and together they set up a steady barrage of fire. Two wolves stepped up and darted out when Delilah gave them the signal. A few seconds later, a scream rent the air quickly followed by silence.

"All clear," Delilah called. The rest of the team flared out in twos, ensuring it was indeed clear to proceed. Delilah held out her arm, stopping Luke when he readied to step out. "Jimmy, you're with the lead team."

He swallowed and nodded, then stepped out into the hall.

Luke approved of the way Delilah was running the team. Her actions and choices were calm and professional. He hoped it would be enough to keep casualties down and they could get out before the vampires organized any kind of serious defense. Maybe enough of the elites had fled to leave those left in chaos.

"Alright, let's go, Luke." Delilah stepped out in front of him, swinging her shotgun wide.

Luke followed her, darting across the hallway into the corridor Jimmy had led the advance team down. They found the shooter, now a corpse, with a stake sticking out his chest—a human thrall.

Yesterday's explosions from above must have done some damage to the power system in this part of the arena. Some of the lights were out, while others flickered. Luke tried to squint his eyes against the flickering light, feeling the beginnings of a headache coming on from the noise of the guns and bad lighting combined with his poor health.

He startled when Delilah put her hand on his shoulder.

"You OK, Luke? You're looking a bit peaked." Her brow furrowed in concern.

"The blinking lights are giving me a headache," Luke replied, looking toward the ground to lessen the effect.

Delilah turned and called over her shoulder toward the front of their group. "Jimmy, how close are we?"

"Not far, next corner," he replied.

"We're almost there, Luke. Hopefully the lighting is better there."

Luke nodded and forged forward until the rest of the team bunching up forced him to stop.

"What's the hold up?" Delilah asked.

"I grabbed a keycard off the…the thrall we killed down the hall. I didn't want to open the door until you were ready," Jimmy replied.

"Guns ready. Jimmy, the door, please." Delilah fed a couple shells into her shotgun.

The door beeped, then Jimmy shoved the door open before backing out of the way as the first two folks poked their guns in the door, sweeping the room. As they disappeared into the door, more wolves followed until a minute later, someone called clear. Delilah led Luke into the room. Soft, low light emergency bulbs sent up a delicate glow anywhere light reflected off metal. The collection, while not huge, was impressive in its diversity and potential antiquity, although Luke would have to properly assess anything he wasn't familiar with to determine its authenticity.

"What do we want, Luke?" Delilah asked.

"Let me take a look." He stepped further into the room before he stopped at a blocked aisle.

"OK, half of you need to clear the room. Go secure our exit," Delilah ordered.

Delilah's command of the team was excellent. He'd have to remember to compliment her later. Her confidence, already solid when it came to her own personal abilities, had really grown. She was turning into a top-notch commander. He sighed; a lot had changed while he'd been missing from the world. Shaking his head lightly, he pulled his head back to the task at hand and walked around, inspecting the trophies stolen from their rightful owners. The vamps had everything from swords of various styles to elaborate stakes, firearms, and armor.

"Delilah, can you have someone take a photo of every exhibit? And make sure to get a readable photo of the plaque listing what the weapons are and who they were taken from," Luke said as he strolled around the room.

"I'll take care of that."

After he made a circuit around the outer edges, he stepped into the center of the room to examine the central exhibit, with its plinth set higher than the rest to mark its importance. In the middle, they displayed beautiful steel scale mail armor with bronze accents at the neckline, sleeves, and hemline. There was also a matching helmet. Bending over, he scanned the plaque listing the vile deeds of the Terror of Tehran, the Murderer of Mumbai, and the numerous other aliases they'd assigned to Roxi.

"Luke, do you want to pick up the pace here? We're on a timetable," Delilah said, stepping in to take a picture of Roxi's exhibit.

Luke straightened and turned to Delilah. "Do you have them all photographed?"

"Yeah. What now?"

"I think this calls for some muscle. I want to take everything. This glass looks heavy. Have them take it off carefully and set it aside, but start with this one." He pointed over his shoulder with his hand. "This is Roxi's gear."

Delilah barked out orders, and everyone jumped into motion to execute them. Together, Luke and Delilah backed out of the way as two wolves stepped up on either side of Roxi's exhibit and lifted the thick glass case from the top. As soon as the glass parted from the case, alarms blared to life. Trying to ignore the hideous noise, Luke reached in and grabbed Roxi's sword and the scabbard next to it, a baldric unfurling as he moved it from its stand. He slung it over his head and shoulder, letting it hang on his left hip, before unbuckling his belt and removing it. Holding his pants up so he'd avoid a repeat of his earlier humiliation, he slid it back through the loops, making sure to go over the baldric on the way by.

"What do we do with the rest of it?" Delilah took down the rest of Roxi's armor and carefully packed them into a duffel bag pulled from someone's backpack.

"Let's take it all. We'll be able to test it later to see if it's good or if we can reunite it with their rightful owners, so they may continue to employ it and pay back the assholes who took it." He tried to ignore the hole in his heart he'd hoped to fill by reuniting with his own gear. It was clearly not here. There wasn't even an empty display marking that it had ever been here.

"Luke..." Delilah started. "Do you think your stuff is being kept somewhere else here?"

"I don't know." He turned to Jimmy. "Is there anywhere else special gear might be? Mine specifically? Roman gladius and banded armor?"

Jimmy shook his head. "I mean, maybe in the study."

"What study?" Delilah asked.

"It's where the Dominus has audiences while he's here."

"Fuck." Luke slumped. "It's not there, or at least it wasn't..." He turned back to Jimmy. "How long ago was the big battle with Le Mousquetaire and his musketeers?"

"His what?" Delilah asked, eyes going wide. "Sorry, that's a story for later."

Jimmy swallowed. "That was a couple weeks ago."

"It wasn't there when I was taken there."

"I'm sorry, Luke." Delilah squeezed his shoulder.

He nodded, frowning. He hadn't seen Roxi's rudis in her display case. "Do you see a rudis? It should look kind of like mine?"

No one said anything or acknowledged seeing it. The growing pit in his stomach opened a bit deeper. If they couldn't find her rudis... He didn't want to think about it. Maybe his would work for her. He allowed a bit of the anger he'd been struggling to keep at bay through, hoping to use it to keep from falling down the pit. Luke whipped his head around to the exit as gun shots blasted out in the hallway.

Delilah pumped a shell into the shotgun's firing chamber. "Jimmy, you help get the rest of this stuff packed up. Ramon, protect Luke. Once the room is cleaned out, you four are responsible for getting everything back up and out to our caravan." With the orders issued, she darted out of the ransacked museum to check in with her advanced elements.

Ramon stepped in between Jimmy and Luke, baring his teeth at the thrall. Jimmy, taking the hint, backed away from Luke and started grabbing stuff to hand to the four people packing up everything. Ramon must be one of the newer team members, activated after his capture.

"We're done here!" called one of the people moving the gear out.

Luke headed for the exit, but Ramon grabbed his shoulder and stopped him, stepping out the door first. Luke followed his hulking nanny out the door. Shotguns blasts were intermixed with small arms fire, mostly handguns, but Luke thought he heard the distinct crack of an AK-47. After using it on the vampires at their battle at Timberline Lodge, he'd grown fond of the weapon. He pumped a shell into the firing chamber of his shotgun and flipped the safety off.

It felt good to have one of his Winchester M12s in his hands after so long. The weapon had done yeoman's duty since they'd integrated it into their mix prior to the freighter assault. The ability to create custom shells made for a versatile anti-vampire weapon. As anger at not finding his gladius and lorica filtered through him, his desire to put the M12 into action grew. He needed to strike back for himself—and for Roxi.

TWENTY-TWO

"**G**o!" Delilah yelled. Two people stepped out and laid down cover fire while two others carried their plunder across the hall and into the stairwell back up to the upper level. When they were clear, she waved up the next quartet. "Go!"

Delilah turned to them. "Ramon, you and Luke are next."

Luke let the wolf clear the way through the hall as everyone pressed themselves up against the wall.

"Go!" Delilah pushed Ramon.

The wolf sprinted across the hall into the stairwell. Luke, following, stepped out and fired off a shot down the hall. He didn't hit anyone but was gratified all the same when someone dove out of the way. With Ramon still in front of him, they made their way down the stairs to the next floor landing and their next objective.

Delilah pointed to a handful of wolves. "You six, hold this door. If you have to bug out, three up and three down."

"Got it, Delilah," replied a deep voice.

Delilah pushed through to the front of their little crowd, now much diminished by leaving six people to hold the stairwell. The gun fire, while not intense, was still steady as both sides tried to take out the other.

They descended another level, then busted into the hallway.

Flashlights flicked on as people pulled them from belts, pockets, and backpacks. A few people affixed specially designed flashlights to the bayonet lug of their shotguns. Once again, Delilah pushed Jimmy to the front to lead them into the recesses of this level. Luke knew they were on the right level to find the other hunters when they turned a corner and the stench of sewage buckets rolled out to greet them.

In the lead, someone fired their M12. The muzzle flash illuminated figures moving deeper in the hall. Luke, stuck in the back, kept his eyes averted to protect his night vision as more shots rang out. When the distinct scream of silver penetrating the flesh of a vampire drifted back, Luke smiled. His smile was quickly extinguished when a handgun shot was followed by the yelp of one of their werewolves.

"Make room!" someone called from in front.

Luke pressed himself against the wall as the shot wolf walked back, cradling a bleeding arm. As long as it hadn't opened a major artery or broken the bone, the wound would heal quickly and they would be able to keep fighting if only somewhat weakened. When the gunshots stopped, Luke looked down the hall.

"Clear," someone called.

"What were they doing down here?" someone else asked.

"Hey! Get us out of these fucking cages!" one of the hunters yelled.

"Keep it down in there," Delilah yelled. "We'll get you out shortly. Luke? I need you up here."

Luke stepped out and pushed his way past the few werewolves and human form teammates. He didn't recognize a lot of people and wasn't sure who was in human form and who might be an actual human. When he made it to the front, Delilah swung her shotgun through the open door of the first cell. Luke gritted his teeth. The vampires had been down here to kill the hunters. A woman lay in a heap inside the cage, her skin slashed from vampire claws, though the vampire had finished her off by wrenching her head around, snapping her neck.

He and Delilah found the same scene in the next two pens. The fourth and fifth were empty. The two after those held fresh cadavers. When they arrived at the last three, the doors remained locked. Delilah grabbed a free flashlight from someone and peered into the pen. A hunter scrambled away from the light, blocking their eyes.

"Can someone find the keys?" Delilah asked, moving to the next to pens.

A similar scene greeted her and Luke when she aimed the flashlight into the last two cells.

"Is anyone injured? Can you make it out of here under your own power?" Luke asked. When he got no answer, he added, "If you are injured, we'll get you out and to medical treatment."

"Just keep those monsters on a leash," one of the hunters said.

At the word monster, several of the werewolves responded with growls.

"The wolves are our friends and will protect you, so don't insult them," Delilah replied.

"At this point, I'd take death from a werewolf over this hell," a woman said. "I just want out of this cage."

"Got the keys!" A man pushed her way through and handed them to Delilah.

The man who'd found the keys stepped up to Luke and placed his lips near his ear. "There's a vamp body back there if you want it. I had them hold off before staking it."

"Thanks." Luke patted his shoulder and stepped toward the back of the cell block, pulling his rudis as he picked his way through the mess of the others his team had killed.

Luke drained the vamp, turning it to dust, and returned to find the three hunters freed from their cages. Delilah ushered them out, sending out the squad to make sure the way remained clear. Every sound, real or imagined, drew flashlights, guns, and eyes followed by relieved sighs when nothing was found. When they reached the stairwell, Delilah reduced their squad by two more, sending them up to escort the hunters back to the entrance. She pulled a couple spare boxes of shotgun shells from her backpack for them to drop off on the way up as their squad holding the stairwell two floors up was still engaged, firing off shots at semi-regular intervals.

Delilah looked around the crowd as she pushed shells into her shotgun until she found who she was looking for. "Jimmy, take us down to the level for the last objective."

"Yes, ma'am." While still keeping a subservient pose, it looked as if his back had straightened some as his usefulness had proven valuable.

Delilah waited until Luke caught up and pulled him into a one-armed hug. "We'll get her out, Luke."

Even in the low light, she'd seen the worried look on his face. He returned the hug. They were getting close.

"Thank you for your support, Dee. It means a lot," Luke replied. He couldn't be truly free until Roxi was free.

"I know, now let's go get your friend."

THEY'D FREED a few hunters from the main pens and sent them out with some of the wolves. Jimmy was taking them through the lower reaches of the arena into its deepest and darkest bowels. Delilah, with a can of spray paint from her backpack, had been spraying symbols on the wall so they could quickly find their way out again.

"This is as far as I've ever gone," Jimmy said, addressing Luke, "but I've seen them taking you and that woman down this corridor. Beyond here was off limits to us low-level thralls."

Luke nodded and stepped in front of the group.

Delilah grabbed his arm and stopped him, stepping in front of him. "Rhonda, you're with me. Luke, you stay behind us in case we come on anyone feeling belligerent. Ramon, you're still on Luke."

Luke reluctantly conceded to Delilah. He felt they were close, and he wanted to run ahead and find Roxi. Restraining his anticipation was proving difficult, but Delilah and the hulking wolf that was Rhonda effectively blocked the hallway while Ramon breathed down his neck. They'd blocked it so effectively, Luke could barely see anything in front of them.

"Luke, we have a problem here. There's no more hallway. It just a dead ends up ahead," Delilah said.

"Let me by, please," Luke said.

Delilah and Rhonda backed up against the wall, making a narrow corridor between them for Luke to squeeze by. He looked over the end of the hallway, and sure enough, it ended in a wall made from the same gray stone as the rest of the arena.

Closing his eyes, he lowered his head. *"Please let me find her. It can't end like this."*

Opening his eyes, he systematically searched the walls, starting from where they met the ceiling all the way to the floor. With his heart falling down a deepening pit as each second ticked away, he'd nearly given up when he noticed a floor stone at the wall's edge. It featured more scruffs and scratches than any floor stone tucked along a wall should have. He ran his boot over the stone, feeling the texture through the sole of the boot.

"Get ready…" Luke said.

Rhonda and Ramon slid by him and crouched, ready to pounce if anyone appeared behind the wall. Luke set this toe up against the wall stone above the scuffed floor stone and pushed. At first nothing happened, then it gave way slowly until smoothly sliding the rest of the way in.

"Always secret doors with you," Delilah mumbled behind him.

The false wall capping the hall receded into the wall sideways, revealing a dark stairwell. Either there were no lights in the hallway, or they'd been knocked out when the levels above had failed. Rhonda led the way as Delilah joined Luke behind her.

"Your friend better be worth all this trouble," Delilah said.

Luke didn't answer, angst eating at his stomach. After finding vampires upstairs killing hunters, he feared the worst as they descended into the abyssal darkness where even the flashlights worried about what they'd find.

Delilah squeezed his hand briefly before releasing it. When they reached the bottom of the stairs, they turned into a small hall, their flashlights illuminating heavy wooden doors. Luke walked up to the first door and pulled on the handle. Locked. "Shit." He hadn't thought about what they'd need to enter the cells.

Delilah handed the keys to Luke. He took them and thanked her with a nod. He tried every key, his despair threatening to overwhelm him more and more with each failed key until he was left with no more to try.

He looked down, noticing the crossbars along the bottom of the door. The lower crossbar blocked a shorter door that had been used to slide through trays. The second cross bar was the bigger one for the bucket exchange.

He sank to his knees and with shaking hands, tried the keys in the padlocks. When the last key failed, he hung his head, tears burning in the corner of his eyes. He reached for the shotgun and tried to bash the lock off the crossbar but failed to make a solid contact in his current condition.

Ramon stepped up and extended his paw to Luke. Nodding, Luke handed the shotgun over. Ramon flipped the safety on, then pulled back and brought the butt of the gun down on the first padlock, sending it tinkling to the ground in pieces. Another quick bash and the lock on the other crossbar joined it. He stepped to the next door and started on its padlocks.

Luke pulled the crossbars off, tugging the flap doors open. When he looked in, it was empty. He moved onto the next door and found it empty as well. His frustration and fear grew. What if there were other special cells in a different part of the arena? What if they'd taken her with them? What if she was dead inside her cell?

He violently yanked the bars off the next door and tossed them aside—the cell was empty. He slammed the flap door shut, then stared at the floor while he stood there on his hands and knees, his breathing growing uneven as his fear deepened. He took a deep breath and held it, then let it out, holding it again. In the silence between breaths, he thought he heard a soft voice singing raggedly. His heart sped up when he heard a couple of muffled screams accompany Ramon's lock bashing, followed by a melody he recognized as one of Roxi's.

Not bothering to get up, he crawled to the next door, and put his ear up to it, then moved to the next one. Finally! He pulled the crossbars off and set them aside. Casting a quick prayer to Selene, he lifted the flap, ducking his head in.

"Roxi," he whispered.

The women he'd spent the last several months with sat in the corner, her knees tugged up to her chest and her arms wrapped around them, as her head hung down. She rocked as she sang the words to a sad song, tears staining the words.

"Roxi," he spoke louder. "It's me, Roxi."

She lifted her head and looked through the sheets of her shaggy black hair and screamed, trying to push herself through the wall.

"Roxi, I've come to get you out. It's Luke."

Once she stopped trying to escape through the back wall, she sat back down, breathing heavily. "Luke?"

"Roxi, come here. I'm with friends. They're breaking us out. We have to go," Luke pleaded, hoping to break through to her. He could understand. He'd nearly lost what was left of his grip on reality when she'd been missing. The last thing she saw in the arena was people taking him away, away from her. "Please, Roxi."

She crawled toward him until she was nearly within arm's reach. He wanted to reach out to her and pull her into his arms, but he was afraid he'd spook her and send her scrambling back into the depths of her cell. She lifted one arm and slowly moved it toward Luke's face. At the last moment, she paused then pushed a trembling finger into his cheek. Once he didn't disappear, she placed her palm on his cheek.

"You're real…"

"I'm real. We need to go, Roxi." He pulled his head out and looked back at his friends. "Can you hold the flap door up?"

Delilah walked up and pushed it against the door, then lowered a hook into a loop to secure the door. "There ya go, buddy."

He wasn't thinking clearly. Roxi's presence robbed him of the little clarity he'd achieved after Selene's healing and draining some vampires. Without the door propped on his head and back, he reached through the flap door. Roxi extended her arms and Luke took them, gently pulling her out the flap door. Once she was out, she collapsed into Luke's arms, sobbing. He held her tightly, caressing her hair as she cried into his neck.

"Ma'am, there's something in this other cell too." Jimmy pointed to the last cell in the hall.

A mangy dog's head poked out of the flap, its hair a matted mess, sticking out in all directions in mats and filthy strands. As he crawled out, patches of missing fur exposed rashy skin and too many ribs. His tongue lolled out as his tail wagged weakly.

While Luke had been trying to coax Roxi out, Jimmy and the wolves had been opening the flap doors to ensure they were actually empty. Hearing the commotion, the dog must have decided to see what was up.

"Why is there a mangy old dog down here?" Delilah asked.

"Did he pee on the wrong vampire's leg?" Rhonda asked, standing naked with her arms folded over chest after she shifted from her bipedal wolf.

Jimmy, staring at the dog, shook his head and shrugged.

After the dog cleared the flap door, he rolled over onto his side, exposing his belly, his tail swishing slowly back and forth.

"At least he doesn't seem aggressive," Delilah said.

Luke turned his lips toward Roxi's ear. "Can you stand? We need to go."

She nodded, reluctantly peeling herself away from Luke. He rose and offered both his hands to help her. She squeaked in pain as he levered her up, hopping on one leg until Luke steadied her.

"Can you put any weight on the other leg?" Luke asked.

She delicately put the foot down and nearly collapsed when she tried.

"Someone is going to have to carry her, Luke," Delilah said, walking toward him.

Roxi shrunk away from the strangers. Hoping he'd drained enough vampires and that Selene's strength would hold, he squatted down and scooped her into his arms. She wrapped her arms around his neck, clinging to him tightly without chocking him.

"Are you sure this is a good idea, Luke?" Delilah asked.

"No, but we have to get out of here." Luke adjusted her to secure his grip on the woman.

Delilah nodded and pointed toward the stairs. "Ramon, help

Luke if he needs it." She took a few steps forward and turned back to the dog. "Are you coming?"

The dog got up a bit unsteadily and moved toward the group. Delilah and Rhonda, back in her wolf form, took the lead while the rest split up so Luke, Roxi, and Jimmy were in the middle. The dog trailed behind, his nails clicking on the stone floor. By the time they reached the stairs, Luke's lungs and legs burned from carrying the slight woman, but he didn't complain. When they found a couple of the vampire bodies they'd left, Luke set Roxi down.

Pulling his rudis, he stabbed one and drained it, feeling a bit of the burn leave his limbs. When he skewered the second one, he guided Roxi to it, helping her get set up. She spoke the incantation, the same one Luke has spoken so many times over the last two millennia. When nothing happened, she collapsed to the side, her sobbing renewed. Luke quickly drained the second vamp, then scooped her up again. He'd hoped his would work for her. Maybe they'd have to try it again, just in case.

They ran into more of their allies the closer they got to their exit point, pulling the six who were still holding the stairwell. Delilah sent them to the middle to reload, assigning teammates with more ammo to bring up the rear and keep the vamps from rushing them from behind.

Soon, it was a flood of werewolves running out of the arena. Luke could see the light of the moon ahead—they were nearly out. Sweat poured down his forehead, but he didn't have a spare hand or arm to wipe it away.

"We're almost out, Roxi," he whispered.

The woman had gone silent in his arms, the only movement her shallow breathing. She'd calmed some as they wound their way out. They hadn't made any stops after the first pair of vampires. The bodies they'd left had been staked by their allies.

"Go!" someone screamed from behind. "Incoming! Lots!"

Luke stepped to the side, letting his squad mates move to the back. They opened fire, sending up a din of shotgun blasts met with screams and small arms fire. After the first shot, Roxi trembled in his arms, squeaking and clasping tightly around his neck. The stop in momentum to get out of the way had robbed him of forward progress as he struggled to move again. Every muscle in his body screamed.

As the wolves in front of him climbed up the rubble leading out of the corridor and out of the arena, Luke's lungs heaved in and out, trying to get air to his burning muscles. He wasn't out yet, as he tried to ignore the shouts of his team behind him fighting a running retreat as they covered the withdrawal. Luke focused on putting one foot in front of the other, escaping the arena with Roxi his only objective. They'd gone through months of hell in this arena. They'd survived fire and death. Now they were nearly walking in the free light of the moon and whatever waited beyond.

CHAPTER
TWENTY-THREE

As Luke caught his breath while waiting for the path ahead to clear, something oppressive touched around the edge of his awareness, niggling at his brain like the beginnings of a rash he couldn't quite reach to scratch. Turning to look down the corridor they'd just run down and where his friends were holding off a surge of vampires, the deepest recesses pulled his eyes in, robbing them of light. He shook his head and focused. One by one, the overhead lights blinked out, exploding in showers of sparks. When the sparks faded, the area they'd illuminated seemed darker than dark—unreasonably dark considering there were still lights running down the section of the corridor closest to the exit the team had blasted into the arena wall. It looked like a wall of vantablack creeping down the corridor, undulating from the edges to the middle. The longer he stared, the more he thought it faintly rotated counterclockwise like someone had opened a star gate into the deepest darkest corner of the unknown universe. And it was now advancing toward them. Before it, the vampires fled, their organization crumbling, heedless of the werewolves blocking their paths with steel, silver, and wood.

Inside, sheer terror warred with his impulse to wall off his emotions and analyze the new threat. Instead of going one way or the other, his mind ground to a halt at the enormity of staring down the maw of a sentient black hole.

"Luke…" Delilah said. "Luke."

"Yeah, I see it. Get our people out of there. The vampires are more scared of whatever that is than us. Tell them to cease fire and run!" Luke ordered.

Delilah pulled out a whistle on a string and blew it sharply three times. "Full retreat! Disengage, and retreat." She emphasized it with three more blasts of the whistle.

Luke started up the rubble pile, slipping over the rocks while trying to keep Roxi safe in his arms. To his right, someone gave a little yip, wrapped a strong arm around his back, and propped his right elbow in a clawed paw. Ramon had stepped in to help so Luke could carry Roxi. When they reached the top, Luke cut across the open land toward the line of hills used to approach the arena earlier.

Exhausted and weak, he struggled with his reptilian brain to keep control. It wanted him to drop his burdens and flee before the hungering maw, to run until his heart exploded. Instead, he stopped and turned, his jaw clenching as he stared back into the ragged hole in the wall. The first hints of the horror slithered out, its tentacles absorbing the light of the stars and moon and darkening the surrounding area.

Ramon yipped again, and tried to tug at Luke's elbow, but not enough to drag him or unbalance him. His friends poured out of the entrance to the arena, trying to outpace the creeping entity pursuing them. Delilah stood at the entrance waving her arm in a circle, encouraging her teammates. When she judged the last one out, she tore off after them, pelting toward Luke. Soon after Delilah had sprinted away, vampires piled out of the hole, tripping and shoving and pulling each other down to get away from whatever was coming down that corridor.

"Luke! Run, fool!" Delilah yelled. "Ramon, take the girl. Luke, give her to him."

The slithering pressure in the back of his awareness throbbed dully, expanding and contracting, seeking. Finally, Delilah's words sank in.

Luke kissed Roxi's forehead quickly. "Roxi, I need to give you to Ramon. He'll take care of you."

She nodded quickly. Ramon held out his arms as Luke transferred Roxi into his gentle grasp. As soon as she latched her arms around the werewolf's neck, he turned and sprinted away. Delilah grabbed Luke's arm and tugged him after her. He tripped and stumbled, trying to get his exhausted legs under control. Digging deep, he went in search of his last reserves, finding them nearly empty, but the desolate presence, pushing aside all other concerns, prodded his legs forward. He'd nearly used up the bit of strength Selene had spared for him. He turned his head, looking over his shoulder. Where they'd blasted holes through the arena's ceiling the previous night, the light-eating darkness rose like an inky steam, blotting out the bright stars from the sky.

He didn't have enough energy left to scream, nor did his teammates as they found a new gear, running at a dead sprint. When they put the first hill between them and the arena, they kept running as fast as their legs would allow them to—too fast for the dark night with only a thin crescent moon and stars to light the rough terrain. The longer they ran, the further behind Luke lagged, his body depleted of everything. As he rounded another hill, he could see the light of their camp ahead. A shadow emerged from the light, running back toward him. As it got closer, it resolved into Delilah.

"Luke, come on," she said, sliding in next to him and helping him along.

When they made it into the circle of their camp, it was a hive of activity as everyone loaded weapons. He hunched when a rifle shot cracked into the night, followed by a second.

"We have Jung-sook and another sniper watching the approach to the road. Don't want any uninvited guests deciding to pay us a call," Delilah said by way of explanation.

"Roxi?" Luke asked between gasps for air.

"Ramon took her to Maggie," Delilah replied.

Luke nodded and followed Delilah as best as he could as she made her way to the forward command post. When they rounded the hill along the side of the road leading up to the arena, they found Sam staring through a pair of binoculars.

"What's going on?" Delilah asked.

"I don't know. It's…scary," Sam replied.

Someone stepped up and handed Luke and Delilah their own binoculars. The darkness hovered around at the hole in the side of the arena. A few figures streamed out, scrambling desperately over the rubble and debris, trying to escape. As soon as a few tried to break out of the growing darkness, they floated into the air, lifted by the invisible force. Once they left the ground, they let out an unholy screech of agony and despair. Luke could see them physically losing mass as something drained their stolen life essence before pitching the dried-out husks to the ground. Soon, nothing escaped the pulsing shadow as it drained everything trying to flee the arena.

"Whatever it is has been destroying every creature that's come out of there since you all made it out." Sam's voice trembled.

"We need to get everyone loaded up and moving before whatever that is decides to come see who's been causing all the ruckus." Delilah pulled the binoculars away from her eyes and turned around to issue orders.

Sam turned to flag her down. "Delilah, we've moved space around to get the hunters and thralls out of here."

"Where'd we find the space?" Delilah asked.

"We're stacking them in the back of every pickup. We've moved out any extra ammo and weapons, so the beds are open." Sam returned her attention to the arena.

It had been a minute since the last vampire had attempted to flee the arena only to be drained by the entity. Without anything else to do, it seeped out like a rolling fog, but thicker and oilier. Advancing slowly, more and more darkness poured out of the arena until it began shrinking and coalescing into something more corporeal in the middle.

"Delilah," Sam yelled back into the camp.

A minute later, she jogged up to join them. "What's going on?"

"That evil fog is condensing into something—or someone," Sam replied.

It didn't seem to be in a hurry as it pulled the edges of its mass in toward the solidifying form in the center. As the entity grew, the wider, more translucent mass shrunk, turning into something about six or seven feet tall and about two or three feet wide. When the form in the middle absorbed the last of the outer mass, Luke could still see through it, but only shapes and shadows as it flexed and contracted until it finished solidifying. In its place stood a tall, thin man with a long gray beard that reached down nearly to the belt of his black cassock. His long gray hair fluttered in the cold night wind of the Absaroka Mountains.

"Holy shit..." Luke muttered.

"Do you recognize...him?" Sam was unsure how to refer to the being that had formed out inky darkness.

"Yeah. In Portland, not long after we met—on the St. Johns Bridge. He came to collect Cassius's body before I could kill him." Luke tried to moisten his mouth, dry from dehydration and fear.

Someone thrust a bottle of water at him. He took it and popped the top, taking a big swig. "Thanks."

The man lifted one hand up to shoulder height, rubbed his thumb over the ends of his fingernails as he inspected them then lowered his hand, clasping them both behind his back. Strolling forward, he looked about casually, as if he were enjoying a pleasant walk through the park. When his eyes ran over the various vampire husks he'd created, his body gave a small shake, as if he'd just chuckled.

"Who or what is he?" Delilah asked.

"I don't know," Luke replied. "All I know is I saw him in Portland, and he speaks Latin with what I think is a Dacian accent. That and he's a spooky bastard—"

"Spooky?" Sam said, her voice rising. "Spooky? That was fucking terrifying."

"I guess I should say, I thought he was spooky then." He took another drink of water, attempting to wash away the taste of fear clinging thickly in his throat. He nodded nervously. "Terrifying is a more accurate term at this point."

"We can figure out how to describe him later. He's walking right at us." Delilah shuffled nervously, kicking a rock her foot bumped into. "What are we going to do? Can we run away?"

"From something that can turn into a gas or whatever it is?" Sam asked.

Luke drained the rest of the water bottle and handed it off to whoever was standing nearby. *"Selene, my mistress? Do you know what that is?"*

"No, but it's wrong, very wrong."

"Luke? What do we do?" Sam asked.

"Get everyone loaded up who can't hold a shotgun. Make sure we're loaded with silver shot. If you have some that's heavier silver, use that. I want everyone to stay back until I signal." Luke set his hand on the unfamiliar hilt of Roxi's Parthian sword.

Taking a deep breath, he stepped around the corner of the hill and into the middle of the road. He tripped over a rock and nearly lost his balance but caught himself before going down. His body was exhausted, but he'd have to ask a bit more of it.

"Oh for fuck's sake, Luke. What are you doing?" Delilah asked. "You can't go out there."

Luke's forward progress startled himself too, but he ignored Delilah, straightening his back and striding forward.

"Get your ass back here. You're in no shape to fight whatever the fuck that is!" Delilah called after him.

"Dee, let him go. We've got to get everyone loaded up and ready. Now," Sam said.

Behind him, he heard his friends issuing orders, which caused more voices to join the growing cacophony as the camp sprang into action.

Seeing someone had emerged from the camp, the being stopped in the middle of the road, watching Luke. He gripped the handle of the sword. The circumference of the handle felt a bit smaller than his, like the hand that normally gripped it. Thoughts of Roxi's hand in his tugged the corners of his lips slightly. He'd managed to get her out. Now he had to secure their release.

Luke debated whether to draw his sword or not, deciding to

leave it sheathed. He could have it out quick enough. When thirty yards separated him from the being, he stopped.

"Who are you?" Luke asked in English. It seemed the best place to start.

"Centurio? What are you doing here?" The man's voice seemed higher than the last time they'd spoken. "Were you a guest at my children's little arena?" He casually waved to the arena behind him.

Luke wasn't expecting the light and airy way the man spoke and acted. The man he'd met on the St. Johns Bridge felt ominous. Dangerous. This man had terrified those he'd called his children, yet seemed to be chatting at a cocktail party. The incongruity unnerved Luke, increasing his wariness as he narrowed his eyes.

"I wouldn't say I was a guest so much as a prisoner of your *chil-dren*," Luke replied. "I repeat, who are you?"

"Who I am is of little import. It is you who I'm curious about. Of all those set against my will, you have been the most burdensome — killing my children, thwarting my plans, setting back my efforts. I thought if my agents got you kicked out of the empire, it would have left a free path to the greatest resources in the west…"

Luke's mind ground to a halt at the claim. "So you've been pulling the puppet strings for all these centuries?"

If what this man claimed was true, he wondered how much of his life had been manipulated by this being directing the vampires.

A high-pitched cackle escaped into the night. "You must think bigger than that. I am not some puppet master. I am… What do the Christians say about their little stick god? Ah yes… To the vampire, I am the alpha and the omega. I am where all things begin and all things end. Alpha and Omega sound so much more impressive, though mortals are easily impressed with old things and the Hellenic alphabet is quite old. Could you imagine if I said it with the Canadian alphabet? 'The Eh and the Zed?' How ridiculous would that be?"

Amused by his own joke, he cackled again. Luke, his brain already slow, had trouble comprehending what was going on. This being had just claimed to be the god of the vampires while making terrible jokes.

"My mistress, he claims to be the god of the vampires."

"He does not feel like Ahura Mazda's counterpart..." Selene avoided speaking the name Ahriman, the creator of the vampire.

The being allowed time for Luke to join him in laughter, but when Luke didn't, he continued. "But what am I to do with you? I cannot have you destroying my works. Creating rebellion among my first born. You would be a most welcome addition to my cause, a true general. Together, we could usher in a glorious future where my creatures dominate the earth, and feast upon what they will, free from the tyranny of petty hunters and masters of destruction such as yourself. What say you, Centurio? Will you put aside your hatred of my children and lead them?"

Luke's wobbly knees almost betrayed him at the offer of the immensely powerful being standing in front of him. "How can I join you if I don't know who you are?"

He cackled again. "Skeptical and wise." He unclasped his hands from behind him and gestured, presenting his body to Luke. "For a while, this body was Vezinas, advisor to Decebalus of Dacia. That was a fun time. Your Trajan did quite well at countering our thrusts. Before that, during this flesh's first time walking the earth, I was known as Zalmoxis. Did you know I was a student of Pythagoras before I became a god? For what else would you call a man who died and was resurrected three years later?"

Zalmoxis straightened his arms, sticking them out to the side with his palms facing Luke, and lowered his chin, tilting his head to the side—the pose reminiscent of the crucifixion. When he got no response from Luke, he straightened and shrugged, placing his hands behind his back again.

"What say you?" He extended a hand. "Join me?"

"No." His left hand on the pommel, he slid it down, grasping the scabbard, and reached across with his right hand and drew the sword. "I have no interest in serving the master of the vile creatures who steal souls from humans. Be gone and return to your sniveling, conniving parasites. I want nothing to do with either you or them."

Zalmoxis shook his head slowly. "So short sighted." He looked up and past Luke. "Ah, I see we have more visitors. I sense power. Perhaps one of them will feel differently." Squinting, something he saw drew an evil smirk to his lips. "I see you've found my wayward pet."

Luke dared not look back, not wanting to take his attention off Zalmoxis.

"We come, my brave soldier," Selene said. *"Hold your place."*

"Since you do not wish the carrot, perhaps the stick may guide the choice of others," Zalmoxis said.

The Dacian god, if he was indeed who he claimed to be, extend his hand out, palm down, and flicked his fingers up and out.

Pure, unadulterated darkness plowed into Luke, freezing his body in place. His jaw stretched open as a terrible scream ripped from his throat. One by one, as if he were frozen in a stasis so he could feel each, his wounds opened slowly, all traces of healing Selene and the vampires had provided dissolving and steaming from the open wounds. When Zalmoxis finished, Luke collapsed into a heap, moaning piteously.

Pain radiated from every inch of his body, yet he couldn't pass out and seek the embrace of unconsciousness. Zalmoxis still had hold of his mind, forcing him to feel every excruciating detail of all the pain he'd absorbed over the last several weeks and more.

"Unhand him, foul creature!" Selene's voice sounded throughout the area, vibrating off the mountains and through Luke's mind.

A wolf, larger than any Luke had ever seen, stepped up next to Luke, growling low and dangerously.

"Foul creature? My pet there has become quite foul indeed." He clucked his tongue and shook his head.

The wolf looked mangy, covered in mats with bald spots taking more space than fur. Each rib poked out through his skin, his body emaciated and sickly. Yet, his teeth gleamed sharp and deadly, his growl furious and potent.

Around Luke, on both sides, dozens of shotguns pumped, loading shells into firing chambers.

"Hold your fire, my children," Selene said, standing tall in the center of the advancing line of werewolves. "Creature, you may not have him."

"Why?" Zalmoxis reached out his hand and squeezed it into a fist.

Agony tore through Luke's body as he screamed, his vocal cords ripping apart. More pain than he'd ever felt before decimated his body as every nerve fiber in his body burned with fire and electricity. His muscles cramped into one solid mass. Yet Zalmoxis kept his grip firmly on Luke's consciousness, preventing Luke from escaping.

Around him, gentle silver light flowed, illuminating the gravel until it seeped into his skin, soothing the agony, turning it down from bright white-hot torture to a dull cherry red.

"Now!" Selene cried.

As one, the shotguns belched fire, silver, and wood into the night sky. And like that, Zalmoxis's control disappeared, releasing Luke. The evil god blinked back into his incorporeal, oily, dark cloud as silver and wood flew through him. Luke thought the cloud pulsed and jolted as the shots hit it. Zalmoxis must have decided he was done with them for the moment, the oily cloud roiling and rolling toward the arena.

The shotguns stopped firing since the cloud appeared to be retreating. The great mangy wolf ceased its growling, its tongue lolling out in a wolfy grin. Luke wasn't sure if his eyes played a trick on him, but the wolf seemed to shift into the dog they'd found imprisoned with them.

"Reload," Delilah called out.

Someone sank down next to Luke and gently lifted his head, cradling it in their lap.

"Oh, my poor Luke," Maggie said, tears falling from her cheeks, one of them landing on his forehead.

He couldn't say anything, sure his voice had been destroyed in the screaming. As the oily cloud slunk away and slithered down into the hole in the arena, eventually disappearing, the stars above twinkled brighter without the malevolent force driving their light away.

The suffocating weight of Zalmoxis's presence lessened until it disappeared from Luke's mind. The mangy dog turned around and snuffled over Luke's body.

Maggie extended an arm and tried to swat it away. "Go away, you…"

Selene reached down and placed her hand on Maggie's shoulder. "Let him. Trust me, my child. I have a feeling."

Maggie lowered her hand and used it to stroke Luke's head. The mangy wolf resumed his snuffling, sniffing up Luke's wounded body until they were nose to nose. His tongue lolling out, the wolf licked his face from the tip of his nose to the top of his forehead, then laid down, resting his head next to Luke's on Maggie's leg.

"The bleeding is stopping," Maggie said, shocked.

Luke's pain receded to a dull roar, bring with it some relief. Selene's head snapped up and looked toward the arena.

"You must flee, my children. Now!" Urgency stained Selene's voice as she stood up. "Someone pick up Lucius and the wolf."

"Can't the wolf walk back? He got here alright," someone said.

"He's not faring much better than Lucius," Selene said. "Hurry!"

"You heard her! Ramon, pick up Luke and get him to the ambulance. Ahmed, grab the wolf. Everyone else, move out! Let's get off this mountain," Delilah ordered.

Ramon, in his bipedal wolf form, bent over and scooped up Luke gently and started back toward their caravan. Luke's head flopped to the side, his eyes pointing backwards. He had no idea why the entity had fled from them after ripping Luke to shreds, and his brain had lost its ability to function enough to do more than tamp back the edges of his terror. The dark, oily cloud rose ominously from all the holes blown in the arena, pulsing and throbbing in the night sky.

The air around the arena expanded and shrunk with the pulsing of Zalmoxis's smoke until it contracted violently, ripping the arena down with it like a kraken had risen from below and pulled down a mighty ship.

The air went dead still and silent, then exploded violently as the stones of the arena were expelled into the sky. The shock wave knocked down several people and drove Ramon to his knees as he cradled Luke. A moment later, Ramon surged to his feet and took off at a run, deciding speed was more important than gentleness. Stones of various sizes, gravity reclaiming them, thudded to the earth around where the arena had been.

He heard a scream of pain, followed by others yelling to summon help. Then, again, screeches of pain, and calls for aid. Other screams of terror filled the air as they fled from the entity and the falling stones. When the hills that blocked their camp from the arena bounced by, Luke knew he was close to Maggie's ambulance.

"Ramon, set him on the gurney gently," Maggie ordered. "Patrice, get me plasma. O-positive."

Maggie ripped open an alcohol pad and carefully wiped down a spot below the inside of his elbow. In another second, she had an IV line placed.

"Ramon, put the gurney in the ambulance, then get to your escape vehicle," Maggie said.

Some more jostling, and the ceiling of the ambulance appeared above Luke. Maggie pulled some straps over his legs, waist, and chest, securing him to the gurney. Next, she locked it down, hung the plasma from a hook, and fixed the line to Luke's IV line.

"Luke?" It sounded like Roxi's voice, but weaker and strained.

He turned his head toward her voice, letting gravity take over once he'd moved far enough. Like him, Roxi was strapped to a gurney with an IV bag hanging above her. He tried to smile weakly but had no idea if he'd managed to move his lips. He couldn't speak.

"Luke, I'm going to give you a little something for the pain, but I don't want to give you anything too strong in your condition," Maggie said.

"Maggie, do you need me to ride back here with you?" Patrice asked.

"No, but ride in the passenger seat. If I need you, we can stop. It looks like his wounds have stopped bleeding miraculously. I don't know how, but I can clean and close them on the road."

Patrice stepped into the van—reaching past him—and squeezed Maggie's shoulder before existing and walking around the ambulance. Then the weight shifted, and a door closed. All around them, cars and trucks fired up, crunching on the gravel as they got moving.

His pain receding further with the addition of the pain meds, his eyes drifted lower until they closed, sending Luke into a semi-conscious twilight.

Luke rocked on his gurney, partially aware as the ambulance tore down the mountain with their caravan. Despite the rocking, Maggie's hands felt steady and secure as she cleaned his wounds and closed them with butterfly bandages.

Seeing him dozing in and out of awareness, Maggie kept up a running commentary. "When we get somewhere safe, I'll inspect everything, then stitch him up."

"Will he be alright?" Roxi asked.

Luke realized she wasn't commenting for his benefit, but talking with Roxi.

"I think so. He's tough, and he doesn't quit. Without any vampires to drain, he'll have to heal naturally, at least until he can find some. Though I suspect his natural healing is better than a regular human's…" Maggie said.

"Yeah, that I know," Roxi said. "I see they found my sword. Do you know if they found my rudis?"

"I don't know. I wasn't part of the rescue party. I didn't see what all they brought back, other than you and the other hunters."

"How many did they free?" Roxi asked.

"Only three. I guess they caught the vampires in the middle of killing the others," Maggie replied.

"I'm glad your people at least got them out…and me," Roxi said.

"Well, that should hold him for now." Maggie pulled a blanket over Luke, tucking it under his chin. Maggie unlocked her stool and rolled to the wall separating the bay of the ambulance from the front seats and transferred to a jump seat, buckling herself in. "You're from London, aren't you?"

"Yeah, I've lived there for a long time. How did you know?" Roxi replied.

"Your accent. I lived in London before moving to the United States. I met my partner in London."

"You're Maggie, aren't you?" Roxi asked.

"Mhm. How did you know?"

"Luke talked about you; his description was pretty accurate. Pretty, blond, Polish accent, kind eyes. You are a lucky woman."

"Thank you. You should try to get some sleep," Maggie replied.

"Sorry, I'm a nervous talker, and I've been stuck in a tiny cell for months, and I don't like windy roads."

Maggie chuckled. "That's understandable. I'm not fond of these roads myself. If you start to feel some motion sickness, let me know."

Roxi started humming one of her melodies quietly, probably to manage her nervousness about everything. The soothing tones worked better than the drugs Maggie had given him, putting him the rest of the way to sleep.

LUKE WOKE to the sound of a heart monitor. It took him a while to force his eyes open, afraid he'd find himself in his cell and everything that had happened was just a dream. But would it be a bad dream? He'd suffered enough against dark terrors for it to qualify as a nightmare, but at the end of it had been Maggie and Roxi and freedom. Instead, he found himself in a small hospital room.

When he opened his eyes to a find a room he'd never been in before with a window opening out to the world, he grew hopeful that it had all been real and he was free. Grievously wounded, but free.

"And he wakes," Pablo said nearby.

Squinting, Luke turned his head toward the sound. As his eyes adjusted to the light, Pablo's form clarified. His best friend sat in a chair, his back leaned up against the wall and his legs stretched out in front of him, a book in his hands.

"Hi," Luke tried to say. It hurt. Even speaking that much felt like razors running down his throat.

"Try not to talk too much, buddy. Maggie says your voice will take a while to recover from the screaming. That dude fucked you up pretty badly." Pablo sounded relieved.

"Phone?" he mouthed, pantomiming a phone to his ears with his pinky and thumb extended.

"I don't know if we have yours here. I guess you can type on the screen and show it to me, at least until we find a phone for you to use." Pablo stood up and picked up his chair, moving it to the head of the bead near Luke so he could sit and they could hand the phone back and forth. "I'm glad you're awake. I really missed you."

Luke made grabby hands at Pablo.

"Oh, here." Pablo handed him his phone, opening it and bringing up a notes app.

I missed you too, Pablo. I thought about you a lot. He tipped the phone to Pablo so he could read the screen.

"That's sweet. How do you feel?"

Like shit. I hurt all over. Where are we?

Pablo chuckled. "I bet you do, buddy. We're currently guests of the Wind River Reservation, courtesy of Owen's friends."

How is everyone else doing? Anyone hurt?

"We had a few broken bones from stones falling and one death. That was bonkers. I've never seen anything like that before. I'm still having nightmares about it." Pablo shivered. "Gives me the willies just thinking about it. Who was that?"

I don't know, not really. He claimed to be Zalmoxis. Seeing Pablo's confusion, he elaborated. *A god to the Dacians and Getae. But I don't know. He felt…wrong. Evil. I'm going to have to think about it. Where's Maggie?*

Pablo chuckled. "Nice way to change the subject. She's out

getting a bite to eat. We've all been taking shifts with you so she could get a break and you'd always have company."

Why? I'm not great company right now.

"She didn't want you to be alone, not after being alone in a cell for so long. She wanted to make sure there'd be someone here for you when you woke up. I just got to be the lucky one that you woke up to. Why don't you ask the question you want to?"

Luke shook his head, giving Pablo a weak smile. *Is Roxi OK?*

"Yeah. She's got a pretty bad limp right now, is using crutches to get around. Maggie says she'll be fine—says she's like you, drains vampires to heal."

Good.

Pablo looked around, making sure no one was headed into the room. "Is there something going on with you two? The way you two clung to each other was…pretty intense. When it's her turn to take a watch—she insisted even if she wasn't much better off than you—she always holds your hand and sings or hums to you."

We were all we had in there. She was literally the only person I could trust. I'd have lost my marbles if it wasn't for her. The last few weeks before you rescued us were…intense on a lot of levels. Being able to get her out of there…

"I'm here if you want to talk about it." Pablo reached out and squeezed Luke's hand.

When I can talk, we'll sit down and talk it out. I promise. I need to, but I need to think about it when my mind is actually clear enough to do it.

Pablo chuckled. "So, looks like we picked up another misfit for your ragtag band of ne'er-do-wells?"

I hope so.

"Well, if she's even half as good as you are, she'll be a welcome addition, unless we have to spend all our time keeping her out of trouble like we do you." Pablo smirked, a twinkle in his eyes.

I'm sure she'll be easier to work with. I think she's a bit more low key than I am. I guess I don't know, though, not outside of our prison cells.

The door opened and a din of voices poured into the room as people jostled to get through the door. A blur pushed through the group and nearly flopped on top of Luke, pulling back at the last moment to give him a gentle hug.

It took him a moment to realize the skinny teen sobbing into his hospital gown was Gwen. He still felt weak, but he lifted the arm not hooked up to lines and dropped it across her back. He patted it, wanting to tell her how much he'd missed her. He thought about risking it, but when he opened his mouth, Maggie smiled and shook her head.

"I missed you so much, Luke." Gwen squeezed him.

Maggie walked up and took Gwen by the shoulders. "Luke's still weak, Gwen. And he can't talk. He hurt his vocal cords and throat pretty bad."

Gwen pulled herself back and stood up, squeezing Luke's hand. Once he was free, he picked up the phone and typed in a message for Gwen.

I missed you so much, little one. I'm so happy to see you. He looked her up and down. *You're not so little anymore.*

Gwen had grown several inches since he'd last seen her. He hoped she fared well in his absence, though he was sure Zel and Maggie had done an excellent job raising her. One by one, his friends came up to touch him and welcome him back to the world of living. He wished he could get up to hug and talk to them, but he'd have to make do with listening to them converse, just basking in being among friends.

One person he didn't see, and missed, was Roxi. Maybe now that she was free, she didn't want to see him.

Sam, always observant, slipped through the crowd as everyone talked, happy to be together with their friend, rescued and alive-ish. She bent over and placed her lips near his ears. "She said she'd be in later to see you. I don't think she's very comfortable with us yet."

Luke nodded and mouthed, "thank you." While it soothed the burning worry, he still wished she were there with them. He'd long lost track of the thread of the conversation going on around him when a knock on the door silenced everyone. They turned to see who it was. Owen, a broad grin on his face, poked his head inside.

"Hey, Luke. Nice of you to grace us with your presence," Owen said.

Luke waved with the hand unencumbered with IV lines.

"My friends and I have a little present for you." Owen stepped through the door and made way for three others to join them.

Like Owen, the three people were Indigenous, though he guessed they were probably not members of the Coastal Pack—he didn't recognize them from the various times he'd met them—or the Chinook tribe Owen belonged to.

Owen started with the woman. "This is Kelly Brown."

"Hello." Kelly waved, smiling. She stood about five foot seven and had long, straight, dark brown hair and a light brown complexion. She wore tight, faded jeans, cowboy boots, and a black and red plaid shirt.

Owen stepped up to a man who was even taller than he was. "This is John Sleeping Bear."

John nodded. He wore a straw cowboy hat with the brim folded up tight to the crown along the sides, along with a tight black T-shirt that showed off a muscular physique and a pair of jeans and cowboy boots. His brown complexion was tanned darker. His hair was long and black; he wore it braided down his back.

Owen slid his arm around the last man's shoulders. He was by far the shortest, probably about five-five. He had a wispy black mustache and a goofy smile that paired well with his picture T, baggie jeans, and black Chuck Taylor high tops.

"This is Ronnie Smiles, also known as Grinning Ron," Owen said.

Ronnie gave a two-handed wave. "Heyo!"

The room smiled, waved, and said hello.

"Don't worry, they're all werewolves. You can speak freely," Owen added.

"Is Smiles really your last name?" Gwen asked.

"No, it's Chavez. Ronnie Smiles is just a nickname." Ron spoke quickly, managing to talk around his eponymous smile.

"I'll have to speak on Luke's behalf for now," Pablo said, "since his voice is jacked up. What's the gift?"

John spoke first, his voice deep and rich. "A few of those fangy bastards that've been sneaking around our land made the mistake of crossing onto the reservation. He said..." He hitched his thumb toward Owen. "You might be able to help us dispose of them properly."

"Hopefully, they're not too lively. I'm not sure he's up to running them down right now." Sam stared at Owen, her eyes narrowed in suspicion.

Kelly laughed, shaking her head. "Probably a good thing to check on with this joker, but in this case, they're not doing much moving anymore."

Ronnie made a wet, slicing noise and dragged his finger over his throat.

"Excellent. Not that Luke talks a lot anyway, but it would be nice if he could talk some. How are you situated for drains?" Pablo asked.

"Not sure we want to wash that down the drain. I've got a backhoe. We'll dig a trench, then bury the mess. They're not toxic, are they?" Kelly looked between Pablo and Luke.

No. Once the vampire magic leaves the body, they dissolve into organic matter. It'll be fine. Luke showed the phone to Pablo. *If we're free to do it now, per approval from Maggie, let's get it done. I can't be confined to this bed.*

"Maggie? Can we take him outside and vamp him up?" Pablo asked.

"Sure. If someone can find the wheelchair, we can roll him outside and we can do it the way we did after Timberline." Maggie took down the IV bag and set it next to Luke.

Someone stepped out of the room and brought a wheelchair back in. Pablo solved the problem of moving Luke by simply scooping him up and setting him in it.

Wait. What about Roxi? Luke typed on Pablo's phone.

"What do you mean?"

She could probably use a vamp or two. I'm assuming we found her rudis in all the stuff we took. How many did they get? He didn't understand why everyone seemed uncomfortable about his questions.

"Ah, I understand," Pablo said. "How many did you get, Owen?"

"Five."

Luke waved Maggie over. *Is Roxi in better shape than me? How should we divide the vampires?*

Maggie turned to the room. "If you can give us some privacy?

Most of you have seen how Luke's rudis works, but I'm sure if our hosts are curious, Luke wouldn't mind your assistance with the bodies."

Gwen tried to slide up behind Luke and Pablo inconspicuously.

"You, young lady, may not see this," Maggie said.

"Ugh, fine," Gwen said, flopping onto the bed.

Luke could practically hear her roll her eyes with her groan of annoyance. He did his best to restrain his laughter to protect his throat and her dignity. A wave of sadness swept over him at how much she'd grown and how much he'd missed. He hoped he'd get some time to learn everything that had happened in her life since he'd been gone.

Owen and his friends filed out of the room and then down the hall to the exit. Pablo, Sam, and Delilah followed them out. Maggie followed them, pushing Luke in the wheelchair. She stopped halfway down the hall once the door to his room and the exit both closed. Squatting down in front of him, she took his hands.

"Luke, she's refusing to take any of the vampires. I couldn't get the reason from her, but she said you can take them all. I tried to convince her that a few would be enough to get you back in shape, but she was adamant. When you have your voice back, you can talk to her and find out what's going on for her."

Luke frowned but nodded, wondering why she would refuse something she needed to heal faster. He made to open his mouth, but Maggie put a couple fingers over his lips.

"You need to take these. If need be, you and the team can take her out and get a few more. Having both of you weakened does nobody any good."

Sighing, he nodded. Maggie squeezed his hands and pushed him out of the small clinic building into the parking lot, then around back to a sagebrush-covered field. Aiming for the backhoe, Maggie pushed him through the dirt and slalomed around the brush until they found the trench.

As soon as Maggie parked him nearby, Pablo and Owen grabbed a vampire from the back of a beat-up old pickup. Before they pulled it off the tailgate, Delilah stepped up with Luke's rudis and shoved it into the chest of the dead vamp. Together, Pablo and Owen held up the body while Maggie helped Luke get situated. Once Luke drained it, Pablo and Owen carried it to the edge of the pit. Delilah snagged the rudis, and the guys dropped it in to explode into a pool of reddish-black goo. Within a few quick minutes, they went through the remaining fangers. Luke, after three young vamps and two old vamps, felt like a new man, nearly. But it'd been so long since he'd felt one hundred percent, he wasn't even sure what that felt like anymore.

He braced to stand up, but Maggie placed a hand on his forearm.

"Let's stick with the wheelchair until we get back inside to level ground, just to be on the safe side."

"OK," he said, his voice raspy but not pained. "I'm thirsty."

"We'll get you something cold when we get inside," Maggie said, a smile spreading across her beautiful face. "How does your voice feel?"

Luke couldn't help but match Maggie's smile, the radiance of her relief palpable. "Not bad. Not painful."

"You sound like you've got a two-pack-a-day habit," Pablo said, smirking.

Luke laughed. "Hey, Dollface, would ya get me a pack of reds and a bottle of Jack?"

Pablo and Owen laughed while Maggie and Delilah shook their heads. But they smiled, indulging Luke and his moment of levity.

"Maggie? Do you think my throat's good enough to get some solid food? I'm suddenly famished now that I don't feel like death warmed over."

"Let me do a proper exam when we get inside, then we can discuss meals and drinks." She stepped around to the back of the wheelchair and pushed him back to the parking lot and the clinic while Kelly fired up the backhoe to bury their vampire mess.

Maggie wheeled him into an exam room and checked him out, determining that his throat looked good enough to handle solid food. Then, she removed his IV line and had him get up, helping to pull him out of the chair. His legs still felt weak and wobbly, but they would recover quickly with more rest and good food to fuel his body. He decided to sit down until he felt certain of his body.

"Luke, can I drop you off at Roxi's room to talk with her?" Maggie asked.

Luke nodded. "Of course, I'd like to see her anyway. After being the only face I saw for months on end, I miss her." He hoped he was able to hold the longing he felt from seeping into his voice.

"I'm glad you're feeling better. It hurts to see you in pain like that." She stroked his cheek.

"I'm sure my breath is dreadful, but I'd love a kiss. I've missed you so much, Maggie."

The longing and sadness in Maggie's eyes floored him, sending a surge of emotions through him and landing in his stomach. She leaned down, cupped his cheeks, and brushed a soft kiss over his lips before pressing her mouth against his, letting out a soft moan as she pulled him into the intense kiss. When she drew back, they both were left breathing heavily as she tipped her forehead against his.

"Luke, I was so scared I'd never see you again. I was so scared I'd lost you. I don't want to lose you…" The relief in her eyes was mixed with fear.

He reached up and pulled her in for an awkward hug due to the angle, but he clung to her tightly, nearly as tightly as she clung to him.

"I'll take you to Roxi now." Maggie stood up and pulled the door open, letting the magnetic hold click and hold it open.

Zel's words from the farm came back to him. "Please be gentle with Maggie's heart." He hoped Maggie wasn't scared of Roxi, afraid she'd take Luke away from her. He couldn't explain his feelings even to himself after being with her for over a year and relying on her presence so much, but he didn't want to be cruel with Maggie's heart. He still loved her. Seeing her again confirmed every feeling he'd experienced since he'd been forcibly taken from her.

"Ready?" Maggie asked.

Luke nodded. She pushed him out of the room and took a right instead of the left that would have led to his room. She left Luke outside and poked her head in, asking if it was OK to let Luke visit.

When she got Roxi's consent, she pushed the door open and rolled Luke in. Before she left, she leaned down and whispered into Luke's ear.

"I'll give you some privacy." She turned, closed a blind on the door's window, and left.

Being outside of their tightly contained world, Luke felt awkward with her lying in her hospital bed and himself sitting in a wheelchair. Roxi looked at him briefly, her eyes making contact before flitting somewhere else.

"Hi, Roxi. It's nice to see you outside in the real world."

She chuckled nervously. "Yeah. There's no stone wall separating us, or vampires, or werewolves trying to kill us so vampires can get their kicks."

Awkward silence followed and dominated for a while until Luke rolled forward and took her hand in his. "Roxi, why did you refuse the vampires? You need them as much as I do after being in there."

She looked away. A few moments later, she sniffed, her chest shaking lightly as she cried.

"Roxi, what's wrong?" he asked, when she refused to look his way.

Her other hand slipped under the covers and drew out something long, thrusting it toward him when it cleared the sheets tangling it up. Luke yanked back, his too tired body protesting. When she dropped it on the bed between, she pulled her hand from his and covered her face.

It was Roxi's rudis—charred black with cracks riddling the wood. The silver of the blade and the filigree was warped and blackened with a healthy dose of tarnish covering the spots not blackened. An ominous sense of wrongness rose from it in delicate tendrils. Reaching out to pick it up, he hesitated before forcing his hand onto it.

It not only felt lifeless, but dark and hungry, thirsting for things to corrupt and twist. He wrapped his other hand around the hilt of his rudis, tucked next to his thigh in the wheelchair. With the two connected, Luke's hands separated by his body, he could feel the angry war between their two essences. Some piece inside of himself, lingering from Zalmoxis's blast of darkness, called toward Roxi's warped rudis.

Something malevolent and ugly rose inside him, reaching toward the warped tool. He lifted the wooden blade from off the bed and heaved it away from himself and Roxi, sending it clattering into the wall and onto the floor. He kept hold of his rudis, letting its rightness push aside the darkness called upon by the warped rudis.

Once her rudis was tossed away, no longer nestled next to Roxi's body, she visibly relaxed, the tension leaving her body. With its influence diminished—though Luke could still feel its oily influence calling to him—her tears turned to sobs.

Locking the wheels of the chair, he pushed himself into a standing position. "Roxi, scoot over."

She wobbled her head in an affirmative and wiggled over to the edge of the narrow hospital bed. He climbed onto it and laid next to her on his side, pulling her quivering body close. He hummed the melody to the Gaulish song he'd sung to her all those weeks ago as he ran his hand gently over her messy hair. He gave her a kiss on the cheek, and she rolled onto her side, clinging to him fiercely.

When her tears calmed, she kissed Luke on the cheek and rolled onto her back. "Oh, Luke. What am I going to do without my rudis?"

The pain in her voice stabbed into Luke's heart. "I don't know, Roxi, but whatever we need to do, I'm here for you."

"Thank you, Luke, for getting that away from me. I couldn't do it. It called to me, wanted me to use it. It was trying to seduce me. It promised me dark things." Roxi shivered.

Luke shivered in response, feeling the same call from the twisted weapon. "We'll get it away from you and make sure it can't talk to you."

"Did you hear it? When you touched it, did it call to you?"

Luke nodded. "It did." He left it at that, needing to explore why something inside him had answered when it had called.

"I don't know what would have happened if I'd used it on one of the vampires your friend offered. It wanted me to do it. Wanted me to draw the essence from the vamp through it and into me. I can still feel it reaching toward me even now. Do you?" She sounded anxious and scared, clinging to Luke for comfort and reassurance.

"Almost. It's like a whisper in the breeze—I'm not quite sure if it's there, except the part of me that raises the hairs on the back of my neck."

"I tried to call to Mithras, but I didn't feel him call back," Roxi replied.

"We're not in lands he's ever walked through, and within the land of a people with their own practices. He may not be able to respond here. I have a shrine at my house. When we get to Portland, we'll see if he answers you there. If not, Selene can convey a message to him. She'll answer me."

Roxi took a deep breath and held it, and with it, the silence growing between them. When she next spoke, it was in a whisper Luke almost couldn't hear. "Do you still want me to come with you to Portland now that you have your friends and...and Maggie back?"

"Of course I do, Roxi. We've been through too much together to part now. Besides, it's too dangerous out there for hunters to try to go it on their own. We'll need to talk to the few we rescued from the arena to see if they'll join with us."

She lowered her face so Luke couldn't look into her eyes. "I was scared you'd not want to be...friends anymore, now that you were free and had everyone else."

He pulled her head closer and kissed the top of it. "Now that there aren't stone walls and armed vampires between us, we can be friends because we want to be, not as a survival tactic, though I never felt that we were kind to each other because of proximity and lack of options. I'm sad we never met until then."

"Me too." Roxi sighed, snuggling into Luke's shoulder. "Can we be real friends? Not just prison buddies?"

He chuckled. "I'd like that very much. How are you feeling, Roxi?"

Friend. It seemed like the easy word to say, the safe label to use, but it felt inadequate. The thought of Roxi choosing not to go back to Portland with him felt wrong as it tightened his chest. He tried to push the yawning pit closed before it pulled him in. Confusion filtered through his awareness as he tried to figure out how to place her in his life. Everything was too jumbled up with the hell of the prison and the softness of her lips.

"I feel weak, my leg hurts, and I'm tired of being in this room alone," Roxi replied.

"Would you like to meet everyone? Or have they come into introduce themselves yet?" Luke asked, stroking her hair.

"I met your girlfriend; she's been checking on me, got me topped up with fluids. She's very sweet and kind."

Someone knocked on the door, then Pablo poked his head in the door. "Hey, Luke. We got you a snack, but everyone's thinking about transferring our base down to the Shoshone Rose Casino. It's got a hotel and a restaurant. Plus, it gets us further away from any vamps hanging around the northern and eastern border of the reservation. Maggie says you're both good enough to travel, and she wants to free up the tribe's clinic. Hello, lady!" Pablo said the last words in his best Andre the Giant accent.

"Pablo, this is Roxi. Roxi, that's Pablo. He's my best friend and full-time sidekick." Luke grinned at his silly friend.

"Dude, everyone knows I'm the hero, and you're my plucky comic relief."

Chuckling, Luke shook his head. "I'm not sure I've ever been described as either plucky or comical."

"It's very nice to meet you, Pablo. Luke's told me a bit about you. I'd like to get out of here. I'm not a fan of hospitals of any kind." She looked down at her body. "Um, I don't have any clothes other than his hospital gown."

Pablo laughed. "Yeah, we burned your clothes from the prison. They were not pleasant. I'll see what we can figure out. There are enough people around here—we can get you some clothes that'll fit well enough. What size do you wear?"

Roxi shrugged. "Um, I don't know anymore. I lost a lot of weight in there, and I have no idea how American sizes even work."

"Hmm, I'll send in Sam or Delilah. They can help you out. Luke, you need help back to your room so you can put on some clothes?"

"Did you bring me anything else?" Luke asked.

"Yeah. We got you a few changes. We figured it would be at least a few days before we got home, though I bet they're all as baggy as the ones we burned after the little fracas we had to get your friend here out," Pablo replied.

Luke slid out of the bed and braced himself, taking a couple unsure steps until he figured out his balance and if his legs would hold him.

"Need some help there?" Pablo asked.

"No, I think I can manage a short walk. We'll leave the chair for Roxi if her leg's still bothering her."

As he walked away, Roxi snickered. Pablo opened the door for Luke, but before he stepped through, he turned around.

"What you laughing about?" Luke asked.

"Cute bum!" Roxi grinned.

Luke shook his head and reached back, holding the gown closed over his exposed ass. "Thanks."

Closing the door behind him, he pointed for Pablo to lead the way down the hall. Nodding, his best friend did his best, but he failed poorly at keeping in his laughter. Pablo kept his pace reasonable as they made their way down the hallway. When they stepped through into Luke's room, everyone made way.

"Alright everyone out! Luke's shown his ass around town enough for one day," Pablo called.

Luke squeezed the gown tighter. Seeing what he was doing, they laughed and headed out of the room. Pablo rustled around in the back of the room, pulled out a backpack, and tossed it onto the bed. Once the room was empty, save for Pablo, Luke fished out a pair of boxer briefs and slid them on, though they fit more like boxers. With some underwear on, he pulled the gown off. Fishing around inside the backpack, he pulled out a T-shirt and pair of jeans, throwing them on.

He looked around. "Is there a belt in here?" he asked, not seeing one.

"I don't think so. We burned your old one. It didn't survive either." He stripped off his belt and handed it to Luke. "I want that back when you're done."

After Luke looped the belt around his waist, he sat down and reached for the socks and shoes packed for him.

"You two looked pretty cozy in there," Pablo said.

"Yeah. Not a lot of room in those beds." Luke wasn't sure he was ready to dive into the Roxi topic with Pablo yet.

Pablo walked over and said, "I know you said there's nothing going on, but you looked pretty intimate."

Luke sat, elbows on his knees, staring at his hands. "I'm being honest when I say there's nothing of that kind going on. We became very close. For maybe a year we just had each other to talk to. Then they started dragging us into the arena. After the first few rounds, they paired us together against a group of werewolves. When we managed to survive"—he looked up, making eye contact with Pablo—"we kissed. We'd survived a brutal fight, and she asked and I said yes. After everything we'd been through, we both just needed a little human contact and tenderness. It happened again after the last battle we fought together, the one where she took her wounds."

Luke reached back and grabbed a bottle of water on the side table and took a drink. "The throat is still a little rough and dry." He swallowed. "After that, I didn't see her until the day you rescued me. She was a guest of the emperor's, brought to his box to watch me die fighting against an old friend of ours. Then you and the rest of the crew interrupted the fight before I could mount my triumphant comeback."

"Ha!" Pablo slapped his thigh. "Were you going to bleed on him to death?"

Luke chuckled. "By the time you guys showed up, that was about the only strategy I had left, and I was quickly running out of ammunition even for that."

"Yeah. You were a few pints low. Who were you fighting?"

"Le Mousquetaire."

Pablo whistled. "Good thing Pieter didn't hear about that, or he'd set the world on fire to get to him."

"Yeah, but who even knows if he was even still there. I imagine he was one of the first rats out on a lifeboat. I'm damn sure that little shit *Emperor* Flavius wasn't around by the time we went in to get Roxi out."

"Flavius? Emperor? You're going to have to fill me in on some details," Pablo said.

Luke chuckled. "Yeah. I don't think I told you that story, just Maggie." He took another swig of water. "My throat's getting a little tired. I'll save it for when we have everyone in a place so we can go over the details."

Pablo sighed dramatically. "I suppose I'll let you get away with that as an excuse for now. Besides, I want to get to that hotel, maybe see if they have some poker games going…"

Extending a hand to Luke, he smiled. Luke took it and let Pablo help him into a standing position only to be pulled in for a tight hug.

"I'm glad you're alive." Pablo patted Luke's back.

"Me too, Pablo. It's good to be back in the world with you." Luke grabbed the backpack and slung it over his shoulder. "Oh, I need an important favor."

"Sure thing, buddy," Pablo replied.

"Before we go, I need you to get Roxi's rudis from her room. We need to put it far away from either her or me. Something…bad happened to it and warped it."

"Can we just bin it here?" Pablo asked.

Luke shook his head. "No, we need to take it with us. I don't want to leave this kind of waste behind. Besides, we may need it."

"OK. I'll make sure it gets stashed."

"Thanks, and if you can keep it locked down until we get back to Portland, I'd appreciate it," Luke said.

"No problem."

Talk of the rudis brought another piece of thought from the arena. "Where's that dog we found in the arena? I don't think he should be left unattended."

"The pack is taking care of him. Don't worry. We've got it covered." Pablo pulled the door open and held it for Luke.

Still wanting to keep an eye on both of her patients, Maggie assigned both Luke and Roxi to the back seat of Pablo's pickup along with herself. Gwen, excited to be old enough and tall enough, claimed shotgun so she would ride with Luke.

"I get to pick the music!" Gwen called, hopping her way to the pickup, excited about reuniting with Luke.

"So that's your ward?" Roxi asked from the wheelchair Pablo was pushing.

"Gwen," Luke called. "I want you meet my friend Roxi. Roxi, this is Gwen."

"Hi, Roxi!" Gwen said, sticking her hand out to shake. "It's nice to meet you. Are you a vampire hunter like Luke?"

Luke was surprised by the kid's boldness. She'd always been reticent, but another year off the streets and surrounded by people who cared about her seemed to have done wonders for her confidence.

Roxi chuckled, shaking the girl's hand. "Yes. I am a vampire hunter. It's nice to meet you, Gwen."

Once at his black Toyota Tundra, Pablo helped Roxi into the back. Rolling the wheelchair back to the clinic, he stopped by Luke before proceeding. "I'll take care of that thing you wanted me to."

Luke nodded, then turned to watch the vehicles of their caravan take off, though it looked much smaller than he'd anticipated based on the numbers he'd seen during the rescue operation.

"This can't be everyone," he said.

"No. There aren't enough spare beds around here to house everyone. We sent the bulk of the pack toward the south end of the reservation so they could get hotel rooms," Maggie replied.

"That makes sense."

"Everyone mount up!" Pablo called. "It's time to blow this popsicle stand."

Luke pushed Roxi's door shut, then walked around the back of Pablo's truck carefully, waiting by the door for Maggie. She slid her arm around Luke's back and squeezed him before tipping her lips up for a kiss.

"I see you found the toothbrush we packed for you." Maggie's blue eyes sparkled in the afternoon sun. "Why don't you hop in the middle so you can sit next to Roxi? It'll be more comfortable for her."

Luke hesitated, checking Maggie's eyes but finding nothing but her usual warmth. Nodding, he climbed in, groaning at having to make the step up. He slid in next to Roxi and buckled himself in while everyone else got situated. When the last door shut, Pablo fired up the truck and pulled into line with the rest of their friends.

The arid terrain had an austere beauty to it, an occasional sandstone hill breaking up the flat high desert with its layered tans and reds. As they left the little town, more a small collection of buildings and houses including the clinic, the fence separating the road from the wide-open range was the only sign of human hands on the land.

"This kind of reminds me of home," Roxi said, staring out the window. She slipped her hand into Luke's.

Thinking back to the times he'd been on the Tigris River, it had the same dry arid flatness. "Yeah, it kind of does resemble the land around Ctesiphon."

"I guess," Roxi said then sighed. "But I meant Parthia. I was born in Ctesiphon, but Parthia was home."

"Where's Tisafawn?" Gwen asked. "And Parthia?"

"Ctesiphon was on the Tigris River in Iraq, south of where

modern Baghdad is. I guess you can still see the ruins. Parthia was in northeastern Iran and southwestern Turkmenistan. Ctesiphon was a city of learning and poetry with temples dedicated to Ahura Mazda, Mithras, Buddha, all the Greek gods, as well as synagogues and some early Christian churches. Over half a million people lived there. They're now dead and gone." Roxi laughed before turning to look at her car companions. "Did you know this is my first trip to the United States?"

Pablo laughed. "Not sure back country Wyoming is the best introduction to the United States, but welcome to America!"

"Thank you, Pablo. I guess I'll get to see more of it now, since I'm here." She turned her face back to the window.

"Horses!" Gwen called from the front seat.

Roxi turned her head in the direction Gwen pointed. "Look how they run, wild and free. I miss being on the back of a horse. It's been too long since I've ridden."

"You know how to ride?" Gwen asked. "I've never gotten to ride a horse before."

"She used to be a Parthian warrior, little one," Luke said. "She could fight from horseback with bow, sword, and lance."

"Really? That's so cool! I'm gettin' pretty good with a sword and a naginata. I wanted to help rescue you, Luke, but the adults wouldn't let me." Gwen pouted, put upon by unreasonable adults.

"You did enough to help rescue Luke. You're still a bit young to go to war," Maggie told her.

Gwen made a disgusted sound. "See. Adults."

Roxi chuckled, relaxing, her eyes following the horses as they ran across the landscape. Maggie slid her hand into his, squeezing it. Luke turned his gaze toward Maggie. She watched him, a question in her eyes. Smiling at her, he slouched into the back of the seat and stared forward, the first edges of motion sickness touching his stomach from staring out the side window and not being well in the first place. With Roxi holding one hand and Maggie the other, he had trouble concentrating on the scenery. Fortunately, exhaustion supplanted his anxiety as the steady road lulled him to sleep.

Luke woke when Pablo slowed and pulled into the parking lot of a large stone building with large red panels. On the end of the building, a sign with a rose in the center proclaimed that they'd arrived at the Shoshone Rose Casino, one of the gaming establishments owned by the Eastern Shoshone Tribe. Once Pablo parked, he headed into reception to get their keys. After he returned, he moved the truck to a side entrance with a few other vehicles Luke recognized as cars and trucks owned by various pack members.

Together, they helped Roxi in as she crutched her way to the elevator. The luggage for the party was minimal since neither Roxi nor Luke had much in the way of possessions with them after their stint in the vampires' prison arena. They had a bank of rooms near each other.

As they showed Roxi around her room, she kept eyeing the large jacuzzi tub. "I'm going to move into that tub, and I may never leave."

"I don't blame you, after what you've described, a proper bath has to feel like the height of luxury." Maggie smiled. "Are you going to need some help?"

Roxi shook her head. "I can manage. Wouldn't be the first time I've had to move around by myself while injured."

"OK." Maggie reached inside her bag and pulled out a phone and a charger, then looked at Luke. "Sorry, we raided your stash of burner phones in case we might need them. I have one for you too until you can get home and get set up again. Roxi, I've programmed in my number, Luke's, Sam's, Delilah's, Pablo's, and my partner Zel's. If you need anything, reach out to one of us, and we'll take care of it."

Roxi smiled weakly, her eyes relaying her tiredness. "Thank you again, for everything. I think I'll be alright for now. I've got a few changes of clothes thanks to everyone's generosity. I should be good."

"Pablo says they're arranging dinner in one of the private banquet rooms for us—we'll come collect you when it's time," Maggie said.

"Thanks, Maggie."

Luke nodded at Roxi and smiled before turning and following Maggie out. It felt weird to not be sleeping with their little window in the stone wall between them. After Maggie shut the door, she went into the bathroom and started running a bath.

"I brought your grooming stuff, if you want to trim your beard, although you'll have to wait until you get home to see your stylist for your hair, unless you want to risk a barber here." Maggie spoke quickly, seeming nervous now that they were finally alone in a space that was safely theirs.

"Where's Gwen staying?" Luke asked.

"Zel has volunteered to keep her for tonight so we could have some time together, if you want me to stay with you…"

"I'd like that, Maggie. I've dreamed about feeling you in my arms so many nights. I didn't think I'd ever get to hold you again."

Maggie smiled, a mischievous twinkle in her eyes. "You can hold me as much as you want, but I'd take it as a personal favor if you'd freshen up a bit first."

Luke chuckled. "I've got to be pretty gamy smelling by now. I haven't had a proper shower or bath since Luxembourg."

Holding up her thumb and forefinger with them spread apart, she said, "Only a little smelly."

Luke stripped down and found the kit Maggie had assembled and took it into the bathroom. Stepping in front of the mirror, he heaved a sigh. It'd been a long time since he'd looked at himself in the mirror.

"I'm surprised Pablo didn't bring me a volleyball with a face drawn on it," Luke called.

Maggie popped her head around the door frame. "You've definitely got some deserted island Tom Hanks vibes going on. Do you mind if I join you in the tub when you're ready?"

"Not at all. I'll let you know." He picked up the scissors and cut the first hunk of beard hair away. After a few minutes, he had a passable shaping done. His hair, now draping down his back, would have to wait until later. He jumped into the shower to give himself a quick clean, then stepped out and called to Maggie before sliding into the tub and sinking up to his neck in the thick bubbles.

Maggie joined him a moment later, striding naked into the bathroom. At the sight of Maggie's curves, his eyes went wide, and he made a longing noise.

"I never tire of hearing you make those kinds of sounds." She sighed as she slipped into the hot water.

The heat felt great as it seeped into his muscles. For the first time in a long time, he relaxed. His eyes drifted closed as he hummed one of Roxi's melodies. When he heard splashing, he opened his eyes to see Maggie moving toward him.

"You're so far away… Can I sit between your legs? I just want to feel your chest on my back and have your arms around me."

Nodding, he made room for Maggie, wrapping his arms around her when she got settled. Kissing her cheek, the melody returned to his lips.

"That's a pretty tune," Maggie said. "What is it?"

"It's a song Roxi would sing in the cells while we worked on our stone or were feeling sad." He chuckled harshly. "Which I guess was most of the time. She sang or hummed a lot; she has a lovely voice."

"I'm glad you weren't alone in there. When you're ready, you'll have to tell me about the stone." Maggie paused for a while, idly tracing her fingers lightly over the back of his hand. "Will you tell me what happened after they forced me onto the plane?"

Luke took in a deep breath and held it. He'd wondered if he'd want to talk about what had happened to him when the time came, but now that Maggie had asked, he needed to excise the poison of the last year and a half. And he needed it so he could clearly examine Roxi in a world in which they weren't clinging to each other desperately for survival, both physical and emotional. Breathing slowly, he started his tale, haltingly at first, but steadier as he grew more confident and comfortable with the reality that he was free and held Maggie in his arms.

Luke paused his story at the moment he and Roxi defeated the werewolves in their first fight together. "Maggie, I need to tell you something. I kissed Roxi. We'd survived the fight together, and we were going to be separated back to our cells. She asked if she could and I said yes. Then, and again in our next fight when we were both badly wounded."

"That's OK, Luke. Everything about that place sounds terrible, and you both needed the comfort. Is that why you seemed so nervous around us both?"

Luke chuckled. "Yeah. I mean, I'm still not certain that I'm actually free and this is all an elaborate dream I'll wake up from and still be in the cell. And another part of me is scared to be under the open sky after being in a tiny stone cell for so long, but also about Roxi and you."

"I'm glad you had each other and were able to provide some respite from the unmitigated hell for each other. Do you want to see where things go? Maybe try dating? You know that's an option. I never wanted you to be exclusive to me." Maggie's body tensed as she spoke quickly, as if hurrying to get out the words she knew she was supposed to say.

"I don't know, Maggie. I invited her to move to Portland and join us. If vampires are rounding up hunters to use for entertainment, it's too dangerous for us to go it alone. We talked about trying to be friends, but my feelings are too tied up in the circumstances to be able to really make a decision right now."

"Now you're afraid the intimacy you forged will fall apart without the circumstances that created it?" Maggie asked.

"I guess. It's all too fresh. We haven't really escaped; we're at a way point along the way with vampires still hounding our trail. I'm still weak as a kitten, and Roxi's weak and injured. We're guests in another people's land who I'm sure don't want this war brought to their home. Even with Owen's reassurance, who knows where their loyalties ultimately lie? And frankly, my brain is still foggy. This little stop in the bathtub is a bit of paradise, but we're a long way from home and there's a lot of potentially hostile territory between here and there."

"Yeah, that's a lot to hold." Maggie leaned to the side and looked up at Luke. "I just want you to know that I still love you, Luke, and I still want to keep seeing you if you want to keep seeing me."

Luke sighed in relief, staring into Maggie's eyes as she laid herself bare in them. He knew she'd been broken up with in the past when partners moved on or started seeing a primary partner. He tried to internalize the fear she must be feeling with the sudden introduction of Roxi into their world. "I'm glad. I was scared you might have had a change of heart in all the time I've been gone."

"My heart is not so fickle as to put aside my feelings for you. I love you, Luke."

"Neither is my heart capricious. I love you too, Maggie."

Maggie's body untensed. "Good, now let's get dressed and go get some food in you. Besides, the water is getting a little cold." Maggie stood up and slipped into the shower for a quick rinse.

Luke pulled the stopper on the tub and stood up, handing Maggie a towel when she stepped out of the shower. Taking a cue from Maggie, he rinsed off, took an offered towel from her, and dried his hair before running a brush through it.

He frowned as he looked at the meager choice of ill-fitting clothes available to him. "I'm going to have to get some new clothes when I get home, at least until I get back to my normal size."

He ended up with the same jeans he'd worn there and a clean black T-shirt. He threw on a hoodie, zipping it up. Maggie wore her typical outfit—jeans and a lightweight sweater. While she finished getting ready, he stood watching her, a content smile on his face. And though he loved seeing her naked, the image of Maggie in her curve-hugging jeans and her sweaters had filled his dreams and fantasies about seeing her if he ever escaped the arena cell.

"You ready to go?" Maggie asked, smiling.

He nodded and followed her out of the room, stopping across the hall at Roxi's room. Luke knocked on the door. When no answer came, he knocked again.

"Roxi, it's Luke."

"Coming," she replied.

A moment later, she opened the door. Someone had loaned her a jersey knit dress with thin blue and white horizontal stripes that fit pretty well. The dress's hem dropped to a few inches above her knee, partially exposing the angry red scar from her arena wound that ran over the top of her thigh. A pair of borrowed Chuck Taylor low tops finished off her outfit. She rubbed her hands over her arms, the sleeves only covering down to mid-bicep.

"Are you cold?" Maggie asked.

Roxi nodded. "The air conditioning is a little intense."

Maggie pulled out her phone and called someone. "Hi, Sam, do you have a spare cardigan you could bring with you? You do? Great. See you in a minute." She put her phone away. "Sam has a cardigan you can borrow."

"Thank you, again. Seems like that's all I'm saying," Roxi replied. "I owe you all."

"Don't worry about it. A friend of Luke's is a friend of the pack, and we take care of our people," Pablo said, stopping behind Luke. "Hey, buddy, I see you trimmed your beard. What do you think, Maggie? If we get his stylist to feather his hair a bit and get him some plaid to wear, he'll look just like Sam Winchester."

"He'd have to shave too," Maggie replied.

A moment later, Sam exited her room and joined them, handing a black cardigan to Roxi. "Here you go, dear. You can return it when you get some clothes of your own."

"Sam, I don't know if you've officially been introduced," Luke said. "This is Roxi. Roxi, Sam."

They shook hands.

"Owen says the room is ready," Pablo said, waving everyone after him.

"Are you OK without your crutches?" Luke asked Roxi as they headed down the hall.

"Yeah, it's flat and level, and I'd like to give my leg a little exercise," she replied.

They followed at the tail end of the group as they chatted noisily. At some point, Zel and Gwen popped out of one of the rooms and joined them. Gwen made her way to Luke and grabbed his hand. As they walked through the halls of the hotel down to their banquet room, being surrounded by the good-natured chatter of his friends felt surreal after what he'd been through. He forced his shoulders down, wondering why he felt so tense. It could be relying on another pack's good auspices or being out of the tight confines of his stone cell. Taking a deep breath, he tried to draw in a modicum of calmness.

He couldn't imagine how Roxi felt being surrounded by strangers, most of whom were werewolves, in a foreign land on a reservation for two of that land's indigenous peoples.

Luke leaned over and spoke lowly. "How are you doing, Roxi?"

"That's a loaded question. Fine, I guess." She hesitated before continuing, "This all feels like a hallucination or a fever dream."

"Yeah. I know what you mean, and I know all these people."

"Also, I'm famished," she replied.

Pablo led them to the banquet hall. Owen and John Sleeping Bear were standing outside the door, waving them inside. As soon as they stepped into the room and the smell of food wafted over them, Gwen dropped Luke's hand and ran to the chafing dishes. She opened and closed them, inspecting the bounty.

"Gwennie, leave the dishes alone," Zel called.

"Yes, Auntie Zel," Gwen replied, sulking her way toward the table.

"Just sit anywhere, please," John said, his deep voice filling the room.

Luke stepped up behind a chair, waiting for everyone to situate themselves.

Gwen approached him, fidgeting. "Luke, can I sit by you?"

"Of course you can, little one." Luke pulled her into his side with a one-armed hug.

Maggie, who'd been chatting with Sam, walked over to them, touching Roxi's shoulder. "Roxi, why don't you sit with Luke. I'm going to have dinner with my partner Zel." Taking in Luke too, she added, "You two should probably be careful what you eat, too much rich food might not be the best idea until you've had more time to get your stomachs accustomed to a more varied diet."

Luke smiled. "That's probably a good idea. It's been so long since I've been able to choose my food, I might go a little overboard when given the opportunity."

Roxi nodded and gave Maggie a nervous smile. Luke pulled out the chair next to him for Roxi, who sat to give her leg rest. Still tired and not fully recovered, he joined her. They sat quietly while the rest of the pack filtered in. Luke had no idea if the people he didn't recognize were North Portland Pack, other allies, or what. His eyes kept flicking to the unknown people, watching and wondering. He twitched his shoulder but didn't feel the weight of his sword on his back.

Although, he was reasonably confident the indigenous folks with hats and boots were probably from the local tribes. The Chinook and other Oregon indigenous folks in the Coast Pack tended to dress more like fishers or loggers.

"You have a lot of friends," Roxi said, looking around at all the people.

"I don't know a lot of the people here, but the pack has a lot of friends."

"Either way, they saved us from that hellhole." Roxi looked around nervously as if to make sure no one was listening then leaned in close. "I keep worrying it's all a dream, and I'm going to wake up back in my cell."

Luke moved his lips next to her ear. "Yeah, me too. Every time I doze off, I'm afraid of what I'll see when I wake up, but every time, it's not been our cell, so I keep hoping. Oh, looks like we might be starting here."

Kelly Brown raised her hands to shush everyone to silence. "Welcome to our friends from Oregon! We hope you enjoy your meal tonight. It's been great getting to know some of you, and I hope to get a chance to meet more of you. Please, go dish up while the food is hot."

Sam rose, getting everyone's attention. "I just want to briefly say thank you on behalf of the Northwest Oregon Council of Packs. You are all welcome in our territory anytime. Before everyone crowds to the buffet, let Luke and the rest of the hunters go first."

"I guess that's us, Roxi," Luke said.

Gwen groaned. "Does that mean I have to wait?"

"Why don't you come with us? We'll probably need some help." Luke stood up and helped Roxi to a standing position.

The other three hunters were already scooping spoons full of the delicious smelling food onto their plates, so they tucked in behind them.

Luke bent down to whisper into Gwen's ear. "You should fill your plate first, then go put it on the table and come back. Roxi will probably need help carrying her food."

"OK!" Gwen bounced on the balls of her feet, staring around the hunters to see what all there was in case something new had been added since her earlier perusal of the options.

As soon as space cleared, Gwen picked up a plate, scooped all the things she wanted onto it, and ran back to their spot, rejoining them to help Roxi. When they finished, they sent the kid ahead with the plate.

"Gwen is adorable," Roxi said as they walked back.

The kid had set down Roxi's plate and dug into hers, scooping fries through a pool of ketchup. After Luke set his plate down, he pulled out Roxi's chair, helping her down.

"Thanks. I guess I'm not quite as healed as I thought I was. That was a long walk on a bad leg."

"Yeah, if you need to, we can see if the hotel has a wheelchair we can borrow, or I can run up and get your crutches," Luke replied.

"That's very thoughtful. We'll see how I'm doing after dinner." Roxi took a drink of water, then looked down the table, snorting and coughing as she tried to keep from choking.

Looking to see what had startled her, he found Gwen looking at them with two French fries tucked between her top lip and teeth, hanging down like fangs. At the end of them, ketchup dripped.

Doing her best Count Dracula accent, she said, "I want to suck your tomato blood. Ah. Ah. Ah!"

Luke snorted with laughter as one of her potato fangs fell from her lip, falling into her lap. Once Roxi got her mouthful of water managed, she joined Luke in laughing at the kid's antics. His eyes flicked across the table to see Maggie smiling indulgently and Zel bordering between wanting to tell the kid not to play with her food and laughing at Gwen's antics.

"Careful, Gwen, don't draw the ire of a Desi auntie," Roxi warned.

"Don't worry, Auntie Zel loves me."

Roxi laughed. Luke looked down at his food, his stomach

rumbling. He was famished, but Maggie's warning ran through his mind. He wasn't interested in having a stomachache, so he'd picked the items likely to be the easiest on his stomach. Finally, his stomach won out, and he grabbed a fry and popped it into his mouth. He'd only grabbed a few, sticking to non-fried items hoping that would work better, but when a server came around to get their drink orders, he ordered a local pale ale to go with his water. A cold beer after a year and a half in captivity was too good of an opportunity to pass.

Roxi, overhearing him ordering, requested one for herself. "Not a lot of good beer in India."

"Is that where you live?" Gwen asked.

"No, I live in London mostly, but I was hunting some vampires in Mumbai and had been there for a while when I was captured. I miss all the good beer from London," Roxi lamented.

"Well, if you come to Portland, we'll take you to Pablo's. He makes beer. You'll have to ask the adults if it's any good." She picked up her buffalo burger and took a huge bite.

"Pablo makes excellent beer, at least he used to. Who knows, he might have slipped without me around to taste his beer for him," Luke said, making sure Pablo, who sat a few seats down, could hear him.

Pablo stuck his tongue out at Luke. "Hey, my beers are better than ever. We'll have to pour a few in you when we get you home."

"Looking forward to it, Pablo." A sly smile spread across Luke's face. "Once my stomach gets used to good food again, I wouldn't say no to one of Aunt Maria and Tony's Mexican feasts."

"Me either." Pieter said, sitting next to Pablo. "I can never get enough of your aunt's food."

Pablo laughed and nodded. "I think we can make a welcome back feast happen after you get settled in."

As his friends joked around him, Luke relaxed, taking in the convivial atmosphere, though he couldn't entirely put away the anxiety running through him like an undercurrent. Gwen seemed giddy to have Luke back. The once shy kid was pulling out all the stops—clowning around, trying to make Luke and his new friend laugh. At first, he could feel the tension pouring off Roxi while surrounded by strangers in an unknown land after a very traumatic experience, but the good-natured group and the silliness of Luke's ward seemed to defuse that tension. Mostly.

Luke and Roxi were among the first finished eating, quickly filling up on their meager meals. Even though the beer was respectable, it tasted amazing, sixteen ounces of luxury. The alcohol quickly worked its way into Luke's veins, affecting him more than it normally would. He hadn't planned on a second and decided that was a good plan to stick with, all things considered. When Roxi slid her hand up his thigh to grab his hand, he inhaled sharply until he realized what was going on.

Luke leaned toward Roxi, speaking the middle Persian they used when they didn't want anyone to eavesdrop. "How are you doing?"

"I'm doing alright," she replied, then opened her mouth before closing it again.

"What?"

"I think I'd like to go back to my room. I'm feeling a little peopled out. Would you be willing to help me get back? I'm worried I might need a little help with this leg."

He nodded. "Sure. I'll be right back, and we'll get you to your room."

Standing up, he found Pablo talking with Owen and John. "Hey, Pablo. I'm going to escort Roxi back to her room, then I think I'm going to call it a night myself. Too much excitement."

"Sure, buddy. Since you're here, we've got a meeting scheduled for tomorrow late morning to figure out our next move. Feeling up for that?" Pablo asked.

"Yeah, just come get me when it's time." Luke patted Pablo's shoulder and walked to the other side of the room to find Maggie with Zel, Sam, Delilah, and Simone. He bent over and kissed Maggie's cheek. "I'm going to help Roxi back to her room, then retire to the bedroom. I'll see you whenever you're done here."

"Sure, Luke. Getting a little too noisy down here?" Maggie asked.

"Yeah. It's a bit of an extreme change from complete isolation or the crowds of vampires and werewolves cheering for my death. I'll have to work at my reentry into society."

"I'll let you know when I'm headed up."

Luke nodded and returned to Roxi, helping her up. Gwen, scraping the last crumbs of cobbler from her plate, stood up to join them.

"You don't have to go to bed now," Luke said.

"I know, but I've got a book waiting for me in Zel's room that I'm really into, and it's getting a bit loud with all the olds."

"So you're choosing to go to your room to read, leaving with the two oldest people here?" Roxi asked, a twinkle in her eyes and a teasing smile on her lips.

Her full lips looked quite nice with the smile on them. It wasn't an expression he'd seen on her face much in their little prison, nor was it one that she'd seen on his face — not one that wasn't forced or strained due to the circumstances.

"Someone has to make sure you don't get lost on your way back; old people are forgetful," Gwen said, holding her head high and lofty as if she were above their petty old people jokes.

Roxi laughed, the sound a bright bell tinkling. "I'm glad we have such a young and mentally spry guide."

Luke followed them out of the room, Gwen slowing once she realized she was walking too fast for Roxi to keep up. After they turned down their hall, Roxi slid her arm through Luke's, leaning on him a bit to help take some of the pressure off her injured leg.

"Are you sure we don't need to get you something to help you back to your room?" he asked.

"As long as we don't go too fast and our intrepid guide can keep it slow for us old fogies. So what is this book that sends young teens to their room to read instead of staying out at a party?" Roxi asked.

Gwen dropped back to walk along Roxi's other side. "It's called 'The Blue Sword,' and I've got the sequel with me if I finish it. It's super cool! It's about a girl and horses and swords. The next one has a dragon on the cover."

"'The Hero and the Crown,' right?" Roxi asked. "I like Robin McKinley; she's a great writer."

"Zel bought them for me. They said they were a couple of their favorites."

"Zel has good taste," Roxi said.

Once Gwen figured out she and Roxi had similar tastes in books, the flood gates opened, and Gwen chattered away about 'The Blue Sword' all the way to her room. When they arrived, Luke gave Gwen a tight hug.

"I missed you, little one. When we get home, we'll do something fun together and you can tell me all the things you did while I was gone."

"I'd like that." Then she looked up at Roxi. "You can bring her along if you'd like. Maybe I can talk her into teaching me how to be a horse and sword girl."

Roxi chuckled. "I'd like that."

"Goodnight," Gwen said.

"Goodnight. It was nice to meet you."

Gwen waved and then shut her door. When they stopped at Roxi's room, she stood inside her threshold while Luke stood in the hall.

"Would you come in and sit with me for a bit?" she asked.

Luke nodded, stepping into her room. "I like the dress. You look very nice."

"Thank you. Your friend Delilah's girlfriend Simone let me borrow it." She kicked the shoes off, grabbed a T-shirt, and headed into the bathroom. When she emerged, she wore the baggy t-shirt. It dropped down to almost mid-thigh. The scar was entirely visible, a jagged red gash across the front of her thigh a couple inches above her knee.

Seeing where Luke's eyes were, she shuffled nervously and clasped her hands in front of her. "In the past, I've been told I have nice legs."

"They're still nice legs. What are scars to people like us?" Luke replied.

"My leg is tired, do you mind if I lay down?"

He shook his head. She walked around to the side of the bed and sat down, swinging her legs up and onto the covers before relaxing into the mound of pillows.

She patted the empty spot next to her. "Come sit with me for a bit."

Luke slipped off his shoes and crawled into bed, propping himself up on the pillows. As soon as he was settled, Roxi rolled over and lifted his arm, sliding under it and resting her head on his chest.

"I hope this is alright, Luke. I just need to be near you for a little bit. It's been so long and I've gotten used to being near you."

"It's OK." He relaxed, enjoying the warmth of her body.

Running his hands over her long, wild, black hair, he listened to his own heartbeat as they sat in silence. After a while, Luke became aware of the soft melody Roxi hummed as she stroked her hand over his chest and stomach. He wasn't sure how long they sat there, but the peace and tranquility let his mind empty for the space of time they shared in each other's arms.

Yawning, she looked up at him, a sad smile on her lips. "I'm sleepy. Would you tuck me in and kiss me goodnight before you have to go?"

He nodded. The radiance of her smile increased, but the sadness didn't quite disappear from her eyes. Sliding out from under his arm, she limped into the bathroom and shut the door, reemerging a few minutes later. Luke rolled out of the bed and lifted the covers for her. Before she got back into bed, she slid her arms around his waist and pulled him in for a hug, then pushed back and slid under the covers. Once she seemed to settle, Luke pulled the covers over her shoulders, then leaned down and kissed her on the lips.

"Goodnight, Roxi."

"Goodnight, Luke. Thank you for coming back for me."

"I'd have come back by myself if they hadn't brought me back."

Roxi reached up and patted his cheek. "You're a sweet man."

He kissed her forehead, then left her as she slipped into sleep.

LUKE WOKE to the smell of coffee and pancakes as Maggie readied the room service she'd ordered. He'd nearly been asleep by the time Maggie made it back to their room, the TV providing a distracting noise in the background, but her smile woke him enough to enjoy some quality kissing before he surrendered to sleep.

"How'd you sleep?" Maggie asked, bringing him a cup of coffee.

"I was kind of afraid I wouldn't be able to sleep in a soft bed after spending so long sleeping on a stone floor, but you're going to have to drag me out of here at gunpoint. I live in this bed now."

Maggie laughed, sitting on the edge of the bed and kissing his forehead. "If I pour enough coffee into you, that'll get you out of bed, eventually."

Luke shook his fist at the cup of coffee cooling on the nightstand. "Damn you coffee and your diuretic effects!"

"You're silly this morning."

Luke wrapped his arms around Maggie and pulled her onto him and then rolled her over into the bed as she squealed, laughing.

"I'm alive. I saved my friend. I have my friends and family with me, and I slept in a real bed. It's a good morning. And best of all, I have a beautiful woman who I love in my arms."

Maggie, smiling broadly, reached up, pulled his head down, and kissed him, starting slowly. When they parted, Luke breathed heavily.

"If you're going to keep kissing me like that, our breakfast is going to get cold," Luke said, sliding out of the bed and heading to the bathroom.

"I've had plenty of warm breakfasts. A cold one won't bother me," Maggie replied.

Heat surged through Luke. He'd eaten cold breakfasts for over a year and a half. One more day of cold food wouldn't matter, not when he had Maggie with him and she kissed him that intently. Unfortunately, they only had enough time before the planned meeting to do some kissing, but it went a long way toward rejuvenating his spirits.

CHAPTER
TWENTY-SIX

After their meeting, they determined to get on the road as fast as they could, hoping to get ahead of any armed vampires trying to blockade their exit. By the time their vehicles were packed, refueled, and ready, the sun was creeping toward the horizon, a victim of daylight savings. Also, they didn't want to overstay their welcome with the local tribes, trying to avoid bringing their vampire war onto the Wind River Reservation, at least any more than they already had. They slipped out of town as quietly as possible, hoping not to draw attention to themselves. An hour later, they discovered their efforts had been misspent.

They were nearly to the reservation's border when a row of headlights flared to life, showing a row of cars blocking the highway, spread wide onto the adjacent prairie. Pablo stopped the truck, sending a cascade of brake lights flaring to life down the line of the caravan.

Luke exhaled, exasperated. "Fucking vampires."

Roxi, sitting next to him, nodded. "I feel them too."

"Looks like we didn't make it out unnoticed," Pablo said. "So what's the plan?"

Luke'd been removed from the battle map for nearly two years, yet it was still his job to make the plans. Shaking his head, he couldn't be angry with them. He'd been their leader, and he guessed they still thought of him as one.

"I guess we see what they want," Luke said, getting out of the truck.

He strode forward about ten yards, standing in front of Pablo's pickup, the headlights washing around him.

"What do you want?" Luke shouted.

Someone stepped out of the shadows. A crunching noise behind Luke drew his attention. Owen had pulled up with his pickup.

"We want our property back. You stole some things that belong to us," the shadow shouted.

"I belong to no one. Move out of our way, or suffer the consequences."

"You were a guest in our home, but yet you still destroyed it. We can't let that stand. You will pay. If you don't want to come quietly, we'll take you by force and kill all your friends while we do it."

Luke turned around and stormed to the back of Pablo's pickup, pulling it open too aggressively as he looked through the totes for weapons, grumbling angrily the entire time. Rage surged through his veins, and hatred burned in his eyes. He just wanted to go home and yet they wouldn't leave him be. Finally, he found something useful—a Kevlar vest that looked about the right size. While he searched, his friends had gathered around him.

"Oh, shit, Luke's pissed. Everyone get ready!" Pablo called.

Luke yanked the Kevlar vest over his head and strapped it tight, then grabbed Roxi's sword, shoved its scabbard under his belt, and clipped the rudis next to it. In another second, he had a bandolier of shotgun shells wrapped around his chest.

"Luke." Delilah lofted an M12 over to him.

He snagged it out of the air and pumped a shell into the firing chamber. "Owen, get the .50 caliber mounted."

Owen turned to his friends from the reservation. "You're about to see some shit go down. Kelly, you want to get on the wheel? John, Ronnie, I need you to lock the hubs in for four by four."

Luke stalked forward, his crew fanning out to either side. Once

Luke was within what he thought would be hearing range for a vampire, he said, "This is your one chance to live."

Someone stepped out in front of the headlights, creating a black silhouette. "What can you do to us? We have you outnumbered."

"Yet I'm still here. I took everything you fuckers threw at me and came out on top. The blood of thousands upon thousands of your brethren is on my hands. I have no mercy for vampires. If I pull the trigger, I won't stop until ever last one of you is a smudge on the pavement. You're the expendable trash your masters have cast in my way."

"I like our odds," the vampire called back.

Luke turned his head back toward his caravan. "Owen, play me some music."

He smiled at the sound of Owen pulling back the cocking lever. The muzzle flash lit up the night, shattering the quiet with its heavy "thump, thump, thump" as half-inch wide bullets ripped into a car pulled off onto the shoulder of the road. In a few seconds, Owen had rendered the car into scrap metal.

As the car burst into flames, vampires scrambled out of the car next to it. One or two tried to crawl out of the wreckage, but a .50 cal bullet can do a lot of damage to even a vampire body.

"Do you think our masters will be satisfied with letting you go because you have a big gun?" The vampire almost sounded like he was pleading with Luke to give up instead of pep talking his soldiers.

"Fuck it," Luke mumbled. He looked at the vampire and the vampires obscured by the headlights of the armada of cars blocking the highway. He drew in a full breath, filling his lungs. "Flee now! Run fast, and when you get back to your masters... Tell them I'm coming for them. Their time is done! Their destiny lies at the end of the Centurion Immortal's sword. Stand in my way and suffer their fate. Run and hide, find the deepest hole, because if I see you, you die. Where I go, I'm only leaving your bodies. Run and tell your masters they're about to become an endangered species!" He raised his arm. "Owen, light 'em up!"

Owen opened fire, but a second gun joined it, this one not quite as robust. Luke guessed it was one of Owen's .30 caliber guns.

Spraying bullets in wide arcs, they tried to pepper as many of the vampires' cars as possible. The screams of vampires being hit or diving for cover pulled a vindictive smile from Luke's lips. One vampire, braver than most, charged at Luke, pulling a pistol from a pocket. Luke raised his shotgun and vaporized him.

"If you're going to shoot, shoot. Don't charge me." As another ran within range of his gun, he pumped a shell into the chamber and fired it off, taking down the vamp but not killing it, adding its shrieks of pain to the rest of the chaos.

As mayhem reigned in the vampire lines, Luke stood front and center, watching his enemies be shredded. By the time movement stopped along their lines and Luke held up his fist to signal a cessation to the guns firing, the vampires' cars and trucks were scrap. A few burned. Pushing a few shells into the magazine of his shotgun to replace those he fired, he waved everyone else forward. Once they joined him, he stalked forward, gun at the ready.

To his right, someone fired their shotgun, ending a vampire. Another one flashed out of its hiding spot, but Luke tracked it and fired just as someone else fired. Between them, the vampire exploded into goo as silver or wood pierced its heart. Down the line, his wolves cleaned up whatever vamps Owen's machine guns had left, some with a shotgun, some with a stake.

Once Luke entered the fray, he stopped to drain a few, feeling better than he'd felt in ages. Buoyed by fresh vampires and an over-sized portion of rage, Luke went looking for trouble. He needed to make bastard fangers suffer the way they'd made him suffer. When he emptied the shotgun, he pulled Roxi's sword from its scabbard but found no one to plunge it into. The sounds of shotguns barking into the night slowed down to a trickle, then to nothing. A few random groans of vampirish pain were silenced with a stake, returning the dark road in the middle of nowhere to near silence. The flames licking the darkness crackled over cars, the occasional pop or explosion punctuating the sound.

"We all clear?" Delilah called.

Cries of "clear" and "yup" ran down the line.

"Let's get a gang of wolves on these two cars before they catch fire so we can clear a path and get through," Pablo called.

Luke, even after both fighting with and against werewolves, still felt surprised at the raw strength they could muster. As a small gang surrounded the first car, they lifted on the count of three and carried it further off the road, throwing it aside with a sad crunch of metal, plastic, and glass. In another minute, they'd tossed the second car onto the first, mostly to make more crunching noises, Luke suspected.

As his raw anger subsided, a smile teased the corners of his mouth as he shook his head at the wolves giving each other high-fives after further trashing the already destroyed cars. He admired their ability to take joys in the simple pleasures; he hoped he'd get back to that place someday. Sighing, he turned and walked back toward their caravan, head hanging. Only fear, anger, and loneliness registered in his brain now that he'd been freed, even surrounded by all the people he loved most in life. He was having trouble escaping the stone cell he'd been kept in for over a year and a half. His body might be free, but his mind and soul were having trouble breaking out.

"Hey, everyone be quiet," one of the wolves called out, holding a hand up to emphasize the request.

Soon, all around Luke, werewolf ears perked up as heads turned toward the northwest and the roadway they'd just unblocked.

"Shit," someone else said.

"What's going on?" Luke asked.

"Lots of noise coming at us. Kind of sounds like dirt bikes," a wolf Luke didn't recognize replied.

"Well fuckety fuck," Luke mumbled.

"You said it, brother," the wolf replied.

"Hey, Luke. Get back here," Owen yelled.

Luke jogged back to Owen's pickup. "What's up?"

"Kelly said the reservation has a couple snowplows in a yard not far from here. She knows where the keys are, so she and Ronnie went back to grab one when they saw the blockade. Don't know how long before they're back." Owen looked forward as Delilah, Sam, and Pablo ran up to Luke.

"We've got to keep this gap open," Delilah said.

"Should we get the caravan moving?" Pablo asked, running his hand through his hair.

"One of your wolves said it sounded like dirt bikes. I don't think we're really set up to go Mad Max on this situation. We can't afford to have cars picked off one by one or lose any of our wheels." Luke looked around, assessing their current deployment. "Try to bunch up the cars for now. We'll need to protect them and keep the dirt bikes away. Owen, can you move the truck into that gap we just made? Anything crosses that bridge, light them up."

"Can do." He slapped the roof of the cab a couple times. "You heard the man. Move us into that gap."

"Delilah, you organize our front line. We need to stop as many as possible before they can break through and shoot up our vehicles. Sam, you organize our vehicle defense. We have to protect them at all costs." Luke pulled shotgun shells from the bandolier and pushed them into the entry port of his M12.

Roxi stepped out of the back of Pablo's truck and limped over. "Is there anything I can do to help?"

Luke's brows narrowed as he contemplated the question. "Sam, we got enough guns to arm everyone?"

"Yeah, I think so," Sam replied.

"OK, pair them up with experienced people and keep them around the caravan." He turned back to Roxi and handed her his shotgun. "Can you protect Gwen? Make sure she stays out of trouble? I don't want her mixed up in fighting yet. She's too young. You know how to use one of those?"

Roxi turned the gun around in her hands, checking out the various parts. She didn't look scared of the weapon, and the way she held it looked natural as she flipped the safety off, then back on.

"Yeah. I've used shotguns before. Not this model, but I should be fine."

Everyone's heads snapped toward the front as the sound of a rifle announced the beginning of round two. It sounded like Jung-sook had broken out the Steyr SSG69 sniper rifle and was going to town. A moment later, Sam popped out from the back of Pablo's pickup, carrying two of Luke's old friends.

"My sawed offs!" Luke took them from Sam and hooked them to his belt before tying them around his thighs.

When his hands were free, Sam handed him her shotgun. "I'll grab one of the spares. Also, you'd better grab another ammo belt."

Luke nodded and snagged one from the back of the truck as Sam called everyone not currently armed to grab a gun. Delilah had taken off and was shouting orders to the front-line squad, organizing them. Shrieking metal drew Luke's attention back to the front as the wolves moved cars to form barriers.

Roxi took the ammo belt hanging from Luke's hand and buckled it on for him. When she finished, she kissed his cheek. "Go kill some vampires for me. I wish I could join you to pay them back."

"I know. I'll be sure to repay them for you too. Please keep my kid safe." He ran his hand over her cheek. Pulling the door of the pickup open, he poked his head in the door. "Gwen, keep your head down and listen to Roxi."

Gwen crossed her arms. "I can help. I know how to fight. I'm so much better than when you last saw me."

"I know you are, but you're still too young for this mess." Luke smiled kindly at his ward.

"Can I go help Maggie?" Gwen pleaded with her eyes.

Luke shook his head. "You're also too young to see the kind of carnage a gun can do to a body, even a werewolf who's likely to heal."

"Fine." She turned away from him. After she let out a deep sigh, she crawled out of the pickup and hugged Luke. "Be careful, Luke."

"I will, little one." Periodic bursts from Owen's heavy machine guns joined the lone cracks of the sniper rifle. "I'd better get back to the front. Back in the car, Gwen." Once she hopped back in, he shut the door. "Thank you, Roxi."

She nodded and leaned up against the side of the pickup, taking the weight off her bad leg until it was needed. Luke nodded and turned around, jogging to the little command post Delilah had set up a few cars from Owen's pickup truck. She handed Luke a set of night vision goggles.

"Wait for a break in the shooting. Owen's muzzle flash is nasty," Delilah said.

Luke put the goggles up and quickly scanned the distance. "Looks like they're holing up." He stopped along the road. "Ah, they've got more people coming in the distance."

A shot fired off from the Steyr, and someone tumbled off a motorcycle.

"Damn, Jung-sook is good with that thing," Luke said.

"Yeah, she's put in a lot of time at the range with it," Delilah replied.

"If they wait much longer, she'll pick them to pieces. Whoop. They're moving out now," Luke commented.

"Hold your fire," Delilah called as a shadow sprinted forward, rising out of the bank of the Wind River.

Whoever it was leapt over the car and skidded to a halt near Delilah. "River's not deep, they can probably cross it on a dirt bike if they're careful."

"Thanks, get to your spot," Delilah ordered.

The wolf nodded, ran to the bed of Owen's pickup, and grabbed a gun laying on the tailgate of the truck, disappearing on the other side.

"Watch the river," Delilah called. "It's shallow."

The sound of revving motors and yelling washed over the river and their line as the vampires rallied and kicked their next assault into action. The first riders breached the line of the bridge, then flared out as they exited. A few shotguns barked to life, sending a bike skidding across the pavement. Luke wasn't sure if the shot actually hit at that distance or just scared the biker. He didn't have long to contemplate it as the first wave drew within range.

Down the line, shotguns opened fire, sending a few bikes tumbling to the ground. Luke barked a quick laugh as one vampire vaporized into dust in his clothes—his bike kept moving forward, smashing into one of the destroyed cars. The vampires, now within range, pulled guns of their own. Most likely handguns, but a few sounded like they held shotguns as they answered the wolves.

Luke lifted his gun, readying to pick a target, when a motorbike sounded from behind him. He whipped around, taking aim, but quickly lowered his gun when he saw the face of the rider.

Luke held up an open palm. "Shit, sorry, Rhonda."

"No worries, kind of a poor choice on my part, but I thought you might want to join me since you've got bike experience. Took this from one of the ones we downed. I drive, you shoot?" She waggled her eyebrows at him and grinned.

Luke couldn't help answering Rhonda's wicked grin with one of his own. He jumped on the back of the big dirt bike, bracing his feet on the foot pegs. With the shotgun in one hand, he wrapped his other arm around Rhonda's waist. She took off, sending a rooster tail of dirt behind her and a whoop of excitement into the air as they tore down the back of the line, making for the edge so they could hunt.

"One ahead!" Rhonda shouted, her words audible over the sound of the noisy engine and dirt and rocks flying behind them.

Lifting the gun, he pulled it into his shoulder and took aim the best he could with only one arm. He waited until the barrel bumped up from the bounce and squeezed the trigger. The vamp went down, splashing into goo. Rhonda cackled loudly with delight. Carefully, Luke maneuvered the gun to pump out the spent shell and place a new shell into the chamber as Rhonda cut a wide curve.

He hoped she stayed out of the line of fire. He didn't want to get accidentally shot because they looked like vampires on dirt bikes, but it looked like Rhonda's plan was to work the edge to keep anyone from flanking their line to attack their vulnerable caravan. Luke took aim and fired, missing. However, the shot forced the biker to swerve off, allowing one of their wolves on the front line to take it down.

Rhonda pulled the bike right into a hard turn as they curled by the line of cars their people were using for cover. In the distance, at least one vamp biker had made it across the river and was coming in away from the bridge. Rhonda made a beeline directly at them. The vamp had the jump on them as he barreled toward their vulnerable friends in the caravan.

Tucking in behind the vamp, Rhonda turned her head slightly and shouted, "Rest the barrel on the handlebars."

Luke slid the barrel under her arm and laid the barrel down in the crook of a couple instruments along the bar and center. Rhonda stabilized their approach. Adjusting his aim slightly, Luke fired off a shot, missing. Rhonda grabbed the pump quickly before Luke could pull it back. He pushed it forward and then back, reloading the next round. After Rhonda let go, he settled the barrel and drew his aim. The vampire's arm raised, light glinting off the metal of the machine gun in its hands. Before the vampire could finish raising it, Luke lowered his aim and squeezed the trigger, blasting the back tire to bits. As the tire disintegrated, dragging the back of the bike into the dirt, the biker's momentum carried him over the handlebars.

Luke, holding on tightly to both the gun and Rhonda, held his breath as the tall woman did some fancy maneuvering to avoid the fallen bike and biker, sliding to a swerving stop next to the vampire as it struggled to get up. Luke jumped off the back of the bike, pumped a shell into the chamber, and ended the vampire before quickly reloading the gun. He paused for a second, then slung it around his shoulder and pulled out one of his sawed-off Stevens 311 before climbing back onto the bike. Rhonda barely waited until he was settled before taking off after the next target that had made it around their front line.

The sawed off felt much better in one hand; he'd be able to reload it easier on the fly as well. These were the guns he'd used when he went after a vampire biker gang in the 1970s. As they pelted back toward the front line, Luke saw their people wave at him, cheering as he and Rhonda zipped by. This time, she swung wide, putting some distance between themselves and the caravan, and aimed for the shadows of a few scrubby trees.

Rhonda slowed down, not wanting to overshoot too closely into what was, for now, enemy territory. Luke scanned the horizon, trying to pick up their next target, when Rhonda gunned the gas and sent the bike surging forward. Four bikes in a cluster had broken through their lines and were speeding toward the caravan. Once they saw the bike heading toward them, two bikers split off and aimed toward Luke and Rhonda.

Luke flicked the safety off while he adjusted his feet on the pegs so he could push himself forward into Rhonda's back. He pulled the other shotgun from its holster and flicked off the safety. As the vampires raised their guns, Rhonda swerved back and forth to throw off their aim. As soon as they reached the effective range of the gun and ammo, Luke waited until the apex of the swerve to the left and pulled one of the triggers on the shotgun in his right hand. It caught the vamp full in the chest and flung its body backwards off the end of its bike. Luke smiled as the vampire puffed into dust as it hit the ground, and its riderless bike rocketed by them before catching and tumbling end over end.

The fanger on his left was tangled up in the strap of his machine gun as he tried to aim across his body. Luke raised his left gun and pulled a trigger. As the fanger's body disintegrated, it lost control of its bike, the front tire jackknifing and sending the fanger over the handlebars in a disgusting rainbow of goo. With the two sent after them down, Luke and Rhonda looked for the other two, but only saw two downed bikes—the wolves protecting the caravan had done their job.

Rhonda throttled back. Squinting, Luke leaned his head forward, wondering what the people of the caravan were gesturing at. Realization dawned as Rhonda pulled a hard left. He brought his arm in and braced it along Rhonda's side until they straightened out. Another group of bikers, this time three, had evaded the front line and were making their way back to the caravan.

Rhonda gunned it, making straight for the middle. She turned her head and shouted, "Right gun, middle biker, then hold on tight!"

"Got it!" Luke yelled.

The helmetless vamps stared at the bike barreling toward them, their eyes widening as they entered a direct collision course. Luke took aim and squeezed the trigger as soon as he felt the range was right, then clamped his arms around Rhonda as she brought the bike into a barely controlled sweeping turn to the right, sending up a wave of dirt and rocks toward the cluster of vampire bikers. As they slowed, Luke raised the gun in his left hand and fired off the last shell into the cloud of dust and mayhem toward what he thought was the shadow of one of bikers.

"Go!" Luke screamed as the lead bike tumbled, taking out the two behind it and sending them flipping and flying toward where he and Rhonda now stood.

He shoved the empty guns into his holster and wrapped his arms around Rhonda as she pushed the bike to its full power, popping a wheelie as the bike's tire bit into the soil and threw them forward. He grunted as the front wheel hit the ground and shook his head at the sound of laughter coming from Rhonda. If they survived this, Luke was going to have a serious talk with the woman about her driving when he was on the back of one of her bikes. Though, he had to admit, she was a superb rider, even if he always felt about an inch from death.

Slowing down, she carved a much slower turn to head back in the right direction. Since they were no longer riding for ruin, Luke pulled his right shotgun out and raised it over his head, leaning into Rhonda's back, and pushed the lever to release the barrels. He snapped the double barrel open, and pulled the shells, shoving them into his hoodie pocket, and grabbed one from the ammo belt on his chest. He pushed it into the barrel carefully, nearly fumbling but securing it after a second, then grabbed another. Once loaded, he shoved it back into its holster and repeated the process on the other. After he managed it without dropping a shell, he thought he deserved an award for reloading two shotguns while on the back of a speeding dirt bike. He snorted at the idea of buying himself a trophy.

As they passed the heap of bikes and vampires they'd just created, a few people ran out from the caravan to finish the vampires before running back to the cars. Luke didn't see any more bikes in their zone as Rhonda slowed and rode a serpentine pattern to increase their field of vision.

"Take us back to the command center," Luke shouted.

Rhonda nodded and pushed the bike faster, aiming toward Owen's truck. Skidding to a stop, Luke stepped off the back of the bike to the relieved faces of Delilah, Sam, and Owen.

"What's the situation?" Luke asked.

"They're pulling back. I only hear a few dirt bikes moving around. They've got some vans or other large vehicles parked out there blocking the road. Looks like about three of four, so if they're full of vamps, there's probably another forty-ish to deal with," Delilah replied.

"Sam?" Luke asked.

Sam stretched her neck to one side, then the other. "Some injuries down the line, mostly on the side of the caravan you weren't on. Maggie and Patrice are treating them, but nothing too serious, as far as I can tell. Vehicles seem to be in good shape, though there are a few bullet holes in doors and quarter panels."

Luke nodded, looking at Owen. "Any word on that snowplow?"

"Ronnie called and said—"

An air horn went off down the caravan line, alerting them to something new. The small group walked to the other side as a giant snowplow chugged along the road's edge.

"Is that mounted on a dump truck?" Luke asked.

"It does appear so," Owen said.

A wicked grin spread across Luke's face. "I want some empty glass bottles and some gasoline. Also, some volunteers to ride in the back of that dump truck. Owen, I want you to bring up the rear. Start spreading the word to the caravan. I want guns left and right if they can manage it."

"What's the plan, big guy?" Owen asked.

"Kelly's gonna slam that snowplow down the center of the road and clear those vans. We'll torch them on the way by with Molotovs and shoot anything that moves, then run everyone else through fast. You bring up the rear and finish tearing up those vans and anyone stupid enough to stand still."

Sam chuckled. "When delicacy fails…"

"Be a big fucking sledgehammer," Luke finished. "Owen, run back and tell Kelly to hold back. Let's not spring the surprise quite yet. You'll back out of the way, then she can barrel through."

Delilah chuckled, then it turned into a full laugh. Everyone stared at her while she tried to get herself under control. "I know where we can get some flammable bottles."

Sam's jaw dropped and her eyes widened. "Oh, no!"

"What am I missing?" Luke asked.

Delilah grinned. "Pablo bought a bunch of whiskey and liquor. I think a lot of it's cask strength."

"So, over one-hundred proof?" A smile spread across Luke's face as he understood the reason for Delilah's laughter.

"Yup," Delilah said.

"Pablo's not going to be happy about you torching his hooch," Owen said.

"He can bill me," Luke replied. "Delilah, you keep the front-line alert. I'll go organize the dump truck gang. I'll have Kelly blow the air horn three short blasts and a long blast. At that point, get your people to their vehicles."

Delilah nodded firmly. "Right. Good luck, Luke."

"You too, Dee." Luke turned back to Rhonda. "Rhonda, mind running me down the line?"

"Sure thing, handsome. Climb on." Rhonda gestured behind her with her head.

Luke climbed on the back and situated his feet, wrapping his arms around Rhonda's waist. This time, she kept their pace to more respectable speeds since there were a lot of people buzzing about, readying the caravan to roll out. Rhonda slowed to a stop next to the dump truck with the huge "V" snowplow blade. The blade looked mean and ready to fuck some shit up.

"Rhonda!" Owen called. "Take me back up front?"

"Sure, get your ass on the back," Rhonda replied. "But after this, I'm finding a place to stow this bike. I'm taking this baby home."

Luke chuckled as she spun around and took Owen back to his truck. "Hey, Kelly, Owen fill you in on the plan?"

"Yup. I've always wanted to bash into something with one of these, so I'm really looking forward to this." Kelly grinned eagerly, her eyes twinkling with delight at the thought of all the destruction she was about to perpetrate.

Luke shook his head. "Well, you're definitely Owen's friend."

Kelly laughed. "Yeah, he collects us troublemakers, but you do realize you're Owen's friend as well?"

"Did I ever say I don't like making trouble?" Luke replied, smirking.

"Ha!"

"So I hear I need to send the bill to you?" Pablo asked, stepping out from the shadow of his nearby truck, pulling his shirt on after shifting back from his wolf form.

"Yup."

"Well, if I can't drink it, I at least get to throw some of it," Pablo replied.

Luke nodded crisply. "OK, you're in charge of the team in the dump truck. Kelly, I'm riding shotgun."

Pablo jogged to the back of his pickup and crawled into the bed, reemerging with a couple cases of liquor and some rags he kept for various purposes. He set the boxes down and rifled through the bottles, taking out a bottle of whiskey. Pulling the foil off, he pulled the cork and lifted it to his lips, tipping his head back for a pull. With a happy sigh, he handed it to Luke, who poured some in his mouth, letting the fire burn down his throat.

"Cask strength will kick you on the way down." Luke handed the bottle to Kelly.

She took a pull, then squatted down and grabbed a rag to shove down the bottle's neck. When the bottle was effectively plugged, she tipped it upside down, letting the whiskey soak into the rag. Luke and the rest of the people riding in the snowplow joined Kelly in turning the bottles of booze into Molotov cocktails.

"What about these lower proof ones? Eighty proof gonna light?" Kelly asked.

"It will when the higher proof stuff goes off. There's enough hundred proof plus stuff to light their asses up," Pablo replied, taking a pull from the bottle he'd just opened.

In short work, they'd turned two cases of liquor into two dozen Molotov cocktails. Pablo and his team loaded them carefully into the back of the dump truck, then loaded themselves. The heavy metal of the bed walls and the snowplow should provide solid protection for anyone riding in the front or back.

"Kelly, give the air horn three short blasts and a long one."

"Righto." She stepped into the cab and pulled the cable attached to the big horn on the roof, blasting the relative quiet of the night.

Wolves from the front line appeared, sprinting toward their getaway cars. Down the line, vehicles fired up. With everything progressing, Luke jogged around the back of the dump truck and climbed up its steps, propping his shotgun against the dash.

"Pablo, give me a couple bottles. I don't want to miss out on the fun," Luke called.

Laughing, Pablo handed a few over. "See you on the other side, buddy."

"Yup. We'll sit and drink some good whiskey, my friend." Luke ducked into the cab and pulled the door shut.

Kelly fired up the truck, the cab rocking to life under the powerful rumble of the big diesel engine. Creeping forward, she brought the behemoth up to speed slowly as she maneuvered down the side of their caravan, but as soon as Owen's truck moved out of the way, she became more serious and coaxed as much acceleration out of the beast as she could. Approaching the gap left by Owen's pickup, she lowered the snowplow so it rested just above the pavement.

"Hold on to your ass, that gap isn't big enough…yet." Kelly leaned forward, excitement on her face.

Luke braced himself as the snowplow slammed through the gap, throwing the bullet-ridden heaps out of the way. Kelly whooped happily at her first piece of vehicular mayhem. With the line of shot up cars passed, Kelly aimed straight down the middle of the road, lining up the leading point of the plow with the dotted yellow lines. Once they cleared the bridge, Luke looked in the side mirror and saw a line of headlights behind them.

Kelly kept accelerating, grabbing more gears, and urged the dump truck toward the upper range of its speed. Reaching down, Luke pushed in the cigarette lighter, glad the truck wasn't so new it no longer had a lighter and just the plug for a power cable.

With a gleeful cackle, Kelly pointed toward the vans they were charging. "Look at the little ants scurry. I'm so looking forward to kicking over their anthill."

Ants scurrying proved to be an apt description as the lined-up vampires waiting to execute their orders scrambled away from the impending destruction. A few tried to get to their vans in an effort to move them out of the way of the snowplow. Luke rolled down the window as the lighter popped out. He grabbed the first bottle and put the cherry red lighter tip to the alcohol-soaked rag. As soon as it caught well enough, Luke stuck it out of the window and hurled it forward to smash against the nearest van. It exploded into a cascade of liquid fire.

He quickly lit the other and hurled it out the window, catching another van just as Kelly plowed their snowplow into the vans blocking the road. The impact rattled Luke's bones, but the first vans parted like the Red Sea just in time to slam into the next line of vans. All around them, more bottles shattered as the crew in the bed of the dump truck hurled their payload far and wide, taking out every van they could hit and any random vampires in the way. Soon, shotgun fire joined the cacophony of destruction as the pack took their opportunity to payback the vampires for all they'd done to the packs—and to Luke.

Luke grabbed his shotgun and pumped a shell into the chamber, resting the butt against his left shoulder so he could shoot effectively. As soon as he drew the bead he wanted, he fired, taking out the vampire. He fired his entire magazine, hitting something with all six shots, destroying four vamps.

Pulling the gun back through the window, Luke reloaded it, his old dexterity returning as he went through the practiced motions. "Slow us down a bit. I want to make sure the line behind us makes it through."

Luke flipped the safety on and set the shotgun aside, then twisted in his seat and poked his head out the window. "Hey, Pablo!"

Pablo poked his head and shoulders over the corner of the dump truck wall. "Hey, Luke!"

"How's it looking back there?"

Pablo cupped his hands around his mouth. "Our caravan is moving fast, so tell Kelly to pick it back up."

"Any vamps moving on them?" Luke shouted.

Pablo shrugged. "Not really, seeing a few shots coming from cars. Owen is weaving his way all over the place now that he's across the bridge, so that's keeping the fangers scurrying about."

Luke gave Pablo a thumbs up. "Let me know if anything changes."

"Got it!"

Luke lowered himself back into his seat. "Let's pick up our speed so we don't have a traffic jam. Keep it topped out as fast as you can go safely. We can slow it down when we're sure everyone's past their line."

"Roger that." Kelly gave him a sassy salute as she mashed the pedal.

The diesel engine roared as it reached the top of its performance. Kelly could probably push it further, but they didn't want to blow the engine out on their blockade smasher—he had no idea what else the vamps might have in store for them, and he was loath to needlessly throw away tools he could use to get his friends to safety.

"What's the road like ahead?" Luke asked, speaking loudly over the engine.

Kelly cast a quick glance Luke's way. "We're about to slide into some hills, river on one side, steep hill on the other side of the road. A bit windy. Why?"

"Just want to be prepared."

Luke jumped when something hit the roof of the cab above his head. He popped his head out the window to see Pablo hanging over the corner.

"Looks like Owen is through!" Pablo yelled.

Luke gave him a thumbs up and turned to Kelly. "We're through the line."

With both hands on the wheel, Kelly kept her eyes locked forward. "Good, I want to slow us down a bit. I'm not sure this old beast can handle much more of this, plus the roads up ahead aren't made for speeding in one of these things."

As they advanced down the road, the overwhelming feeling of "vampire" decreased until they drove around a bend, and it faded to nothing. Without the miasma pressing on his brain, his shoulders relaxed as he heaved a sigh of relief.

"Feeling good there?" Kelly asked.

Luke chuckled. "No—I mean yes. I can't feel vampires anymore. We're passed them."

Kelly snorted and shook her head. "Well don't get too content, we got a lot of lonely road in front of us."

"I won't, but…" He squinted, looking ahead.

"I don't like the color of those flashing lights." Her knuckles whitened as she squeezed the steering wheel.

"No. Me either. Nor do I like the feeling I'm getting." He turned to face her. "How do you feel about local cops?"

"Ain't no reservation cops out here. Probably state pigs," she replied, a sneer on her face. "They like to harass us when we cross the line out of Wind River since they're usually not welcome on the reservation."

"How do you feel about vampire cops?" Luke asked.

In response, Kelly let the roar of the diesel engine accelerating answer Luke's question. When someone pounded on the roof again, Luke was expecting it. He popped his head out the window. Pablo once again hung over the corner, but this time pushed up his nose making a pig face.

Luke chuckled. "I see them. Vampire cops. We're going through. Have everyone pass the word."

Pablo nodded and ducked down. Pulling his head back in, he cinched down the seatbelt and focused his concentration forward. As they swept around the gentle corner, they saw the pair of cops parked across the road, blocking it between the fences separating the road from the surrounding land.

"Down the pipe?" Kelly asked.

"Let's keep them on the hook for now. Stay in your lane. Keep the pedal down, but can you tap your brake lights to give them a flash of red?"

Kelly chuckled and nodded.

As they got closer, the head lights mounted on the top of the hood, since the blade blocked the truck's regular lights, illuminated figures moving behind cars. They looked like they were getting into a shooting pose. He counted about six or so.

"Can you raise the blade a few inches so we get a little coverage here in the cab?"

Kelly reached over and pulled the lever, activating the hydraulics to raise the blade. "There, that should do it. Should still be able to hit them just below the bumper."

Once she had the blade where she wanted it, she slouched down lower. Luke followed suit, not wanting to catch a stray bullet in his teeth. Once the cops figured out they weren't actually going to stop, Kelly moved into the center of the road. The cops opened fire, bullets pinging off the blade until the vampires calculated they'd better move out of the way. Even with their vampiric speed, they barely dove out of the way as Kelly slammed into the cars. The sound of a cop car screeching against the "V" shaped blade made Luke smile. As the wheel on the car to the right caught, the blade scooped it up and flipped it off the road. The crew in the back fired off several shots after the vampires trying to scramble out of the way. After a few seconds, they were out of range.

"Hey, Luke. Do you think this is their last roadblock?" Kelly asked.

He turned toward her. "Maybe? That was a pretty weak one. Why?"

Her eyes flicked down to the instrument panel. "We don't keep these things topped up on fuel in the summer, not if we've left the blade on them, and we're looking like we're awfully close to the big fat 'E' on the gauge here."

"I guess we're going to have to look for a place to ditch this beast. Will using the tribe's snowplow bring down some heat on y'all?" Luke asked.

"We'll just say some drunk college kids lifted it. You better wipe down your side for prints, though. I'll be fine. Mine are all over this thing, anyway. I'll wipe the wheel down so it looks half-assed. If Pablo has any of that booze left, we should tip a bottle over inside the cab to back up our little ruse." She pulled a phone out of her pocket and handed it to Luke after unlocking it. "See if you can find the next turnout. It shouldn't be too far, but I'm not sure. Don't come out this way much."

Taking the phone, he pulled up her maps app and centered in on their current position. After scrolling for several seconds, he found a likely spot.

"Looks like about five or so miles ahead." Luke handed the phone back to her.

Kelly took a second to zoom out then looked down at the gauge panel, a frown furrowing her eyebrows and bringing the corner of her lips down. "It'll be close. We chewed through a lot of fuel going as fast as we were."

Nodding, Luke pulled his hands inside his sleeves and wiped down everything he thought he'd touched, finishing up just as Kelly slowed down and pulled into a scenic turnout. When Kelly parked as far to the edge of the scenic pullout as possible, she let out a heavy breath of relief as she lowered the blade to the ground and turned the key off. Grabbing the hem of her shirt, she started wiping things to smear her fingerprints. Luke opened the door with his sleeve and stepped out, pulling his shotgun out and gathering the spent shells ejected into the cab.

"Why we stopping?" Pablo called from the bed.

"Out of gas, or near to it. Plus, this thing will be a dead give-away to anyone looking for us," Luke replied. "You better gather up our shells and wipe down the bed for prints as best as you can. They'll report it stolen by college kids. Also, you got any of that booze left?"

"Yeah, we got a few. Why?" Pablo looked suspicious after donating so many of his prizes.

"Pick the one you care about the least and dump it in the cab. We need some seasoning for the story."

Pablo sighed. "Alright. You owe me, dude."

"You know I'm good for it. I'll make it right."

The caravan packed into the small scenic pullout, waiting for the members of the snowplow brigade to clean up and rejoin their cars.

Owen took the opportunity to tear down his machine guns and stow them out of sight.

"Hey, Kelly, great driving there," Luke said.

She grinned broadly. "Thanks! I've always wanted to do something like that. Oddly enough, when people pay you to use heavy equipment, they expect you to be kinda careful and not commit carnage with it."

Luke laughed and patted her on the shoulder. "Thanks for letting us help you fulfill your dreams of vehicular destruction. It was really great to meet you."

"You're not getting rid of us that easily. We're going out to the coast. Owen promised to take us fishing on the Pacific. Might try to catch the tuna if it comes in close enough to shore. You should join us. There'll be a bale of pot big enough for a Harold and Kumar movie." Kelly smiled.

"I might take you up on that offer after I get settled back into life a bit."

"Cool. See you later!"

"Yeah. We better get on the move before anyone sends out trackers. Owen, great job on the guns." Luke smiled at his friend, weariness tugging at the edge of his awareness.

"No prob, Luke. See you out on the coast," Owen said, jumping out of the bed of his truck.

Luke waved and headed toward Pablo's pickup. Maggie joined him, finished in the ambulance van for the time. Sam popped out of the driver's seat and made her way around to the little group gathered at the back.

"Patrice driving the van?" Sam asked.

Maggie nodded. "Yeah. She volunteered so I could ride with Luke for a bit. Now that Rhonda stashed her new prize, they'll trade off driving it for a while."

Delilah strode over purposefully and opened the back of Pablo's truck, pulling herself onto the tailgate. Putting her fingers between her lips, she let out a shrill whistle. "Great job, team! Now get to your assigned vehicles. You all know your routes and destinations. Stay in communication. Don't stretch your groups out too far. Good luck and see you all at home."

Everyone who'd stopped to listen let up a cheer, turning to high five or hug whoever stood nearby. Now through the immediate chaos, Luke's energy drained from his body as the adrenaline worked its way out of his system.

Pablo walked up and patted him on the back. "Let's get moving, dude. We got miles to eat."

Sam handed Pablo the keys and headed toward Delilah's car. "See you later, gators!"

"In a while, crocodile!" Gwen shouted from the window of Pablo's pickup. "You're riding in the back with me, Luke."

"Sure thing, Gwen." Luke climbed into the back and took the rear passenger side seat since Gwen was in the middle and Roxi was on the other side. Maggie climbed in the front while Pablo walked around to the driver's door.

Pablo pulled out first, going slowly as a few cars worked their way out of the caravan to join them. They were the lead group and would continue up Highway 26 until the split at Moran, where they'd head south to Jackson Hole and then through Idaho and Oregon. Some of the groups would head north through Yellowstone and Montana or west into Idaho.

"So… How was the ride so far?" Luke asked.

"Besides the Mad Max caravan of flames and destruction?" Roxi asked. "Gwen has been teaching me about Billie Eilish."

"What or who is Billie Eilish?" He focused his gaze on Gwen as her face lit up.

"She's the best!" Gwen pulled out her phone and opened it to her music app and hit play. "She's kind of this cool, trippy alt-rock singer. She's only like a few years older than me. This is 'Bad Guy,' it's her best song. It's got over a billion streams."

"Billion with a b?" he asked, incredulous.

"Yeah. Um, one-billion-eight-hundred-million and some," Gwen replied.

"That's impressive. Lay it on me, little one." Luke smiled, happy to see the enthusiasm of his ward.

After the heavy electronic bass intro, an airy young woman's voice filled the truck as they got up to speed. Soon, Gwen was belting out lyrics. Some of the songs had explicit lyrics which Gwen didn't change, singing them out slightly louder.

"Gwen, what are we?" Maggie asked, turning in her seat to look into the back of the truck. She was trying to keep a straight face.

Gwen sighed, then Pablo turned, a huge smile on his face, and together, he and Gwen yelled, "Werewolves, not swearwolves!"

"Isn't 'What We Do In The Shadows' a bit much for a kid?" Luke asked.

Maggie smiled indulgently at Gwen. "We only let her watch that one scene. We told her she'd have to get your permission to watch an R-rated movie."

"Come on! I've seen plenty of scary stuff," Gwen protested.

"I know you have, but you shouldn't have had to live that at your age," Luke said. "It's my job to give you a childhood if I can." Seeing the disappointment on her face, he nearly relented. "Let me watch it again, and I'll decide if you can get away with it. It's got vampires though…"

"I know. But they're stupid vampires and only a little evil." Gwen held her finger and thumb a bit apart to demonstrate.

"We'll talk about it, but for now. What other new music do you have for me?" Luke asked.

Gwen rolled her eyes. "Fine. Let me see what else you haven't heard of. Oh! Future Islands released a new album. I know you really like them."

Luke smiled, feeling loved and appreciated. "I'd love to hear it."

CHAPTER
TWENTY-SEVEN

They drove straight through, trading drivers when they stopped to refuel, pick up snacks, or take a pit stop. Roxi offered, though warned that she hadn't driven on the right side of the road in ages.

"I guess if we need to wake up and scream in terror!" Gwen said.

"Be nice. It's all interstate from here on out, so she'd probably be fine," Maggie replied.

They opted to put off Roxi's first American driving lesson until she was healed and feeling up to it, but between their little mini caravan, there were plenty of people who could take driving shifts to give the others rest. Toward the end of the trip, Luke fell asleep, resting up against the door. He jolted awake when the truck pulled off the paved road onto a gravel road.

"Birkenfeld?" Luke asked, yawning.

"Yeah," Sam said. "We decided you could use a slow reentry into life, so we figured the farm would be the best place to start."

Luke nodded, a content smile tipping his lips. He had many happy memories at the farm, including his first kiss with Maggie. He'd enjoy the quiet solitude of the Coastal Range.

"Feeling up for a burger down at The Birk?" Pablo asked, once again behind the wheel.

"I'm always ready for a Birk burger. Mind if I take a shower first?" Luke asked.

Sam stretched, rotating her neck. "Sure, we got time. I'm sure everyone will want to take a moment to freshen up after everything."

Once they parked, Luke slid out and made room for anyone else coming out of his side of the truck. "I hope there's some clean laundry, I think I used all the clothes you brought me."

Maggie stepped up next to him, sliding her arms around him. "I have some more clothes up in my room for you. Figured it was better than dragging everything all over the country."

Luke squeezed Maggie, kissing the top her head. "Hopefully, we can spot Roxi some more clothes until we can get her some new ones of her own."

"We keep a store of clothes up here. We'll get her set up until we return to town," Sam said. "We'll have to find a place for her to stay while she's in Portland."

"I figured I'd offer her my guest room until she figures out what she wants to do," Luke said.

Sam nodded, holding Luke's gaze for a few seconds longer than Luke felt was normal. "Well, I'm eager to tuck into a Birk burger, and I need a shower before that's tenable. I'm heading in. Besides, I see Holly's car, and I'm in need of some sugar."

Pablo opened the back of the pickup and lifted out the dog. He'd been eating the kibble they'd purchased in Wyoming and was looking a little less wobbly, but like the rest of them, he still had a long way to go.

"Who's Holly?" Roxi asked, joining the huddle by Luke.

"Sam's wife and the packleader," Luke answered.

"Ah. So what's this I hear about a burger?" Roxi stretched, twisting her torso.

"Oh my god, they're the best!" Gwen said. "I'll go find you a room so you can get ready!"

Gwen grabbed Roxi's hand and dragged her toward the house. Roxi did the best she could to keep up, hopping twice on her good leg for every one on her bad leg.

"Slow down, kiddo," Maggie called.

"Right. Sorry, Roxi," Gwen said.

Luke chuckled as they disappeared into the house.

"Gwen seems to be taken with your new friend." Maggie gave Luke a last squeeze then grabbed his hand, leading him into the house.

Luke and Maggie retired to the room they used when they visited the farm. Luke made his shower quick, his stomach rumbling, so he could let Maggie get a shower of her own before heading to dinner. He knew the company would keep him awake, but he couldn't wait to sink into the bed with Maggie's body next to him.

They met downstairs. Typically on a lovely evening, they'd walk in, but no one mentioned it with Roxi unable to join them due to her leg, so they piled back into the cars and drove the mile down to The Birk.

"I'm very excited to have my first proper American diner burger," Roxi said, dressed in a pair of ill-fitting jeans loaned by Simone. Roxi was a couple inches taller, but the closest in size at the hips and thighs to the Senegalese French woman.

Luke had missed the entire development of Simone and Delilah's relationship while he'd been a prisoner. He'd been looking forward to seeing if the spark witnessed in France and Belgium between the two young women would ignite. It appeared it had and was still burning strong. The two women always seemed to be touching, even if it was as simple as just leaning into each other. Their looks and smiles warmed Luke's heart, briefly pushing aside the hollow anger smoldering inside. He was happy for Delilah and Simone, but not seeing his friend fall in love and start a meaningful relationship with a wonderful woman was just another tally to add to the sheet of what the vampires had taken from him.

Gwen, back in the first place she'd been welcomed and made to feel safe, clowned around with the people who'd become her adopted family. The group they'd left Wyoming with had been reduced to what Luke considered the core of the pack, at least his core—Maggie, Sam, Pablo, Delilah, and Holly, along with the new additions of Simone and Roxi.

Everyone, used to Luke's bouts of quiet, focused on making Roxi feel welcome. They knew she was important to him, plus he could see they genuinely liked the woman as they coaxed pieces of her story from her in between attempts to make her laugh. Despite his physical and spiritual exhaustion, the friendly camaraderie of the people he loved most wore away the edges of his funk, drawing him into laughter and jokes. A few beers didn't hurt either.

When they finished, everyone did what they usually did at the farm. Sam and Holly retired to their room to reconnect after Sam's time away on a mission. Pablo went to his room to watch movies on his laptop. He was flying solo for the week or so it took to free Luke and get him home while Tony was in charge of the pack and Holly waited at the farm for the team to return.

Delilah went to her room, but now had Simone to join her. Gwen, still a ravenous book worm, slid away to the quiet of her room and whatever story she was currently tearing through. Roxi, exhausted for her first night at the farm, escaped to the room she'd been assigned.

Luke and Maggie grabbed a bottle of whiskey and a fuzzy blanket, then planted themselves on the couch where they'd first kissed, outside on the porch.

"Are you sure you wouldn't rather head to bed? You're practically falling asleep on your feet." Maggie stroked his cheek.

Luke captured her hand and brought her palm to his lips, kissing it. "I know, but I need to have a glass of whiskey with you on this couch."

"For strictly medicinal purposes?" Maggie asked, her tone teasing.

Luke affected a mock serious face. "Yes. As a medical professional, you can see it's the correct diagnosis."

Maggie laughed, then she leaned to the side and poured two glasses from the bottle they'd brought out. Once she handed him his glass, they touched them, then took a sip. The burn of the whiskey felt amazing after months on end of bland monotony and loneliness punctuated by terrifying struggles for survival, but the warmth of Maggie next to him felt even better.

"Damn, I missed you so much, Maggie." He took another drink. "It's…it's really real, isn't it?"

Maggie tipped his chin toward her so she could look into his eyes. "What, Luke? What's real?"

"I'm out. Free." The corners of his eyes burned as he breathed shallowly, trying to get his emotions in check. "Aren't I?"

Sensing his distress, she took the glass from his hands and set it down on the end table along with hers, then pulled him into her arms. Luke buried his head in Maggie's shoulder as she stroked his long hair and rubbed his back.

"It's real, you're free. It's OK, Luke, you can let it out."

It was the gentle, soothing tone that finally broke the dam of Luke's tears as he sobbed into her shoulder. Making soothing sounds, Maggie let him cry himself out, the poison of the last many months pouring out in his tears. When they finally dried, he felt empty but clean. She left him to sit quietly on the couch while she fetched some tissues. After he dabbed his cheeks and blew his nose, she handed him his glass of whiskey. For the first time since Luxembourg, he felt free.

LATE THE NEXT MORNING, they met in the kitchen for their usual debriefing meeting. Donuts and coffee awaited Luke and Maggie when they appeared. Holly must have brought the donuts the previous day when she'd met them at the farm.

Luke, feeling greedy for the little luxuries, took a maple bar and an apple bear claw to go with his steaming hot cup of black coffee. Maggie grabbed a maple bar for her coffee. Gwen had already been in to grab her donut so she could return to her book out in the sitting room. Everyone else was already at the table, save for Roxi. No one had told her about the meeting.

"Gwen, dear," Maggie called into the other room.

"Yes?" Gwen replied.

"Can you run up and see if Roxi would like to join us, please?"

"Okelie dokelie," Gwen replied.

Her footfalls thundered across the sitting room and up the stairs as she ran. A couple minutes later, Roxi popped her head into the room.

"You wanted to see me?" she asked shyly.

Sam rose and gestured toward the table. "Come on in, grab a donut and a coffee. We're just going to have a little chat so we can all get on the same page after bustin' you out of the hoosegow."

"Hoose-gow?" Roxi asked.

"Jail. She means a jail." Holly playfully swatted Sam's shoulder. "Since we're Luke's friends and he's part of our pack, we like to talk over these incidents to figure out what new dangers are posed to the pack and what we can do to protect ourselves and our city. We'd all like you to join us for your perspective."

Roxi nodded, smiling nervously. "I don't mean to be discourteous, but do you have tea?"

Sam smiled. "You're not being discourteous at all. Let me turn the water on. We have a few different teas. If you'll come over to the counter, you can pick what you want."

Sam pushed the button on the kettle and pulled down a few boxes of tea bags and tins of loose leaf.

"Oh, Earl Grey would be lovely," Roxi said.

Luke smiled at Roxi, glad his friends were doing their best to make her feel welcome and part of the group. He wanted her to feel at home.

Sam pulled a tea strainer from the cabinet, scooped some the Earl Grey leaves into it, and set it in a mug while she waited for the kettle to finish. "If you're feeling peckish, the donuts are quite tasty. If not, we have other stuff in the fridge. Breakfasts are typically a 'fend for yourself' situation here at the farm. We have quite a bit more food stocked, since most of us planned to stay up here for a while to get out of town and take a break after our little trip to Wyoming."

"I see," Roxi said, moving to the donut box and picking up a small plate from the counter. After surveying the options, she picked one and waited for Sam to finish her cup.

"Do you take milk or sugar?" Sam asked.

Roxi shook her head, her wild black hair swishing back and forth. "No thank you, not with a proper cuppa Earl Grey."

When the kettle beeped, Sam poured it over the tea, then set a timer on her phone before handing a small bowl to Roxi. "When my phone goes off, pull the strainer."

"Thank you, Sam." Roxi turned to survey the table.

Pablo, who'd been sitting next to Luke, slid over to the empty chair next to it to free the spot for Roxi. She gave him a light nod and an awkward smile before taking the offered seat. Luke gave her what he hoped was a friendly and reassuring smile. He longed to reach under the table to take her hand. After so many months of holding it as the only form of human contact, he felt oddly wrong without it. Maggie sat on his other side, and he yearned for her, missing the time they could have had together. The last handful of days, she'd been there, but he'd only been able to engage with her on the most surface level. Despite their physical proximity, there'd been…not a gulf, but a gap between them he couldn't explain—although he guessed it was probably himself feeling it or causing it. Maybe both.

It had only been a handful of days since he'd been freed and regained a portion of his strength, yet he wanted too much of himself. He couldn't put his entire life back together after only a few short days. He hadn't been on vacation. It would take a while, a long while if he was being honest with himself, to return to some semblance of normalcy.

He closed his eyes and took in a deep breath, holding it until he thought his chest would explode before letting it out, trying to keep the exhale from being a noticeable sound at the table. With a small shake of his head, he tuned back into the casual chit-chat of his friends as they nibbled on their donuts and drank their caffeinated beverages.

"So, Luke." Holly fixed her intense gaze on him. "What hell have we gotten ourselves into this time?"

It was odd that Holly was trying to be somewhat jocular while entirely accurate about the depths they might have sunk to.

"I don't know, Holly, but it's not good. Bad might be a more accurate descriptor."

Holly, normally the poster child of stoicism, seemed to shrink in on herself. Luke wasn't sure what she'd been told about the incident in the mountains of Wyoming, but the internal scars he still felt attested to their danger.

Luke looked down at the table, his hands clasped there. "Holly, I've walked this earth for nearly two thousand years and fought the evilest creatures that have been created, but I've never felt anything like what happened outside that arena. Zalmoxis, if that's who he was, felt deeper, eviler, worse than anything I've ever felt."

He closed his eyes, trying to breathe his way to stability, his fingers intertwined and knuckles white with tension. He stared into Holly's eyes. "I've never been laid more bare like that in my entire life. I can still feel the absolute desolation right here." He hit himself with his fore and middle fingers in the middle of his chest. "Whoever he was, he stripped me of all the juice I'd taken from the vampires and even the blessing Selene had given me."

"Selene?" Holly asked, her brow troubled.

"The goddess of the moon." Luke chuckled humorlessly. "She's your goddess too. The goddess who brought the pleas of your progenitors to Artemis. The beautiful light who blessed werewolves and welcomed them out of the darkness they were born out of. She's the velvet glove that surround's Mithras's fist." Luke took in a shaky, deep breath and let it out. "She is gentle and has given me strength and her kindness more times than I can think of or have deserved. And it was all stripped from me painfully, agonizingly so. I don't know who we face, Holly, but it's bad."

Maggie's hand slid up his right arm, taking his hand and giving it a gently but firm squeeze. He momentarily startled when he felt Roxi's hand on his left leg, the hand giving a gentle pat.

"W...w...who is Zalmoxis?" Holly asked, her face blanching.

Luke squeezed his eyes together, letting a harsh breath out through his nostrils. "He was a Dacian god. Supposedly, he was a man and studied with Pythagoras. When he died, he rose three years later, alive."

"Do you believe he was a god?" Sam asked.

"I don't know." Luke shook his head. "I know a few gods." He laughed harshly. "Such an odd thing to say and mean. I'm having trouble gauging the power of a god. He stripped me bare, then tore down a massive stone arena. Pulled it down like it was crumbling into a black hole. I've never felt anything like that in my entire life. He was amused by us, but profoundly hateful. Utterly evil. He drained the vampires, drained them and left husks. Frankly, I'm amazed any of us left there alive and weren't crushed and condemned to utter oblivion."

Luke's words left the room silent, the life sucked out of it as they contemplated his words and the tenor he'd placed on them. Holly, desperate for something substantive to grasp, looked around the table at the members of her pack council—Pablo, her second, Sam, her wife, Maggie, her medical leader. Luke, watching Holly's eyes as they moved from person to person, could see she found no comfort or reassurance from the people who'd witnessed what had happened firsthand.

"Is there anything we can do?" she asked, looking pleadingly at him.

He'd never seen Holly anything less than confident and self-assured. Her seeming helplessness startled him. He'd rarely met someone as deservedly self-confident, but to see her confidence shaken? It didn't sit right with him. He didn't realize how much responsibility and leadership he'd abdicated to her since he'd become involved with her pack. From the moment Luke formed the Black Legion, he'd operated independently of military control, but he'd always subjected himself to civilian leadership, such as it was in the Roman Empire. He'd always sought to place himself under a civilian leader whenever possible. When he didn't have someone of appropriate gravitas, he fell into a habit of keeping his operations confined to himself as much as possible. Once Pablo interjected himself into Luke's life and mission, Luke welcomed Holly's authority as the final arbiter of his status. With the potential for such destruction and unfathomable power, the veil of Holly's authority disintegrated as she looked to Luke for answers on how to protect her pack. Her family.

And he couldn't provide them.

"I don't know, Holly. I need to speak with Selene. This is beyond me, and I'm afraid it may be more than even she can address. I won't know until I can speak with her. I may not be able to avoid Mithras anymore. I may have to give myself over to him again. I just don't know, Holly." Luke pleaded with her, focusing his lack of confidence into his gaze.

They were the leaders at the table. The ones everyone else looked to and looked up to. They grasped at each other for a straw they could present to the people who looked to them, finding nothing in the other. Holly sighed and nodded.

"What can we do in the meantime?" Holly asked. "Until we know what we're facing…"

"Keep driving the vampires out of Portland. We need to make this a total no-go zone. It's time we expand beyond our little corner. We need to figure out what packs we can bring in on our side. We need to watch for plants. There were a lot of werewolves serving and fighting for the vampires. If we let the vampires bring over a lot of packs to their cause, we're going to be in serious trouble. How do you feel about diplomacy?"

"We've largely been working in that direction during your absence." Holly nodded, looking more confident having reasonable things she could accomplish. "This pack wouldn't be here without it. I'll reach out to my allies and feel them out. I'll have anyone in the pack with good contacts in other packs start opening those lines of communication. Besides reaching out to your…uh…contact, what will you be doing and how can we help?"

"Right now, I need to do some healing, but I need to see where my gear is and we need to see about getting Roxi's rudis fixed." He turned to Roxi. "Do you have contacts with other hunters? People you've run into in your travels?"

Roxi nodded. "Yeah. I can try to track some of them down. Have you spoken with the hunters you brought out of the arena?"

Luke shook his head. "I haven't spoken with them yet. I will as soon as I'm back in town."

"Why didn't you bring them out here?" Roxi asked.

"They aren't pack. They're unknown commodities." Sam got up and refilled her cup of coffee. "You're here because Luke trusts you. This is the pack's retreat—where we celebrate and mourn. We don't just invite anyone up here."

"I feel honored." Roxi gave a close-lipped smile.

"I wish Pieter was up here," Luke said. "I want to talk to him about Luxembourg."

"He wanted to get back home and didn't figure you'd be in any shape to really discuss things for a while," Pablo said.

"We've been getting an influx of Belgian refugees fleeing the pack there," Sam said. "He's been working on settling them."

"Ah, I see. He's probably right. I'm almost two years out of date on what's been going on. I guess I'm going to need you all to fill me in. We're going to need to set up a worldwide intelligence and communication network. Playing it local isn't on the table anymore." He sighed and shook his head. "I'm sorry I got you all into this before Wapato, but…"

Holly straightened in her chair, fixing a stern gaze on Luke. "As you told us then, we were involved in this without even knowing it. I can't say I don't wish for the quiet times, but the people of this pack fought to just exist in our world. If it's our job to protect that world, I guess that means we widen our operations." She looked around the table at her packmembers, the werewolves and the humans. "You've helped us fight and made sure we stayed alive. Luke, you've earned our trust and then some. We've got your back."

Luke nodded. "Thank you, Holly. I'll do right by you and the pack."

"I know you will." Holly leaned across the table, narrowing her eyes. "Now, one last question. What is that stinky dog, and why do you have him?"

"I don't know." Luke shrugged. "He was in the special prisoners' section with me and Roxi. I don't know why or what he is, but he seems to be able to shift between that dog and a giant wolf, bigger than any I've ever seen before."

"He kind of looks like a Grampr," Roxi said. Seeing everyone's confused looks, she added, "It's a large Armenian breed of herding dog."

He sighed, mulling over the problem for a moment. "I'm going to have to move him into the house. Whatever he is, I think it's best I keep an eye on him."

Delilah laughed. "Good luck with introducing him to Alfred."

"Oh my, that could be trouble." Maggie chuckled, as did a few other people.

Pablo laughed and stood up. "You better get him groomed. He's one stinky mutt."

Holly shook her head, smiling. "I wish you luck with your weird pets. It's good to have you home, Luke."

The room was silent as they all looked at each other, smiling and nodding. The clink of glasses broke the silence as Pablo pulled whiskey from the cabinet and filled glasses. "I know it's still early, but we're not driving anywhere. I bought something special to celebrate for when we eventually found you. It's been sitting up there for a year."

Sam and Delilah grabbed glasses and passed them out until everyone had one, save for Pablo, who filled one for himself. Holly pulled out a bottle of sparkling apple juice and poured a glass, taking it to the table.

"Gwen," Holly called. "Come in here, please."

When the young teen poked her head in, they waved her to the table and handed her the sparkling juice.

Pablo raised his glass. "Luke, buddy, it's good to have you back home with your family. I missed you, and I know everyone else here did as well." He turned his gaze to Roxi. "I also want to welcome Roxi to our little group. If you ever need anything, just ask any of us."

They all touched classes and took drinks. Luke sighed at the burn of the fine whiskey, taking another sip.

"Now, I have a question that I've been dying to get an answer to," Luke said. "How in the world did you find me? I thought I was going to die in there."

Everyone turned their heads toward Gwen. The kid blushed and lowered her eyes.

"So I have you to thank for my freedom?" Luke asked. "How did you know where I was?"

Gwen paused, swallowed, then gathered her strength, looking up and into Luke's eyes. "You remember when you were in Belgium, and Maggie and I couldn't get into your house?"

"Yeah."

Roxi looked confused since she was the only one who wasn't around then.

Luke looked at her. "When I went into my Mithraeum in Belgium, it activated my shrine in my house in Portland."

"Well, when that happened, I, uh, I went into the basement and found it. I wanted to see it. After I opened it, a woman's voice started talking to me. I closed it real fast and ran away, but..."

Luke chuckled. "But you were curious and went back?"

"Well, not at first, but one night when I was outside and the full moon was out, she talked to me again and told me who she was. Is it true?"

Luke tipped his head to the side, brows furrowed. "Is what true?"

"Is she really the goddess of the werewolves?" Gwen asked.

"Selene?" Luke smiled encouragingly at the teen.

Gwen nodded.

Luke nodded slowly, contemplating his answer. "It's a complex story, but yes. She took in the werewolves after they'd been created. She and Artemis took them in and accepted them when they fled their cre...a...tors..."

"Luke?" Holly asked.

He held his hand up to forestall her. Settling his elbows on the table and resting his chin in his hands, he stared into blank space. While Luke sat quietly thinking, Pablo topped up a few glasses, including Luke's when he didn't wave Pablo off.

After a few more minutes, Maggie rubbed his shoulder. "What's going on up there, Luke?"

"I'm having some thoughts about who that might have been at

the arena—Zalmoxis. I'm going to need to do some research first, but..." He shook his head to clear it. "Sorry for the interruption. Gwen, please continue."

"Well, Selene started talking to me. When you disappeared, I asked her to find you. She said she didn't know where you were. She said she looked but couldn't find you. The only thing she knew was you were alive. Then a few weeks ago, she found me and told me she'd found you and knew where you were."

"Did you tell anyone you were talking to her?" Luke asked.

Gwen shook her head. "Who would believe me?"

"I would have," Maggie said. "Pablo, Delilah, and Sam all met her in Belgium."

Gwen crossed her arms, looking petulant. "But did any of you tell me that? You never tell me anything."

Sam snickered, covering it with her hand. "She's got a point there."

Gwen rushed forward with her explanation. "So when she told me she knew where you were, I told Maggie, and she told Sam."

"And then she guided you to Wyoming?" Luke asked.

They nodded.

"What I don't get is why she was able to find you all the sudden," Sam asked.

Luke chuckled and shook his head. "The arena had a retractable roof. They opened it during one of my fights, and she was able to find me."

"Ironyyyyy..." Pablo said, laughing.

"All the same, I'm glad they decided to be fancy with their design," Luke said.

"Me too," Roxi added quietly.

Luke patted her leg under the table.

"Unless there's anything else to add to the discussion, let's call it until we can get going on what we've talked about here. I'm feeling like taking a walk with my wife." Holly slid her hand over Sam's.

"I think I've got a nap on the old schedule," Pablo said, tipping the last of his whiskey into his mouth. He waved and headed upstairs.

Holly and Sam followed him out, heading upstairs to put on some walking clothes. Maggie stood and moved the empty glasses to the sink.

"Luke," Gwen started tentatively. "Would you like to play cribbage?"

"That sounds lovely," Luke replied.

"Maggie?" Gwen asked.

"Of course, Dear."

Gwen looked at Roxi. "Do you know how to play, Roxi?"

Roxi smiled and nodded.

"Yay, we can play teams! I'll go set it up."

Luke helped Roxi up and led her to the sitting room so the four of them could play cards, so he and Roxi could begin the process of healing. He knew they both had a long way to go. A game of cards with some of his favorite people seemed like a good first step toward finding himself again. He just hoped it would be a step on Roxi's journey, and that she'd let him walk it with her.

EPILOGUE

They spent a week at the farm, resting and rehabilitating. After a couple days, Pablo, Sam, and Holly departed for Portland, leaving Luke, Maggie, Roxi, and Gwen. Pablo promised to watch over the giant dog and bring him by the house along with Roxi's rudis after Luke returned to his house and felt settled.

By the end of the week, Roxi felt well enough to make the walk down to The Birk for their last dinner before heading to Portland, though they had to go slowly not to tire her weak leg.

Still, the long walk back and forth wore her out, so she went to bed after a game of cribbage. Gwen took her book upstairs, leaving Maggie and Luke.

"You wait here, Luke." Maggie disappeared into the kitchen and reappeared with a bottle of whiskey and a couple glasses. She held them up and tipped her head to the side, silently asking the question.

Luke stood, took the bottle from her, and replaced it with his hand, leading her out to their favorite couch. She'd already taken a blanket out. When they got their drinks situated, they curled into each other sharing touches and soft kisses. After a week of the farm's peace, Luke finally felt a bit more human, the numbness that had settled in after their rescue starting to warm.

"Maggie, I love you," Luke said.

"I love you, too." She caressed his cheek and beard-covered jaw before giving him a kiss, then deepening it.

Luke's heart fluttered, as warmth surged through his veins. He took a moment to look into Maggie's blue eyes, the intensity of her gaze doubling the feelings he'd not felt in months and months. He'd kept them bottled up to preserve himself. He pulled her in tightly, hungry for her lips and affection.

When they pulled back, Luke grabbed his glass. "Maggie. If you're amenable, I'd like to take some time on this couch and finish this glass. And while we work on it, I'd like to make out with you. Then, I want to take you upstairs to your bed and renew our physical intimacy?"

"Renew our physical intimacy?" Maggie chuckled teasingly.

Luke smiled at the vibrant sound. "I want to make love to you, have sex. I want you, Magdalena."

"I want you too, Luke." She struggled to erase her smile and affect a serious expression. "I find your proposal acceptable."

After more than a year's worth of deprivation, Luke felt positively decadent sipping a wonderful whiskey in between moments of kissing with his girlfriend. When their glasses were empty and Maggie's eyes burned into his, he grew nervous about what would come next. It had been so long since he'd been intimate with Maggie and considered asking for another glass. Sensing his anxiety, Maggie stood up and offered her hand, leading him upstairs to her room. Smiling his relieved thanks, he took her hand and followed, pulling her into a passionate kiss as soon as the door closed.

AFTER A LONG NIGHT, Luke stayed in bed late into the morning, dozing. It wasn't until a gentle knock at the door and Gwen's voice informing him breakfast was ready that he crawled out of bed and pulled on a robe over his pajama bottoms.

When he arrived downstairs, he heard laughter from the kitchen and the voices of Maggie, Roxi, and Gwen. As soon as he stepped through the entry of the kitchen, Gwen brought a cup of coffee for him as he sat at the table. Soon, a plate of pancakes and chicken sausages joined his cup of coffee. As he shook off the last of his sleep and enjoyed his breakfast, he listened to the banter between his ward, his girlfriend, and Roxi. When they finished, all four joined in cleaning up the kitchen and picking up the house so as not to leave a mess for the cleaning crew and whoever from the pack might be up that way next.

Luke wasn't sure if he was ready for life in Portland after being absent, especially considering how he'd been dragged away from it. But he wanted to see his cat Alfred and be in his home once again, though he was afraid it might not feel like his home anymore. Feeling quiet, Luke let Gwen sit in the front with Maggie and control the radio of the pretty Polish doctor's car. Stealing quick glances at Roxi, he watched as her tension rose, her hands fidgeting as she picked at her nails and cuticles absentmindedly. Her eyes flicked about the landscape, the wooded hills of the Coastal mountains turning into towns and then Portland.

"Hey, Maggie. Do we have to go pick up Alfred from somewhere?" Luke asked.

"No. Zel dropped him off this morning and set him up. He's been with us since… You know."

"Please give Zel my thanks for taking care of Alfred and letting us have some time together." Luke smiled at Maggie.

"Of course. When you get settled in, we'll invite you all over for dinner and you can personally thank them. They prefer their thanks in the form of red wine," Maggie replied.

Luke nodded. "That sounds excellent."

They turned onto Luke's street, then, after a few houses, pulled into his driveway. He'd missed his home. It'd always been a comfortable place to live but had truly become a home when he added Gwen and the constant stream of his friends coming and going.

"And we're here," Luke said quietly, more to himself than anyone else.

Maggie popped the trunk, then everyone piled out, grabbing their stuff, what little of it there was for Luke and Roxi, whose bag was filled with clothes borrowed from others and the pack. The gear they'd stripped from the museum in the arena had been taken somewhere else, at least that's what Luke assumed. He hoped they hadn't dumped it in his house.

Out of old habit, Luke reached into his pocket but came back empty, his keys most likely tossed by his captors. Maggie smiled and handed him a key on an empty ring.

"I had a copy of mine made for you," Maggie said.

The sounds of eager meowing on the other side of the door drew a genuine smile to his face. Before he could get the door all the way open, Alfred ran out the door and wound his way around Luke's legs, still meowing incessantly.

"Hey, Alfie!" He bent over and scooped up the cat, hugging him. "I missed you too, buddy."

He stepped into the house, cat in his arms, to clear the doorway for everyone else. Once he stepped into the living room, he looked around, expecting layers of dust and cobwebs from the house's lack of inhabitants.

"We hired a cleaner for the upstairs. Gwen, Zel, and I cleaned up your...office." Maggie's eyes momentarily flicked to Roxi when she called his basement lair an office.

"Thank you, Maggie. I can't thank you enough for all you've done for me while I was gone." Luke pulled her into a hug.

"It's what we do for the people we love. I'm glad you're back." She pulled him in for a kiss. "If it's OK, I need to get home. I miss Zel."

"Of course. Please thank Zel for me. I'll do it in person as well, but I appreciate them so much," Luke replied, scratching Alfred's neck as the giant orange tabby purred in his arms.

Maggie pulled Roxi into a friendly hug. "It's really nice to meet you, Roxi. Welcome to Portland."

"Thank you for making me feel welcome," Roxi replied.

"Bye, Gwennie." Maggie hugged Gwen, giving her a kiss on the forehead.

"Bye!"

After Maggie left and closed the door behind her, they stood around in the living room awkwardly until Gwen took matters into her own hands.

She grabbed Roxi's hand and pulled her down the hall. "I'll show you your room."

Luke set Alfred down and searched through the kitchen. The cabinets were stocked with some of Luke's favorite staples, as was the fridge, including some cans and bottles of beer. He pulled out his French press and found a canister of fresh beans.

"Coffee?" Luke asked when he heard Roxi shuffle into the kitchen.

"Yes, please."

Gwen passed through the kitchen, heading into the office. "Hey, Luke, I'm going down to the gym."

After he set the timer, he turned around and leaned up against the cabinet. Roxi stood on the other side of the kitchen, her hands nervously clutched in front of her.

"Thank you for letting me stay with you. I'll try to figure out what to do next," Roxi said, shuffling from foot to foot.

Luke pushed off the counter and walked up to her, running his hand down her arm. "You can stay here as long as you want to."

Roxi took a tentative step toward him. "May I hug you?"

Luke nodded as Roxi closed the space before he'd even finished the affirmative gesture. "Are you doing OK, Roxi?"

"I'm...fine." She sighed. "I'm not fine. I'm struggling."

Luke kissed the top of her head, then pushed back when the alarm went off. "If you go into the room Gwen just went into, I'm guessing you'll find the door open. Head downstairs, I'll be down in a minute with coffee. We can put some music on and talk."

Roxi gave him a weak smile. "Alright."

Luke found the carafe and filled it. Roxi was gone when he turned around. Grabbing a couple cups from the cabinet, he headed into the office and down into his secret lair. When he reached the last step of the metal spiral staircase, Roxi stood in the doorway looking into his training center. He set the cups down on the end table between the two mid-century Danish-style chairs and filled them up.

Roxi turned and sat down, picking up her cup. "How do you have all this hidden? It's amazing."

"I'll show you which book triggers the door. You can come down here anytime you want." He walked to the door and poked his head in. "Gwen, I'm going to shut this door so Roxi and I can talk. If it's closed, please knock before entering."

Gwen stretched in the middle of the giant room. "OK."

Luke shut the door and sat down. "I'm struggling too, Roxi. Would you like some music?"

Roxi nodded, blowing over her coffee. Luke slid back the panel hiding his record collection and went to the B section, pulling down Beck's Mourning Phase LP.

Roxi stared down at her coffee, finally looking up, her eyes filled with anxiety and fear. "Luke, I don't know what I'm going to do. I don't have any paperwork. I don't have any way to access any of my money. I'm completely helpless. And…I don't have a rudis anymore. It's only a matter of time before…"

"The pack can make you a passport so you can get back to London. I have plenty of money to get you set up again. As far as the rudis, I don't know, but I promise we'll figure it out. When you're feeling up to it, we'll see if we can use my shrine to contact Mithras. You don't have to do this alone. We can't afford to fight this battle by ourselves anymore, Roxi." He swallowed, and stared into her dark brown eyes, pouring his earnestness into his eyes. "I'm hoping you'll move here. Together, we can fight this war better with my friends and the connections of the pack."

Roxi swept her shaggy hair from her eyes. "Is that the only reason you want me to stay?"

He shook his head. "No. It isn't. I want you to move here because I…I like you, and I want you to be part of my life. I've missed you the last several days since we're not constantly close to each other."

"I feel ashamed to say this, but I almost miss being in that cell where we could just talk and hold hands whenever we wanted. I've felt so scared and lonely, and you haven't been there."

Luke's stomach dropped. "I'm sorry, Roxi."

"It's selfish of me to say that, but it's also true. I'm so happy we're free and you've got all your people, but I'm scared that now that you have your life back, you won't need me in your life anymore."

"Roxi." He set his cup of coffee and leaned closer to her.

She set her cup down and moved closer.

Luke took both her hands in his, holding her gaze. "When you said if you found me, you wouldn't leave and would stay by me. Now that we've found each other. I don't want you to go. The last year and half were hell, but you weren't. Roxi, I need you to stay."

Staring into her eyes, he thought about her leaving. He didn't want to fall down that pit. Still having trouble seeing through the confusion of being in the arena, he knew his feelings for Roxi were more than just friendly, but he didn't want to leap when his thoughts and feelings were still shattered and jumbled from the hellish year and a half.

She slid to the floor. Luke joined her, pulling her into his arms. It felt good to have her body against his. Reaching down, he tipped her chin up. His breath caught in his throat when he saw the longing in her half-lidded eyes. Licking his lips, he swallowed and lowered his lips to hers.

The first two times they'd kissed, it was under the duress of the arena. When their lips touched, Luke melted a little inside. Her lips were warm and soft, and the electricity felt intoxicating, the intensity overwhelming as if all the longing and relief of being free merged and exploded into the kiss.

When they pulled back, Roxi rested her head on Luke's shoulder. They sat in silence holding each other until she fell asleep in his arms. Setting her gently against the edge of the chair, he scooped her up and carefully took her upstairs and to her room. He laid her on top of the covers and pulled a blanket over her, then bent down, kissed her forehead, and left.

Attraction and confusion warred as he looked at her for a moment. He sighed and closed the door, walking across the hall to his room. Putting on his workout clothes, he went down to join Gwen, hoping exercise would help center his mind and bring clarity to what was happening with Roxi. Besides, he'd missed training with

Gwen and was eager to see what new moves she'd learned while he'd been gone.

Despite the awkwardness and confusion, it felt good to be home.

322

**Luke Irontree will return in Blood Empire Infiltrated
Available Now!
Keep reading for a short preview.**

LUKE IRONTREE WILL RETURN IN

BLOOD EMPIRE INFILTRATED

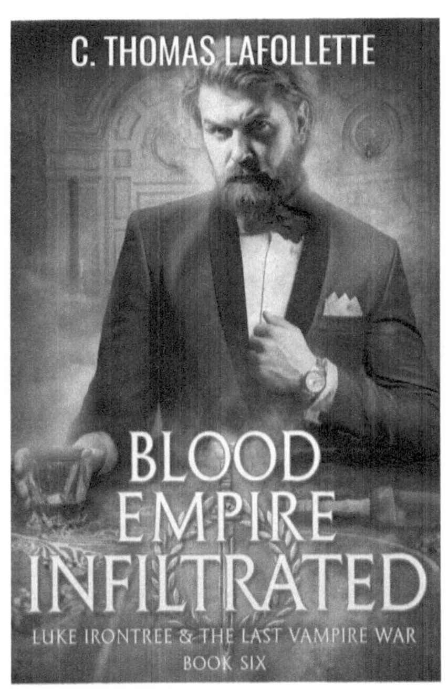

BLOOD EMPIRE INFILTRATED: BOOK SIX

CHAPTER ONE

The black Volvo tore down the windy, narrow coastal road, the driver pressing the souped-up engine for all it was worth. The weight of the car pushed the suspension side to side as it leaned around corners. At least the roads were dry, the fall rains taking a brief night or two's break. Each peek to the rear revealed a pack of cars burning south down Highway 101 in pursuit of the Volvo.

Luke and his crew hoped to stay ahead, making it to the Astoria-Megler Bridge and back into Oregon. They needed to get to their nearest allies, the Coast Pack. If they could make it across the Columbia River, through Astoria, and a bit further south, they could divert the chase pack onto private land where a brutal response awaited any vampires stupid enough to mess with the pack's friends.

"They're gaining, Luke!" Delilah said, watching the lead car slowly close the distance.

"I know," Luke said. "This isn't as easy as it looks." He focused on the road ahead, eyes squinting in concentration as he planned his lines around the corners to keep the heavy vehicle from spilling too much speed. Every mile per hour mattered.

"We're not going to make it to the bridge…" Pablo said.

"I know. If we were using your truck, we'd have more muscle." He loosened his grip on the wheel, his knuckles gripping too tightly. There was a lot of road ahead of them, and he didn't want to tire out his hands.

One of the pursuit cars tried to pull into the lane running the other direction, but its steering wheel was quickly yanked to avoid the oncoming delivery truck. As soon as the truck passed, the car tried again to make its way around their Volvo. With a bit of a straightaway to work with, Luke pushed the speed as hard as he could with the old car. Even with all the upgrades Jorge had implemented, it wasn't a thoroughbred vehicle like some of the luxury sedans and sport cars trailing him. Fortunately, another car in the oncoming lane forced the vampire attempting to pass to return to its lane.

Luke snorted and laughed when another car, pulling up to take the place of the one that'd darted into the oncoming lane, swerved off the road, flying off the edge and down into a thick Doug Fir tree. One down, but still enough to cause a lot of mischief. Giving the chase cars a quick look, Luke thought they might be opening a bit of space between each other to avoid another such mishap.

"How far are is it to the Astoria Bridge?" Luke asked, his voice tight with the strain of keeping the Volvo on the road.

"About seven miles," Delilah replied, anxiety lacing her voice.

Luke eased the Volvo into the center of the road as they approached the Chinook River Bridge, effectively cutting off any attempts to move around them. As they rocketed over the short bridge and returned to regular highway, Luke swerved slowly back and forth, taking advantage of a lack of headlights coming at them. One of the pursuit cars tried to use the left shoulder to move around him, sending up clouds of dirt and rocks, but it tipped and rolled over when one of its wheels caught in the ditch. It slammed into a tree trunk.

"Another one bites the dust." Luke smirked.

"Luke… We warned you about bad quipping," Sam said, shaking her head.

"Come on, you've got to let him have that one. There was dust and everything," Pablo said.

Delilah turned to Pablo, shaking her head in disappointment. "I hardly think you're a neutral advocate, Pablo."

"I calls 'em like I sees 'em. That was a funny pun. Punny, if you will." He reached up and patted Luke's shoulder.

"If I had a newspaper and it was safe to do so, I'd roll it up and swat Luke on the nose for that one." Delilah pantomimed rolling up paper.

Pablo shrugged. "Sorry, buddy, I tried."

Luke grunted, concentrating on swerving the Volvo back and forth over the middle line, the tires occasionally hitting the rumble strip augmenting the yellow paint and vibrating the car. Since they had the entire road but only a skimpy portion of the shoulder, the vampires took advantage and flared out, trying to find an open gap. Every time one tried to make a move, Luke would yank the wheel over to cut off the pursuer. One got close enough that Luke rubbed bumpers with it before the pursuers jammed on the brakes.

They were lucky it was as late as it was, and most of the sparsely populated Long Beach Peninsula was in bed asleep. That didn't mean there still weren't other cars on the road, like the one pulling around the corner into the oncoming lane. Luke kept barreling down the center of the road, the driver blaring their horn at Luke. The vampire cars weren't as brave as Luke and pulled into the right lane. Luke stayed put until the last moment, bouncing over the rumble strip as the car whizzed by.

As they rounded the corner, Luke crept back into the middle, slowly adding more speed until the road straightened. Then, he put everything the Volvo had left onto the road. After a bit, the Volvo vibrated oddly as it flew down the road.

"I'm not liking this shimmy. I gotta back it down some or we're going off the road. We can't get to the bridge if we're dead in a ditch." Luke slowed down until the Volvo stabilized.

"Luke, slow it down some more. You got a curve, then a town… Chinook," Delilah instructed.

Luke nodded and followed her instructions. So far, their luck had held, and the road stayed free of traffic. Seeing the approaching town, he grumbled. The road widened, adding thicker shoulders as they breached the town limits of Chinook. The sidewalks weren't making him feel any better.

Luke returned to his swerving pattern, but this time a few of the cars chasing flared out wide. "Fuck."

"Luke, they're uh…on the sidewalks." Pablo's voice rose, a sign of his growing anxiety.

Giving up on the swerve in favor of speed, Luke pushed the gas back down, aiming straight down the road. The shimmy returned, this time adding a weird knocking.

Luke gripped the wheel, his knuckles white. "Come on, baby, keep it together."

Everyone kept quiet, letting Luke concentrate.

"Oh no…" Sam said. "We just passed a parked cop."

"Hopefully, the car's just parked and empty… And no, lights are on," Pablo added.

"Nothing we can do about it now," Luke said. "They'll be behind the fangers."

The high-pitched oscillation of the siren filtered through the engine's increasingly loud noises. Scanning his peripherals to check the cars on the sidewalks, a slight sense of relief washed over him as he saw them fall back. Turns out a car half on, half off the sidewalk wasn't going to be a real speed demon, even if driven by one.

Delilah looked at her phone, expanding the image on the screen. "Once we get out of town, the road is looking narrow without a lot of passing opportunities. There's a tunnel, then we're running by the water."

"Cop still back there?" Luke asked.

"Yeah. Still there," Sam replied.

"Almost out of town." Luke pulled back into the right line. "Car coming."

The tension ratcheted up as everyone checked the cars behind him. This time, the vampires didn't tuck back in behind them.

"Come on, move over." Luke's eyes flicked up to the rearview mirror. "Damn it." The car honked at them, then held it down. His eyes drifted back to the oncoming car—still moving toward them.

"Luke…" Delilah said, the edges of panic seeping into her voice.

"I've got it," he bit out as he yanked the steering wheel to put the Volvo back into their own lane.

The oncoming car screeched to a halt and swerved off the road into someone's yard. The vampire cars didn't let up. They'd have likely plowed headfirst into the oncoming car.

"At least they didn't crash," Sam said.

Now that the extra space evaporated as the sidewalks and wider shoulders disappeared in the rearview mirror along with the town of Chinook, they were on the last stretch, assuming they could reach the Astoria-Megler Bridge and make it out of Astoria. And that was becoming a bigger assumption by the mile as the Volvo picked up new sounds, knocks, and rattles. The poor old beast wasn't meant to be pushed so hard for this long, even with the upgrades.

Luke did his best to mix in aggressive driving to box out any cars trying to get around him and using any straightaway to scrape all the speed he could from the struggling engine. When the tunnel came up, Luke hogged the middle of the road. When they blasted out of the tunnel, he resumed swerving. The only worrying moments were when they drove over a section with a middle turn lane.

A pair of cars—a white Suburu WRX and noisy, souped up Honda Civic—tried to flank him and pass on both sides.

"Hold on," Luke called.

He hit the brakes just enough to drop them back so the nose of the Volvo was lined up with the rear end of the two smaller cars. Before the vamps could adjust, he pulled the wheel hard to the right, slamming into the rear quarter panel of the Subaru. Its driver wasn't expecting it and overcompensated, spinning into the boulders that served as a guardrail along the right side of the highway above the mouth of the Columbia River. Luke managed to evade the Suburu's demise, only taking a scrape and bump from its front bumper as he passed.

Before the Civic to his left could do anything, Luke used his momentum to plow into the rear of the Honda. The driver jammed on his brakes, the car's tires screaming in agony as the car went sideways. Luke eased his speed back, disconnecting from the fanger's car. The tires bit into the ground and the momentum took the Civic onto its side and into a roll, spraying destroyed parts as it tumbled off the road into a ditch. As soon as the road was clear again, Luke accelerated. The Astoria-Megler Bridge was just visible in the near distance. Luke focused on the road while his crew focused on the bridge—a long metal and asphalt runway to freedom.

"Almost there…" Luke mumbled. "Alright, get ready!"

Luke swung the Volvo to the left side of the road and braked, hitting the turn onto the Astoria-Megler Bridge with the best line possible to keep speed. As soon as he entered the bridge, the Volvo's line carried them over to the left oncoming lane.

"Luke…headlights."

"I see them." Luke waited until the car had settled from the long, wide turn and eased back into their lane. "Fuck!"

The oncoming car pulled into their lane, coming head on. Two sets of headlights bore down on them.

"Why are we slowing down?" Delilah asked.

"Shit, shit, shit… I'm losing the car," Luke said.

A loud thunk shook the car as the rattle turned into screeching metal. The smoke and stench of burning oil and grinding metal filled the cabin. The Volvo had reached the end of its range, slowing as it bled its power out onto the Astoria-Megler Bridge.

"Get your guns ready!" Luke cried, yanking the wheel and using the last of the car's momentum to bring the car broadside to both lanes, effectively blocking the bridge.

"Hold on!"

The last thing Luke saw before the car slammed into his Volvo was the feral face of a vampire, fangs extended in a grim smile of destruction. Sam screamed behind Luke. A second car plowed into the other side of the Volvo, sending it spinning between the two cars in a grim ballet of screeching metal and shattering glass. A third car plowed into the Volvo, followed by a fourth. Horns, stuck in a rigor mortis, blared without the hand of a driver. An engine sputtered. Another revved but had nothing to apply power to. Flames licked at the crumpled hood of one of the vampire's cars. Wedged between four destroyed cars, Luke's poor Volvo looked like it'd gone through a car crusher.

As the cabin of Luke's Volvo filled with smoke, cutting down on visibility, Luke's throat felt raw as he tried to blink the burning sensation from his eyes. Two vampires, shocked by their impacts, stirred in the crumpled cabins of their cars. One kicked out the shattered glass of the windshield and crawled onto the wreck of Luke's Volvo.

"What the fuck!" The vampire stared into the Volvo, his eyes wide with shock.

Guns opened fire on the vampire from inside the wounded Volvo, splattering the vampire into a pile of goo that temporarily tamed the flames before igniting them further. So far, the fire remained on the outside of the car, but it was only a matter of time before the flames found ingress.

Gun fire poured out of the Volvo from all directions as more cars stopped on both sides of the collision, vampires scrambling out armed and angry.

As one, the fangers opened fire on the five car pileup without regard for what car they hit—or whether they took out Luke and his friends or one of the vampires who'd finally brought the car chase to a spectacular end. A couple vampires pulled grenades from their pockets, pulled the pins, and lobbed them over their friends to land and roll into the heap of twisted steel that lay across the Astoria-Megler Bridge.

"Down!" a vampire yelled.

A few seconds later, the grenades went off, sending shock waves of steel, glass, and shrapnel everywhere. A few vampires, unlucky to take wounds, groaned and crawled back toward their cars, cursing the idiots who hadn't waited for the crowds to clear before throwing the grenades.

"Everyone back!" boomed a voice.

The vampires scrambled to their feet, helping those near them, and hid behind their cars. Two vampires pulled out rocket-propelled grenades from the back of a truck, took aim, and fired them into the burning hulk that was the Volvo 240DL wagon. When the rockets hit and exploded, the shock wave knocked vampires onto their asses and shattered a few of their windows.

The twisted corpse of the Volvo burned along with the four bodies inside.

Blood Empire Infiltrated is Available Now!

NEWSLETTER

The Centurion Immortal is a Luke Irontree prequel novella and is exclusive to the Dispatches from C. Thomas Lafollette news-letter. Please sign up for your free copy and you'll also receive a twice-monthly news-letter with news, book updates, recipes, drinks tips, and other fun stuff. Your email will never be given out, rented, or sold.

CThomasLafollette.com/newsletter/

ACKNOWLEDGMENTS

I'd like to thank all the people who made this book possible.

Suzanne, your editorial eye has made this book and series infinitely better. Your belief in my vision for these characters has made this a kick ass team effort.

Ravven, your covers are amazing and really capture the essence of Luke and his world.

Amy, you're my alpha reader and my proofreader. These books wouldn't be possible without you.

C.D. Tavenor, you stepped up when I needed to change my copy editor and did a fantastic job.

Doochie, you've been my earliest reader and a great hype man as well as a wonderful friend.

To my critique group, thank you for all your hard work. Your eyes and efforts have made my writing better.

ABOUT THE AUTHOR

C. Thomas Lafollette is a writer of Urban Fantasy and Historical Fantasy and is the author of the forthcoming Luke Irontree novels. He earned a degree in Ancient History with a specialization in Classics at The College of Idaho. He's read poetry on stage with Yevgeny Yevtushenko and dined with the Belgian Prime Minister. C. Thomas has lived in Portland, Oregon for over Twenty years. He lives with his wife, fellow author Amy Cissell, his stepdaughter, and his three jerkface cats. He and Amy also run their own freelance editing business - Cissell Ink

twitter.com/CTLafollette

facebook.com/CThomasLafollette

tiktok.com/@cthomaslafollette

instagram.com/CThomasLafollette

bookbub.com/authors/c-thomas-lafollette

amazon.com/C-Thomas-Lafollette/e/B09JMTR7W7

goodreads.com/cthomaslafollette

ALSO BY C. THOMAS LAFOLLETTE

Luke Irontree & The Last Vampire War

Book 0 - The Centurion Immortal

Book 1 - Dark Fangs Rising - March 22, 2022

Book 2 - Dark Fangs Raging - April 19, 2022

Book 3 - Dark Fangs Descending - May 17, 2022

Book 4 - Blood Empire Reborn - August 23, 2022

Book 5 - Blood Empire Avenged - September 20, 2022

Book 6 - Blood Empire Infiltrated - October 18, 2022

Book 7 - Blood Empire Burning - November 15, 2022

Book 8 - Ancient Sword Falling - March 21, 2023

Book 9 - Ancient Sword Unyielding - August 22, 2023

Book 10 - Ancient Sword Shattering*

The Luke Irontree Historical Adventures

Rise of the Centurio Immortalis - April 5, 2022

Fall of the Centurio Immortalis - May 31, 2022

The Moonlight Centurion*

The Highway Centurion*

Red City Reaper - A Dark Urban Fantasy Adventure

Book 1 - A Shot For Death* - Winter 2024

Book 2 - Death Orders a Double* - Winter 2024

Book 3 - Death on the Rocks* - Sprint 2024

*Forthcoming

Titles and release dates may be subject to change.